FRENCH TWIST

A dark shape shot up through the ladder-well opening and hovered in front of Austin, wing-flaps spread. It hissed at him, red eyes glinting, then drifted slowly forward. Austin dodged to the right as it pounced, but it caught him easily. He struggled wildly, striking out at the huge alien, then froze as it poised a taloned hand directly over his throat.

"One more word, Faon," the Avelle declared in rather decent French, "and I'll slash you to shreds."

By Paula E. Downing
Published by Ballantine Books:

RINN'S STAR
FLARE STAR
FALLWAY

FALLWAY

Paula E. Downing

A Del Rey Book

BALLANTINE BOOKS • NEW YORK

A Del Rey Book
Published by Ballantine Books

Copyright © 1992 by Paula E. Downing

All rights reserved under International and Pan-American Copyright Conventions. Published in the United States of America by Ballantine Books, a division of Random House, Inc., New York, and simultaneously in Canada by Random House of Canada Limited, Toronto.

Library of Congress Catalog Card Number: 92-97044

ISBN 0-345-37763-X

Manufactured in the United States of America

First Edition: January 1993

Acknowledgments

My thanks to Sara Wojciehowski for her friendship and her help with this book; to my editor at Del Rey, Shelly Shapiro, for her continued enthusiasm and encouragement; and to my husband and fellow-writer, T. Jackson King, for his love in all the ways.

FALLWAY

❦ Chapter 1

IN THE DEPTHS of the asteroid Quevi Ltir, all valued the shadows of tier and fallway. Jahnel Alain paused in the First Turning and looked behind her at the Faon emerging from the fallway leading downward to the City. Her companions seemed strange in gray vacuum suits instead of their usual black caped aals and pale bodysuits that mimicked the appearance of the alien Avelle who owned Quevi Ltir. In the light gravity of the asteroid, the human descendants of the French colony-ship *Phalene* moved with an Avelle grace in the asteroid's low gravity, with an Avelle liking for shadows. Instinctively, her companions moved to the deep shadows along the walls, flowing past her in a double stream on either side, rising toward the surface to battle at Avelle bidding. She floated in midcorridor, waiting for Sair Rostand, her senior husband and kin-leader today in their kin-group, the Louve. She did not like the choosing on this day, for all its necessity. She did not like it at all.

She puzzled over her uneasiness. It was not the imminent danger of attacking the miin's intruder ship now hiding in a crater near the surface ruins—the Faon were brave enough and had fought in the City's tier wars when Lejja, the Principal of Songs, bid them. Nor could she deny the necessity: as cleverly as Koyil, the Principal of Laws, had managed his machines, the surface defenses had not driven away the miin from Quevi Ltir. This next attack required guile and flexibility, the workings of a truly living mind, not mechanical inflexibility. Nor could she deny the choosing of the Faon: her people owed a great debt to the Avelle and were better suited physically to attack and feint on the asteroid surface. Yet still she distrusted.

She grimaced at her reflections, uneasy about uneasy truths she had rarely questioned, a complexity typically Avelle in its

1

convolutions. I value the safety of shadows, she thought, but shadows can also conceal dangers. What is Koyil's purpose in sending us? The Principal of Laws had opposed the rescue of *Phalene* eighty years before, had remained adamant in that opposition. As well as she knew the Avelle, she could not solve the puzzle today of the Principal's machinations—or, rather, suspected the obvious. Could it be as simple as sending Faon to a slaughter? She thought about that, frowning.

The Avelle of Quevi Ltir had more reason than most to guard their hidden City. The Songs of the City's walls told of an aging world long since left behind, that first Home-Space of the first Brooding now faded even in long Avelle memory, where other shadows like these had birthed a proud and virile race with a strength that had carried them to the stars. There for millennia the Avelle had warred with each other in great Predator ships, an endless strike and counterstrike of craft and guile and naked force that expanded the racial Home-Space from star to star in Carina star-cluster, a territory held by all but disputed at every point. Among the Predators, the great starship *Quevi'ali* had won preeminent place in the wars for centuries—but even the great could suffer chance misfortune, odd disaster, a tumbling from the heights. Mortally wounded, *Quevi'ali* had fled its four pursuers to the very edge of Carina cluster, losing them at last among a scattered spray of suns.

In Rhesaa star-system, a binding of twelve stars dominated by a great blue-white star, *Quevi'ali*'s four kin-alliances, called iruta in Avelle speech, sought a refuge to repair their ship and to rebuild their breeding numbers, not only for *Quevi'ali* but for a daughter-ship, doubling their strength for the return to the Predator wars. On a large asteroid circling a lesser companion of the blue-white star, *Quevi'ali* had concealed itself beneath naked rock and begun a great building of a subterranean City. For decades, then centuries, the Avelle brooding grew steadily, the original four iruta fracturing into a dozen new bondings, each building its own great tier of two hundred levels, expanding outward and downward into the rocky depths, tempering their strength in tier wars for territory and influence. Yet the Avelle of Quevi Ltir did not rebuild their ship nor begin their daughter-ship; instead, they lingered in their City past all accounting, until even the Avelle servant classes, conditioned by gene and rank never to question their superiors, wondered why the Song of Returning seemed forgotten.

For five centuries *Quevi'ali* had lain in its subterranean cavern, a dark hulk rarely visited. The Star Leader, hereditary captain of *Quevi'ali* and the Principal vested with the charge of its rebuilding, found other reason in the City for other affairs, without explanation. Among the six Principals who ruled Quevi Ltir, the Principals of Law and Song rose to new influence, supplanting the primacy of the Star Leader, and contested with each other, deftly building shifting alliances with Mind and Battle and Science, never trusting the other, growing crafty and wise as they subordinated lesser kin-alliances to their purposes. The tier wars grew dangerous and more frequent as the Principals contested, threatening extinguishment of whole tiers and the ending of brood-lines, but still the Avelle did not rebuild their ships.

Then, in the fifth generation of the new Brooding, a stranger human ship named *Phalene* had entered Rhesaa system, its fragile ship-world dying from radiation and meteor impact. For reasons only Lejja knew, the Prinicpal of Songs had ordered the Avelle upward and had rescued *Phalene*'s human survivors, taking the humans into her own tier and giving them two levels for their own, and defying the other Principals to challenge her choosing. The resulting tier war was ferocious but short-lived, and terrifying to the shocked humans under Lejja's protection; when Lejja prevailed by narrow victory, the thirty survivors of *Phalene* swore kin-bonding to Lejja and, at her bidding, adopted Avelle ways to keep their place among the kin-alliances of Quevi Ltir, forgetting the human that differed, becoming the Avelle that preserved life and brood, naming themselves the iruta Faon.

Only in the names they took for their kin-groups within their iruta, memories of Earth in rock and water, star and wolf and owl, did the first Faon keep a human heritage. As a new generation was born to the Faon and as Lejja's kindred grew accustomed to the humans in their midst, Lejja permitted certain liberties based on practicality. At her direction, Kiiri, the Science Leader, devised heavier gravity fields for the Faon levels to ease Faon bone damage from the asteroid's low gravity; adjustments were made in atmosphere and humidity and lighting to give the Faon a Home-Space more similar to their native world. When limited parts of Avelle speech proved physically impossible for human articulation, Lejja permitted the Faon to resume their own language and encouraged her Avelle to learn francais. As the third Faon generation was born, Lejja openly promised the Faon their own Song among the Avelle, and cham-

pioned them against the continued malice of Koyil, and protected them and gave the Faon her own strength.

A fourth Faon generation had now begun, with new children
in the Faon levels. Jahnel thought of her own daughter, Luelle,
now three, and her infant son, Didier, and worried for them.
Lejja was visibly aging and her strength had begun to wane: was
this bidding today the first failing of her protection? How to tell
in a society where even the Avelle could confuse themselves with
their own subtleties?

Her father, Faon Leader Benoit Alain, had agreed to this, had
agreed quickly. She distrusted that quick agreement, doubting
her father's judgment. They had contested, she and Benoit, all
her life, but never on essentials. She tightened her hands on her
dis-rifle and shook her head slightly, as if to shake away the
doubts. When you are old and white-haired and maybe Faon
Leader in your own right, she chided herself, then nose-wrinkle
and sniff and flip your wing-flaps: a nestling does not question
his elder. But still she felt uneasy. She watched more Faon
emerge from the fallway, wishing for Sair.

Jahnel nodded to friends of the Hiboux and Etoile as they
passed, touched hands briefly with Eduard and Melinde, her cohusband and sister-wife, then watched them follow the others
around the Turning to the gathering-room beyond. Her vayalim,
her marriage-group, risked four of its six adults today, an un-
lucky chance of the lot; only teenaged Evan and pregnant Solveya remained below in safety with the children. The Avelle
practice of multiple marriage gave strength to the Faon in a
dangerous City, though some Avelle of Lejja's tier still complained, even after eighty years, that all Faon adults entered
vayalim as breeding adults, an oddness the Avelle found unnatural. Three-quarters of adult Avelle remained in servant class,
nonbreeders ruled by vayalim kindred who repressed their in-
feriors' sexuality with chemical inhibition and conditioning,
methods not readily available to the human Faon—nor wanted,
though the Faon did not voice that too proudly. But it was a
difference easily concealed within the privacy of the Faon's
home-levels, a tolerance Lejja could permit the Faon and had
permitted. Jahnel had grown up with several parents and the
company of a dozen siblings; it was a comfort to her that Luelle
and Didier would not be wholly orphaned if she and Sair, and
Eduard and Melinde, died today.

She quickly shied from the thought, not liking to think of her
beloveds' deaths, not liking to think of her children deprived of

anyone. Uncomfortable beneath the dim central light of the corridor ceiling, she moved upward to the shadow of the far corner of wall and ceiling, hovering there on the gentle push of her belt jet. She stretched gracefully to a horizontal position and cradled her dis-rifle across her arms, face downward, watching for Sair.

How to tell? she wondered. I am Avelle in mind and purpose, but even Avelle sometimes are confused by their own inverts. Certainly I confuse myself at times, all by myself. I am confused today. Sair would tease me if he knew; perhaps I will tell him so that he might enjoy the teasing. She smiled. You are late, my beloved; I will tease you about that if you delay much longer.

What was Koyil's purpose—and why had Lejja agreed? Though generally truthful when flatly confronted, the Avelle Principals knew the value of partial truth and often warred with deceit and multiple purposes. Even Kiiri, the Science Leader who knew the Faon better than most, had his secrets and would not answer some questions put to him. Kiiri had sought out Jahnel since her childhood, attracted by something in her he would not say, or perhaps merely kin-bonding with Benoit's likely heir for its possible future advantage to himself. Kiiri never did anything without a reason and his reasons were always Avelle, turned on themselves, pointing a half-dozen directions, maybe tangible or intangible, maybe deliberate or impulsive, sometimes bordering on no reason at all. In her private thoughts, Jahnel believed that not even Kiiri always knew which was what. Would Kiiri know what Koyil intended? And how could she provoke him into telling her what he knew? She considered ways to provoke Kiiri, smiling slightly.

The last of the Faon passed her, moving toward the Downlift and its access to the asteroid surface. Jahnel bit her lip, vaguely irritated at Sair and his lateness, then saw her husband rise into view, Rodolphe Tardieu of the Etoile beside him. Rodolphe had the overall leadership of the battle today with Sair as his second, supported by kin-leaders of the other three kin-groups. An older man with proven ability, Rodolphe had a calmness she trusted; she felt some of her tension relax. Sair saw her and waved, then murmured some words to Rodolphe. The older Faon moved past Jahnel, nodding to her politely, then vanished around the turn.

"You didn't have to wait," Sair said. Jahnel smiled and moved to kiss him, but Sair quickly shied away. "Niintua follows," he warned her.

Jahnel promptly increased the distance between them to several meters and turned to face the fallway exit. The Avelle did not understand the Faon's habit of easy embracing, and themselves touched closely only in combat and mating. Blundering into an Avelle's body-field invited instant punishment, including death if the rank difference was great. Faon children, like Avelle children, learned early about the dangers of slash-attack; only later, when they understood the subtle rankings among the Avelle adults and had gained the physical agility to extract themselves from bad mistakes, could they begin the play of deliberate insult that Avelle rank-peers sometimes enjoyed in such invasions. But Niintua as Principal and Battle Leader was beyond such friendly insult; even the other Principals took care to not tempt his ferocity.

Niintua rose gracefully into view, his black wing-flaps spread slightly as he ascended on the fallway's updraft. An Avelle's size belied his grace in low gravity: over three meters long from a squarish pallid-skinned head to the double flange tipping a segmented tail, Avelle rode the air currents of the fallways by sculling with their large and intricately muscled wing-flaps, deft in their maneuvers, capable of flashing speed. In the beginning, both races had had difficulty accepting the physical appearance of the other, the Faon alarmed by Avelle size and threat-displays, the Avelle struggling with attack instincts still partially linked to visual clues. Both had tried to adapt to the other. With two clawed hands, a small flexible lipped mouth, vestigial ears, and wideset dark eyes set centrally in the face for bifocal vision, the Avelle vaguely shared a few human physical arrangements; the Faon had adopted dress and certain postures in flight to mimic the Avelle. Later, in the tier wars, the Faon had devised infrared goggles to lessen their visual disadvantage in Avelle lighting, and had fought with studded poisoned gloves to match the poison of Avelle talons and tail-tip; both races took Kiiri's battle drugs to increase agility, reaction time, and resistance to pain. The common defense of tier and Home-Space had kin-bound the Faon and Lejja's Avelle in ways the more deliberate change had not—but still the Faon would always be alien in ways irreducible, even to the Avelle of their own tier. How much more so to an Avelle of another tier and kin-alliance, who had chosen to bind himself to Koyil and shared that Principal's loathing of everything Faon?

Niintua's deep-set eyes flashed as he saw them, his reflective retinas gleaming redly in the dimness of the corridor lights. The Battle Leader hesitated in obvious distaste, his small mouth drawn downward and pinched, then glided forward, sculling with the flexible edges of his dark wing-flaps, two servant-guards following him at respectful distance. He flicked his segmented tail, flashed an edge of his wing-flap, and hovered motionless in front of the two Faon, glaring at them. Jahnel and Sair returned the look impassively, waiting on the Battle Leader's intentions. After a few moments, Niintua drifted forward toward them, wing-flaps slightly spread, pressuring them. Jahnel promptly edged forward herself, pushing back at him, for all it was unwise. She lifted her chin defiantly.

"Lejja has asked and we are here, Battle Leader," she said. "Give your orders."

Niintua flicked his tail irritably, his aversion to the Faon visible in the tenseness of his body, his obvious temptation to slash-attack. Behind him, his servants hesitated, watching their master for direction, their tail-tips twitching nervously. For five decades, Niintua had held his rank as Battle Leader with unbridled ferocity, a cruelty unusual even among Avelle, and had long allied himself with the Principal of Laws, becoming Koyil's creature with little independent will. Jahnel idly wondered if Niintua enjoyed his subjection, relying on the Principal of Laws to control the violence in which Niintua reveled—and wondered if Koyil found his ally an uncomfortable burden. When snaring a great-claws, Jahnel reminded herself, thinking of the food animal common to both Avelle and Faon food tanks, wear gloves and extra eyes.

Niintua gestured with a clawed hand. "The Faon sent too few," he said harshly in Avelle speech, omitting any courteous greeting.

"Ah, you counted," Sair retorted. Jahnel threw him a quieting glance. Sair detested Niintua, believing him careless of Faon lives in the tier wars—or, like his master, bent upon Faon deaths.

"That has been discussed," she said calmly, "by all the Principals and all Faon. The Faon will risk not more than one-third of our breeding adults in this new attack on the miin lander, but that forty we will risk." She raised her dis-rifle before her chest, saluting Niintua without mockery. "Command us, Battle Leader."

Niintua flicked his tail and pointed a clawed hand at her. "You will inform us what the miin do. Have you swallowed the suval?" he asked, referring to Kiiri's new battle drug.

She scowled at him. "Not yet. When we leave for the surface, I will take it, as will the others who take suval today. Kiiri has tested it only twice and found it has a distance limitation—and it wears off quickly, Battle Leader. Would you waste Kiiri's new psi-drug on stirring speeches in the Downlift?''

The Avelle chose to ignore her sarcasm. ''Still, you will inform us of what they do.'' He moved forward with purpose, and Jahnel and Sair quickly moved to the sides of the wide corridor, granting him the passage he merited by his rank. As Niintua's servants followed, the Faon drifted inward again, decreasing the distance between them until they edged on the aliens' body-fields. The Avelle nearest Jahnel hissed at her and flared his wing-flaps in angry display.

''I am a breeding female,'' she told him sharply. ''Mind your courtesy.''

The servant-guard hesitated, then spat a word at her. She bared her teeth, confusing the Avelle badly, who lacked such gesture.

''Hardly,'' she mocked. ''But you leave your master unguarded. Do you so easily forget your duty?''

The servant flipped his wing-flaps indignantly and soared onward, then flashed around the Turning after Niintua.

''Hmmm,'' she said, wondering if she would regret her provoking later. ''Niintua's servants grow bold.''

Sair took her elbow and drew her onward. ''Niintua's kin-brood has always been bold, with few courtesies to us. It means nothing.''

''You don't believe that, either,'' she commented.

Sair shrugged. Dark-haired and dark-eyed, one year older than herself, Sair had a lean strength she still found irresistible even after four years of marriage. Though she tried not to show partiality for courtesy to her other husbands' feelings, Jahnel could not deny the effects of Sair's glance, his smile, the way he moved. She wished suddenly that she and Sair were alone in safety, for talk and unhurried lovemaking through the idling hours, not abroad on this desperate idiocy—a stupid thought, perhaps, but a thought she kept. Thinking of Sair's caresses always had value, she told herself, whatever the context.

He smiled at her, his dark eyes intent. ''We are all alert, beloved.'' He moved off, heading for the Turning, and she followed him, struggling again with her uneasiness.

They turned the corner and joined the gathering in the large room beyond, the last chamber before the vertical Downlift leading to the surface. Jahnel took her place with Sair among the six Louve along one wall, and saw the other kin-groups gather in their own places: Ruisseau and Hiboux, Roche and Etoile, eight each. In room center, Niintua turned slowly to look over the Faon in the gathered semicircle.

"You are Faon," he declared in badly accented francais—perhaps courtesy, probably insult to Faon comprehension of Avelle speech. Few of the Avelle outside Lejja's tier had bothered to learn francais, rarely used it even if they knew it. Niintua paused, flaring his wing-flaps in emphasis. "You are an iruta within the City. You owe the Avelle a debt for the rescue made of your ancestors. You owe kin-loyalty to the tier in which you reside. You owe a debt to *me*, Principal and Battle Leader."

"This is known," Rodolphe said calmly from his place among the Etoile.

"Good. Do not forget it." Niintua gestured more calmly. "The miin have landed another craft in a crater beyond the surface ruins. They erect machines to counter my machines—"

"Our machines," Sair murmured, earning himself a vicious glance.

"You *will* destroy their machines and their ship. You *will* destroy the miin associated with the machines and ship. You will exterminate all the intruders as the Principals command."

"As they ask," Rodolphe amended, "and the Faon, as kin-alliance, offer." He smiled grimly. "Niintua, we are not servant Avelle at your beck and call. We are a kin-alliance with full rights within the City, however Law protests it—but Song protects us and today we will do this thing for her sake."

"Lejja is senile," Niintua spat.

"Not yet. And she is Principal of Songs, superior to Law in influence and power. We go against the miin for her, not for you."

Niintua swelled in rage but managed to control himself with an effort, violence flashing in his eyes. Several of the Faon nearest him edged prudently away.

"You will go," Niintua declared.

"We will go," Rodolphe agreed. He raised his chin and glanced from group to group. "Faon, we travel by kin-group through the routes discussed this morning. The alpha talents, those on suval, will coordinate our advance, and Jahnel of the Louve will provide what data she can about the miin. We attack simultaneously from shadow, first what miin we see, then their machines in general. Is that agreed, Battle Leader?"

Niintua flicked a wing-flap. "Agreed."

"Suit up." The Faon put on their helmets and checked their

vacuum suits. Jahnel quickly swallowed the tablet of suval, Kiiri's strange new drug that brought an indistinct knowledge of other minds, and saw the other alpha talents make the same quick gesture. The other battle drugs, human-adapted substances from the tier wars that brought strength and stealth and speed, had been taken at breakfast by all. She turned to her husband Eduard, the Louve's other alpha talent that day.

"Remember, my love, what Kiiri said about the suval side-effects."

"I remember." He pointed a finger at her in mock sternness, drawing his eyebrows together. "You remember, too, Jahnel, this once. You forget dangers, a trait I wish Luelle hadn't inherited."

"What? Would you have her soberly sedate like you, Eduard?"

"I merely make my mischief in other ways, wife," Eduard replied with dignity. Short and stocky, blond like herself, and three years younger than her twenty-three, Eduard had a cheerfulness on all things that Jahnel sometimes envied; it was Eduard's strength to be so and perhaps a better kind of willfulness than her own. The combination in their daughter made safeguarding Luelle a busy task.

She heard Sair chuckle, and saw Melinde toss her head irritably, humorless as always. Jahnel's youngest sister had a sour side her siblings had endured since Melinde's infancy, and the trait had not improved with marriage. Jahnel spread her hands, looking at all the Louve. "Good faring, my own. Be careful: we would grieve to lose any of you. Be brave and ruthless, quick in your movements, daring in your speed." She gestured the Avelle blessing, then fastened her helmet, breathing in the cool dryness from the suit's air tank.

As she fastened down the last connection, she felt the first ripple of suval through her body, oddly different from Kiiri's other drugs, and clamped her jaws against her dread of it. The trials of the new battle drug had not been pleasant and had been based only on partial dosage; even Eduard and Jean-Luc of the Etoile, who tolerated battle drugs well, had reported physical problems with this new chemical. Kiiri had long experimented on Faon with the Avelle's battle drugs, coldly fascinated by the new combinations that resulted as the Avelle enzymes interacted with human biochemistry. For some years several Faon adults who fought frequently in the tier wars had reported strange mental sensations while under battle drugs, a blurring of mind that disoriented and had caused two deaths through the distraction. Intrigued, Kiiri had investigated, located those most sensitive to the effect, then had defined his tests and sought others less poisoned among the younger Faon.

Only recently had Kiiri isolated the human enzyme he named suval, a chemical byproduct of the human pituitary gland stressed by three of the minor battle-drugs. Faon bodies had built up residues from other battle-drugs, and these, too, played some role in the suval chemistry. Among those particularly sensitive to the pure drug, suval could create a telepathic link to certain other Faon, sometimes along kinship lines, sometimes not, and not always predictably—but often enough to be useful.

Of all those tested, only Jahnel had sensed miin thoughts instead of Faon, a fact that disturbed Jahnel more than Kiiri suspected. She heard much less than the alpha talents who heard other Faon; she had to struggle more to listen and suffered worse afterward. To bind mentally to Faon was easier; to bind to miin hurt in ways Jahnel could not describe. Kiiri had professed himself unsurprised that Jahnel heard miin but wouldn't say why, however she provoked him. When do the games stop, Kiiri? she thought irritably, provoked herself by the memory. When all Songs end?

She waited as Sair checked their equipment by eye, carefully and one by one, then followed him with the others toward the Downlift.

One by one, the Faon cycled through the atmosphere lock to the airless fallway beyond. Above them stretched a dark emptiness lit with dim watchtale lights at each level; beneath them the darkness narrowed to a single dark point in the depths. The Downlift, the only surface entrance to the City, was two kilometers deep and paralleled the now-abandoned First Tier. As the Faon soared upward, the metal walls gleamed in the dim light of the watchtales flickering past, faintly marked with power leads, paneled squares, the worn covers of antique control panels. At intervals, the boxy shapes of defender robots stirred warningly, then stilled into immobility as the Faon's suit belts sent a recognition signal to their silent electronic challenge. Melinde turned her head nervously as a robot cannon tracked them overlong as they passed it; then it, too, abandoned the scan and returned to ready position, looking upward. A cross-tunnel loomed its inky blackness, concealing other defenders and traps.

As they passed through the lower reaches of the Downlift, the words of the Avelle Songs gleamed on the smooth walls, fitted between the later-added defenses, inscribed in their loops and graceful whorls into the metal, proclaiming the upper limits of the Home-Space, the place to be defended. The City the Avelle had built in the depths gave them warmth and air, deep shadow for safety, and life-warm space to rear their young and sing the Songs of life and star-home; gladly they had left behind the dangers of vacuum and starlight on Quevi's bleak surface—and of other Predator ships that might rove too close to the star cluster's edge and discover *Quevi'ali*'s hiding space. How long since a living being had passed upward through this dark and silent space? Until the Avelle rose to *Phalene*, perhaps centuries, and likely not since.

Jahnel saw signs of disrepair in some of the defender-modules they passed: robot-canisters that did not respond to their approach, a flickering arc-current of a short-circuit in a sensor-panel, scorch-marks from system failures decades old. In all the centuries since *Quevi'ali* had taken refuge in Quevi Ltir, no Avelle Predator ship had entered Rhesaa system; it appeared not even *Phalene*'s more recent intrusion had reversed Avelle carelessness about the surface defenses. Pakal, the current Star Leader, was not the only Principal who had grown indifferent to traditional duties. Jahnel touched Sair's arm and pointed at another scorched panel.

"I see it," he muttered. "If the other Principals knew how badly Koyil maintained these defenses . . ."

"No Avelle comes into the Downlift; not even we came this far in exploring the First Tier. If the Downlift is so poorly kept, what of the surface machines? How many mobile robots are still functional? Did an attack on the lander even occur, Sair?"

"Almost certainly. Lejja wouldn't let us go into this danger without demanding some kind of proof—and Kiiri would see that Koyil's proof *was* proof, not fakery."

"You think," Jahnel said sourly.

Sair turned his head to look at her curiously, his dark eyes glinting through his faceplate. "Are you doubting *everything*, beloved? Even Kiiri?" She saw the gleam of his teeth.

"I hate suval," she muttered. "I hate the touch of miin. I'm feeling it now—excuse my grumbles, love."

Melinde moved closer. "I'd like other grumbles excused sometimes, too, Jahnel."

"Not now, Melinde," Jahnel said tiredly. Of late, her sister-wife had grown peevish, increasingly infatuated with Sair in a bride's single-minded sexuality and jealous of Jahnel's seniority.

Somehow the seven years' difference in their ages seemed a gulf, temperament and grievances and unintended tiffs a gulf, Jahnel's motherhood and Melinde's lack of it a gulf, though Melinde was still in her bride-year and there was no shame yet in that. Adolescents, even married adolescents, can be trying, Jahnel thought—especially when they're married to you. "Not now," she repeated.

Melinde moved off, affronted. Jahnel sighed. I'm too young to be a senior wife, she thought. I don't have the wisdom. Maybe Kiiri has a wisdom pill, she told herself. Is wisdom chemical?

"I try to give her enough attention," Sair murmured in frustration, watching Melinde soar upward.

"She'll grow out of it," Jahnel said, though not believing it. "She wanted so much to conceive your first child, Sair, you know how badly. Solveya's pregnancy was a great disappointment, and now Evan is jealous of you, too, wishing Melinde felt about him as she feels about you. If she did, we might have more balance." She frowned, worrying about a problem that had festered for weeks since Solveya's genetics test, nothing truly serious in the marriage—Melinde had always been passionate about her wants—but still . . . troublesome. "*Phalene*'s custom was two-person marriage, not six or eight. Maybe we should go back to two-people vayalim and forget Avelle sensibilities."

"What an idea!" he exclaimed. "Besides, if we did that, how could I bed three different women, all of it properly? I'd hate to give that up. And how would I choose whom to keep?" She swiped a hand at him, making him dodge. He laughed at her.

Heads turned toward them, and Jahnel saw a few disapproving glances, more others amused. She had forgotten, she realized ruefully, that the helmet radios broadcast even quiet conversation. The entire battle group had heard; even Melinde had heard. If we lose the battle today, Jahnel thought defiantly, then I'll be grim.

"Vayalim tiffs on the edge of battle?" a nasal voice drawled. "Aren't we relaxed, Louve? Amazing."

"Brood bond is all-important, Roche," Sair answered placidly, reciting an Avelle maxim everyone had learned in infancy. "Always topical."

"Louve are always relaxed," Eduard added. "Comes with the bloodline."

"And none of your business," Melinde said, ending it. She

swooped back downward to Jahnel and linked arms shyly. "I'm a problem," she murmured.

"A most beloved problem, yes."

"I'm sorry, Jahnel. I'll try to do better."

Jahnel squeezed Melinde's arm against her ribs, smiling at her.

"I'm sorr-eee, Jahnel," the nasal voice mocked over the radio circuit. "Great claws!"

"You want your air line yanked out, Philippe?" Eduard asked heatedly. "Just keep it up and I'll oblige."

"That's enough," came Rodolphe's calm voice. "Battle Master says shut up, everybody."

Jahnel heard a ripple of laughter over the radio circuit, then only the sound of soft breathing, multiplied many times. As the uppermost Faon neared the top of the shaft, a voice ordered the invert. The first rank flipped neatly and turned into the wide doorway to the left, followed seconds later by the next ascending group. The Louve came last and joined the other defenders in the top of the Downlift. Jahnel looked around curiously at the pale metal walls and faded inscribed panels, at the side room with the shadow of machines through a doorway, and at the shimmering energy curtain over the Portal. Dimly through the curtain, she could see the blue-black glare of Quevi's sky, a rock-strewn street between high walls, and the huddled shadows of ruined buildings beyond. Never before in her life had she seen Quevi's sky; she gawked at the strangeness. Rodolphe moved into the side room, then gestured to Sair to join him. A few moments later, the energy curtain vanished.

Rodolphe reemerged and raised his hand for attention. "By battle groups. You've seen the map; you know the approaches. Yves, you remain here on guard; keep two of the Hiboux with you. All others will keep radio silence until the attack." He glanced around at the faces, his expression sober. "Our lives may depend on that silence, Faon. The miin have clever machines of unknown capacity—our strength is total surprise."

"Won't they expect a new attack?" asked a Faon of the Ruisseau, a younger man who swallowed nervously.

"They've had time to grow used to the surface robots, perhaps to think themselves safe. Niintua gave us the data from the surface machines, the same proof he offered Lejja." He shrugged. "Be prepared for anything. Be swift and deadly." Heads nodded. "For the Home-Space we defend."

"For the Home-Space we defend," a dozen voices echoed.

Gracefully, the first group moved through the Portal, darting into shadow along the walls, heading outward. Rodolphe gestured to Jahnel.

"Remain with me and the Etoile, Jahnel, if you will. I'll need what you hear of the miin. Do you sense anything yet?"

Jahnel watched Sair and Eduard leave with the rest of the Louve. The Etoile lingered, waiting for Rodolphe. "Only vaguely. I don't think I'm within range."

Rodolphe grunted noncommittedly, then signaled Etoile's advance. They passed through the Portal, following the other kin-groups into the shadows.

Above them, the star Rhesaa spread glowing tendrils of luminescent blue-white gas across half the horizon, dimming the array of its several red and golden companions, muting shadows, touching all with a faint bluish light that bore a deadly radiation only partly deflected by their vacuum suits. Jahnel stared for several moments at the wideness of the sky and the blazing magnificence of Rhessa-system's suns, then hurried after the others. The surface ruins straggled across a square kilometer around the Downlift, some walls broken into random pattern to better conceal the sentient order of regular angles from prying eyes out-system. But the miin had found Quevi Ltir—how? Against the glow of the sky, she glimpsed the distant black shape of the orbiting miin ship, the temporary home-space of the miin in this remote star system. What do they want? she wondered as she watched the speck move slowly across the sky.

Why do they invade us? She stared at the shape, as if the looking could bring answers. How could one small ship of stranger miin hope to take all of Quevi Ltir for its own—and why else is it here? To take Home-Space from *Quevi'ali*'s extensive Brooding, a fierce stock that had held primary rank in the Predator wars for a millennium? How could the miin think they could? It seemed not even miin could be so stupid. It baffled her and worried her, the not-knowing.

Jahnel abruptly sensed the miin's strange shadows within her mind, growing steadily stronger as the suval penetrated more deeply into her brain—alien presences that thought and moved, planned and determined. She wished Kiiri's psi-drug brought more than a knowledge of movement and vague intent, wished she had certainty to protect the Faon in this battle. The miin did not think like Faon: she had sensed that much in the trials and knew it now for certain as thoughts not her own teased just beneath her consciousness. She swallowed uneasily, disliking the alien touch.

She watched the speck move slowly across the array of stars, lost it in the glare of the morning, then glimpsed it once more as it swept downward and vanished behind the horizon. Why? she wondered. Who are they? Her uneasiness returned in full force, magnified by the suval's pernicious influence on her emotions. She did not like this; she did not like this at all.

❧ Chapter 2

RODOLPHE SIGNALED THE ADVANCE. Jahnel followed the Etoile down the ruined street, hugging the shadows of the wall. They moved quickly through the ruins, picking their way over broken stone, slipping lightly from shadow to shadow, cautious of any miin observer that might have been waiting ahead within the surface structures. Occasionally they crossed the path of a surface robot on patrol, single-mindedly following a deep track worn into the naked stone by centuries of ceaseless vigilance. Near the edge of the ruins, Jahnel saw a dozen laser-blackened metal hulks; the miin had advanced this far in pursuit of the machines that had destroyed their first lander. Perhaps they lingered still. Rodolphe signaled more caution, leading his group into deep shadow on the very edge of the ruins. They waited then, studying the terrain ahead. In other shadows, the other kin-groups also studied that broken expanse of stone and dust stretching to the tumbled rock of the crater lip. The starlight glared on whitish stone, striking at the eyes even through the protective faceplates. Jahnel squinted and felt her temples begin to pound with the glare of this place. Miin voices jibbered on the edges of her mind, taunting her with their nonsense.

Rodolphe snapped off his radio and signed for Jahnel to do the same, then touched his helmet to hers. "What do you hear, Jahnel?"

Jahnel closed her eyes obediently and listened, awkward in her fumbling toward those odd voices. She turned in her crouch, trying to focus first on the edge of the ruins, seeking any miin that might stand guard. She heard nothing to either side, only ahead, a strong murmuring that beat upon her mind, odd

thoughts that occupied themselves with instrument boards,
friendly contention as they talked to each other, a subtle alertness without fear. She heard the confidence of these miin
with their machines, a bitter anger about the first lander,
the prick of strong grief in a few—and a vague wish for
revenge. And an odd lust for Quevi Ltir—not a need for
territory, a need she understood too well among the Avelle
and her own kindred, but something else. She puzzled about
that, trying to amplify the unnatural sense given to her by
the suval, but the answer eluded her. What did the miin
want? Even this close, she could not say.

Rodolphe touched her arm, recalling her attention. She bent
to him and touched helmets. "I don't sense any miin on guard
in the ruins, only ahead in the crater—but I'm not certain of that,
Rodolphe. Using the suval is like fumbling in a dark tunnel."

"Do your best. So they have no guards out—odd." In the
City, absent guards invited immediate invasion by an adjoining
tier, a mistake that rarely allowed repetition by the careless iruta
who made it. Rodolphe frowned, uneasy with that difference.
"Do they have devices that might hear our advance?"

"Of what kind?"

"Hell if I know. Am I a miin?" He smiled slightly at his own
joke, his eyes only inches from her own. "Do they?"

"I'll try." She concentrated, trying to sort out the alien
minds ahead, biting her lip in frustration as they merged
and separated, like oil sheen on the surface of a water tank—
single yet multiple, eluding her. She sighed. "I can't hear
that. They are confident, angry about the earlier attack, busy
with their affairs, whatever those might be. I sense instruments, miin working together, an alertness—but they don't
sense us, not yet. I do know that."

"All right." Rodolphe turned to Etoile's alpha talent, Nathalie Jouvet, and gave her instructions to pass to the other
groups. Jahnel looked beyond him to Louve's position forty meters away, but could see nothing in the blue-black shadows. All
to the good: if she could not see her kindred, neither could the
miin—unless the miin had some strange machine that could penetrate shadow. She worried about that, and stretched out again
toward the miin, seeking the answer. In her concentration, she
nearly missed Rodolphe's chopping gesture, signaling the attack. She surged forward with the others, skimming over the
surface with the speed and grace only light gravity could lend,

crossing the intervening plain within a dozen breaths. The Etoile threw themselves down at the base of the crumbling talus beneath the crater rim.

She heard the click of the radio circuit. "So . . ." Rodolphe whispered.

Three dozen vacuum-suited bodies skimmed upward and found new positions behind the boulder ring lining the rim. Jahnel slid sideways to peer between two large rocks and steadied her dis-rifle in the crevice, aiming it at the miin ship below, and waited for Rodolphe's next command. The intruder's lander glinted under Rhesaa's glare, a squat shape of metal twenty meters long, its splayed legs gripping the rocky floor of the crater. A rung ladder extended downward from a closed hatch. Above it, halfway up the sleek sides of the ship, a wide panel glowed in yellow shades, moving subtly as if miin were walking back and forth behind it. She saw nothing moving outside the ship and waited with the others, memorizing every part of the lander, her hands tight on her rifle. A babble of voices drifted underneath her mind, nonsense mostly, an occasional sharp clear thought. *All clear, chief,* she heard suddenly, as if someone had spoken immediately beside her ear, then only the low murmuring.

Then a miin came into view from behind the ship, and her finger almost squeezed the trigger in shocked reflex. She heard several audible gasps over the helmet circuit and knew that she, too, had made that quick withdrawing of breath. Two legs, two arms, human proportions, and, more subtly, a human way of movement, a skilled adjustment to low gravity she had seen all her life among the Faon. Astounded, she watched the spacesuited figure reach up and pull on a projection above his head, testing something, then walk lightly back around the ship, heading for the ladder. Human?

She turned to look at Rodolphe, but the older man was focused on that single figure. He bent over his dis-rifle, aiming carefully. "This should bring the others out," he said. "On alert, Faon." His dis-rifle flared, crumpling the miin in midstride. A puff of atmosphere burst outward from the huddled shape, freezing instantly into a slowly expanding cloud of crystals. Within seconds, the hatch-door slid open and another miin appeared in the lock, holding something long and thin in his hands. A dis-bolt from Jahnel's far left lashed out, throwing the second miin backward out of sight. The hatch flashed shut an instant later.

"What the devil?" Rodolphe said in surprise.

"They aren't Avelle," Jahnel reminded him, surprised that he expected Avelle response. "No slash instinct. It's a different pattern."

"Open general fire," Rodolphe commanded.

"They won't come out," she told him urgently. "We're too exposed, Rodolphe. Rodolphe!"

He ignored her. "Concentrate fire on the lander legs." A turret on the lander swiveled toward their position.

"Fire incoming!" Jahnel cried out, as she sensed a mind's intention behind that machine's movement. An instant later, rock exploded around them, shattering into fragments. She clung to the ground, trying to bury herself in the small crevice beneath her body, as a cloud of dust drifted down on her. The lander's weapon spoke again, targeting to the left, then again and again, demolishing the edge of the crater with mechanical precision. Jahnel slid hastily backward down the talus, dragging her rifle with her, then looked up to see Rodolphe's suit shredded, his body blown half apart. Another Etoile lay beside him, also dead, and other bodies lay beyond along the crater lip, alive or dead, she couldn't tell.

"Sair!" she called, forcing down a stab of fear that Sair lay among those too-still bodies. "Sair! Rodolphe is dead!" She heard the panic in her own voice and struggled for self-control as the lander's machine spoke again, showering her with dust. "Sair!"

"Retreat, Faon," Sair said, his urgent voice crackling over the radio band. "Back to the ruins. *Now!*"

A new concussion rained down rock fragments all around Jahnel and the surviving Etoile as they scrambled backward. Jahnel stumbled to one knee, then ran across the flat ground to the nearest building and its shadows. She swerved instantly as another missile exploded directly ahead, skipping lightly out of range of the rocketing stone. Another projectile exploded, blocking their way to the right.

"Etoile!" she called, and ran to the left, ducking another concussion of stone as she and the Etoile escaped into a shadowed gap between two buildings. They darted from shadow to shadow down the alleyway, trying to outrun the miin barrage. She heard a cry of pain as another bomb exploded only meters behind them, then a horrid gasping over the radio circuit as the Faon's vacuum suit collapsed. She responded instantly and bounced hard against a jutting stone, reversed neatly in midair on the rebound, then ran back to the body writhing on the stone street. Another missile exploded far to the right, then another to the left. As she threw herself down beside the injured Faon, two pain-startled eyes looked dazedly at her through the fogged faceplate.

"Leave me . . ."

"Shut up, Nathalie," Jahnel said furiously. She hurriedly slapped a repair seal on the long gash in Nathalie's suit leg, then moved her hands aside as Jean-Luc sealed the rest of the gash from his own belt kit.

"I can't breathe . . ." Nathalie gasped, her face dusky with lack of oxygen. Her head lolled backward.

"Turn up your airflow, Nathalie." When the woman did not respond, Jahnel shook her hard. "Nathalie! Key your airflow!" Jahnel shook her again, rocking Nathalie's head inside her helmet, then saw Nathalie dazedly nudge the neck-ring control with her chin. "Good. On your feet, Faon. Help me with her, Jean-Luc."

Together they lifted Nathalie by her arms and half dragged her several meters. Nathalie began to help then, gaining strength with each stride, her breathing ragged with pain—but breathing. We forget how precious breath can be, we in our City, Jahnel thought, and heard again the mutter of miin voices deep beneath her mind. With a flush of anger, she hated those voices, that taint within her and within her world, and wished death for the miin. We will kill you all for this, she promised fiercely. All. As they reached the next street, the other Etoile closed around them and together they fled deeper into the ruins, seeking shadow to conceal and regroup.

Near an open square by the Downlift, Jean-Luc took Nathalie downward for tending in the First Turning; four other wounded followed, supported by their kindred. Jahnel looked for Sair and found him with the other kin-leaders in the alcove of a small building on a side street off the square, where the thick stone and metal walls would block revealing radio transmissions as they debated. She slipped among them and settled beside Sair. Her husband's face was flushed with anger as he faced Philippe Sarrat, kin-leader today of the Roche battle group, also an angry man. Neither Sair nor Philippe liked to lose, chafing even at minor setbacks in the tier wars—and this quick reverse already bordered on humiliation.

And what else in this defeat? Jahnel wondered, looking out through the doorway at the blue shadows of Quevi's deadly surface. What would Niintua do if they took him this news—and how would Koyil use it against the Faon? She frowned.

"Niintua didn't tell us about that ship weapon!" Philippe said hotly. "Or the bombs!"

"Quiet!" Sair said. "That doesn't help now, Roche. The weapons are fact: accept them." He grimaced. "Rodolphe expected the miin to swarm out like Avelle do, like they did the first time. But the miin learned, changed their tactics. So will we." He looked around the faces. In the distance, the miin barrage had stopped, an ominous forewarning of the enemy advance. "I want scouts forward," Sair said. "One from each kin-group, to watch for the miin. When they come deeper into the ruins, we can ambush them from shadow."

"If they enter the ruins," Philippe said. "Why should they?"

Sair smiled thinly. "Because we are here. They pursued the robots to wreak their punishments—why not us?"

"And bring what other weapons, Sair?" Philippe demanded. He lifted his dis-rifle and shook it in frustration. "Laser rifles against bombs and cannon—how can we expect to win a battle like that?"

"Maybe we won't win," Sair said calmly. "That's always a possible fortune of battle. Do you suggest we return to Niintua and not try further?"

"Of course not," Philippe said with a sniff.

"Then get constructive. I'm angry, too. We have dead we could not retrieve—I don't like leaving them for the miin to violate. I don't like the tactical situation, the vacuum, the radiation. I don't like being forty of us against a ship full of miin, while the Avelle idle below." He looked around the group bleakly. "But it's more than our personal survival, my kinbrothers: what we do today counts on all Faon. Don't deceive yourself. We agreed to fight—we must fight, to the last Faon if necessary." Jahnel shifted uncomfortably.

"Sair . . ." she began.

"Do you hear the miin?" he interrupted, turning to her. She blinked, startled by his abruptness.

"Vaguely. Wait a minute." She looked away toward the crater, as if her eyes could penetrate stone and metal, bringing other sensations to bind with the muttering voices beneath her mind. Anger, excitement: they were coming now, cautiously, heavily armed. She heard a burst of emotion as the leader reached the crater rim and found a Faon body, then confusion and dismay among the miin as they gathered around the body. "Something's happening . . ." she murmured. Two miin bent and carried the body back into the crater, stumbling with the weight, while the others disputed.

"What?" Sair demanded. When she didn't answer immediately, he grabbed her arm too roughly and she jerked away irritably. She glared at him.

"Sair," she said with asperity, "forge ahead if you must, but leave me follow at my own pace. 'To the last Faon?' Are you crazy?"

Sair set his jaw at her tone, his eyes glinting angrily. "Don't start, Jahnel. For once, just once when it's important, give some kin-obedience."

"Pfui, beloved. Am I that bad? And when have I ever denied you kin-obedience—when it's important? You're thinking in too narrow a pattern, Sair—Avelle patterns, which is how we got in this great-claws den in the first place. Avelle die to the last tier soldier—if you're servant-class—which is probably just what Niintua and Koyil are hoping we'll do. Slash these forty, then send up forty more Faon, slash them, and then . . ."

"All right," he sighed. "You've made your point. No dying to the last Faon."

"Thank you. The miin are now leaving the crater, by the way."

Sair sent her a sharp look that promised a few discussions later—if they had a later, she thought grimly.

Philippe stirred impatiently. "Their weapons . . ."

"Which we don't have," Jean Tardieu of the Hiboux said, then quelled Philippe with a look. "Listen, Sair: we do have our dis-rifles and a detailed map of these ruins—and we have the surface robots. Do we know about any other surface defenses? Surely Koyil has more than mobile robots. Where are *our* cannon and bombs?"

"Niintua chose not to share details." Sair hesitated, scowling. "Maybe he told Rodolphe, but I wasn't there if he did. Our dis-rifles were to be more than enough."

"Typical," Jean snorted. "Blinkered Avelle thinking. I think Jahnel's right about what Niintua really has in mind." He frowned, his brown eyes abstracted, then glanced at the Ruisseau and the Etoile. "I doubt if the miin have explored as far as the Downlift or we'd have found signs of their tampering at the

Portal. So they won't know these shadows and we do, another advantage. If we can ambush several of them, maybe circle back around to the lander . . ."

"Against bombs?" Philippe asked incredulously.

"Oh, stuff it, Philippe," Jean said, obviously out of patience. "For once, just pitch in and stop squawking." Jean pushed him off balance, and Philippe went sprawling on the stone floor. Jahnel reached over and yanked Philippe off balance again as he started for Jean.

"Great jittering claws, Philippe. Do you think with your mind or the battle drugs? Calm down."

"You—you—" Philippe sputtered.

"Calm down," she repeated firmly. "Use all that zeal on stalking the miin." Philippe muttered at her, but contented himself with a glare at Jean. Jean smiled nastily and nearly started it all over again. Jahnel raised her hands and chopped them down, ending it. "That's enough, you two. Do we have your attention? Ruisseau? Etoile? I suggest we try for some sort of victory today—do you agree, Sair, my kin-brothers? But we won't win everything, not with this balance of weapons."

"We need equal weapons," Philippe muttered.

"We will get them," Sair said firmly. "Out of Niintua's hide, if necessary. Are we agreed?" He looked around at the faces, receiving their nods one by one. "Then let us prepare. Alpha talents will coordinate, and I expect data from you, Jahnel."

"You'll get it."

"Thank you," he said ironically, and scowled at her fiercely. Definitely discussions, she thought, and smiled back.

He grunted, unappeased. "Then to battle, Faon. Attack and feint."

Two hours later, the miin had pushed the battle nearly to the Downlift, forcing the Faon to group dangerously close among the tumbled ruins near the shaft. Jahnel could see a dozen Faon shapes in nearby shadows, hidden behind stone and tortured metal. If the miin cast another of their destruction bombs, a quarter of the City's defenders might fall. Yet still Sair would not retreat into the fallways.

She flinched as another cluster bomb exploded far to the right and reverberated through the stone beneath her prone body. In the distance beyond the crumbling building that sheltered them, a cloud of pulverized rock shot upward in a smooth bell of dust, then drifted downward, scattering loosely onto crumbling roofs and ancient walls. A second bomb fell on ruined stone farther to the right, sending another concussion shuddering through the ground. Dust drifted downward from the roof above them, lazy in the light gravity of Quevi Ltir, coating their vacuum suits with a powdery mist. The miin fired their bombs in scattered pattern now, no longer certain of the Faon positions and wary of hitting their own forces advancing into the ruins. The Faon had harried the miin fiercely from street to street, shooting from cover and then moving quickly away before the ship retaliated with a new barrage—but air tanks were low and all fatigued, the battle drugs fading. She saw Sair's frustration, sensed the rage among the Faon—and still the bombs came too close.

"We must go down, Sair," she whispered into her voice mike.

Sair's helmet turned toward her and she saw the flash of alert eyes through his blue-shadowed faceplate, nearly lost in the glare of Rhesaa's morning. "Have they targeted the Downlift?" he asked.

"No . . . not that. I'm losing contact in the afterhaze." She swallowed uneasily, feeling the first wave of nausea as the suval faded from her system. This time the drug had faded sooner; it would hurt her more afterward.

"We'll push them back," Sair said.

"Not today, Sair," she said. "Ask the other kin-leaders if you must; we're too exposed in this position. We must go down."

"I agree." Jean's strained voice sounded in their headphones. He turned and looked at them, his own frustration written plainly on his face. "We must go down, Sair," he said.

Sair clenched his hand on his dis-rifle, then nodded a reluctant assent. She knew he had hoped for a better victory today, if only to give the defenders a reprieve before the next. Rodolphe might have hoped for honors; Sair thought more narrowly of exhausted men and women, of the dangerous vacuum of the surface that allowed no mistakes, of a surface battle that leached strength from the Faon. It was his gift, to think in such terms, one of the reasons she loved him. She heard the click of the all-group circuit.

"Into the Downlift, Faon. Regroup at the First Turning."

A sigh of soft acknowledgments sounded in Jahnel's ear, then an echo as the other kin-groups received the order. Etoile, Hiboux, Roche, Ruisseau, her own Louve: of the thousands of kin-groups in Quevi Ltir, bound within their rankings into the great kin-alliances that ruled each of the City's fourteen tiers, only five tiny kin-groups were human, bound together into the kin-alliance Faon, an alien presence in the City. She swallowed uncomfortably as the suval nausea struck again, her head spinning with too much knowledge, too little.

Sair moved to her across the slide of crumbled stone and pressed her arm through the tough fabric of her vacuum suit. "I'll help you, beloved."

"Please." She reached out to him, comforted by his familiar touch.

"Can you sense anything at all?" he asked anxiously.

Jahnel looked into Sair's dark eyes, the effect of the suval adding an uneasy halo to her vision. His lean body, enshrouded in the smooth dark gray of his vacuum suit, seemed bathed in a stretched light, more than starlight. Beyond him, the others of the Louve vanished into a drug-induced haze. Her time was running out quickly now; already the suval threatened other hallucinations. She swallowed again and tried to concentrate.

"Four to the right," she said, "near the Hiboux—two miin move forward toward Building Twenty-seven." She closed her eyes, reaching out again with her unnatural sense toward the enemy. "Six still near the lander-ship, guarding it. Three . . ." Her head sank forward on her arms as yet another wave of dizziness swept over her. Demonic shapes gibbered at the edge of her mind, then reached toward her, displacing Sair's comforting presence.

"Jahnel?" His fingers pressed her arm, bringing her back.

"Two on the left, waiting—the leader is thinking of bombing our sector. We *must* go down!"

"We will, beloved. Hold on now." The gentleness in Sair's voice comforted her, reminding of other times long before the miin came to attack Quevi Ltir and Koyil worked his plots against the Faon. All had been innocent then, especially a young bride named Jahnel Alain. She sagged against him.

"Melinde, help me with her." Jahnel felt the slight vibration on stone as her sister-wife joined them, then Melinde's touch on her other arm.

Together they helped Jahnel to her feet and moved toward the Downlift, their boots catching awkwardly at the iron subsurface beneath the puff of soil. Other Faon flitted across the tumbled stone, keeping to the black shadows of the airless surface. Al-

ready half their force had vanished into the Downlift; others
followed, moving with the quick speed possible only in the light
gravity of the asteroid's surface. Like a stream of shadowed
smoke, the Faon flowed back into the depths of Quevi Ltir.

Halfway to the Downlift, a warning lashed suddenly across
Jahnel's mind as a distant miin stabbed at a control button.
"Missile incoming!" she screamed, and turned automatically
to look upward. Sair dragged at her roughly, forcing her to turn.

"Jump!" he shouted.

Melinde tightened her grip on Jahnel's other arm, and together they leaped madly for the Portal. As they soared through
the metal frame of the doorway into the safety of its shadows, a
blazing light shattered the darkness behind them. Hands grasped
them quickly and pulled them aside, a scant second before a
concussion of pulverized stone rocketed through the open doorway. Jahnel heard a scream of agony that abruptly ended.

"Down!" Sair ordered. "Carry the injured with us!" He
turned, searching for Eduard among the nearby Faon. "Is everyone here, Eduard?" he asked.

Eduard paused a moment, his expression abstracted as he
mentally called to the other alpha talents. A sheen of sweat
covered his broad face, visible through his faceplate, and Jahnel
became aware of the prickle of sweat on her own skin. Eduard,
too, had little time left under the drug. Then others would take
the burden, and then more, if the Principals insisted on sending
new Faon to the surface . . . But Kiiri had not yet found another
like Jahnel, one who heard miin instead of Faon. What will we
do if he cannot? she wondered. She closed her eyes, surrounded
by strange miin thoughts only she could hear, as the miin spoke
strange nonsense to each other with great urgency, hiding anger,
half-sensed intention.

Go away, she told them fiercely, hating them for their intruder's taint, and for the deaths they had made among her kindred.
Go away.

Already the miin ground forces—four, six, eight miin—were
scurrying toward the Downlift entrance, wary of ambush, crafty
and clever in their weapons, intent on their intrusion into what
was not theirs. The miin leader in front hesitated, scanning the
black shadows ahead, his hands aching with the tightness of his
grip on his weapon, fear uppermost in his mind. Yes, fear us,
she wished him. Fear us until your heart flows to water, your
strength vanishes into shadow. Take your taint away.

"We lost Marc Jouvet of Hiboux," Eduard reported. Jahnel

blinked and jerked back to here-and-now away from miin whispers, like a tether recoiling into its case. "Genevieve says he disappeared during the last skirmish. Unconscious, probably dead. She doesn't know which—her suval sensitivity is limited, even among her own kin-group. The Hiboux couldn't reach Marc's position again." He curled his gloved fingers into a fist, his face anguished as he shared Genevieve's grief through their drug-induced contact. Jahnel looked around distractedly, her head spinning as she automatically counted faces among the Louve, anxious for her own loved ones. "Stefan says four of the Ruisseau were blown to fragments in the bombardment . . ." Another pause, as Eduard linked with the other alpha talents and completed the grisly tally. "Those five also, including Rodolphe; the Etoile brought in the bodies we could reach."

"Very well," Sair said wearily. "Raise the barrier."

Jean slipped quickly into the shadowed alcove nearby. An energy screen shimmered into existence across the doorway, visible only in its faint distortion of the broken street beyond. They were safe . . . for now.

"At the First Turning, Battle Master?" Jean asked when he returned, his face grim.

"If the miin come that far and can find the Portal," Sair said. "If they do and if they're smart, they won't—we've shown them enough of the City defenses to make them think about it." He glanced at the energy screen, his face strained. "If we have to, we can destroy the Downlift. A few dis-rifles on overload could do it."

"They won't try," Jahnel said with certainty, drawing on the last embers of her enhanced psi. Already she could hear the baffled anger beyond the doorway, the hesitation as the miin realized their prey had again escaped. The miin still feared Quevi Ltir's subterranean mystery and would not try the Downlift, not yet.

With that last touch, her gift flickered and vanished, leaving her clammy-skinned and empty; she sagged against Melinde and felt her sister-wife take a stronger grip on her suit belt.

"Jahnel needs tending," Melinde said worriedly.

"Take her to Kiiri," Sair ordered. "And you, too, Eduard, all the alpha talents. We can't risk losing any of you."

"I'm all right," Eduard said, straightening his slump.

"That aside, that's an order."

"Yes, Sair."

Melinde tugged on Jahnel's belt to get her moving. Jahnel felt

Eduard's strong arm slip around her from the other side as she limped to the Downlift, and turned her head to smile up at him, then thought better of the effort when she saw a flash of alarm cross his face. "Do I look that bad, Eduard?" she asked ruefully.

"Not good, my love. I look the same, no doubt." He scowled, dragging together his bushy eyebrows, as if puzzled at the reason. He pressed her closer to him, and she felt his chest rumble with a low chuckle. "Maybe it's old age," he suggested lightly. "We're too many years past twenty now, both of us. Another year or two and we'll be doddering around the fallways. Don't you agree, Melinde?"

"Definitely."

"Ah, youth," Eduard said, and tweaked Melinde's arm in a playful caress.

Melinde shook him off irritably, tossing her head. "Cut it out, Eduard," she said with a ferocious scowl that mixed unpleasantly with her sharp-angled face. If only I could blend them a little, Jahnel thought feelingly, making one more serious, the other less so. Life might be easier. She sighed and closed her eyes.

Eduard pressed her still closer to him, comforting her. Melinde left off with her snit and intertwined her arm with Eduard's across Jahnel's back, enclosing her sister-wife still closer in a mutual embrace. Jahnel relaxed into the arms of her beloveds, supported by their strength against the aftershocks of the suval. Several paces from the edge of the shaft, her feet slipped into a long-trained rhythm with her companions and all three simultaneously launched themselves over the wide shaft of the fallway. The asteroid's light gravity snatched at them, and they fell into the blackness.

They fell several meters feetfirst into the Downlift, tracked by the defense robots in their one-minded attention. "Invert," Jahnel ordered weakly, and the three jackknifed gracefully toward the depths, still linked arm in arm. Melinde touched her belt-jet controls, increasing their rate of fall by a meter or so per second. Jahnel took a ragged breath, her head pounding "Left turn . . . invert."

The three landed neatly on the landing of the First Turning, then cycled through the atmosphere lock. Yves Rostand, Sair's birth-brother, stood guard by the air lock, a dis-rifle in the crook of his arm; other Faon clustered near the other end of the gathering room, waiting, several too-still human forms at their feet.

A woman knelt close by one of the dead, shoulders shaking as she clasped the limp hand in her own. All looked exhausted, depleted by too many hours on the surface, the grief of too many kin-deaths, the waning strength of the battle drugs. Above them, the surface thundered as the miin vented their rage on ruined stone.

"How many dead today, Eduard?" Yves asked quietly.

Heads turned toward them, anxious for the answer, all knowing what even one death meant to what truly counted in Quevi Ltir. Even into their fourth generation, the Faon could not afford such losses from their levels; the deaths in the surface battle, but a minor number in any skirmish between Avelle tiers housing thousands, had taken nearly ten percent of Faon adults. The Faon could not afford such losses, not and expect to hold their Home-Space against the territorial pressure from nearby Avelle levels, for all the Principal's favor and the friendships with the Avelle of her tier. In Quevi Ltir, an iruta held its territory by breeding numbers or perished.

"At the moment, twelve," Eduard said grimly. "Two more may die from decompression injuries, four others from burns." He scowled. "Niintua won't be pleased," he muttered, and glanced beyond the gathered Faon to the Turning.

Niintua drifted into view in the far shadows of the Turning, his emotions apparent only in the steady flicking of his segmented tail beneath his wing-flaps. The Avelle Battle Leader shivered in agitation as he advanced, menacing the Faon near him. Several Faon shifted away, moving out of his attack-threat range; in this mood, an Avelle had few controls over his instincts, and Niintua was not known for wishing any.

"Why have you retreated?" Niintua rasped, his francais barely understandable in his rage. "Return to the surface—*now!*" He drifted closer, advancing on them, wing-flaps spreading in threat, revealing the pallid segmented body beneath.

Eduard faced him calmly. "Our position became too exposed," he replied in Avelle speech, adding the aftergesture of necessity. Niintua glared all the more, further insulted by Eduard's choice of language—though apparently anything would insult Niintua today. Eduard lifted his chin and defied him; Jahnel felt Melinde start to edge backward and checked her.

"Hold," she whispered. "Don't back away."

"But he's showing attack-threat," Melinde whispered back frantically. "This is crazy. What is Eduard trying to prove?"

"Stand still, Melinde!" Jahnel insisted.

Niintua quivered in rage and seemed to puff himself to twice his size, his tail flicking as he moved still closer. Jahnel felt Eduard's body tense and tried to shake off her own fogs, tensing for flight—but she knew they had already let Niintua come too close. As Niintua came within a few bodylengths, shivering with agitation, Yves calmly raised his dis-rifle and steadied it on his forearm, centering Niintua in his riflesight.

"Do that, Battle Leader," he said softly, "and it's the last you do."

Niintua halted abruptly, his pupils widening in shock. "You threaten a Principal?" he asked incredulously.

"You threaten the Louve?" Yves countered. "Jahnel is kin-sister to me; I claim brood-right. You have no cause to attack. Back off!"

"Brood-right," Niintua spat. "You?" He made the question sound like an obscenity. His eyes shifted to Jahnel. "Reprimand your kinsman. I demand it!"

Jahnel set her jaw. "We are the Faon," she declared proudly. "We are guest-brothers of Lejja, Principal of Songs, and reside in her tier. Protest to her, Battle Leader, and hear her answer yet again—and back off."

Niintua's jaws worked convulsively as he hesitated; then, in a flash, he abruptly flipped his wing-flaps and inverted back-ward, vanishing around the far turning. Everyone immediately tensed, wary of a feint for quick return and slashing attack, but Niintua did not reappear. After a few moments, a Faon slipped to the corner and looked, then signed reassurance.

Eduard blew out a breath. "Thanks, Yves," he said. "I thought that was the end of us. Has he been showing attack-threat all morning?"

Yves shrugged. "What else is new? One of his servant-guards chased Lucien halfway down the fallway when she drifted too closely—let's say Niintua was a little slow in calling him off."

Melinde tossed her head. "I think if Niintua wants the right to an opinion," she said, "let him fight on the surface with the Faon. It's time the Avelle ventured their own bodies, as well as ours." Jahnel heard an angry murmur of agreement.

"Melinde," she murmured reprovingly.

"Well, it's true!" Melinde said hotly. "Why should we be the only warriors? What do we win? How long until the Avelle use our losses as their excuse to drive us from our levels and take them for themselves? How long do we *really* have left, Jahnel?"

"Later, Melinde, please." Jahnel pressed her sister-wife's arm warningly. Sound carried easily in the warm air of the fallways, and Avelle had acute hearing, better than human.

Melinde glared at her in baffled anger. "So what if the Avelle hear? 'Later, later.' When is 'later,' Jahnel? When the Avelle have no more human bodies to send to the slaughter?"

Melinde's shrill voice jangled unpleasantly in Jahnel's ears. She closed her eyes and swayed against Eduard, suddenly exhausted by the younger woman's emotions. Too close. "Let me recover, Melinde, and we will talk—this time. I promise." An odd sensation shuddered up her body, as if her limbs were writhing subtly beneath the skin, flashing pinpricks of heat into her fingers. Kiiri had warned her of the progressive damage; soon the drug would kill brain tissue even beyond the Science Leader's capacity to repair.

Would Kiiri regret her death? she wondered groggily. The Avelle felt emotions differently than did humans. Perhaps. Too close. She felt another wave of heat flow from her feet upward, weakening her.

"Help me . . ." she said faintly.

Melinde and Eduard caught her as she sagged. "I'm sorry, Jahnel," Melinde murmured in quick regret. "I forget when I get angry."

"Hold on, love," Eduard said. "Philippe—you report to Sair what happened here with Niintua. I'm taking Jahnel to Kiiri. All alpha talents to go below—Sair's order."

He waited impatiently as four others moved forward and joined them. Together the Faon passed around the Turning and approached the wide opening of the next fallway. At its edge, they launched themselves into another graceful descent, falling into the light and warmth of their adopted City. Jahnel tightened her grip on Eduard, clinging to his sturdy strength, and felt him respond immediately, but lost her struggle against the chaos in her mind.

Betrayal . . . death . . . the loss of everything: the demons gibbered in the distance, taunting her, walking with miin bodies, laughing with miin voices. Who are they? she wondered weakly. What do they want here? She moaned as her body began to shudder convulsively.

"Jahnel?"

For a moment, Eduard's anxious voice nearly called her back, but no—too close. She fell helplessly into unsafe shadows, defenseless against their terrors, lost in the darkness of her own mind.

Kiiri, help me.

ℜ Chapter 3

"JAHNEL!"

The whispering voice was insistent, and Jahnel slowly returned to the here and now, conscious of the press of a pallet mattress against her back, a movement of cool air on her face, the sounds of quiet movement nearby. She opened her eyes and looked into Kiiri's wideset pupils, the depths blood-red like a flickering flame. The Avelle floated nearby, his broad fleshy wing-flaps wrapped tightly across his body, shielding his soft abdomen. She looked at the broad naked head with its vestigial ears, at the thin-lipped mouth nearly buried in the folds of his lower face, the flickering eyes, and tried to assemble them into a memory.

Who?

The alien stared at her dispassionately, watching her face. Then those flickering eyes, twin flames of intelligence and a cold curiosity, bound the image together for her. She knew that gaze.

"And who am I?" he asked, responding to the shift in her expression.

"Kiiri."

"Good." The Science Leader stretched out a thin, clawed arm from beneath his wing-flap and tapped the portable monitor at her feet. He studied the reading on his machine, then snaked his arm back into concealment, drifting slightly aside in the light gravity. He pushed himself back casually against the bedframe with his tail-tip. "Life readings nearly normal. You recover—this time."

"Thank you, Kiiri. The others?"

"Others are not as poisoned—yet. You have an innate sensitivity to suval, both gift and deficit. Is why you can reach so

34

far—even to the miin.'' The thin lips twitched, caught in some
quirk of Avelle humor.

"Funny?'' she challenged him.

"Rude to ask,'' he said with a sniff. Kiiri edged slowly down
the bed, checking other underframe readouts that measured skin
temperature, blood flow, and muscle tension.

"I'm still asking,'' she said.

"Persistent, you. Maybe indigestion, caused Kiiri's lips to
writhe.'' Kiiri flicked his segmented tail irritably, then curled it
from view under his dark wing-flaps.

She ignored the gesture. "Faker,'' she accused. "You only
scramble your francais when you're hiding something.'' She
allowed her own mouth to turn upward, mocking him. "Faker,''
she repeated.

Kiiri snorted. "Am not.''

"Faker.''

Kiiri grimaced and gave in. He drifted back along the bed.
"I was thinking maybe we could steal some miin to listen to the
miin; would save using up the Faon so rashly.''

"Is it rash?''

"Very rash. But since when does the Battle Leader listen to
the Science Leader?''

"Only when there are no battles.''

"Yes.'' Kiiri's eyes flickered a moment, a regret quickly concealed. "Melinde is unhappy?''

Jahnel sighed: so Niintua or his guards had overheard. "She
doesn't understand.''

"Do you?''

"No. But I trust in you, Kiiri.''

Kiiri seemed to shudder, and turned away. "Humans can be
foolish,'' he said gruffly.

"No more foolish,'' Jahnel countered, "than Avelle who lock
themselves inside a stone prison and sing vainly of the Returning.''

Kiiri swelled himself and huffed. "What does a Faon know
of the Greatest of Songs?'' But the protest was halfhearted. He
wrapped his wing-flaps more tightly around himself and idly
rubbed one tip against his ear, slowly rotating back to face her.
A self-calming gesture, she thought, recognizing it from other
times. Or today maybe only an invert, who could tell? The Avelle delighted in misdirection.

"You must speak to Melinde,'' Kiiri said at last. "Niintua

will tell the Principal of Laws. Koyil will not tolerate her anger.''

''Perhaps, Science Leader, you have heard of what I said to Niintua at the First Turning.''

The Avelle's eyes flickered, confirming nothing. She made a gesture of minor defiance, tempting him.

''Let Koyil explain himself to Melinde and others. I will not.''

Kiiri tightened his wing-flaps around his body, ignoring her challenge—or refusing it. Who could say? She hadn't the mind now for deciphering Kiiri's word games. She closed her eyes wearily.

''Yet you do not doubt?'' he insisted.

''No . . . not yet, Kiiri.''

''Still, you must speak to Melinde,'' he persisted. ''You are a senior wife, influential among the Louve; she will listen.''

''Perhaps. The Faon are human, Kiiri, not Avelle—you of all Avelle should know that. Kin-dominance isn't bred into our genes, whatever heresy you think that and shudder to admit.'' She lifted herself onto one elbow and accused him. ''A convenient reality: what is, isn't—by Avelle decision. We are Faon: you wish us Avelle.''

''I do not wish any such thing,'' he said gruffly. ''I have never asked that. You confuse your Principals.''

''Oh? Then why are you twitching?''

''I do *not* twitch,'' Kiiri said loftily. ''I'm a Principal of long tenure with four dozen kin-sons: twitching does not fit my dignity.''

She made a rude noise, then sank back on the mattress and studied his flickering eyes, probing for the hidden meaning that lay there. ''What is disturbing you, Kiiri?'' she asked. ''Our differences? After all this time? Our kin-groupings are by convenience, Science Leader, as easily rearranged as you cannot rearrange your own. You've never complained before, not you. What else disturbs you? That the Faon choose to obey and to breed as they will? You know that will not change. We gave up our other customs and took yours, learned the ways of your City as our way, but we will not change what we kept. Hasn't Lejja allowed us that Song for a generation?''

Kiiri shrugged, then idly returned her earlier gesture, granting her a respect of sorts in the implied equality. ''So she said, but even a Principal of Songs can forget. Lejja grows old. New voices speak in the inner city, until Law may rise to constrain even the Songs, especially yours, Faon. The battle did not go well.'' Kiiri's eyes flickered.

"And Science? Will Science also speak against the Faon?''

Kiiri gestured gently. "I? What have I to say about Law and Song? Few listen to me now, except to ask for more weapons against the miin." His eyes flickered again. "Once they asked Science to understand a ship of strangers, to build a home for them among us as Song decreed. Only Law disputed, keeping to the older ways. Be careful, Jahnel: change can be swift, even among an ancient people.''

A clawed finger brushed her arm gently in a near caress, quickly withdrawn. "Rest there. In a few hours I will return you to the Louve." He drifted to the doorway and left her.

The room was quiet and shadowed, her bed comfortable beneath her; in the next room, she heard a low rumble of voices as Kiiri instructed his servant, then the hiss of a door and silence. She closed her eyes, listening to her own heartbeat, conscious of the slow rise and fall of her chest as she breathed.

She rested, still lightheaded from the suval aftereffects, and worried about what troubled Kiiri behind his subtleties—and what he had meant to warn.

After an hour, Jahnel grew impatient with lying abed and determinedly got herself up. Kiiri's servant, Alavu, disputed, insisting that she wait until his master returned. They had a brief argument as Jahnel put on the hooded aal and bodysuit Eduard had left for her. In the end, she pushed Alavu gently aside and then darted out of reach as he reacted to her physical intrusion into his body-field. He made a halfhearted attempt to catch her as she headed for the door; as she danced out of range to the far wall, he flipped her an exasperated word with his wing-tip. Jahnel promptly touched her belt jet and turned upside down in Avelle mockery, then flipped a ruder word back.

He maneuvered toward her, eyes glinting.

"I'm going back to the Louve," she informed him sternly. "Tell Kiiri I feel fine.''

"The Science Leader told me to keep you here until he returned," Alavu protested, and grabbed at her. Again she darted out of range. Alavu puffed himself in threat, for all his lack of breeding rank to give such discourtesy to a breeding female, Faon or not. Jahnel lazily inverted a full circle, unimpressed, and saw Alavu give it up, though he still glared.

"Stuff it, kin-brother," she said, and headed for the door. "Don't worry—Kiiri knows me well enough not to blame you."

"I'm *not* your kin-brother," he groused after her, twitching his wing-flaps indignantly. "Song perish the thought."

Jahnel laughed, and left the lab. She quickly handed herself down the wall rungs of the connecting corridor, slipping deftly to the exterior doorway and the tier's central fallway beyond. Kiiri's science lab, which occupied an entire level near Lejja's complex of administrative offices, brooding chambers, and City-Net communications, opened onto the fallway only a dozen levels below the great Gate and the broad common thoroughfare bisecting the City. Several meters from the doorway, she could hear the muted roar of the thoroughfare traffic, a busy stream of commercial exchange and messengers protected by custom from challenge. Before launching into the fallway, she put out her head past the doorway frame and prudently inspected upward for approaching Avelle, then edged out on the level's entry platform to look down. Although Lejja's iruta accepted the Faon after long acquaintance, even the Faon's home Avelle sometimes jerked with the attack-threat impulse if approached too suddenly. In other fallways elsewhere in the City, the Faon kept well away from other Avelle, and fled for their lives if they inadvertently strayed too close. It was a lesson of the fallways and why Jahnel so relentlessly pursued her small daughter, Luelle, when Luelle made another of her escapes from the Faon home-levels: the child was too young to understand the danger. It would come in time, as it had come to Jahnel, but Luelle was only three.

She positioned her boot on the doorway frame, then pushed off. A full bodylength from the level platform, she inverted downward and cut in her belt jet. She fell gracefully into the shadowed depths, her arms slightly outspread to display her aal cape, her eyes flicking in all directions at the grayish Avelle forms aloft in the fallway. As she fell, she looked downward into a shadowed depth of a thousand meters, flickering with the movements of Avelle busy with their own affairs among their kindred. The tier descended a hundred levels to the lower gate and the service tunnels that ran the length of the downward bank of tiers; beneath the common lower levels and their environmental supports, sealed underlevels held the massive nuclear reactor that supplied power to the City. In the low illumination of the fallway, distant Avelle resembled only shadowed blurs, sparked by an occasional flash of the white underbelly, the slow graceful movement of their dark wing-flaps.

Avelle vision extended well into the infrared, and so even a fallway fifty meters wide required discretion. She inverted a quarter turn to glide farther around an ascending group of Avelle, then darted toward a nearby doorway as they suddenly veered in her direction. The guard Avelle within the doorway promptly challenged her, his tail flicking in anger.

"Intruder!" he shrilled, though he knew her by name. In her youth, she and Sair had often played catch-a-tail with the nestlings of the guard's home-level. Tuan, long past his own youth and such frivolous games, had watched the children's play in the fallway, sour and irritable and unamused as only an Avelle guard could be, but had tolerantly not intervened.

"No threat, Tuan," she reassured him hastily. "I'm leaving."

She checked herself on an overhead fitting, pushed off hard, and shot out of the doorway again at an angle beneath the approaching group. She was well below them before they had time to react. Rude, perhaps, but a discourtesy common to lesser-ranked Avelle in inconvenient fall patterns. She descended onward, the levels flickering past her as she accelerated. Halfway down the tier, she flipped vertically and began to brake with her belt jet, then landed neatly on the wide apron of the uppermost Faon level. The Faon on guard stirred, then relaxed as she recognized Jahnel.

"Greetings, Aunt Francoise," Jahnel said, smiling. Francoise Alain, now in her fifties and Jahnel's father's oldest sibling, had shared in the raising of Faon Leader's wayward eldest child when an entire vayalim had not sufficed to curb the girl's explorings into the tier; Jahnel regarded her with deep affection, liking her tart speech and practical attitudes. For Francoise, she would reconsider almost anything—though not always to her aunt's preferred conclusion.

"Welcome, Jahnel." Francoise moved aside in courtesy and saluted her, then peered concernedly into Jahnel's face. "How do you feel?"

"Covered with spines."

"I'm sure of that." Her aunt snorted. "You've always had that gray color. Matches your bodysuit just fine."

Jahnel spread her arms to puff her aal in threat, then pretended to lunge at her aunt. Francoise laughed and caught her hands; they tussled briefly, then broke it off as they both drifted over the doorway threshold. Her aunt toed herself back outside to her station. "I caught Luelle sneaking out this morning," she said casually, "and paddled her for the gesture she gave me when I did—just like I paddled you more times than I'd like to think of."

"I remember." Jahnel gestured an Avelle word at her, then blinked innocently. "Was it that one?"

"No." Francoise glowered.

"Then maybe this one . . ."

"Jahnel, spare my old bones, please. All right: you're just fine. I believe you. Go inside and find Sair; he wants to talk to you."

"I will. Thank you, Aunt."

"Any time, dear." Francoise sighed and shook her head, only half pretending her despair, then turned back to watch the fallway.

Jahnel drifted forward across the threshold, then inverted feet-down as she passed over the farther threshold of the entry, landing neatly as the higher gravity field of the Faon levels grabbed at her. She pushed back her hood from her blond hair and gathered her cape around her, then walked down the central hallway of the upper level, squinting against the brighter light as her eyes adjusted, sniffing appreciatively at the familiar human scents on the air, glad to be home. The miin could rage on the surface with their bombs and destructions, but all here was still unchanged, safe. Strange that it could be so, she thought, so unchanged—but it will stay so, she promised fiercely.

She paced past the open doorways of the vayalim quarters on this level, mostly Etoile and Hiboux, surrounded by the soft murmur of muffled voices, then the piercing shriek of a child. A young girl rocketed out of a nearby door, chased by a younger boy, then three other children, their voices high with excitement. Jahnel spread her aal and hissed at them in mock threat, then smiled as they taunted her with their laughter. They danced around her, shouting, then darted away as an adult appeared abruptly in the opposite door. He scowled at the children, then saw Jahnel and bowed respectfully; she returned the courtesy and walked onward, sobered by the implications in that respect. Though Benoit had not formally named Jahnel as his heir, she had lately received such respect from several elder Faon, even Benoit's own senior councilors. Her father had six children of his begetting for his choice and wasn't bound to bloodlines if he chose otherwise—yet she saw the assumption about his choosing in this recent respect. Benoit himself refused to say, whether to deny Jahnel the affirmation or to keep a stubborn silence against elder pressures, she didn't know. She frowned, not knowing what she thought about either reason, then shook it away.

I forgot to ask Kiiri about the wisdom pills, she reminded herself lightly. Don't forget again. She walked onward, her arms wrapped comfortably in her cape, relishing the sounds and tastes of home.

Forty meters farther, the hallway divided around a large central stairwell leading to the second Faon level below. The Faon had asked for the accessway connecting the levels, though the Avelle had clicked and bothered about the asking for reasons the Faon could only guess. Avelle kin-groups never shared levels, even when joined within a kin-alliance and its dozens of family connections up and down the tier. Iruta even traded breeding females with other tiers as a practice of good genetics, but all Avelle guarded their levels, absorbing the subtleties of Home-Space and kin-rankings from the nest onward; even after eighty years, the Faon had not identified all the permutations. But Lejja had consented to the stairwell, and Kiiri had helped in the building, though even he shook his head wonderingly, probably pretending. She clattered down the stairway to the central section on the second level that belonged to the Louve.

There, too, she heard a murmuring of voices, the play of children, the familiar sounds of home. She nodded to a passing group of neighbor Louve, then turned into the open doorway of her vayalim's home-space. She walked down the short corridor to the central common room and its four radiating hallways to her family's sleeping rooms, nursery and storage rooms, and tank room. A large metal table and chairs stood in room center, with other comfortable seating along the walls; above a long couch to the left, environmental monitors flickered on a wide wall panel, bracketed by two of Solveya's abstract paintings.

Luelle's pet fur-bird, Smart-Mouth, watched from a ceiling light bracket, its four black eyes gleaming malevolently. As Jahnel stepped into the room, it squawked angrily and flashed its eye patches, then hitched itself indignantly out of sight behind the bracket. Avelle did not keep pets and thought fur-birds merely a tasty food animal among tastier others, but the first Faon had missed Earth animals and saw another possibility in the irascible creatures. Nearly every vayalim kept one of the animals for their children.

"Smart-Mouth, you'll singe your fur up there," Jahnel said.

Muttering grumpily, Smart-Mouth called her vile fur-bird names and stayed put. "You silly thing."

"Mama!" Luelle barreled out of a hallway and threw herself into Jahnel's arms, then gave her an elaborate smack of a kiss. Jahnel ruffled her daughter's blond hair and set her on her feet, then bent down to bring her face to Luelle's own.

"You went out into the fallway again, Luelle. How many times do I have to tell you . . ."

"Aunt Francoise ratted on me," Luelle declared indignantly. "That's not fair!"

"Of course it's fair. More eyes mean greater safety and—"

"—safety preserves the Louve. I *know* that, Mother." Luelle rolled her blue eyes dramatically. Jahnel repressed a sigh, remembering other conversations between Francoise and a very young Jahnel that had proved as ineffective. "Luelle . . ."

Luelle set her jaw stubbornly, her eyes defiant. Jahnel regarded her small daughter ruefully. Do my eyes look like that when I'm stubborn? she wondered. She felt a new empathy for her kindred.

"I'm glad you're back," Luelle trilled happily, deftly switching tactics, and spread her arms wide for another hug. "I missed you." She gave Jahnel a second smacking kiss, then giggled. As Luelle danced away, chortling, Jahnel swatted her lightly on her bottom and sighed.

"Yes, dear. I missed you, too. Where's Papa Sair?"

"In the tank room, I think. Mama Solveya threw up again," she added brightly.

"Yes, dear."

Luelle stopped and stared up at Smart-Mouth, her mouth slightly agape. Smart-Mouth gaped back, then sneered. "She throws up a lot," Luelle commented, still watching her pet. "Won't Smart-Mouth get burnt up there?"

"Probably." Jahnel checked the City-Net monitor for any general tier announcements and noted that Lejja had recently summoned her father to her chamber level. Why? she wondered, worried at Lejja's calling a personal meeting out of its proper time.

"Why?" Luelle chimed.

Jahnel turned to face her daughter. "Why what?"

"Why does Mama Solveya throw up?" Luelle was fascinated by Solveya's condition, and repeatedly ran her data back to zero so she could ask everything again.

"She's going to have a baby, a little brother like Didier. I've told you that, Luelle."

"If I throw up, can I have a baby?" Luelle puffed out her cheeks and squeezed her middle, trying to belch.

"No, Luelle," Jahnel said firmly. "Reverse your terms."

"If I have a baby, I can throw up," Luelle recited obediently.

"Yes, dear."

"Why doesn't Smart-Mouth care if he gets burnt?"

"Mystery of the universe, sweetie." She tore off a 'Net print-out of the last several hours' messages, then folded up the thin paper to look at later. "I doubt if even Smart-Mouth knows."

Luelle swiveled to look up at Smart-Mouth, totally confused. "*Smart-Mouth* doesn't know? Really? Why *not*?"

"Go ask your father," Jahnel dodged. Eduard had an inventive mind and secretly despised Smart-Mouth; the combination might provoke a colorful answer she'd like to hear herself. Smart-Mouth swore at her as she left the common room.

Her daughter followed her partway down the hallway, and Jahnel shooed her back to play with Smart-Mouth or find Papa Eduard, whichever pleased her, then stepped into the low-ceilinged tank room. A dozen long food tanks on heavy pedestals ringed the room, with the deeper tanks standing in long rows in room center, their occupants flashing silver-sided among the waterweed crop or creeping cautiously over gray bottom shingle. Sair was bent over an open tank on the near wall, his back to the door. As she walked toward him, a great-claws paced her for several steps in the tank beside her, its stalky eyes waving malevolently; she flipped her fingers at it, and it darted away into a clump of waterweed. Sair heard her step and turned, then pulled her against him and buried his face in her hair. She put her arms around his waist and pressed close.

"Are you well?" he murmured.

"I feel much better, Sair. Luelle got loose."

"So I heard," he said resignedly. "Eduard never did all that as a boy; I quite agree with him—why can't she take after him instead of you?" He released her and smiled, then turned back to the tank and finished his adjustments on the current-flow meter. "Niintua wants another Faon attack on the miin lander-ship."

"Do we get new weapons?"

"Yes; Benoit insisted and the Principals agreed. We're to assemble and draw lots in a few hours. But not you, Jahnel. You stay here until the suval has completely worn off. I don't like your color, however alert you're trying to look right now."

"I will go with the Louve."

"Beloved . . ."

Jahnel set her jaw. "The suval worst is past. If the lot chooses, I will go with the Louve—and you, Sair. I won't take suval, but I will be there."

Sair sighed and turned to glare at her. "Arguing with you never goes anywhere. When will I learn that? I can be the voice of reason, and you still do what you want."

"Of course," she retorted lightly. "What's the point of being senior wife? That's why, after all, I talked Papa Benoit into letting us start a new vayalim." She fluffed her hair and grinned at him. "How else could I be senior wife at twenty-three?"

"Listening to your senior husband at twenty-four, that's the point."

Jahnel made a rude sound at that, then pulled his head down for a kiss to distract him from his scowl. She let the kiss linger. "That won't work, Jahnel," he muttered, not very convincingly. So she kissed him again and let her hands wander; after a time, so did his. She stepped back at last and laughed up at him.

"Love you, Sair."

"Love you." He suddenly tightened his embrace, all lightness gone. "If I lose you, I don't know how I'll live, Jahnel," he said in a broken voice.

"Please, Sair, don't." She caressed his face, her own fear catching at her throat, then flushed into hot anger at the miin who risked such desolation to them both, who threatened the Faon and all they had won of life and Home-Space and the bonding together. "You will live, my beloved, as I will live if I lose you—and you will revenge me."

"Yes." He kissed her passionately, then abruptly released her and turned back to the tank, busying himself with his flow meter for a few moments. He unlatched a dip wand from the wall. "Be careful, Jahnel," he said in a low voice, not looking at her. "Don't be stupid, please."

"I won't. I promise you that." She leaned back on the tank-edge and changed the subject, trying to speak lightly, as if all were normal, without such dangers that threatened them. "Tell me more about the Council meeting."

"Short and sweet, basically, after Lejja's summons to your father."

"I saw that news on City-Net."

"Right—nothing like broadcasting it to all the tier. Lejja demanded to know if we intended to defy kin-obedience, her words. You know how it bothers the Avelle that we can." His dark hair fell over his forehead as he stirred the plants in the tank with the dip wand, chasing the elusive water shrimp that hid there; he flipped his hair back irritably. "It's not a great time to remind her how alien we are."

"Is any time?" she asked ironically. "What did Papa Benoit say?"

"What do you think? She didn't ask, Jahnel; she demanded. She gave him an ultimatum. If we refuse, Koyil will invoke the Law and force Lejja to eject the Faon from her tier: she made that very clear. We don't know if she's been forced to that threat by Koyil or if she agrees with it. Who can tell?"

"At least she had the grace to warn us."

"And conveniently forgets the Song she promised," Sair fretted. "Something's going on among the Principals, Jahnel, something we aren't catching." He shrugged, and fiddled with the flow-meter dial again, then carried his bag of squirming shrimp to the next tank and lifted the lid. "Lejja has always used us as a weapon in her influence wars with the Principals. Now Koyil's trying to outmaneuver her by using us against her. A neat trap, worthy of Koyil: if we fight on the surface, more of our breeding adults die and our levels are put at risk; if we refuse, Lejja drives us out and we get hunted all through the First Tier. I suspect Lejja could adjust easily to either outcome." He dumped the bag of shrimp into the water and stirred briskly with the dip wand, scattering them into the weeds.

"Unless we drive the miin away."

"Yes, that, too." He turned to face her, scowling. "Jahnel, you must talk to Melinde. I know she means well, but she doesn't understand how her words have endangered us. Saying such things among the Faon is one thing; saying it in Avelle hearing is quite another, especially now."

"She is grieving, Sair."

Sair's eyes flashed angrily. "Everybody grieves. Marc Jouvet was my best friend when we were boys—he lived just up-level from my vayalim. God, the times we spent together—and now he's gone, just like that, gone forever. Doesn't she think *I* grieve?"

"I'll talk to her." Jahnel paused, frowning. "Kiiri made a point of asking me to talk to Melinde—I wonder why?"

"Kiiri has his own reasons for doing things, too."

"I trust him."

"I respect that, beloved—I'm just worried. So is your father and the other elders, more than you realize. I thought our problem was surviving the battle with the miin; now I wonder who the real enemy might be."

"Lejja?" Jahnel asked incredulously.

"Freedom of breeding, freedom of obedience: that was the Song given to us. The Third Generation wrote it on our walls, our Song granting us iruta rights to ally or to abstain, even with Lejja. Since when does one kin-alliance tell another to sacrifice itself for another's brood-right? Have any of the tiers ever demanded that of each other?"

Jahnel frowned. "I hadn't thought of it that way. But Quevi Ltir is our home, too—and we owe a debt to Lejja."

"True. We've given fifteen deaths as our kin-debt for *Phalene*. And likely we would have fought again without Lejja's prompting—though it would make it easier for some Faon if a few Avelle helped next time. Only now Lejja hasn't asked—she demands. Why?" He leaned back against the tank beside her, his shoulders bent forward. "It's like watching shadows for the danger, not knowing which shadow threatens death. And I'm afraid we won't know in time. Jahnel . . ." His voice broke again.

She reached out for him, alarmed. It was so unlike Sair to talk like this. Not Sair. He straightened and gave her a crooked grin, his face gray with fatigue. "I'm tired and I want you," he said simply. He tipped his head to one side and studied her with a roguish interest he couldn't quite pull off. "How do you feel?"

"I already told you that."

"I forget what you said."

"Sure you do." She reached out and took his hand, then tugged at him gently. "I can talk to Melinde later."

He detached her hand and moved away. "No, you should talk to her now," he said contrarily, his scowl back on his face. "I hope she listens to you. Evan's tried, but she literally turned her back on him—he's quite hurt. You know how he feels about Melinde."

"I'll talk to Evan, too." She sighed, and rubbed her forehead thoughtfully. "Any suggestions?"

"I've already tried what I could think of." Sair quirked his lips into a rueful smile. "Melinde's raging, Evan's sulking, I'm fretting, Luelle's loose again—I bet you never thought of all this when you decided to be senior wife.''

"Actually, I had my mind solely on catching you. A preemptive move: I overheard Sebastien asking Papa Lucien for you as junior husband for their fourth wife, Raquelle; it would have filled out their eight. I admit I eavesdropped.''

"Raquelle? The redhead with the big . . .''

"Mind your eyebrows, husband.''

"Yes, wife.'' He gave her a slow smile. "Why didn't you ever tell me that before?''

"I didn't have the occasion,'' she said with dignity.

"Oh, sure.'' He grinned. "Melinde's in her sleeping room, I think, and Evan's with Solveya in the kids' playroom. You could talk to Solveya, too—she's afraid for us and still mad about throwing up. It's quite a stew.''

Jahnel hesitated, then pushed herself upright. "Well, I'll try. Does wisdom come in a pill?''

"What?'' Sair looked confused.

"Never mind, love. I'll have to get along with what I have.'' She kissed him quickly and left to find Melinde.

℞ Chapter 4

A T NIGHT-CYCLE THE Faon again regrouped in the First Turning. Jahnel had drawn the lot, but Sair and Eduard had not, giving them a reprieve to take the rest they needed, however they groused. In their place, Evan, a year younger than Melinde, had eagerly joined Jahnel and Melinde, overtly possessed with romantic ideas of battle and oversolicitous for both his senior wives, insisting on inspecting their vacuum-suit connections and trying to boss Melinde on this and that. Melinde ignored him completely, and not graciously, and sought out Philippe of the Roche for muttered conversations in the corner of the gathering room. Jahnel watched her uneasily, wondering what brewed with Philippe, then took time to allow Evan to fuss over her.

"Now, Jahnel," Evan said officiously, "you must be more careful this time." He jiggled his eyebrows and tried to copy Sair's authoritative scowl, not successfully. Only fifteen, Evan had a half-finished look as he filled out his growth; likely he would stretch a few more centimeters by his twenties and overtop even Sair. The interim awkwardness with his adolescent body embarrassed him thoroughly, though he found it hard to discuss, embarrassing himself all over again by that. Evan set himself many goals in his eagerness for maturity; one or two were actually reasonable.

"Yes, dear," she said. He set about checking her vac-suit connections again, and she brushed his hands away. "I'm fine, Evan. Check your own."

"Who knows?" Evan said pompously. "You may be pregnant, and we must be cautious of that."

"Evan, I'm not pregnant."

48

"You're sure?" Evan actually looked dismayed. She squinted at him.

"Who's been talking to you?" she demanded.

"Well . . ." Evan squirmed. "Hell, Jahnel, we've been married for six months now and Roger fathered a child in only two after he got married and—"

"Evan," she said patiently.

"Hell," Evan muttered, and looked away toward Melinde. "Is Melinde pregnant?"

"Solveya is."

"I *know* that," he said, exasperated. "But that was Sair, so she doesn't count. And Eduard has *two*, both of them yours. Honestly, Jahnel!"

Jahnel laughed, and kissed him, then ruffled his brown hair. "Take some time on a few things, Evan. But we'll work on it. How about that?"

"If you insist," he joked, then smiled at her shyly, all his heart in his look. Over his shoulder, she caught another sour scowl from Philippe as he overheard part of their talk; the man had the ears of a brood-chamber female. She scowled back at him, daring him to comment. She had never particularly liked the Roche subleader, a sour-tempered man quick to bitter complaints about anything and everything, and wondered again why Melinde had sought him out. She felt half-inclined to go ask.

Why is it so easy to forget a coming battle? she wondered then, bemused by her own absorption in vayalim priorities. I'm more Avelle than I sometimes think. Or perhaps much in love and much liking my roles—senior wife and mother, Leader presumptive, Kiiri's student, Jahnel and Louve and Faon, all the people I am. But now all that is at risk: it's easier to not think of that. She shook herself briskly. Do think of it, Jahnel; don't give the risk any edge with a stupid inattention. She left Philippe and Melinde to their muttered conferences and tried to focus on the here and now.

A few minutes later, the Faon assembled by kin-group and the Battle Master, an older woman from Ruisseau, gave quick instructions, then led the Faon into the Downlift. As agreed, the Avelle had provided better weapons, tools the Faon would adapt to their own tactics. The Etoile maneuvered the awkward weight of two laser cannons salvaged from a robot station deep in the Downlift; the Hiboux and Ruisseau carried explosives and coils of naked wire to add new deadliness to the broken streets of the surface ruins, traps tripped by the miin themselves and drawing miin fire while the Faon lay safely hidden elsewhere. Destruction of this lander would not bring full victory—the miin ship still orbited high overhead, beyond their reach—but even Niintua had finally agreed to stepped objectives, for all his spleen about the earlier retreat.

Jahnel took a dis-rifle from the cache near the surface portal, then waited with her kin-group as Jean released the energy screen. To Louve and Roche lay the baiting with another dis-rifle attack, in the hope the Faon could lure the miin into the ruins to the destruction awaiting them. With the lander emptied of most of its miin, Etoile could then open fire with the cannon on the lander itself. So went the plan: if it didn't work, she thought confidently, they would devise others. She heard a quick murmur of voices, hoarse with suppressed emotions, then joined the other Faon as they flowed outward again onto the surface, hiding quickly in shadows, Louve and Roche advancing silently toward the miin, the other kin-groups scattering into side streets to lay their traps.

Near the edge of the surface ruins, Jahnel edged prudently into the black shadow of a nearby wall, wary of the bluish light that glanced off broken stone. Once this was a narrow street on the edge of the Avelle dwellings, an alley shielded by metal roofing. Half the metal plates had fallen into the rubble of half-collapsed walls, creating obstacles to the rocky plain beyond. She edged outward, choosing her route among the debris, then relaxed back into shadow, waiting. The sound of her own breathing seemed loud in the confines of her vacuum suit, subtly underlaid by the faint hum of her heat exchanger, the thudding of her heart. She still felt the aftereffects of the suval despite Kiiri's counter-agent, as it tugged her heartbeat into a random thrum, stretched her vision in odd ways. She shook her head impatiently.

She turned in her shadowed space and looked backward, squinting through the glare. If she could not see her kindred in the other shadows, neither could the miin. All for the good. She took confidence in that, for all it had not helped in the first attack.

Against the glow of the sky above the street, she saw the distant black shape of the orbiting invader ship flashing downward toward the horizon, its orbit quickly accomplished. In a few hours, the ship would appear again in the east, rising quickly against the ever-present blue haze. The miin had not yet struck from the larger ship, but Niintua had spoken of other Avelle

weapons that could touch that ship and bring its destruction. Yet
the Avelle had seemed uncomfortable in that confidence, would
not explain why the weapons had not been used. Why not? she
wondered. She suspected a reason beyond malice to the Faon,
something hidden among the Principals, something to do with
the extensive disrepair of the Downlift. She gripped the stock of
her dis-rifle more tightly.

"So . . ."

The word came quietly through her headphones, broadcast
from a tiny drone flashing skyward from the Downlift, then
vanishing as quickly behind the asteroid's horizon. Jahnel moved
instantly, bounding lightly across a lighted space to the next
shadow, then again, choosing her path efficiently, taking every
advantage a native to this asteroid might have over the invader.

Oh her fifth leap, Jahnel reached a new wall-shadow and
stopped, recoiling slightly from the stone until her magnetic
soles gripped the iron-rich surface. She maneuvered herself
quickly, again concealing herself within the safety of the shadows.

She heard a click in her headphones as Melinde began the
linkup. "Jahnel, to your left," she whispered. To better conceal
their approach, the Faon had modified the vac-suit radios to
directional beam, eliminating any careless signals in directions
the miin might detect.

"Here," she answered. She looked to the left and saw a glove
wave briefly in the sunlight, then vanish again into impenetrable
shadow. "How far to the miin?" she asked.

"A hundred meters," the voice whispered. "More bodies to
slaughter."

"Clear your mind, Melinde," Jahnel reproved. "Don't give
them the edge." An hour of attempted persuasion, often heated,
had not changed Melinde's opinions, though her sister-wife had
ungraciously agreed to stop airing them in Avelle hearing.

"This is stupid," Melinde said.

"Probably. But Home-Space asks the sacrifice."

"It's *still* stupid." Melinde's voice was shrill.

"Please clear your mind, Melinde; I don't want to lose you—
none of us do." Jahnel turned right and aligned her radio link
with her other flank-mate.

"Evan, to your right," she called softly.

"Here," Evan answered promptly, his high clear voice trem-
bling with excitement. "How far to the miin?" Evan asked.

"Just beyond the next block of buildings. Steady now, dear one. Continue linkup."

"Yes, Jahnel."

Evan's presence vanished as he turned his helmet out of line of sight, breaking the radio connection. Melinde, too, had withdrawn from link, perhaps staring backward across the blue-lit stone. Jahnel felt a small prick of worry; mistakes happen during distraction, even in the relative safety of the fallways. A small inattention, a distracted mind, and an Avelle might come too close and attack, raging at the strange human shape. She bit her lip.

A silvery globe again shot skyward from the Downlift, quickly lost in the glare of the sky.

"So . . ." came the measured voice.

Jahnel turned and threw herself into the sunlight. She ran lightly to the next shadow, then bounded over the rocky wall. Ahead lay the pulverized stone and rubble of the crater lip, broken in several places by the earlier barrage. She ran forward in lightly bounding strides, in perfect balance, her breath evenly paced. In her peripheral vision, enhanced by the cantilever mirrors in her helmet, she saw the gray shapes of other Faon, each running as easily as she, flowing over the rubble. Together, the line of Faon climbed to the crater's edge and threw themselves down behind the ring of broken stone.

Jahnel brought up her dis-rifle and lowered the telescopic sight, then charged the magazine with a quick flip of her wrist. Beneath her on the crater floor, through a crevice between stones, she saw several miin in their awkward vacuum suits, tiny two-legged figures with bulbous heads clustered about a great machine. To one side stood the missile launcher, attended by a half-dozen other miin. They had grown careless to show such exposure, odd in their choice of mistakes. Did they really believe the Faon could be driven off so easily? She glanced left and saw Melinde focus her rifle sight on the largest group. Jahnel cradled her own rifle against a wedge of small stone.

"So . . ."

A dozen jagged lightnings exploded downward into the crater, each striking its target in mid-chest. Jahnel quickly swung her beam to the right, slicing through the suit arm of another miin. A puff of white emptied the suit of breath and life; the miin staggered, clutching at his arm, then fell face forward into the feathery pumice of the crater floor. A moment later, a third managed a few agonized steps before it, too, collapsed. In a space of seconds, the Faon had counted fifteen miin lives, re-payment of the debt for their own.

Seconds would be all they had.

In a convulsive heave, Jahnel threw herself backward from the crater rim, bounced lightly on her back down the rubble, inverted on the rebound, and landed on one knee. She had scarcely gathered her feet for the next leap when the world exploded in the miin counterattack. She felt a giant's blow to her back, thrusting her forward, then another as the miin again pounded the crater lip with their cluster bombs. She tucked herself into a ball and rolled with the concussion, then tried to run. The third salvo caught her halfway to safety.

Helplessly, she was lifted up and thrown against the rock face of a crumbling wall. "Luelle!" she shouted and tried to cover her faceplate against the imminent collision. She smashed into the unyielding stone and rebounded hard. She rolled, skating across the rubble beneath the wall, then sprawled against a projecting stone. Dazedly, she heard the hiss of escaping air from her broken suit, then felt a sudden lancing pain in her arm where a jagged rock had scraped through the suit-fabric into her flesh. Above her, Rhesaa burned down its blue haze and seemed to rush down upon her, crushing her into oblivion.

No!

She heaved herself on her side and drew up her injured arm, fumbling at the suit-fabric with her other hand in a desperate attempt to close the tear. Black spots danced before her eyes, merging into broader bands of shadow nearer the wall. She tightened her hand on her injured arm and heard the steady hiss of air lessen, but not enough. Her vision grayed still further as anoxia drained the strength from her hand.

Not like this, please, not like this. "Sair . . ." she moaned and clutched at the suit-tear more tightly.

Don't be stupid, Sair had asked. She should not have run so close to stone. Forgive me, Sair . . .

She lost time then, and came to herself inside metal walls. A miin stood leaning over her and reached for the seal of her suit helmet. She raised her hands to ward it off, then struck violently at it, driving it away. It promptly hit her back hard, rocking her helmet hard. She twisted, but the miin caught her and flipped her over easily and laid her on a bench, then bound her hands with a cord, securing it to a railing above the bench. As she struggled, it broke the seal on her helmet and pulled it off. She gasped involuntarily as a wash of blood-warm air swept over her face, then wiggled as the miin passed its hands over her body and paused over her injured arm, probing painfully with its fingers. It left her then, face down on the bench.

Furiously, Jahnel struggled against the cord. She heard the heavy tread of other miin walking beyond the door, then a rumbling noise, a clang, and minutes later a building roar. She struggled against her bonds frantically as a vibration built through the floor plates and the bench, a steady roaring that waxed in noise and strength. An invisible hand pressed her down against the bench, stealing her breath away again, and she fought it for long minutes. Then nothing, and a lightness to her body beyond even the easy flight of the fallways she had always known.

She guessed too well the meaning of the clang, the roaring, the lightness to her body. She grimaced: she had willed the intruder ship to leave, but not with her aboard. Easy now, Faon, she told herself: control your rage. She stopped pulling at the cord and tested its length with her fingers, then patiently worked against it to allow her to turn over and sit half-upright on the bench, though the cord bit through her gloves into her wrists and tugged painfully at her injured arm. She explored further upward, trying to undo the knot, her fingers clumsy in her gloves.

A miin drifted through the inner doorway, then touched lightly off the door-rim and floated toward her. It checked itself against the bench and reached up and pulled off its helmet, revealing its face—a young face shaped like her own, dark hair clipped close to his ears, heavy eyebrows now drawn into a scowl, two black eyes that looked at her speculatively, glinting with anger: human eyes!

She stared at the man's face, a knot of cold anger coiling in her stomach. She would have Koyil's own hide, that one, and mount it on her wall. Four days before, Koyil had broadcast what he claimed was a radio message from the intruder ship, an incomprehensible babbling by a blurred and nightmare image that pointed to itself and named itself "miin." We should have guessed, she thought distractedly, remembering the human shape of the miin at the lander. We should have guessed.

"Why are you attacking us?" her captor said in francais, strangely accented but understandable. Human speech: the miin were human—and Koyil's tape fakery. Her head swam with the implications.

"Do you understand me?" the miin repeated urgently.

She nodded reluctantly, wondering if she gave up an advantage in doing so. It seemed to relax the miin. He snagged a hand through a nearby bracket and smiled at her encouragingly, a smile she immediately distrusted.

"My name is Gregory Austin," the miin said. "What's your name?"

She stared at him coolly, her fingers easing up the cord to the knot. If she could get free, she could leap on this Austin and—what? What could she do on a miin ship with its strange machines? Well, she could crash it. She thought about that a moment, her fingers probing the knot, then put the tempting idea aside for a while. Possible, but she preferred battle plans that left herself alive—not essential, but preferable.

"Are you hurt?" The miin gestured at her arm, where blood had seeped through the tear in the suit fabric. A stupid miin to ask the obvious, she thought: she wondered if the others were more intelligent than this one. Austin scowled again. "Why don't you answer me?"

Jahnel smiled, enjoying the miin's irritation and knowing that her smile irritated him all the more. Adding to it, she looked beyond him at the doorway and wondered how many other miin were sitting in the rooms beyond. Her fingers probed the knot again. The miin sighed, jerking her attention back to him.

"Well, be that way then." He poked his chest with his finger. "For your information, this ship is PAS *La Novia* based out of Buenos Aires and MarsPort—the PAS stands for Pan-American States, Earth. I'm one of the ship's junior pilots on temporary assignment to Contact Team." He looked at her expectantly. She stared back, saying nothing. "You *are* descended from *Phalene*, aren't you? We caught *Phalene*'s distress signal forty lights from here and followed it to this star system. We're here to take you home—do you understand? Home to Earth. Why are you attacking us?"

"You attacked us first," Jahnel countered.

"So you *can* talk," Austin said sardonically. "Hooray. Do you want tending for that wound? I'm not coming closer until you promise to not fight."

"Stay away," she warned him.

"As you wish," he snapped. He crossed his arms and glared at her. "What's going on down there, anyway? We tell your aliens we've come to take you home, and they send *you* up to attack us. Why?"

"Told them . . ." Jahnel swallowed painfully. Sair had thought something was loose among the Principals—and Kiiri

must have known, perhaps even helped in faking Koyil's tape.
She bowed her head a moment, sick with the treachery.

But perhaps the miin lies, she thought desperately, though
she recognized several of his words from *Phalene's* history tapes.
Phalene had launched from a PAS colony world at Mu Carinis.
When PAS had founded three new colonies in Carina, it had
grandly invited colonists from other nations of Earth to immi-
grate to Carina, promising the immigrants a new future on a
new world—only to claim later convenient excuse for the anti-
foreigner laws that trapped non-Latinos into economic peonage
of discriminatory taxes and pay. After years of struggle, a small
group of French immigrants had scraped together the money for
Phalene, hoping for a better start on a non-Latino world in Cen-
taurus, but finding through near-disaster a new world they had
never expected among the Avelle. *Her* world.

She lifted her chin and denied him. "And who should fight
but the lesser iruta who owe a kin-debt to the Avelle? The Avelle
Naalaiku commanded; it was our vaar to comply. Bid you do as
the Naalaiku command, miin: go away."

"Iru—what did you say?"

"You invade the Tiraamu; it is not permitted."

"Tiraa . . . You've lost me, woman. What's an iruta?"

Jahnel bent forward and pulled hard at her bonds. Austin
lunged forward and pushed her back, pinning her against the
wall, bringing his face inches from her own. "Stop that. You'll
just hurt yourself more." She turned her head away, refusing to
look at him, conscious of a sweet tangy odor from his skin, the
faint sourness of his breath, the closeness of his body. If she
only had her hands, he'd regret coming this close.

Behind him, another miin appeared in the doorway and spoke,
a woman, from her voice and slighter body, though little else
could be told in the baggy folds of her odd clothing. Austin
backed away from Jahnel, then replied to the other in words she
didn't understand. The woman looked at Jahnel in distaste, then
quickly smoothed her expression into something she no doubt
thought friendly.

"This is Elena Sanford," Austin told her. "She has questions
she wants to ask you. "I'll translate."

"Tell Elena Sanford to invert herself." Jahnel showed her
teeth.

"Uh . . ." Austin ran a hand through his hair, obviously at
a loss. The miin woman demanded something and he spoke to
her briefly, his tone conciliatory. Jahnel doubted he translated

anything about inverts. The woman pointed at Jahnel's arm and spoke again. Jahnel looked back and forth between the two, trying to catch the meaning in the gestures as they squawked at each other. The woman pointed again and spoke more sharply to the man; she saw a slow flush creep up Austin's neck and heard the tightness in his voice as he answered. Finally, the woman tossed her chin and pulled herself back through the doorway, her boots clanging against the rim as she pushed off.

"You like this woman?" Jahnel asked sweetly.

"Shut up." Austin glared at her.

"Why doesn't she speak francais, too?" Jahnel asked.

"Wrong continent, sweetheart. Our crew is Latino and Anglo, with Espanol and English as ship-official. I have the misfortune of being half-French—that's why I'm stuck with you." He glared at her. "Why are you attacking us?"

"Is that one of the things Elena Sanford wants to know?"

"Not especially—she's more interested in your Avelle's gravity control. What's an iruta?"

Jahnel clamped her lips tight. Austin waited patiently, though she could see his anger building. An angry man could get careless, she reminded herself. An angry man turned his back at the wrong times, and discovered his mistake too late. She considered that, too, and let him simmer. After a few minutes of their silent battle, the miin Elena Sanford returned, and she and Austin discussed Jahnel again with their squawkings.

"Elena will tend your arm," Austin told her.

"Advise her I'll take out her teeth as she does. Say it literal this time, please."

"As you wish." Austin told Sanford; she gave Jahnel an incredulous look, then left quickly. It amused Jahnel immensely.

"Are you always this tough?" Austin asked.

She saw that he, too, was amused, and that irritated her more than she expected. Faon jokes were not shared with miin, especially crafty black-eyed half-French miin who thought apologies meant anything. She gave him a level stare. "You killed fifteen Faon. When their blood has seeped through all of Quevi Ltir, then I might consider you other than I do." She looked away, her jaw set.

"I'm sorry," the miin said awkwardly. "We didn't know who you were—not until it was too late. It was a mistake we deeply regret. Can't you understand that?"

She said nothing.

"Be stubborn then," he said irritably. "When we get to *La*

Novia, you'll talk, believe me.'' He waited another moment, as if he hoped she would relent, then shrugged and followed the other miin through the doorway.

Jahnel looked around the small room, then tugged vainly at her bonds again. Her arm ached, and blood still oozed from the rip in the suit. She leaned forward and tried to inspect the wound, but winced as the cord dug into her wrists; if she had torn an artery, she decided, she would have been dead already. She looked around the room again, studying the walls and strange angles, each component, each detail, fighting her own despair. She was captive among the miin, lost in this strange place . . . and the miin were human.

The Avelle have betrayed us, she thought in anguish. Kiiri . . . She felt hot tears fill her eyes. She shook them away angrily.

You'll talk . . .

Well, the miin could hope for that. She smiled grimly.

After a time, Jahnel heard hissings and a building roar, then felt the lander surge forward to a gentle thud. She immediately felt weight again, and noted her displeasure at the sameness to the gravity Kiiri had fashioned for the Faon. The first generation of Faon, those who had come with *Phalene*, had made a Song about a place named Earth, but their children and their children's children, after waiting in courtesy until the last of the first elders had died, had remade the Song. The Faon now sang of the fallways, not Earth, and had no wish for any other Song.

Or would they? Would the Faon return with the miin to Earth, abandoning all that they were? She thought on that as she waited for the miin to reappear, guessing that Koyil had doubted the Faon answer, however his skin must prickle at the wishing. Even a Principal of Laws understood the Songs and their imperatives, for all his rivalry with Song itself in his lust for Lejja's influence. Yes, he had doubted that easy solution, guessing that some Faon would refuse this ship's offer and remain a waterthorn in his side. A crafty Principal—great-claw feasting was too good for him. Melinde might have some useful ideas later, she thought. She just might.

She lifted her head as she heard footsteps, then watched warily as the miin Austin stepped through the doorway and approached her, his suit helmet under one arm. He raised his other hand and showed her a slender metal object.

"We can do this the easy way or the hard way," he announced. "We want you to walk out of the lander up to the hospital. You either agree to do it peacefully, or I'll put you to sleep and haul you like a sack. You understand me?''

She looked at his determined expression and allowed her shoulders to slump. ''I understand,'' she murmured abjectly.

He hesitated as if he didn't trust her—apparently he had more brains than she had assumed—then grunted. ''Look me in the eyes and say that again.''

Jahnel looked up. ''I understand,'' she said clearly. He studied her face, then nodded and slipped the object behind a flap in his clothing. She made a careful note of which one.

''Okay. But you make one wrong move and it's lights out. Understand?''

She nodded. He moved toward her, watching her carefully all the while, then bent over her to untie her hands and quickly stepped back. She saw him tense, ready for anything, and so sat quietly, biding her time.

''Get up, please. Follow me.''

He stepped toward the outer doorway, then waved the miin Sanford back as she appeared in the other door. She squawked at him awhile; he finally barked at her and she backed off. Jahnel caught an intimation of their kin-ranking in her furious expression—though maybe the Sanford's mother had eaten watergrass during pregnancy and permanently soured her daughter's disposition. If the miin had watergrass. If the Sanford had a mother.

''This way.''

Jahnel rose to her feet and picked up her helmet from the bench, then followed Austin into the corridor beyond, conscious first of the woman treading closely behind, then of the sound of other footsteps as the rest of the lander crew followed them. The corridor led to a wide porthole and a glimpse of a broad metal deck, then a ramp leading outside. More tentatively, Jahnel followed Austin down the ramp, trying to take in the wideness of the room and the bewildering array of machines. The space was nearly as large as the Principals' own Council Chamber, and obviously a room and not a fallway. Miin scurried along the far wall in front of tall panels flickering with lights; other miin hastened toward the lander, giving her a wide berth as Austin gestured at them. She noticed their clothing for the first time: strange tubes around their legs, a short aal around their chests, bound around the arms. And green, like waterweed. She looked up and saw two small ships in brackets on the walls above their heads, each tiny ship barely the width of a fallway, much smaller than the lander. She instantly lusted for one of them—then looked back at Austin. A pilot, he had said, a word she hadn't quite understood as he used it, but she now guessed at the miin meaning. He could fly one of those little ships. Austin turned and looked at her warily; she arranged her face in a pleasant expression.

"Big place," she said, waving her arm expressively.

"The ship bay stretches half the ship's core. Come along."

Jahnel followed him sedately across the metal floor to a nearby wall, then watched with interest as he pushed a button on a control panel. An instant later, a door parted, revealing a small room within. The hospital? And what would they do with her there? He motioned her to step inside. She did so, then edged to the farther wall as he and Sanford crowded in after her. The woman gave her a cool look as their sleeves brushed; Jahnel smiled pleasantly.

"Big place," she repeated, and saw Austin give her a sharp look. He pushed a button on another control panel and the doors closed, followed by a surge of acceleration upward. She looked around in alarm, then quickly hid it before the miin noticed. "Biiiigg place," she drawled.

"All right, already," Austin said irritably. "It's a big place. Bet your Avelle don't have anything like this."

Jahnel smiled. He'd find out.

The acceleration stopped and the doors opened. Austin motioned her out into the corridor beyond, then followed her down the hallway. Small rooms opened up to either side, each with a bed and odd equipment; three rooms had miin in them, looking relaxed. Austin guided her around a turning and down a side corridor, then motioned her into a room. She stepped inside and immediately sidled to the right as she saw the two miin waiting for her. They sat on odd benches with four legs near a long mattress elevated on a metal frame; the miin she had seen earlier had reclined on such mattresses. The hospital, obviously, though again the miin meaning didn't quite track with the Faon word; here it seemed to mean a place to be relaxed. Austin squawked at the two miin, his tone respectful, and the younger one, the one with the black hair and restless black eyes, squawked back; the Sanford walked in then and added her irritable share.

Jahnel wished for proper gravity to show her opinion of them all, but doubted the miin would understand a rude invert if they saw one. Austin squawked some more at the older miin with the silvered hair and long nose, then turned to Jahnel.

"This is Commander Boland. He wants to ask you some questions."

"The same questions as the Sanford?"

"His own questions. That other man is Lieutenant Rivera, his first officer. You can sit down if you want." Jahnel sidled to the abutting wall opposite the miin, then leaned back comfortably, shifting her weight to one leg. "Or stand, if you must." Austin turned back to Boland, who squawked several words.

"What is your name?" Austin translated.

"Wolf."

"Wolf?" He looked confused. "That's your name?"

"Wolf." She paused reflectively. 'Sometimes I'm Rock or Star or Owl. It depends on my ilaipaari and the Naalaiku's concept of reality. In the Tiraamu," she added helpfully.

"Concept of . . ." Austin looked at her in bewilderment, then translated hastily when Boland barked at him. "The commander wants to know—uh, let's back up. What's an ilaipaari?"

"The currents of the apadi."

Austin scowled, drawing down his dark eyebrows, and glared at her. "What's an apadi?"

"The will of the Naalaiku."

Boland started squawking again.

"Naalaiku?" Austin asked, ignoring him.

Jahnel smiled. "The vaar of the Tiraamu. Your commander is talking to you, Austin. Is it wise to ignore him? It's hardly vaar."

Austin grunted, and turned to talk to the miin Boland. She saw Boland scowl, then glance at the miin Rivera. Rivera scowled, too, then scowled at Sanford, who scowled back, who then scowled at Jahnel. Jahnel yawned elaborately, an invert of Faon design that even a miin would understand.

"I told him you're playing games," Austin said angrily, his black eyes glinting. "I suggest you stop it."

"Games?"

"What's your name?" Austin shouted.

"Wolf."

Boland stood up with a disgusted look and gestured at Rivera, then stalked out. Sanford scurried after him hastily, leaving Jahnel and Austin alone. Jahnel braced her hands against the wall behind her, waiting for Austin to make his mistake.

"Cute," Austin growled. "Really cute." He turned away toward the door, and she leapt for him.

Her momentum slammed his head into the wall by the door,

stunning him. She quickly threw her arm across his throat and squeezed, then dragged him backward off balance. He half fell against her and began to struggle, his fingers digging frantically at her forearm as she throttled him. She tightened her throat-hold, then took his weapon from his clothing and jabbed it in his ribs as a warning. When he slumped limply against her, she loosened her neck-hold slightly. Austin took a gasping breath, then another.

"Quiet," she hissed in his ear, then tightened her arm again as he began to curse. He obeyed immediately. She listened for any sound in the corridor and heard nothing—aside from the impact of Austin's head against the wall, her assault had been nearly noiseless. "Now," she whispered to Austin, "you will return me to Quevi Ltir.'

"Where?"

"Where you found me, miin."

"Impossible," he blurted out loud.

"Lower your voice, or I'll throttle you into oblivion. I don't care if the Tiraamu has one less miin to pollute it—but it would take me a while to find another pilot. So you'll do."

"There's no way, Wolf," he protested, and pried at her arm again. "We'll be seen."

"Stop that and drop your hands. Think of a way."

"You'll never even get out of the hospital."

"Think of that, too," she threatened him. "Think of a way." While Austin thought, she listened again, anxious for any approaching footsteps. "Do you have a way?" she whispered urgently.

"In that compartment by the bed. Clothing."

"Come with me." She dragged him backward and probed at the latch, then pulled the contents out when the door snapped open. Still keeping one arm across Austin's throat, she shook out the bundle, finding tube pants and an aal like the miin in the ship bay had worn. She reached inside, found another bundle like the first, and took it for Austin.

"To get dressed in that, you'll have to release me," Austin said, a distinct triumph in his voice. He stiffened as Jahnel jabbed his weapon against his ribs.

"And two seconds to kill you—which I will if I have to. *La Novia* has more than one pilot, does it not? I can always find another. I suggest you behave, miin Austin."

"You don't know how to use that weapon."

"It has one button and one lever. We can experiment—no?"

"You wouldn't do that."

"Test me and see. Likely my vayalim already grieves for me as one of the newly dead; I have nothing to lose."

Austin thought it over and decided wisely to believe her. An intelligent miin. "Listen to me," he said earnestly. "You don't understand . . ."

"Will you behave?" She released her hold slightly, then stepped away from him and tossed the extra bundle at his feet. "You dress, too."

He turned toward her suddenly, then froze as she swung up the weapon and pointed it at his chest, one finger cradling the lever, another poised over the button on its side. It was obviously the right combination; the miin eyed the weapon and swallowed uneasily.

"Okay, okay," he said, raising his hands. "Don't get excited." Moving more slowly, he bent for the bundle and tore open the plastic, then reached for the zipper at his throat. She watched him strip off his vacuum suit and put on the tube pants, then the aal.

"Move over to the wall and lean your hands against it, feet backed out," she ordered. When he had complied, she quickly stripped off her own vacuum suit and put on the other set of miin clothes. Then she wrapped her suit and Austin's around their helmets into a bulky roll.

"Come," she said.

He turned and faced her. "This won't work," he said, fury in his face.

"Make it work, or I'll find another pilot."

"Why won't—" he began. At her warning glare, he lowered his voice again. "Why won't you listen?"

"Take me to Quevi Ltir and maybe I'll listen."

"You will?"

"Maybe."

He hesitated, studying her face. "Okay. This is crazy, but come on."

He walked to the door and looked out in both directions, then signed to her to follow. She walked quietly behind him, carrying their vacuum suits beneath her arm, the weapon concealed beneath them, alert for treachery. A pair of miin approached them; Austin gestured naturally and spoke a greeting, and the miin passed without giving Jahnel a second glance. She smiled to herself—looking human had its advantages in this miin place— then scowled as it led to other thoughts she did not enjoy. At the

next turning, Austin slowed and checked ahead, then walked on
toward the transport room at the end of the hall. Jahnel padded
behind him, trying to keep alert in all directions while focusing
on Austin, watching the tenseness in his shoulders, the first sign
of any move against her. At the wall-doors, he pushed the summons button, then stepped in as the doors opened. She slipped
in behind him.

"This was the easy part, Wolf. Now what am I supposed to
do?"

"One of those little ships in the ship bay. On the walls. You
will think of a way."

"A jitney? You're crazy."

"Do it, miin; find the way."

The doors opened onto the ship bay, and Austin glanced at
her, then headed for the little ships. She followed behind him
casually across the long floor and watched as he poked at a wall
panel. One of the little ships slid outward on a metal frame that
projected, then descended gracefully to the bay floor. Austin
pushed another button and the frame receded; the little ship sank
a few inches to rest on its wheels. A door in the side whined
open.

"Get in," she ordered.

"I have to program the launch sequence first," Austin said,
glancing around nervously. Nobody of a dozen miin walking
about paid them any attention at all. This Austin had good ideas,
it seemed, Jahnel reflected. She intended him to continue having
them.

"Do it," she said.

"All hell will break loose when we taxi into the ship lock.
Boland hasn't authorized any—"

"You will explain to his satisfaction."

"God damn it, woman! You can't do this!"

She bared her teeth. "I already am. Prepare the ship." She
raised her bundle and let him see the weapon beneath. "Then
get in and take me back to Quevi Ltir. Or I will find another
pilot who can. Don't think I can't." Austin muttered an oath
and punched at the panel, then gestured her toward the little
ship. "You first," she said. That earned her another muttered
oath, but he continued to have good ideas and climbed up the
short ladder.

Inside, she found a small room with two strangely shaped
benches, padded and nearly shoulder-high; Austin strapped
himself into the bench on the left. She slipped around the far

side of the other bench and sat down to fasten her own belts over the vacuum suits in her lap, then leveled the weapon at Austin. He reached for one of several control levers on the panel in front of him, then touched a button. The panel lit up an array of lights; a gray view-window above it flickered into life, showing an image of the ship bay. Austin engaged other levers and she felt a low vibration, then movement as the jitney began to roll forward. As they approached a blank wall at one end of the large room, a door irised open. A voice suddenly sounded in the air, barking some command; Jahnel looked around, startled, then spotted the grille to Austin's left.

"Do I answer that?" he asked.

"Find the way, Austin. Your choice."

Austin shrugged and touched another button, then spoke aloud and was answered as the little ship rolled smoothly forward. Austin began another sequence on his panel as Jahnel watched, the grille blatting more incomprehensible words. Austin replied in a soothing tone, then tightened his hands on two levers as a door ahead opened, revealing an array of stars and Rhesaa's blue haze. Jahnel tightened her grip on the weapon, pressing hard with her fingers, her eyes flicking from the grille to Austin's face, watching him for any treachery, hoping she would see it for what it was while she could still act.

A roaring sounded behind them and the ship accelerated outward, surging over the threshold and falling into open space. The voice in the grille was lost in the roaring, then came abruptly back again as Austin moved his hands smoothly over his panel. Austin tipped another lever, and the grille's noise stopped abruptly.

"Where do you want to land?" he asked sardonically.

"Where you found me. At the crater."

Austin shrugged, only the working of his jaw muscles showing the fury he felt. This was a man, she thought, who did not like compulsion—who thought kin-obedience, the vaar, was always a choosing with options. She studied his profile, noting the stubborn line of his nose, the angry set of his jaw, the deftness of his hands as he moved them over his controls. A miin with talents—and an anger she might use further.

Steal a miin . . . Kiiri had said. She smiled recklessly.

"Wolf . . ."

"Shut up."

He seethed at her brusqueness, though he tried to hide it from her. She looked quickly out the little ship's view-window, trying to reckon how long she must keep him off balance with that anger of his, not too much into rashness, not too little into treachery, until the advantage became entirely hers. The Avelle understood such balances, exquisitely well; the Faon had learned those balances from them long before to survive, as she used it now.

The little ship swept downward, then skimmed across the rocky surface toward the ruined city on the horizon. Jahnel moved her hands to rest on her knees, tensing as the ship touched down and rolled jerkily over the rough surface, then eased to a stop near the lander crater. When Austin turned to her and opened his mouth to speak, she struck him with the weapon, connecting with a satisfying thud on his head. Minutes later, she had the unconscious miin dressed in his vacuum suit and had repaired the damage to her own vacuum suit. She left the jitney at a run, dodging nimbly among the robots rolling inexorably toward the little ship, and headed for the Downlift, carrying her human booty with her.

❧ Chapter 5

A USTIN AWOKE WITH a splitting headache and for a panicked moment thought he was blind. He thrust out a hand,
groping against the sudden darkness, and saw the moving gray
blur in front of his face, the shadows of fingers. He tentatively
moved his fingers and, to his relief, saw the shadows respond,
then let his hand fall loosely into his lap. Blearily, he turned his
head to look around him, trying to match his personal reality to
the gloom on every side. The blackness spun for a few moments,
then settled back into perspective of a curving overhead, pitch
darkness to either side. Where was he?

He blinked and tried to remember, then laboriously assembled fragments of the assault in sick bay and his jitney flight
downward. He felt a light pull of gravity, more than free-fall,
and laboriously added it to his data. Important, Greg, he thought
groggily. Think. He noticed the familiar confines of his vacuum
suit, a comforting weight. The current of warm air sighed across
his face, slightly off true air-mix and bearing undefinable odors—
not unpleasant, but strange. He reached out again, touching
nothing in the darkness, then became aware of metal supporting
his back as he half lay, half sat against it. He turned his head
full to the right, trying to peer into the gloom, and saw grayer
shadows in the distance, rounded somehow. To the left was only
a deeper blackness. A tunnel? He couldn't tell.

Shadows . . . He drifted away, his thoughts fragmenting into
memories of other shadows.

He remembered the sunlit shadows on his mother's pale still
face as she sat on their balcony in Caracas, her fingers twisting
unhappily in her lap as his father stood looking out over the city,
his back to them both, his passionless voice rising and falling
as he lectured her, oppressing her with his disapproval, his pride,

his unbending rectitude. That same brilliant Caracas sunlight
had later dappled the carpet in his father's study as he himself
stood mutely listening to his father's intended horror of boarding
school and forbidden contact with his mother, a foreigner who
so little understood her duties as wife, who foolishly thought
she could frustrate a father's rights to his son by leaving her
husband.

At the school, his schoolmates had taunted him, calling him
bastard and foreigner, mocking his foreign name and his mother's disgrace of divorce—Grégoire, Grégoire, they had chanted,
where is your mother? In a French brothel? That's where divorced women go—is she there? What does she do there, little
Grégoire? And they had told him what she did, in graphic and
obscene detail. And he had fought them, an eight-year-old flail-
ing out wildly against a dozen older boys, and they had beaten
him into submission with their fists and their feet. More lectures,
another shadow-patterned carpet, then a summons to his father,
calling him away from important affairs at the ministry to learn
of the disgrace to his name in such a fight with such fine boys
from such distinguished families of the highest social circles of
Caracas. It is your mother's blood, he had told his son contemptuously, a phrase Austin had never forgiven, and had left
him there in that awful school, coming rarely to visit, then not
coming at all.

On his eighteenth birthday, the first day he became an adult
and the first day his father could not undo what his son chose to
do, Austin visited a lawyer to file the legal papers obliterating
his father's name from his own, never again Juan Grégoire
Amaneda-Perez y Austin, only Gregory Austin, the newest pilot's candidate for PAS *La Novia*, the colony bureau's new sleek
survey ship. And he had told his father in dry measured tones,
in that study with the patterned carpet, what he had done and
why he had done it and had watched his father's face as he told
him, then walked out.

He had heard later that his action had been a horrifying scandal for a month and a day in Caracas social circles, then forgotten as easily as his mother had been forgotten years before. On
ship, he kept silent about his birth names in a society that re-
volved on birth names and heritage, and knew his Latino shipmates speculated behind his back about what had happened in
Caracas to make him a nameless man. He told himself it amused
him and ignored their attempts to ferret out the scandal, isolating

himself too much during his three years aboard ship, keeping even his Anglo friends at a careful distance.

Were the memories why he helped Wolf escape? he wondered. Was it some tone in Boland's voice, some tilt to Rivera's eyebrow, that old contempt for the outsider that permeated Latino assumptions? They had looked at her with that unassailable condescension of the Latino male, a judgment further laden by the initial biopsy reports of the strange drugs found in the corpses. Drug slaves, the rumor had swept through the ship, subhuman, alien captives. Whispered eager stories flying from Sick Bay to Command to Pilot Quarters to Tech Basin, hands raised in horror, mouths made into Os, a delicious shudder of it all. And Wolf had defied them, her chin lifted, playing her word games, her pride in every line of her slim body.

Vive les Francais, he thought ruefully—though he hadn't thought of himself as French for years, or known that his self-disownment so long before needed any coda. Surprise to you, Greg, old boy. He had intended that defiance as a finality, the ending of it.

His head still throbbed, scrambling his thoughts and making it hard to think. He felt another puff of warm air on his face and puzzled about it a moment, then touched his face, realizing another oddity. Where was his helmet?

He hunted vaguely beside him, then tried the other side. Nothing. Had Wolf taken it? Why?

He took a deep breath and closed his eyes, willing his head to clear. Think straight, Greg; take your time.

Time: strange how time could foreshorten from the dozens of real-time years that *La Novia* had crossed in a few weeks to the bare seconds of inattention that cut life into death as box-shaped alien machines rolled toward them. Strange how assumptions could turn upside down. For three weeks *La Novia* had searched among the fringe stars of Carina cluster, tracking the wavering distress call that had brought the survey ship so far into space, a message with its tantalizing hint of aliens that had sent pictures, that promised rescue for the crippled ship. Had *Phalene*'s message not mentioned aliens, *La Novia* would not have come at all, not this far in the unlikely chance of rescue: space disasters rarely left survivors to find. It wasn't worth the risks—unless something else beckoned.

For two hundred years, Earth had waited for First Contact with an alien race, ever since the first star-explorer ships had broken the light barrier and escaped Sol system. A primitive doglike race in Gemini had stared at the human spacemen in blank wonderment; Earth archaeologists had stared as dumbly at the long-dead ruins of a master race in Ophiuchus. But nothing else, not in the dozens of star systems within Earth's reach—until now. And so *La Novia* had come deep into Carina, hunting for the aliens as much as for the humans lost here—had come with all the fatuous human presumptions that such Contact would be welcomed.

We expected eagerness for Contact, he thought, the same wish for exchange, knowledge, exploration. We were so sure, so sure of everything.

A mistake, Boland had decided after the robots destroyed the lander. An unfortunate preprogrammed response. Just a mistake, the Contact Team nodded, their chins jerking sagely up and down, deceiving themselves. It didn't matter that the aliens still ignored the follow-up radio messages beamed at them, didn't matter that no one down below had bothered to turn *off* the automatic defenses. Contact is Contact. And so the second lander had waited confidently, expecting aliens to come walking out of the surface ruins any time, hands or flippers or claws extended in welcome. When new attackers had come, moving lightning-swift through the shadows, striking with laser-fire and showing a sapient intent beyond the mere machine, it wasn't so easy to say "mistake." The lander had defended itself, then later found the human bodies in the wreckage of the counterattack. Mistake, right. Big mistake.

Maybe it was Rivera's shrug, that condescending indifferent Latino shrug Austin had seen hundreds of times before, that later made him turn his back, giving Wolf her chance. Maybe it was a lot of things.

My head hurts, he thought irritably. Some Contact man, though no doubt Wolf thought her choice of "contact" had suited perfectly. He fingered his jaw and winced. I'm making contact, he had said to Boland. Let me humor her a little; I'll bring her back right away. Oh, sure. God, she had a wicked punch. He sat up straighter, the fogs finally clearing from his mind.

She had taken his helmet and its radio. He fumbled his fingers along his belt to the emergency transponder embedded in the fabric near the buckle and keyed it on. He preferred voice communication—his Morse was damned rusty—but he had limited options, considering. Activated, the transponder dial cast a halo of ruddy light into the gloom in front of him, glinting on curves of shadowed metal. Laboriously, taking great care with a balky memory, he tapped out a message to *La Novia*. A-u-s-t-i-n-h-e-r-e. R-e-s-p-o-n-d-p-l-z. He waited a few moments, then tried again.

Midway through his repeat, the transponder dial winked briskly in response, lighting the gloom in front of him with quick flashes. Austin concentrated on the flickering pattern, his finger poised over the transponder. B-o-l-a-n-d-h-e-r-e. W-h-e-r-e?

U-n-d-e-r-g-r-o-u-n-d, Austin replied. W-i-t-h-c-a-p-t-i-v-e, he added. Surely Wolf was somewhere around here, he told himself; it wasn't a complete lie. O-r-d-e-r-s? he tapped.

R-e-t-u-r-n-s-h-i-p.

D-i-f-f-i-c-u-l-t.

He waited several seconds for a reply, then shifted position uncomfortably. Boland must be having a fit. There goes your promotion, Greg, he told himself. There goes Elena and her liking for ambitious men on the up-and-up. There goes most of everything, though he might keep his pilot's ranking; Survey needed good pilots. He told himself he hadn't wanted all the rest, anyway, not really. H-a-v-e-l-o-c-a-t-i-o-n, the commander sent at last. D-o-y-o-u-r-e-q-u-i-r-e-r-e-s-c-u-e?

He looked around the narrow tunnel and imagined what lay above for any rescue team. *La Novia* may have triangulated on his position, but that didn't solve the defenders between them. His ship had lost enough people.

N-e-g-a-t-i-v-e, he sent. W-i-l-l-r-e-t-u-r-n-s-h-i-p-s-o-o-n-e-s-t.

R-e-t-u-r-n-b-y-s-e-v-e-n-t-e-e-n-h-u-n-d-r-e-d. W-i-t-h-c-a-p-t-i-v-e. B-o-l-a-n-d-o-u-t.

O-u-t. The transponder dial faded, and Austin turned it off. With captive. Not likely. He checked his wristband. Two hours. Great. And he still had no idea where he was. He was about to explore down the tunnel toward the light when he heard a faint scrabble and tensed, then shied involuntarily as a shadow loomed suddenly in front of him.

"Ah, you are awake," he heard Wolf say. "Good."

Austin tried to hitch himself up to a sitting position and immediately thought better of it as his temples throbbed. He called her a rude name in French, hoping the slang had survived.

"And alert, too. That *is* good." He heard her chuckle.

"Where are we?' he demanded.

"In a side tunnel below the Downlift. You've been sleeping."

"Go ahead, rub it in." He tried to sit straighter again, then stifled another groan. "That was hardly friendly, Wolf—you said we'd talk."

"We *are* talking—and who wants to be friendly, miin?"

"My name is Austin," he said mildly. "Greg to my friends. Why don't you call me Greg?" Maybe he could cajole her into taking him back to the jitney and salvage this mess. She just stared at him, shadow against shadow. "Where's my helmet?"

"In a safe place. I will take you now to the Tiraamu."

"The what?" he asked hopefully. He peered at her, but saw only shadows.

"The Home-Space. Come."

"I don't want to go to the Home-Space. I want to go back to the jitney."

"There isn't any jitney. The nindru melted it." He saw the gleam of her teeth. "Quevi Ltir has excellent nindru, as crafty as you, miin—and longer-lived. Come."

He sighed. "What's a nindru?" he asked, though he could guess from the context.

You speak French, Greg, Elena had said eagerly. Once we contact the colonists, you can be liaison for the Contact Team, move up in rank; I've already cleared it with Boland. Sure, Elena, he thought sourly. Only the colonists don't speak French anymore, not really.

"Come."

He looked at her speculatively. Maybe if he went with her to this Tiraamu, she would take him back to the surface afterward, then let him climb aboard the lander that would be waiting for him. Maybe.

She tugged impatiently on his sleeve and pulled him toward her. He maneuvered awkwardly in the narrow tunnel, trying to get horizontal with his feet in the right direction, and hit his head on the ceiling. "Ouch!" He recoiled and bounced on the tunnel floor, then smashed his elbow into the other wall. Austin gave out a vivid oath, not French, and cradled his aching arm. Wolf clucked in exasperation and grabbed his suit collar. She scooted him several meters down the tunnel, bumping his other elbow and his knee.

"Hey, slow down! Goddamn it! I'm not a sack of flour!"

"Flour?"

Then abruptly they were in open air. Austin looked down into a dizzying depth and clutched at her as they began to fall slowly in the asteroid's light gravity. Wolf laughed and spread her left arm wide, then swung a leg upward, spinning them effortlessly heads-down. The walls whirled dizzily.

"That was a saavi, an invert," she told him.

"It certainly was," he muttered, and held on to her belt, his other hand tight on her forearm. He didn't like heights, for all his pilot's training; after all, in a ship you could pretend the view was just television. They fell at a lazy walking pace, the dim walls flickering past them. In the dim light from glow panels, Austin saw glimpses of metal panel covers, curious markings inscribed in uneven whorls, shadowed openings onto blackness. Sapient construction, he noted absently—well, of course. Too sapient, he thought, as something moved in a shadowed alcove as they passed.

As his eyes adjusted further to the gloom, he saw a box-shaped canister in another alcove swivel its metal barrel as it tracked them ominously, then swivel back to point upward. More automatic defenses, he guessed, like the robot lasers who had destroyed *La Novia*'s first lander. Quevi Ltir, as Wolf called it, was armed to the teeth. Why? More to the point, why didn't the robot fire? He craned his head backward to peer at it.

Wolf touched her free hand to her belt and their speed quickened. He tightened his grip on her. It was rather like flying, he decided a few minutes later—real flying, not in a ship, but like birds fly. He released her forearm and tentatively pushed out his hand to the right, then hastily retracted it as they veered left.

"If you're going to invert," Wolf said calmly, "be definite about it. Faint heart can leave you stranded in midair, ripe for the slash." Slash? he wondered. By what? He eyed a passing tunnel nervously. Then he squawked as she suddenly jackknifed and spun them a full circle before checking them neatly heads-down again.

"I've done free-fall acrobatics before, thank you," he said with gritted teeth.

"Oh?" she asked pointedly. They fell smoothly, still picking up speed.

"How far does it go down?" he asked curiously. He still couldn't see bottom in the darkness below them—this tunnel might be a kilometer deep, maybe more. *La Novia* had picked up subterranean power readings five kilometers square, though the experts had argued against any city that large. They hadn't even thought about how deep. Maybe they should have.

He saw yet another robot track them, then desist, and wondered what kind of surprises these aliens really had, if they decided to use them. A self-sustaining city over a hundred cubic kilometers in size? How many aliens lived in a hundred cubic kilometers? Thousands, certainly. Maybe tens of thousands—and Wolf was taking him right into the middle of them. And something slashed if you didn't watch out.

"How far?" he asked hoarsely.

"As far as it goes. But we will invert onto a landing place before then. Or sooner," she added suddenly, and veered them to the right, then pulled him quickly into an alcove. "Don't move." She pushed him back behind her and he bumped against a rear wall only two meters from the opening. "Quiet," she whispered urgently.

He thought to protest, then gawked as his first Avelle flashed past the opening, a blurred image of dark wings and white underbody three meters long, moving more gracefully than he had thought possible—and fast, he realized the next moment as he noticed the scant second it had taken the large alien to pass. Wolf leaned forward to look out the opening, threw a quick glance upward, then grabbed his arm. "Come! Before he returns!"

She planted a boot on the opening rim and pushed off, pulling him behind her, then inverted in a flash, wrapping her arm around his waist.

"Relax against me; don't resist."

"Okay."

Wolf touched her belt-jet control again, and they accelerated rapidly to a speed fast enough to make him squint against the rushing air, arrowing downward into the black depths. She looked behind them, then inverted feet-first, hauling him around with her, and they slowed quickly. Another invert and they slipped diagonally into another opening, falling several meters before touching down on a crosswise wall. Wolf waited for several seconds, watching the opening of this new tunnel, then seemed to relax.

"What was that all about?" he asked, suspected more games. "Aren't the aliens your friends?" He hadn't seen Wolf worry about much of anything, especially Gregory Austin. Why all the caution?

"Niintua must be inspecting your jitney personally, what's left of it. I prefer to not have him see me in a miin's company."

She settled to her haunches, steadying herself against a wall of their short pit. "We'll wait here awhile until I'm sure he's gone."

"Niintua? Nindru?"

She turned toward him, a dark shadow again in the gloom of the tunnel, and seemed to sigh. "I thought you spoke francais, Austin."

"I do—and you aren't, not always. Half your words don't make sense to me. What's a nindru?"

"An Avelle word. The machines on the surface and in the Downlift walls."

"How am I supposed to know Avelle words, Wolf?" he asked reasonably.

"Oh." She laughed softly. It was a nice sound, he thought, when she didn't put an edge on it. "What's a miin?" she asked suddenly.

"A what?"

"You. Miin."

"People, humans—more specifically, males. Pronounced 'men.' It's an Anglo word."

"Men." She repeated the word curiously. "Hmm. I'm human. Am I a miin, too?" She sounded disturbed by the idea.

"What do you think you are?"

"Faon. I am Jahnel Alain of the ilaipaari Louve, iruta Faon. We Faon are Naalu of Lejja, the Naalaiku of Apadi."

"I caught about two words of that, Wolf."

"Wolf is my ilaipaari," she corrected him absently.

"God damn it!" he declared, totally frustrated. "What's an ilaipaari?" This was ludicrous.

"A kin-group," Wolf translated. "You don't have kin-bonding?" From her tone, she seemed to find the idea rather obscene.

"What's a kin-group?" he asked.

She threw up her hands. "Austin . . ."

She stopped abruptly and lifted her head, hearing something he hadn't caught, then swiveled toward the opening of the tunnel and spat a word. A moment later a shape bulked in the opening, dusty black on pallid white with blazing red eyes. It spoke something to her in a deep rumbling voice, something in whistles and grunts; Wolf immediately lunged upward at it.

"Wolf!" he shouted in alarm. Wolf collided hard with the Avelle, then broke free, a small object in her hand. She flipped backward and darted back into their tunnel; a moment later, a blinding flash lit the abyss, followed by an echoing boom as the sound of the explosion bounced off metal walls. Charred fragments of flesh exploded in all directions, then slowly drifted downward in a nauseating rain past the tunnel opening. Austin heard a whining sound, then saw one of the robots—nindru, he corrected himself—drift into sight. The machine paused in front of their tunnel and inspected them, then flipped a light and resumed its hunt elsewhere.

"Who was that?" Austin whispered. "Niintua?"

"No, one of his salas—his guards. Niintua wouldn't be that easily surprised. And that probe robot has the entire incident in its vid memory, too. Stay here."

"I'm coming with you," he objected forcefully.

"You can't manage the fallways, Austin. You're as clumsy as a baby."

"I'm not *that* clumsy, Wolf. So don't wait up for me. But I'm coming along."

She stared at him a moment, then shrugged. "As you wish." She handed him the object she had taken from the alien. "Clip that to your belt. It wards off the nindru."

"Thanks."

She edged out of the tunnel, then pushed off. Austin followed her more cautiously, getting quickly behind as she used whatever she had on her belt to accelerate. Forty meters beneath them, a boxy shape glinted in the telltale lights as it drifted sideways, its lights winking off and on. Wolf approached it cautiously, slowing to practically nothing as she came within a few meters. Austin watched as she tentatively touched it, then twisted a latch on its cover. The machine beeped urgently and swiveled toward her, then abruptly went dark. Wolf slid the panel open, then touched something inside its innards. All three lazily fell downward as she finished disabling the machine.

"I'll be back," she called up to him, then grasped the robot and arrowed sideways toward another of the ubiquitous tunnel openings. Austin waited, a little anxiously, and slowly fell thirty meters below the tunnel she had selected. He tried flopping his arms but found that inverts did not stop his slow fall; finally he managed to maneuver closer to the walls and caught at a bracket. He clung there, looking up and down for other Avelle, though he hadn't the faintest idea what he would do if one showed. Probably consent to the slash—it was about his speed in this environment.

Odd to live in this kind of gravity. He smiled and pulled lightly on the bracket and bobbed upward, then checked the movement. Well, you can handle that, Greg, he thought. He awkwardly swung himself upside down, half floating, and clanged his boot on another bracket, recoiling a quarter-turn before he could catch himself. Greatly daring, he crossed his wrists and pulled sharply, dizzying himself with the loop-the-loop that made the wall spin.

This was something else, he decided, delighted.

On Luna, light gravity was more a menace than a wonder, with descending ramps his particular hazard; nor had he ever tried free-fall as an opportunity for fun, not with a sour-faced crew chief watching and growling his safety regs. He tried another loop-the-loop and stopped in midspin, half embarrassed, as he saw Wolf above him, watching him.

"Saavi," he said. She grinned and descended lightly to his level.

"What's an iruta?" he asked.

"A kin-alliance. Don't you have kin-bouncing?"

"I don't know what kin-alliance means to you, Wolf. I also don't know why that Avelle threatened you—or why you killed him."

"I didn't kill him—the nindru did."

"Let's not be slippery."

She shrugged. "He was careless—and he would have killed us both."

"Why?"

"You are an intruder. The Tiraamu must be defended. There are no exceptions."

He studied her face. "And this is your Home-Space, too? Is that why your people attacked us?"

"Of course." Her eyes changed and glinted with anger.

"Not 'of course,' " he said patiently. "We're human, too. We're your kind. We heard *Phalene*'s distress signal and tracked it to here. Our intentions are peaceful."

"*Phalene* was wrecked eighty years ago." She looked him up and down, sudden distrust in her face. "You don't look eighty years old, Austin."

"We were a long way from here, and space has different time frames." That puzzled her. "We came to rescue you."

"From what?" she retorted. "So far I've done all the rescuing, miin." He saw her glance quickly upward and down, checking.

"True," he admitted. "And some of the hazards you created, too—those hardly count. Why did you knock me out?"

"Would you have come with me voluntarily?"

He hesitated. "Probably not, Wolf."

"So. My name is Jahnel."

"I thought your name was Wolf."

"Wolf is my ilaipaari, a word you do not understand. You wonder why I killed the Avelle? If you don't even know what a kin-alliance is, I don't dare let the Avelle find you. Home-Space is all they care about, that and increasing their family brood. They don't know how alien you are, miin, not yet—and since you are human, they may think we Faon have the same taint."

"Taint?" Austin asked, confused.

"Come with me." She floated downward to another tunnel, then looked cautiously around yet again, up and down, then gestured him to follow. He moved gingerly after her, awkward in the light gravity. She slipped into the access gracefully, vanishing; he hesitated, then found himself yanked rudely into the darkness beyond.

"Hey!" He shook her off and glared. "Do the other robots have tapes of us?" he asked worriedly.

"The Downlift nindru do not observe, only defend," she answered absently. "Niintua had a prowl nindru with him; it observes and remembers, sometimes thinks. And much has grown old in the First Tier: even machines age and forget." She floated to a stop and turned toward him, her expression intent. "We approach an area of listeners now. I could take you through the Gate, but it is sure to be guarded—so we will go this other way. The Avelle do not waste repair metal on unneeded machinery, but this fallway abuts Lejja's tier, and we believe some of the wards are still active. Do not speak until I speak to you."

"All right." He caught at her sleeve. "Then let me ask now. Why did you bring me below? What are you going to do with me?"

"Had I not brought you, the nindru would have destroyed you with your ship." She stared at him a moment, then shrugged again. "Whatever the fault, it is done. The other I don't know; it is not my decision." She pointed a finger at him. "You will obey me."

"Do I have any choice?" he retorted.

"Hmmmph," she said noncommittedly. "You think in strangely restricted ways, miin. Come."

She twisted gracefully in midair and pushed off the tunnel floor, then built an ongoing momentum by handing herself, much like a swimmer, down the tunnel. He copied her and followed more slowly; after several dozen meters, he started to get the hang of it. Swimming in air. He felt the lightness of his body, her own grace possible within himself, but his limbs moved too awkwardly. He focused on the movements of his hands, the straightness of his body, sculling himself lightly along the tunnel.

They reached a downward turning and descended hundreds of meters, confined within a narrow tube. His shoulders began to ache with the cramped movements, and he gritted his teeth against the pain. A short way further, Wolf suddenly inverted in front of him into a side tunnel bisecting the tube. He tried to slow himself and nearly overshot the turning, then laboriously tugged himself back, lined up carefully, and pulled himself into the new access. She had waited patiently for him. Beyond her silhouetted body, he saw light again, a narrow circle of reddish light that seemed bright after the pitch darkness of the tunnel.

"Wait here," she instructed.

She left him alone, slipped gracefully down the tunnel toward the exit, and vanished from view. Austin waited, then looked upward. You think in strangely restricted ways, she had said; maybe he should try it. He could retrace his way to that first tunnel, find his helmet, get back on the surface—he had a ward-off device now. Boland would send a lander to pick him up, could duplicate the ward-off device to give them all protection. Austin could lead a survey party downward with what he knew, and force Contact. He would be the hero of it all, dauntless Gregory Austin, Contact man extraordinaire.

He hesitated. So far La Novia had made one mistake after another, blundering around not knowing what was going on, assuming things to fit its preferences, acting more out of its lust for alien contact than caution for the colonists. And so had blindly killed Wolf's—Jahnel's—people. Extreme territoriality: had the Contact Team even considered that as a fundamental? What was going on here? And if he was caught sneaking out by the Avelle, would that impact on the Faon? Jahnel had implied as much. Why blame the Faon? Because they share the human taint?

Go on: be the hero, he told himself. Show her. Take the risk. He sighed and rubbed his face, then sighed again. La Novia had made enough blunders; he wouldn't add his share. He shrugged his shoulders into a comfortable position against the wall, settling himself to wait.

℞ Chapter 6

J AHNEL EMERGED FROM the cross-tunnel and propelled herself quickly down the narrow fallway fronting the outer wall
of Lejja's tier. Their descent through the maze of the First Tier
had brought them to within a few hundred meters of the Faon
levels. In the early decades of Quevi Ltir, *Quevi'ali*'s kin-
alliances had lived together in the First Tier while they built
separate tiers for their brooding. The Avelle had built the First
Tier as a maze of close spaces and multiple turnings, responding
out of normal pattern to the stress of iruta in too close a prox-
imity; it was not their pattern of first choice, and few Avelle had
bothered with the First Tier afterward. To the Faon, the First
Tier held endless fascination—as well as a prudent option against
attack, should Lejja's Avelle deny their bonding and invade the
Faon levels. Later the Faon had used the portal to explore the
dark tunnels and wards of the First Tier, even venturing downward into the lower levels that ran the length of the City's seven
double-tiers. In either purpose, the Faon showed themselves all
too human: an Avelle had little interest in spaces outside his own
tier and would never abandon his home-level once he held it,
even upon the destruction of his brood.

In her youth, Jahnel had loved the shadows of the First Tier,
playing chase-and-slash games with her companions through its
bewildering complexity of tunnels and dark fallways, wheedling
her parents for sparé odds and ends to build a pretend Home-
Space in some byway easily defended, creating in miniature
their own world of City and tier, Principal and soldier. Dozens
of times, Jahnel had defended her chosen tunnel from Sair's
blinding attacks; dozens of times, she had led her kin-alliance
in counter-feint and stealthy advance. The children's tier wars
often rivaled the noise and passion of the real wars elsewhere,

bringing an occasional reproof from a Faon adult when the wars
raged too close to the tier walls and gates, but otherwise the
elders indulged the play—if only to preserve adult peace and
quiet within the vayalim.

She had expected to see children playing in the tunnels nearest the portal, but heard nothing. This part of the First Tier lay
as quiet as the rest; it troubled her. She looked upward, half
expecting to see other Avelle descending the fallway, and wondered if Benoit had forbidden the children their usual play because of other encounters deeper in the First Tier. Or was there
another reason? She felt a sudden sense of foreboding.

Until now, she had acted without forethought, determined to
return to Quevi Ltir and to bring the proof of the miin with her;
only now, when she had time to think, did she realize how this
act would appear to the Avelle, an act of immorality beyond
Avelle thinking—and perhaps some Faon thinking, too. No matter what information Austin could give, no matter any other
purpose to his catching, intruders were not tolerated in the
Home-Space. To permit such intrusion risked loss of everything
a kin-alliance possessed; that lesson governed Avelle life. Once
Lejja had dared such a rash choice against all sense, defying her
rivals with the rank and power of her numerous brooding, but
the Faon lived by uneasy tolerance, weak in numbers and resented by too many Avelle. Have you forgotten everything you
knew? she wondered desperately. What ever possessed you to
do such a thing?

She slowed her descent, trying to think coherently. But I
couldn't just leave him for the robots, she argued with herself.
Oh? And why not? He's only a miin—only the miin are human.
Human like us. And she greatly suspected that Austin had aided
her escape, for what reason she couldn't guess. Though he moved
awkwardly in the fallways, she could recognize that as inexpe-
rience—his competence lay in other areas, competence he had
not used to stop her. Why did he help me? she wondered. Would
you have helped him if matters had been reversed? Candidly,
she knew she would not, not for a miin, and suspected that that
difference was a human thing the Faon had lost. What else had
the Faon lost of their human selves?

Why *had* he helped her?

She stopped and hovered in the shadows edging the fallway,
cudgeling her brain, and felt half-tempted to return and ask
him. But asking would not solve her problem; she only now
recognized its serious implications. Idiot, she thought, angry at

herself. But what could she do now? If she took Austin back to
the surface, how would he live? And if Niintua discovered him
in Faon company on their way upward, matters would be far
worse—not even Lejja would defend the Faon then, caught in
the moral ambiguity of condemning an action she had taken
herself. Koyil would love that inverted advantage, she thought
sourly. Yet if she left Austin too long in the First Tier, an Avelle
might find him, especially if he chose to wander—and she didn't
entirely trust Austin to stay put, not indefinitely. He had strength,
and a certain initiative, though why he refrained from acting
confused her. But if she took him into the Faon levels, as she
had intended . . . what then?

She shook her head irritably. How do you arrange this for
yourself, Jahnel? I am committed now, she told herself, and felt
irritated all over again at her reluctance to face her kindred with
such news. Her family would be worried, thought her likely
dead. She could not linger. She touched her belt jet and hurried
downward.

She saw the shadowed shape of the Faon guard in the portal
before he saw her and slowed her descent, then inverted in mid-
tunnel, drifting downward into his range of sight. The guard
jerked in alarm and raised his dis-rifle, then relaxed as he recognized her human shape. Then he saw her face.

"Yves," she greeted him. Sair's birth-brother looked at her
as if she had risen alive from a disintegration vat. Well, perhaps
she had, in a sense.

"Jahnel!" He gawked a moment, then split his face with a
wide incredulous grin. "You are well?"

She caught a projecting tube and pulled herself level with
him. "I am well. Yves, I brought a—"

"You must see Sair right away," Yves interrupted. "We've
been concerned for him. Come."

"Not yet, Yves. I've brought a—"

Yves turned and vanished into the shadowed opening, hurrying ahead to bear the news. News. She floated in front of the
access, chagrined. She supposed she was such news, for Yves
to lose all courtesy for her and to leave his guardpost unattended.
And she brought bigger news, how Jahnel Alain had brought an
intruder into the Home-Space. Benoit would not enjoy this new
dilemma brought him by his daughter. I am an idiot, she thought.

She glanced upward into the shadows and hesitated. Austin
would stay put for a short time, at least, and she saw nothing

above or below. The tier guard's attack had sobered him of any thought he had of escape; she had seen it in his eyes, that fear that every Faon learned in childhood. Had he helped her escape from his ship? For all his awkwardness, he had adapted well, better than she had expected. But she mistrusted his passivity, mistrusted it badly.

You just assume, Jahnel, she chided herself. You think you know what the miin are, what they intend—like Melinde assumed she could say anything she wished in Avelle hearing. For an instant, Jahnel felt another prick of deep apprehension. Had she imperiled all the Faon? And now that she had Austin, what should they do with him?

She reached out a hand and touched the rim-edge of the tunnel, then pulled herself into its confines with a jerk. Consequences must be faced, the sooner the better. You think you're so smart, she told herself angrily.

The portal led to a small storeroom, then opened into the gathering room on the lower level. Here the Faon met to discuss decisions that affected all of them, to watch City-Net broadcasts on the larger monitor, and to meet for public celebrations and other cross-vayalim meetings. Jahnel drifted neatly over the threshold of the gravity field and dropped feetfirst to the metal floor. She heard a murmur of voices ahead and walked toward the lighted doorway ahead, finding a gathering of many Faon, mostly elders. Two levels high and twenty meters square, the conference room could hold an extensive gathering, though soon the Faon brooding would overflow the long ranks of chairs along each wall. In the center of the room stood a wide table and three chairs for the Faon Leader and his two councilors; a wall screen connected to the City's communication network dominated the rear wall. She saw Yves talking to her father and the two councilors at the center table, waving his hands excitedly, quite oblivious to the fact that she hadn't immediately followed. She smiled slightly; that was just like Yves. She saw her father's quick glance toward her, then his gesture to a younger Etoile and quick instructions. The Etoile vanished through the far door into the inner level.

Well past middle age, Benoit Alain had been Faon Leader for three decades, imperious in his leadership but undeniably committed to the benefit of the Faon. He and Jahnel had an uneasy relationship more distant than she wished, for her willfulness offended her father. In all his life, Benoit had never taken action without forethought and great deliberation; he still grieved quietly for Jahnel's mother, blaming her mother's own willfulness for her early death in the tier wars; he saw in Jahnel the same defect. Even so, he had indulged Jahnel in permitting her marriage to Sair, though he thought her too young and impulsive to lead a vayalim—and had told her so coldly. But he had permitted, and for that Jahnel still felt grateful whatever their later quarrels, both private and public.

She waited in the doorway, looking at the faces she had known all her life and relishing the fact that she was home. Although she loved the ease of the fallways, something deeply physical was satisfied by the weight, the air, the warmth of the Faon Home-Space, as if her ancestry remembered through the body the onetime Home, remembered that she was a miin. She wondered if the Faon would feel the disquiet in that thought as she did, reminded again that they did not belong to Quevi Ltir, not in the deepest essentials.

Then suddenly she was in the midst of an enthusiastic welcome as others saw her in the doorway. Francoise rushed over first and took her into a fervent embrace. Others came, overwhelming her with their talk and smiles as she was hugged again and again, words talked into her face, excitement bubbling. She felt overwhelmed and looked beyond them for Sair and the others of her vayalim, knowing she would feel at home truly only when their arms embraced her, their words were spoken. Evan appeared first, bounding through the conference-room doorway on his limber legs, nearly knocking an Etoile elder off his feet. Then Solveya appeared, moving gracefully in her fourth month of pregnancy, her serene young face alight. Eduard came next, carrying Luelle . . . and then Sair.

Sair stopped in the far doorway and stared at her, his emotion naked in his face. She shook off the well-wishers, touched hands briefly with Evan and Solveya and Eduard, gave a smile to Luelle, a kiss to Didier in Solveya's arms, then went to Sair. He took a shuddering breath and held her tightly, and she felt him tremble against her.

"Sair . . ." she whispered.

His throat moved but he didn't speak, only held her closely. Finally he pushed her back and stood her in front of him, his hands holding her shoulders.

"How?" he asked, bewildered. "We saw the miin take you into their ship—but how . . ." He looked her up and down, as if he doubted her reality.

"I forced one of the miin pilots to bring me down—or perhaps he permitted it," she added ruefully. "I've stashed him in a tunnel in the First Tier."

"A miin? You did *what*?" he asked incredulously.

"*What?*" a deep voice echoed from behind her, heavy with shock and displeasure. She turned to face her father.

"The miin are humans," she told him, raising her voice so all could hear. "They come from Earth, like *Phalene* did. You need to talk to this Austin, Papa, hear his words."

"A miin?" Her father scowled, his mouth drawn down in contempt. Contempt for her also? she wondered. Her anger flared instantly, reacting to his coldness.

"*We* may be miin," she challenged him, looking swiftly around the faces near them. "And, yes, I brought him into the City rather than let the robots kill him. I could have given him up, but I didn't."

"This explains why Lejja has demanded a council," Benoit said sourly. "She must know about this miin." He glared at her. "Don't you realize what you've done, Jahnel?"

"Lejja can't know," Jahnel protested. "I avoided the Avelle and brought Austin down through the far side of the First Tier. The Avelle cannot know."

"Hmmph. We shall see." Her father turned to Yves. "Yves, take two Faon and bring this Austin into our levels. I don't want the chance of a probe robot sniffing around and finding him. Where did you leave him, Jahnel? Will he cause any trouble?"

"In the fifth bend of Level Forty-two, farside. He seems cooperative, but he's not stupid. Approach him easily, Yves—do not alarm him."

Benoit glared again. "Who cares about miin sensibilities?"

"He is *human*, Papa."

"A miin—you bring a miin into the City."

"Papa . . ."

Benoit shrugged, dismissing her protest. "Well, there's no help for it. If I could, I'd put him down a disrupter unit, but likely it wouldn't stop the crisis you've created. I told you Lejja had demanded conference. She is coming *here*, Jahnel."

Jahnel tightened her fingers on Sair's. "To Faon Home-Space?"

"Exactly. Let's call it an object lesson on who really owns our home." He pointed at the rank of Louve chairs. "I want you here, for whatever influence you have on Kiiri and his matching influence on Lejja. Yves can bring in your miin and hide him. Move quickly, Yves. Guard says the Avelle party is already descending the tier fallway.''

Yves nodded soberly and signed at Philippe and another Roche, then vanished back into the storeroom and its access beyond. Jahnel exchanged a pained glance with Sair, then gathered Luelle into her arms, hugging her tight. Jahnel moved toward the chairs along the nearer wall and sat down in the middle row beside Sair, Luelle on her lap. Solveya sat down on her other side, Evan beyond her. Baby Didier, Jahnel's son, kicked his short legs on Solveya's knees and looked around placidly, thumb in his mouth, fascinated by the bustle in the room, then smiled winningly at Jahnel as he saw her looking at him. Another charmer, she thought, more of Eduard's charm than her own, and just now showing some personality as he passed his first year. As Eduard joined them, Didier gurgled and reached for him; Eduard raised him high, making him laugh, then sat down with him nearby. My beloveds, Jahnel thought fondly, then suddenly noticed Melinde's absence.

"Where is Melinde?" she asked Solveya.

"Where Melinde chooses to keep herself." Her junior wife's beautiful face settled into great severity. "She has left the vayalim, Jahnel.''

"Left?''

Solveya looked distressed. "She's been talking to certain of Hiboux and Roche—Philippe's at the middle of that. God knows what they've said to each other in their huddlings. Last night she announced she was moving into a Hiboux vayalim and just left.''

"I went to talk to her," Evan said, "but you know how she's been acting." He looked down at his hands in his lap, no doubt blaming himself.

"She won't listen," Sair added. "She never has—you share that with her, Jahnel.''

Jahnel drew in a quick breath of pain. "Not you, too, Sair.''

"Well, what do you expect?" he began angrily.

Sair stopped abruptly as others caught the signal from the conference-room door and hurried toward chairs in their ranks around the room. Benoit and two other elders seated themselves on the low bench near room center. Evan and Solveya left quickly with the children, taking them to the safety of their vayalim. At the end, about sixty Faon remained, all adults and all seniors. She saw a Faon across the room glance through the storeroom door, sign at someone within, then step through the doorway, firmly shutting the door behind him. Yves had not been quick

enough. She twisted her hands in her lap anxiously, wondering
what the Avelle would do if they found Austin here, in the Faon
levels. You don't think sometimes, she told herself angrily. You
just don't think. She waited, too conscious of Sair's disapproving
silence, then felt the gravity change. Kiiri had cut the gravity
controls, and Lejja's party must now be within the level.

A few moments later, a Faon drifted through the inner doorway and straightened himself to respectful attention, then made
way for the Avelle that followed him. An Avelle senior guard, a
high-caste of the Principal's own brooding, drifted easily through
the doorway and looked over all assembled with a haughty stare.

"The Principal of Songs," he announced in a reedy voice,
adding the aftergesture of commanded respect, "ruler of this
tier and of the Faon within it."

Benoit rose. "We salute the Principal of Songs," he replied
in Avelle. "We welcome her presence with glad hearts. Please
bid her enter."

Politics can be interesting in its lies, great and small, Jahnel
thought dispiritedly. She glanced at the storeroom door, wondering if Yves had kept Austin there or had had the good sense
to return him into the shadows of First Tier. Avelle had a keen
sense of smell and knew other things through their electrostatic
senses. Did a miin radiate different fields than Faon? Now several other Avelle servant-guards appeared and advanced into the
room in stately pace, their wing-tips sculling against the air
currents. Then, at the center of their arc, Lejja entered.

She advanced slowly, her movements hesitant with age, then
stopped several meters behind the foremost guard, her deep-set
eyes fixed on Benoit and his two companions at the center table.
Behind her, Kiiri and Lejja's daughter-heir, Nerup, took their
positions, giving the Faon a united front that menaced with their
subtleties of body language. Even Kiiri kept his wing-flaps tight
around his body, though his expressionless gaze roved the room
in casual ease. Benoit was right, she feared: the Avelle knew
something.

Benoit rose gracefully and bowed. "Greetings, Principal of
Songs. Welcome to our Home-Space you granted to us and ours
long ago; the debt is known, the favor recognized in blessing."

"Greetings," Lejja said distantly, her voice barely above a
whisper. She gestured vaguely with a thin-fingered hand, then
seemed to lose attention.

The Avelle matriarch had cruelly aged in recent months, as if
decades had been compressed into a few scant years in their

ravages on her body. The edges of her wing-flaps were whitened
and scored by new disease; her mouth hung open slightly, showing worn teeth and a scabrous lining at the gums: she was definitely in her final decline. She seemed hesitant, soft, a shadow
of the crafty Principal who had held her rank and tier for more
than two centuries against the worst that her rivals could plot
against her. Jahnel's throat tightened into a knot. To the girl
Jahnel, Lejja had always seemed a wonderful figure, a holder of
mysteries, a benign queen to all she ruled, a crafty and subtle
matriarch who protected and blessed the Faon. Now she saw a
ruin of all Lejja had been to her own and to Quevi Ltir, her
death perhaps hastened by the stresses of the miin intrusion and
Koyil's immediate grab for its advantages.

Few Principals enjoyed a leisurely old age, and their inevitable death could put all the City into convulsion, disrupting
whole tiers, throwing all alliances into doubt. Lejja herself had
risen to Principal rank in such disorder two centuries before,
taking the honor from another kin-alliance and crushing the defeated tier into subservience. Among the Principals, only the
Star Leader was immune to such changes, but so long had the
Avelle lingered in their City that the Star Leader's kin-alliance
had failed in its brooding and lost the Principalship to a kindred
tier. Pakal's line had held the Leadership for only two generations, depleted in its authority by a weak successor and his son
Pakal's own indecision, thus making new opportunity for Law
and Song to rise to unusual prominence. Lejja had bound Science to herself by supporting her kinsman Kiiri into the succession; in due course, Koyil had elevated his own kinsman,
Suuryan, to Principal of Mind, strengthening the dangerous du-
ality uncommon among Avelle that had polarized Quevi's iruta
behind its two great Principals.

In a society bound firmly by hereditary rank, change came in
a rush of violent wrenching. The tensions among the Principals
had worsened for decades, so firmly balanced that usual adjustments were too long delayed. *Phalene*'s arrival had nearly un-
done the balance, threatening a major convulsion that was but
narrowly avoided and only put off for a time. Kin-alliances died
in such major tier wars, their home-levels quickly occupied by
the victors. Jahnel glanced around the room, her senses height-
ened with greater tension. Not mine, she vowed, and curled her
fingernails into her palm, pressing hard.

Benoit waited politely, then grew visibly uneasy as Lejja's
silence lengthened. The Principal stared over his head vaguely,

her mouth moving randomly from side to side. Behind her, Nerup's gaze sharpened, calculating. An heir-daughter had a narrow tunnel to keep what her predecessor had built; few caught that slender chance. For an instant, Nerup's eyes met Jahnel's across the room. Jahnel half rose in the intensity of that gaze, then abruptly remembered herself in embarrassment. She re-seated herself, discomfited.

"Jahnel?" Sair whispered.

"Nothing." She raised her eyes again and saw Nerup's gaze still upon her, as if she willed Jahnel to do something—but what?

They know something, her father had said. What do they know?

Then Lejja half started, and the vagueness of her gaze van-ished in a sharp flicker of her eyes. She looked cooly over the assembly, her tail brushing the floor, her wing-flaps pulled tightly around her long body. Her reddish eyes, deep-set in the shadows of their sockets, gleamed almost malevolently, a blend of craft-iness and raw power that Lejja used to intimidate even her own. Benoit faced her calmly, uncowed. His own arrogance served him well with the Faon's powerful Principal.

"I see the Faon, kin-alliance within my tier," Lejja said, her voice whispery but strong. "I see the Faon Council assembled, and representatives of the kin-groups bound with the name of Faon. I see a part of me and mine."

Her father subtly relaxed, the lines in his face easing. "I see the Principal of Songs, kin-mother to us all." He bowed grace-fully, a complicated gesture in light gravity but smoothly done.

Lejja's wing-flaps shivered, then loosened slightly as she, too, relaxed. Kiiri drifted forward to take up a new station slightly behind and to her right; Nerup did not move, though her clever eyes watched everything. After the formal greeting, several others of Lejja's councilors entered the room, arraying themselves in a counter-arc to the proud guards that divided Avelle from Faon. Lejja's thin arm emerged from concealment and gestured slightly to Kiiri.

"Greetings to the Faon," Kiiri said formally. "I bring news—and inquiry. Two hours ago the surface monitors detected a radio signal to the miin ship from within the First Tier. An intruder has entered the City," he intoned. Jahnel pressed her hands together, knowing that Kiiri was carefully ignoring another pos-sibility—that the signal had been Faon talking to the miin. If Kiiri had shared Koyil's faking of La Novia's message, he knew the miin were human and would consider countertreachery. Kiiri always considered everything. She watched his face, not quite forgiving him if he knew, knowing she would be a fool to forgive him if he confirmed he knew. And what else did you know, my clever and beloved Principal? What else?

She saw Lejja's eyes sharpen as she studied the faces of the councilmen, but her gaze did not threaten now. They know, Jahnel concluded as she watched the Avelle faces, bringing all she knew of a lifetime of knowing the aliens—but they aren't sure what they know. Not even Kiiri—or does he? She watched Kiiri's face especially closely, careful to conceal her own scrutiny under blandness.

The Science Leader flipped a clawed finger. "One of Niintua's guards went to investigate but has not returned; we have searched for him briefly in the upper levels. We ask if you have seen him."

"In the First Tier?" Benoit said, feigning confusion at the question. "The Principals know that the First Tier is long-abandoned. Who goes there but probe robots in their ceaseless vigilance?"

The question rested on the air for a few moments as Benoit gazed in dignified courtesy at the Avelle. Jahnel could have sworn she caught a ghost of approval in Lejja's eyes—the Principal delighted in such ambiguity, a statement that neither denied nor admitted, yet hinted at the worst, at bland innocence. Wheels within wheels. The Avelle were masters of subtlety, and the Faon their able students, especially Benoit Alain. She bent her head to hide a smile.

"That is true," Kiiri agreed solemnly. Jahnel rubbed her nose hurriedly to compose her face back to solemnity. "Still, we bring warning. Any intruder, if the miin have penetrated the City with a spy, must be destroyed. The Home-Space will not be violated!" Lejja nodded gravely—and in that acknowledgment repromised her protection of the Faon. Jahnel saw her father stir uneasily, all too conscious of the miin hidden behind the storeroom door.

"I thank you," Lejja said in her whispery voice, "for the sacrifices you have made for our kin-alliance and tier."

Jahnel saw her father relax again as Lejja publicly restored to the Faon their rank of full kin-alliance within the tier, not the subservient kin-group thrown to the sacrifice that she had threatened earlier. She felt Sair shift beside her, reacting also.

"When the miin come again to Quevi Ltir," Lejja continued,

"should they be so rash, four of our tier's levels have volunteered help to you, Faon. May your battles bring victory."

Benoit bowed gravely once again. "Victory," he echoed.

Lejja looked around the room, even half turned to look behind her into the hallway beyond. "It has been many cycles since I visited your levels, my Faon. Does all still please you?"

"We are content, Lejja."

"Should you think of any need, however minor, inform the Science Leader and it shall be crafted for you."

"We thank you for your courtesy."

Lejja nodded, then signed to no one in particular. As she turned, the circle of Avelle foreshortened, some proceeding her into the hallway, the guards last to leave. Jahnel's father sat down with a grunt, looking exhausted, then bent to talk privately with elder Arnaud. Several minutes later, full gravity returned with a sudden heaviness that seemed odd for a moment. A murmur broke out among the assembled Faon; several stood and stretched, then began gathering in groups to discuss Lejja's visit in low voices. Jahnel sat unmoving in her chair, then glanced at Sair.

"I don't believe it," he muttered. "Not wholly."

She reached for his hand, then pressed his fingers. "Security of position would be a boon right now—though few Avelle enjoy it themselves. She is ill—did you see that? The mind-blank has begun."

"But not severely." He looked at her and thought to say something else, then decided against it. "You are alive," he said simply. "We didn't know that for sure when Evan saw the miin take you."

"Yes." She squeezed his hand again. "Well, it's done," she said, answering the comment about Austin he had not added. "Perhaps it will be the right choice."

"Perhaps. We have little certainty today." He stood and tugged her to her feet, then followed as Benoit signaled to Jahnel across the room.

"Yes, Papa?"

"Come with me," Benoit said curtly. "You, too, Sair." Her father turned on his heel and marched toward the storeroom. Councilman Arnaud gathered up the third of Benoit's council, Celeste du Gard, and joined them as they stepped through the doorway. On a low bench on the far wall, Austin sat lumpily, looking rumpled with a smear of blood on his cheek. Philippe and Yves stood on either side of him, a dis-rifle slung in the crook of Philippe's arm. As Jahnel appeared, Austin looked up at her hopefully.

"There you are," he declared.

"Shut up," Philippe commanded. "You will speak when you're spoken to, miin."

"My name is Gregory Austin," Austin said mildly, his voice underlaid by subtle defiance.

Jahnel's father walked to within a few paces of Austin and stared down at him, then inspected him coolly from boots to disordered hair. He looked at Philippe. "He gave you trouble."

"He *said* he wasn't sure who we were," Philippe answered scornfully, "and so tried to escape into a side tunnel. He didn't get far." He touched the muzzle of his rifle to Austin's belt. "The buckle apparently has a transponder." Jahnel bit her lip in chagrin; she hadn't thought to look beyond the helmet. What had Austin done?

Benoit swung toward Jahnel and stared at her a moment, but chose to say nothing. He confronted Austin again, who had watched the exchange with alert eyes. "Did you signal your ship?"

"Yes."

"You fool!" Benoit exploded. "You've endangered all of us!"

"I have since figured that out," Austin said calmly. "I didn't know at the time; I do now. My ship doesn't understand the situation here, but they mean well, sir."

"By killing Faon?" Benoit's voice was frigid with contempt.

"We didn't know who you were," Austin shot back. "How could we? Did your Avelle tell you who we were? Did they tell you they were *talking* to us while you were preparing for battle?" Jahnel saw several startled looks among the Faon, but her father's expression did not change its rigid displeasure. Austin stared back at him a moment, then shrugged. "We asked the Avelle for contact with you. Your 'contact' wasn't what we intended, though obviously the Avelle liked it just fine. Both sides have dead to grieve."

"I am not concerned about your dead, miin."

"My name is Gregory Austin," Austin said defiantly. "Kill me if you wish. Go ahead, act like your bloody-minded Avelle. I'll take comfort that you'll get yours." He crossed his arms across his chest and glared.

"That hasn't been decided." Benoit scowled, then turned to Celeste. "We can't risk keeping him in the First Tier, not with the Avelle searching. I want the access portal closed so it isn't discovered by accident, if the probes come down-tier this far. In the meantime . . .'' He looked at Austin speculatively, then turned to Jahnel.

"Since you created this problem, daughter, you can watch over him until I decide what to do with him. I wish to consult with the elders, examine all sides.'' Jahnel studied his face closely, guessing that Benoit's "examination" already had a likely conclusion. Of all Faon, Benoit thought most like Avelle and had deliberately chosen Avelle attitudes, Avelle choices, to better understand the Principal who protected the Faon. The Faon had benefited from that prudence, she reminded herself, only . . . "I suggest,'' Benoit said, "you keep him away from others of your vayalim to spare them the taint.''

"Taint?'' Jahnel asked acidly, stung by his tone, though she knew she had thought the same word herself. "And since when do you govern my vayalim and its personal affairs? I am senior wife.''

"Then act like one,'' her father snapped.

"Didn't you hear what Austin said? The Avelle have talked—''

"He's a miin.'' Her father turned on his heel and stamped out as Jahnel stared after him incredulously.

"Welcome to the Tiraamu,'' Austin muttered.

Philippe promptly jabbed him in the ribs with his riflebutt. "Shut up.''

"Do that again, Philippe,'' Jahnel warned, "and I'll take it out of your hide.''

"That's enough, Jahnel,'' Councilman Arnaud said, interrupting smoothly. "We must move him immediately. Too many of us in the room knew the miin was in this storeroom, and I distrust the clever eyes of Lejja's guards. Even too great a stillness or too long a refusal to look in this direction would hold meaning for them. They could insist on a probe search, for all Lejja's gracious expressions of trust.'' He made a face. "Sair's and Jahnel's vayalim is as good a place as any—and I think Jahnel has been pricked enough to take the care.'' He raised an eyebrow.

"Austin,'' Jahnel said, "if we bring you into the Faon Home-Space, in which you are now on the periphery''—she gestured at the room—"will you give me your word you will not try escape and will follow orders? Lives could be in the balance if you don't. Otherwise you must be bound.''

He met her eyes without hesitation. "I understand that. Yes, I will give my word."

"Trust the word of a miin?" Philippe protested.

"Quiet, Philippe," Arnaud said firmly. He gestured at Austin's spacesuit. "Get him out of that miin spacesuit and destroy it in the disrupter. Some of Kiiri's probes have molecule sifters and they might track it here. Philippe, I want this air analyzed and scoured just in case—do the fallway outside the portal, too, and back-trace the tunnels to where you found him."

"Yes, Councilman." Philippe turned and stamped out. Jahnel watched him leave, wondering what Philippe was brewing with his group of rebel Faon. Knowing Melinde's opinions, she could guess what the group shared in beliefs—though what the Roche leader would do with such opinions perplexed her. Launch a tier war against Lejja? Challenge Benoit and force him to step down? Or merely oppose any suggestion for the pleasure of the anger? Philippe was capable of that; so was Melinde. Her sister-wife liked her jealousies too much to give them up easily.

And I bring a miin into the City, she thought glumly, to add to my father's problems. Whatever their disagreements, Benoit had the leadership and deserved her kin-obedience. It was the law of the City, the way of things among the Faon; it is what they were as Faon.

But will he throw Austin away? she worried, guessing that he might choose that in his anger and fear.

And if he does, does he throw away the Faon?

🪶 Chapter 7

J AHNEL SHOOK HERSELF out of her distraction and gestured
to Austin. "Come with me, Austin," she said curtly. He
stood up with a nervous glance at Philippe's rifle, then walked
forward stiffly.

"Earth gravity here," he commented. "Who makes it?"

"Faon gravity," Sair said haughtily, correcting him. "Kiiri
does. Take off your spacesuit."

Austin hesitated as if to dispute, then began to comply.
"What's a kiiri?" he asked as he unzipped.

"Who, miin, not what," Sair said. He watched Austin strip
off his suit, then looked curiously at the tube pants and strange
aal. Philippe picked up the vacuum suit and left with it. "Good.
So far you keep your word, miin. You will come this way. Beloved?" As they walked through the conference room, several
Faon turned to look curiously at Austin, then talked quietly
among themselves with more glances. Jahnel's choice would be
much discussed today. She tightened her lips, not liking the
scrutiny.

"He didn't tell me what a kiiri—who—was," Austin said to
Jahnel.

"Hush, Austin. You walk a knife-edge—or don't you know
that?" She pushed him ahead of her toward the central stairway,
placing him between herself and Sair.

"I know it," he said calmly. "I choose to ignore it. Who's a
kiiri?"

"The Science Leader of the Avelle, a Principal of Quevi Ltir.
He made this place for us."

"Gravity control," Austin said, sounding awed. He looked
around with interest as they walked along the second level, as
if he were a visiting Principal himself, so casually he inspected.

"Would you like to know what a few think-tank professors back on Earth, not to talk of whole governments, would give for gravity control?"

"No."

Sair opened the door to their vayalim and vanished within, then waited for them in the common room. He threw Jahnel an enigmatic glance, then pushed the call button on the central table. A mellow chime echoed through the rooms. In a few moments, Evan appeared from one of the side hallways and stopped short to goggle. "The miin," he said.

"The miin," Sair answered tiredly. "We get the keeping of him."

"All right, you two," Jahnel said in exasperation, and put her hands on her hips. "Do we discuss this now or later?"

Sair looked at her, amused. "Love you," he drawled, then grinned at her. "He needs Faon clothes, Evan. He's about Eduard's size—could you go get an aal from his room? Where's Solveya?"

"In the children's room."

"Ask her to stay there for a while with the kids. And clear out the spare storeroom with the extra bed. We'll stash the miin there after he's decently clothed. Are you hungry, Austin?"

"Are you?" Austin countered. He stood where he had stopped by the inner portal, his eyes looking everything over. He focused on Sair. "What's your name? And what are you to Jahnel? And who was that?" He pointed at the hallway into which Evan had vanished. "And who's Solveya?" He worked his fingers into fists, then uncurled them. Jahnel heard the strain in his voice and knew that Austin's control had frayed to a ragged edge.

"Come sit down, Austin," she invited, and pulled out a chair, then slid a chair out for herself.

"We're putting him in the storeroom," Sair objected.

"Not right away. Didn't you ask if he was hungry?"

"Jahnel, he's not a guest to our Home-Space."

"Oh?" She smiled up at Sair.

"Song Above, you'd play the host if the ceiling fell," he said irritably, flashing a disgruntled look at Austin. "Is that how you want it? A guest?"

"Yes, Sair." She reached out a hand to him. "Please."

Sair blew out a breath and studied her a moment, then turned to Austin. "Be seated, please. My name is Sair Rostand, senior husband of our vayalim. That other man was Evan, my cohusband; Solveya is co-wife." He gestured Austin forward impatiently when the other still hesitated.

"Thank you," Austin murmured, and sank down into the chair beside Jahnel. Sair vanished into the kitchen and started a faint clatter. "Co-wife?" Austin asked.

"We have six in our vayalim—that word means marriage-group."

Austin closed his eyes wearily. "Contact is wonderful, but it can get confusing. What's a marriage-group?"

Jahnel leaned forward and cupped her chin in her hand. "Don't you know *anything*, Austin?" she teased him. Austin straightened and threw a few miin words at her, asking her if *she* knew what *they* were, but the effort quickly faded. He looked mortally tired, pale beneath his curious brownness. Evan brought an aal and supervised Austin's dressing of himself, then bore away the tube pants and miin aal to the disrupter. Austin sat down again with a grunt.

"Will they 'disrupt' those, too?" Austin asked tiredly. He looked down and fingered the black cloth of his aal.

"Yes. We can't risk foreign particles for the sniffers."

"Sniffers?"

"More nindru, Austin."

"Ah, yes—nindru. Always nindru." He wiped at the blood on his face with his sleeve. "Some nindru aren't exactly mechanical."

"I'm sorry about that," she said. "Philippe is zealous."

"There are other words to describe Philippe," he growled, then smiled at her without restraint. The smile transformed Austin's tanned face—strange that it should be so brown, she thought irrelevantly. With the smile, he looked far younger than she had assumed, hardly more than Eduard's age. His hands were lean and square like the rest of him, capable hands for all his awkwardness in the fallways; he moved more easily in full gravity, natural to him. A miin he remained with his lack of vigilant eyes toward shadows, but perhaps they shared more than her father would admit.

I was right to bring him into the Home-Space, she decided, whatever the risks. Her spirits rose again, for all the thought might be self-deception, more her wish than truth.

"Thank you for your courtesy," Austin said. "I appreciate it."

"You're still a miin."

He leaned back in his chair and stretched out his legs a little.

"That I can't help," he said complacently. Sair returned with a bowl of chilled great-claws and some greens, then brought water. He turned Austin's chin toward the light and inspected the cut over his eye, then left again.

Smart-Mouth flapped briskly into the room, as ever faultlessly alert to any prospect of food, and landed with a thump on the table in front of Austin. The fur-bird took one look at its first miin and squawked in alarm, then cursed at Austin vividly. Austin started backward, nearly upending his chair.

"Shut up, you stupid thing." Jahnel swiped a hand at Luelle's pet and missed, as usual, but distracted the fur-bird from its imminent attack on Austin. Smart-Mouth redeposited itself on the table and stared insolently at Jahnel for a moment, daring her to do anything, anything at all, then slowly reached out a taloned foot to snag one of Austin's great-claws. With great dignity, the fur-bird flapped off to the ceiling light to dine in splendid isolation.

Jahnel sighed and rubbed her face. Maybe Luelle would consider trading her fur-bird for a nice bowl of water shrimp; it wouldn't hurt to try.

"Who was that?" Austin asked warily.

"A pet."

That seemed to amuse Austin greatly, but he irritatingly kept his reasons for amusement to himself. He pointed at the kitchen door. "And him? He's your husband?"

"One of three—he is senior."

"Three husbands," Austin said reflectively, as if that were strange to him.

"How many wives do you have?" she asked.

"None."

"None? Not even the Sanford?"

He studied her face with surprise. "How'd you guess that? Oh, never mind. Well, Elena and I . . . Not officially—she plays the field. I suppose that's an equivalent to a marriage-group of sorts, though I doubt if Elena would call it that." He twisted his mouth. "It's not considered moral for a woman, not in a Latino culture, but Elena's always done what she wants—though some things are kept more discreetly than others."

"Moral?"

"Not respectable."

"What's not respectable about having several lovers?"

"It's how Latino culture thinks about women. Men can play

around—it's considered manly, expected really, but not women.''

Jahnel scowled. ''Why not?''

''Women should be pure.'' A ghost of a smile twitched at Austin's mouth as he watched her reaction.

''What's pure about not having lovers?''

''It just is.''

''You truly are a miin,'' she said disgustedly.

Now he was laughing at her. ''Don't you have religion? You know, a God above and rules below. Order, the rightness of conduct, the way people ought to be.''

''We call that vaar.''

He sobered then. ''Did you give up everything human to survive here, even right and wrong?''

''I don't understand.''

''Never mind. I'm not that convinced of Earth rectitude, either. Personal history.'' He closed his eyes and dabbed at his cut again, then jumped a little as Sair reentered the room and approached him. ''What do you think they'll do with me—eventually? Will I be disrupted, too?''

''That is a possibility,'' Sair said bluntly. ''The Council will decide.''

Austin looked up at him, then closed his eyes again. ''At the moment, I find it hard to care that much.''

Sair applied a dressing to his cut; by the time he had finished, Austin was nodding, nearly asleep.

''Miin have stamina,'' Sair said, lifting an eyebrow.

''*That* comment we will discuss, too,'' Jahnel said firmly. She rose and together they led Austin to the spare room. Evan joined them there, his face carefully noncommittal. Austin lay down on the bed and closed his eyes, not caring that they watched him—and curiously uninterested in his own danger. Strange, she thought—but then I'm tired, too.

Sair drew Jahnel out of the room and closed the door.

''Keep an eye on him, Evan, will you?'' he asked. ''Not overtly—down the hall a ways. We'll need to see if the miin keeps his word about following orders.'' He took Jahnel's elbow and ushered her back to the common room, then sat down across the table from her. He studied her face a moment, genuinely perplexed—but not judging. She felt a knot of tension uncoil, grateful to him for the trusting.

''Thank you, Sair,'' she murmured.

''For what?''

"Never mind, beloved." She toyed with the food left in Austin's dish, then realized she was hungry. She stabbed a fork into the greens.

"Jahnel, what is going on? Why did you bring a miin into the City? Don't you realize. . . ."

She laid down her fork and looked at him bleakly, realizing that her relief had come too soon. "I already heard this from Papa Benoit. Why can't anybody see its necessity, whatever the risk? The miin are *human*, Sair. They've come for *Phalene*—and the Avelle never told us anything about it."

"If Austin is telling the truth." Sair looked very skeptical.

"Why would he lie?"

Sair's face was troubled as he struggled with his own prejudices, a prejudice ingrained into the Faon by the society of which they were a part. Outsiders were intruders to be fought, the Home-Space an inviolable space where any intrusion risked loss of all. The Avelle suffered similar risks even within their own society, had come from a culture that created Predator ships intent on expansion at any cost. All their lives the Faon had been conscious of the Avelle above and below their levels, their existence dependent upon the variable favor of the Principal. It was not easy to think in another pattern.

"I don't know," Sair said. "Maybe he's not human—he just looks human."

"Sair! How can he speak francais? He has to come from where *Phalene* came, from Earth."

"I don't like it." He reached for her hand and squeezed her fingers. "Don't set your heart on keeping him safe, Jahnel. Don't think we depend on him. You know how your father thinks, and too many of the Faon lost kinfolk in the battles with Austin's ship."

"Are you so sure we don't depend on Austin and his ship?" Sair straightened and scowled, and Jahnel grieved for the lingering division between them. He was not convinced; what else could she say to convince him? She looked away, wondering why she felt so sure about this Austin. Had the suval warped her loyalties, made her favor these miin against reason? Perhaps it was that.

They heard footsteps in the exterior hallway. Her aunt Francoise appeared in the doorway and beckoned, her face as noncommittal as Evan's. All my life, Jahnel thought, I have been one with the Faon. What has happened to me? She rose and walked slowly to Francoise.

"Yes, Aunt?"

"Come with me. No, not you, Sair. Just Jahnel."

Jahnel followed her aunt into the outer hallway. "Go to the fallway," Francoise said. "Kiiri wants to talk to you, asked that it be kept quiet."

"Doesn't my father know?" Involuntarily, she looked toward the stairwell.

"Kiiri asked. I have done him the favor." Francoise looked deeply uncomfortable, not certain where loyalties lay, as if Jahnel's decision were a taint slowly spreading through the Faon. You always do what you want, Sair had accused playfully. Had she that right when all might be at stake?

"Thank you, Aunt."

Francoise turned and headed for the staircase and her guard station at the upper fallway, not waiting for Jahnel to accompany her. Jahnel hesitated, then turned the other way, taking the shorter route down the level to the lower platform. As she emerged onto the fallway landing, she saw Kiiri floating above, waiting for her. He drifted downward, his wing-tips sculling gently.

"Come with me," he invited.

Jahnel hesitated, studying his face, then drifted off the platform to hover beneath him.

"At my speed, please," Kiiri rumbled, perhaps joking to reassure her—he, too, studied faces. "No belt jet antics."

"As you wish."

They soared upward into the flow of traffic in the fallway. As they rose toward a group of ascending Avelle, the other Avelle scattered respectfully before Kiiri's ascent, then she and Kiiri veered around a descending transport. Then Kiiri nodded to a tier guard accompanying a boxy-shaped robot—a sniffer, Jahnel noted with alarm. She looked quickly at Kiiri.

"I hope you hid him well," the Avelle murmured.

"Who? Oh, never mind. How did you know?"

"It is a curious human trait to reveal knowledge best kept hidden—though you Faon can be subtle when you choose. But not you, Jahnel. You give trust too easily."

"It remains my word against yours," Jahnel said, jousting with him. "You can say we have a miin; I'll say we don't. You are Principal, I am lesser-rank—if your lies are truth and mine falsehood, what does it matter that you are believed over me? But Koyil would believe what he wants to believe, Science Leader, even if I were Principal."

"True. But you are fortunate, Jahnel, that Niintua cares little which Faon die in battle. I heard, because I ask on such matters, that you were captured by the miin, perhaps dead." He made a vague gesture with a clawed hand, though she sensed the deeper emotion that he thought he concealed. "Then we Avelle intercept a miin transmission within the First Tier, and I see you reappear among the Faon shortly afterward. It is a principle of scientific inquiry that events have causes, that one thing can lead to another, that similar events have similarity."

"All true—though I don't think that's your reason for talking to me now."

They rose more slowly, sculling through the air. "What is my reason?" he asked casually.

"Don't you know?" she asked impudently. "That is an alarming thought." Jahnel rose even with him and studied his face again. "You've told Nerup."

"Yes."

"Who else?"

"No one. Nerup should know: Lejja will fail soon and Nerup must move quickly to protect our kin-alliance if we are to survive what Koyil will start. But on the telling, Jahnel, I didn't tell you about Koyil's tampering with the miin ship's message. That might be considered treachery."

"And I have countered by not telling you about the miin I don't have. We are even, Kiiri."

"But you did tell me about—" He stopped and gave her a look. "Hmmph. You did well coming down the First Tier. A prudent action to map all the First Tier byways—when did the Faon accomplish that?"

"What?"

"That."

"That what?"

"What is his name?"

"Who?"

He turned his head to look at her irritably and she smiled at him, saying nothing. After a moment, he grunted at her, his deep-set eyes flickering with his own amusement. "The Faon are able students. You improve."

"And the Principals are subtle beyond reason. Where are we going?" she demanded.

"Nowhere, anywhere, so long as it looks to have purpose. I want to know what the Faon intend to do with that miin."

"The Faon, assuming there is a miin, haven't decided."

"This displeases you," he decided, looking at her face. She said nothing. "If you had the choice, what would you do with him? Would you take the offer and leave Quevi Ltir?"

"Was that the miin offer?"

"Would you?"

She reflected, knowing he wanted a considered answer. "I am Faon and this is my Home-Space," she said slowly. "I am kin-sister to the Avelle, and no, I would not leave. Why?" she challenged him. "Do you wish it?"

He sniffed, and flipped her a gesture. "Think to yourself, Jahnel, why I even ask? Why have I come to you to ask such questions?"

"You are Lejja's spy."

"Lejja doesn't know. I told you I informed only Nerup. We both have narrow choices, Jahnel, skirting the brink of an unending depth. If Koyil has an interest in the fate of particular Faon, which he might even if his creature Niintua does not, he, too, can find an effect for a cause. Scientific thought is available to any who seek it."

"Perhaps he will seek it."

Kiiri shrugged. "He has the motive; you are alien."

"So are you, Kiiri of the Avelle; it depends on your point of view. What would you advise about the miin, assuming we have one, ridiculous as that idea might be?"

"Am I a Faon, to make such decisions?"

Jahnel made a rude sound. "You are a master of games, Kiiri, and I'm tired of talking to you. Take me home."

Kiiri chuckled in the low wheeze of Avelle laughter and made a slow invert, then headed back down the tier. Jahnel inverted and spread her aal, flying with him in the graceful swoop past the levels, the warm air rushing against her face.

He left her at the Faon landing. "Take care, kin-sister," he said in parting, and flashed upward, sculling powerfully with his wing-flaps. She watched him disappear into the shadows of the fallway, then turned to Francoise.

"And?" her aunt asked.

"He knows about Austin—but he won't tell, not yet."

Francoise looked shocked and glanced quickly upward. "Benoit should be told this."

Jahnel took her aunt's elbow and pressed it, then looked levelly in the other woman's eyes. "You gave Kiiri a favor; now give me one, Aunt. I will tell Papa Benoit."

Francoise hesitated. "You promise?"

"Yes, I promise—but not the timing." She smiled ruefully. "If I am ever to be Faon Leader, Aunt, there must be a time of training. No?"

Francoise sighed. "You play a dangerous game, sister-daughter. I do not understand you—but I believe in you." She smiled. "Now, *what* I believe, I can't hazard, except it involves you and your rash behavior, which should have killed you a dozen times over by now. Your survival shows a certain defiance of reality I think might be useful to the Faon."

"Oh, Aunt. How would I live without your constant nagging?"

"I haven't a clue," Francoise retorted lightly. "I don't like it that the Avelle didn't tell us the miin were human. It's not proper to hide that kind of knowledge from kin-brothers, if we are such to Lejja's own."

"We are to Kiiri—and when has such a choice ever happened in Quevi Ltir until now? Perhaps the kin-laws don't quite apply."

"You excuse Kiiri too much, Jahnel," Francoise warned.

"I trust him." Jahnel smiled tightly. "Until our advantage lies elsewhere. Treachery can flow both ways when there is great need, even to one much beloved. Kiiri knows that; so do I." She kissed her aunt on the cheek and was swept into a vigorous hug.

"Be careful, Jahnel."

"I shall."

As Jahnel reentered her vayalim, she heard a murmur of voices within, Sair's baritone and Evan's lighter voice. She stopped in the shadows of the entry hallway, her heart pounding. She heard contention and looked down in despair. I don't wish to be separated from my beloveds on this. Is Austin worth it? Not Austin as a person, for all his clever talk and eager interest, his quiet acceptances, but his being miin and what advantage that gave the Faon, that might be worth it—or would it? She clenched her hands and trod hard enough for her bootstep to echo in the hallway. The voices beyond abruptly ceased.

Four pairs of eyes watched her as she entered, all wary. She tightened her lips and stopped in the doorway, hands on her hips. "I can go out and come in again," she said angrily. "Then we can do this again. I can look at you and you can look back, wondering who I am—and what I am. We could do it a third time, too. Why not?"

"Jahnel," Sair began, then stopped. Evan looked distressed and glanced at Solveya.

"You don't have to take that tone," Solveya said slowly. Her dark eyes flashed. "We are a family; no one is excluding you."

"Oh?"

"We just don't understand, Jahnel," Evan said.

"*That* is obvious. I think I will go out—and not come back right away. When you've decided on your common front, I'll be back." She turned on her heel and stamped out, not knowing if she wanted one of them to come after her or not. She blurred the issue by moving quickly up the stairs and out of sight. On the upper level, she hesitated, then heard her name called.

"Jahnel!"

She turned quickly toward her father's voice and tried to compose herself, aware of the issues at stake.

"Yes?" She saw him coming; Celeste walked at his side, her face troubled.

"We have reached a decision," her father said, rather pompously—but then Papa Benoit had a tendency toward pomposity, she thought, her respect warring with apprehension. It suited dealings with the Avelle who ruled this tier, but it boded difficulty now. His eyes met hers and read the rebellion there. "We dare not keep this Austin; if the Avelle discover him, we can lose all."

"Or keep all by keeping him," Jahnel declared.

"That is not for you to decide, Daughter. I require kin-obedience."

"Unquestioning kin-obedience? As if I were a servant Avelle?" She stared at him. "Who has spoken for my viewpoint in this debate? Since when have we become Avelle in even that?"

Benoit took her elbow and pressed it painfully, his face only inches from hers. She could see his anger and felt a giddy temptation to spin it higher, throwing all caution to the winds. She forced herself into control, sensing grave error in that impulse. "And how will we *not* keep him, Father?"

"The sniffers have already been here," Celeste said quietly. "When Kiiri finishes his finer analysis, who knows what he will know?"

"He already—" she began.

"That's enough!" Benoit barked, and gave her arm a rough shake. "You will obey, Jahnel—or risk the consequences!" She stared at him again, not feinting this time, unable to believe he meant it—but she knew he did.

"You will un-keep me, too, Papa?" she challenged him, and flung herself away.

"Jahnel!" Celeste called after her as she threw herself down the stairwell. Jahnel swung around the lower banister and leaned back against the wall, concealing herself in shadow. She heard their voices continue above her.

"Never mind," Benoit said. "Jahnel is only willful. She does not understand the risks."

"One does not teach a nestling by bending the spirit, Benoit."

"Jahnel is not a nestling."

"Exactly."

"Take your mysteries elsewhere, Celeste. You conceded my point. We dare not keep him."

"Dare? Are we then ruled by fear? Need or not, Benoit, I do not like murder of the helpless, even a miin."

Benoit made an exasperated noise and stamped off. A moment later, Jahnel heard Celeste's footsteps retreat in the opposite direction, heading for her own vayalim among the Hiboux.

And thus we hover over an unending depth, she thought fiercely, knowing that Kiiri had the truth of that. Even though Jahnel would not choose to leave Quevi Ltir if she had the freedom of choosing, Austin offered a link to *La Novia*, a possible escape for the Faon if the Avelle turned irrevocably against them. Yet no one had even discussed that option, had even noticed it, a thoroughly Avelle omission. The Avelle *never* abandoned their home-space. *Phalene*'s humans had done it twice, once to leave Earth, again to leave Mu Carinis—and could again if driven to it. Benoit is wrong to throw away that chance, she decided reluctantly, but what can I do about it? Should I do anything?

He will kill Austin, thinking he saves us all. She hesitated, angry with her own uncertainty. What is treachery? she thought in anguish. What is wisdom? What do I do?

❦ Chapter 8

BLINDLY SHE PUSHED off the wall and made herself walk slowly down the hallway. A passing Louve, abroad in the late evening on some errand, nodded pleasantly. "Greetings, Jahnel," he said courteously.

"Good evening," she replied, returning the nod as if nothing were untoward, as if all were normal. She walked onward, not stopping to talk, and wandered down the long hallway between the Louve vayalim. She passed her own doorway and hesitated, then firmly moved onward. She should return and make amends for her anger; it wasn't right—but she could not. She passed the guard at the outer portal and watched the fallway for a time, ignoring the guard's curiosity, then forced herself to make a pleasant greeting, some brief conversation, playing a role she little felt. Never in her life had she been separated in spirit from the Faon; never had she felt at such odds. She could quarrel publicly with Benoit, even bitterly, but such division lay only between two, not between one and many. How many Faon agreed with him, seeing only difference? He had not given her the chance to know.

She suspected her father for not putting the decision to a Council vote, as was custom in such profound choice, and knew that omission troubled Celeste. Celeste had led the Hiboux for nearly a generation, respected beyond all senior women for her quiet thought, her insight into the heart. Jahnel's quarrels with Benoit had distressed Celeste greatly, for both she and the other councilor, Arnaud Jouvet of the Etoile, favored Jahnel as heir and had let that opinion be known quietly among the Faon kingroups, subtly pressuring Benoit to do what he stubbornly refused to do. Among the Avelle, a parent's rank descended to the eldest child, a fact formally acknowledged after the child had lived to adulthood and survived his or her first battle in the tier wars. Jahnel's grandmother, *Phalene*'s captain, had led the Faon from their peonage at Mu Carina through near-fatal disaster to Quevi Ltir; her eldest son, Benoit, had overseen the transition from human to Faon and still guarded it zealously.

But Benoit had waited past prudence to acknowledge his own choice, denying Jahnel the affirmation. Why? Did his eldest daughter remind him too much of the beloved wife so recklessly dead in the tier wars? Did he still grieve that much, for all he would deny such soft emotion, such weakness? Or did he truly fear to make Jahnel Faon Leader, believing that she might lead the Faon into fatal mistake?

Would she? Jahnel shuddered.

Have I?

Did she doubt her father only because of their quarrels? How could she know? And if she did not, who could tell her?

I'm so confused, she thought plaintively. What do I do?

Several doorways inward, she entered a storeroom between two vayalim and waited inside the doorway until her eyes adjusted to the darkness. Here the Faon kept weapons, extra environmental equipment, medical supplies, a host of other things available to all the Louve for their using. Along one wall, she saw the rack of vacuum suits recently supplied by Kiiri for surface battles, an age ago. She walked over to the rack and idly thumbed through the suits, found one that would fit Austin, then chose another for herself. Air canisters, charges for the ward-off belts, weapons—Niintua's Avelle might swarm through the First Tier now, refinding all the hidden places, looking for what she would have with her . . . She chose mechanically, not yet sure if her choosing had any purpose. Finally, the equipment in a carrysack at her feet, she sat down on a metal lockbox and buried her face in her hands. I cannot, she thought. I cannot.

She sat unmoving for an ageless time, until the hush in the corridor outside signaled deep night, though shadows and light had arbitrary meaning in Quevi Ltir. Finally she stood, staring unseeing at the array of shelves and stores across the room. Then, with a quick lunge, she seized the carrysack and lifted it to her shoulder, then moved quickly before she could change her mind, give in to the doubts.

Her own vayalim was quiet and dark; she stole into the common room and paused in the darkness, listening for the breath sounds of any who might be waiting. As her eyes adjusted to the greater darkness, she saw a shadowed form slumped in a chair. Sair. She heard the faint sound of a snore as he slept uncomfortably, waiting for her. She watched the shadows of his body, her own breath coming more quickly, then stole past him into the corridor beyond.

As she keyed open the door to the storage room, she heard a startled movement inside. "Hush!" she whispered at Austin, then quickly shut the door behind her. She crossed the gap between them in two quick strides and pressed his shoulder hard. "Quiet!"

"What's going on?" he whispered.

"Do you promise, Austin?" she said urgently. "Do you promise the chance? Will your ship withdraw, give us a space to find a new balance?"

"Is there trouble?" he asked, sounding confused. Jahnel gave a short bitter laugh and handed him one of the vacuum suits.

"Dress in this. I am taking you back to the surface—to talk to your ship, as you said you could, to make them go away."

He sat immobile, his face a gray blur in the dim telltale lighting of the room's baseboard. "I can't promise you they will."

"But the chance!" she insisted at him.

"That, yes."

"Then come. And quietly—Sair sleeps in the common room." They both put on the vacuum suits and Jahnel helped him with the belt fastening and its ward-off device. At last she pulled an aal over his shoulders and tightened the hood around his head, then re-dressed herself likewise. "Now, we go. And your life lies in your silence, Austin—believe me on that."

"I believe you, Jahnel," he answered, though she doubted he really understood. Men rarely believed in imminent death until that instant when it came and all was too late. Austin had that way about him, of safety and confidence that Jahnel had once had, too, careless with chances.

"Come."

She led him into the darkness of the corridor and past Sair, though the familiar sound of Sair's breath, known through treasured nights beside her as she lay drowsily awake, tugged hard at her. He might think it betrayal, that she did not wake him and tell, might cut himself off from her, two lovers divided by a gulf she had created through her own fault. Sair, she thought, grieving. She pulled at Austin's sleeve and led him into the outer hallway, then stopped in the darkness.

"What's the matter?" Austin whispered after a moment.

"Wait here. I'll be right back." Jahnel stepped back into the common room and approached Sair softly, then touched his shoulder. Sair startled awake violently and she quickly slipped her arms around him.

"It's just me," she murmured.

"Oh." Sair shook his head groggily. "Jahnel . . ." he began, then saw the pack and the dis-rifle slung over her shoulder.

"I'm taking Austin to the surface," she said hurriedly. "Benoit has decided to kill him. I must do this, Sair—please understand."

"I'll go along with you."

"No—please." She put out a hand to stop him from getting up. "There are Avelle at the Gate and in the First Tier; if this goes poorly, I want you here to take care of our family. They shouldn't lose both of us, not when we have a choice. Don't you agree?"

Sair bowed his head and sighed, then kissed the palm of her hand. She caressed his face, then bent to kiss him. "Please understand," she whispered.

"I don't understand, not yet. But if I think more about it, maybe I can. I'll try. Take care, Jahnel!"

"I shall. Good-bye, beloved." She clung to him a moment longer, then hurried back to where Austin waited. As she and Austin stepped into the lighted corridor, she murmured to him to walk normally, then led him toward the fallway entrance, reckless in her choices. Philippe or Yves would know him at the First Tier exit; she would take the bold way, casting the fall as it would.

She guided him past the fallway guard, nodding pleasantly, seeing with a quick glance that Austin turned his face away, concealing his features with the edge of his aal hood. Perhaps the danger pricked finally at him now, prompting that caution. "We've been summoned by Kiiri," she said casually to the guard, a Hiboux less alert than others. Chance already turned its favor. "Returning in an hour or two."

The guard nodded and smiled, then looked beyond her at Austin. "Evening, Eduard."

"Evening," Austin muttered indistinctly, not quite matching Eduard's light timbre but close enough. Jahnel pressed her belt-jet control and rose effortlessly upward. Several meters upward, Austin drew abreast of her and she slipped her hand in his.

"Spread your other arm slightly for balance. Say nothing more."

"Isn't it dangerous to go this way?" he protested.

"Danger is part of living, miin," she muttered irritably, and heard him chuckle low in his throat.

"You are something else, Jahnel. What—I'm not sure."

"Be quiet, you miin," she said, exasperated with him.

"I will be quiet."

They rose steadily upward, hands linked as she steadied his awkward balancing on the belt jet, then gathered speed. Several Avelle passed them, proceeding downward on a late-night errand; a few eyed them without particular interest, disdainful of acknowledgment. Jahnel sensed a difference in the tier, the wariness in posture and movement among the Avelle who saw Faon among them; Lejja might command still, but even servant Avelle thought privately on great affairs.

Jahnel rose with Austin at a moderate pace, not drifting so slowly that an Avelle guard might suspect invasion of his level, not hastening as if in flight from pursuit below. They soared upward, climbing steadily, marked as Faon only by size and the lack of the fluidity that only an Avelle possessed in the fallways. As they approached the central Gate at the top of the tier and its access to the great lateral fallway bisecting the City, Jahnel squeezed Austin's hand in warning, then led him through a slow invert to check their pace. She chose the next-to-center opening in the Gate, one not currently occupied by an Avelle guard in these hours of quiet, and slid through feet first, then inverted ninety degrees and pulled Austin after her, accelerating across the top of the tier.

She heard Austin gasp as he looked at the vista behind them. The City's primary fallway was four hundred meters wide and tall, a vast space that stretched for three kilometers across the tiers, narrowing to a single point in the far distance. Both near and far, even at this hour, Avelle swarmed through the fallway, flying in great phalanxes of a hundred or more, moving among the great transports that drifted slowly up and down the fallway. Along the walls marched the words of the Great Songs shared by all the Avelle, whatever their divisions in other affairs, reminding them of the bonds between them. The rumbling of distant machines echoed along the fallway, underlaid by the rushing sound of the great air currents. Jahnel felt the air current catch them and spread her aal, borrowing its buoyancy.

Austin looked behind them again and swore under his breath in awe. "How far does it go?" he asked.

"The breadth of seven tiers. This fallway divides the upper and lower halves of Quevi Ltir, owned by none, shared by all."

"You could fly a jitney in here," he said, marveling.

She smiled. "A few have. Have the point now, Austin? The Avelle built this place—and greater cities elsewhere."

"Elena's fingers would twitch, wanting it."

"That is why the Avelle twitch, wanting her dead."

"Really dead? Or just gone?"

"Either," Jahnel said, and shrugged indifferently. "Both serve the purpose."

She kept close by the down wall, avoiding the occasional commerce traffic; none challenged. As they crossed the outer quarter of Lejja's tier, the robot housings became more frequent, ancient guardians of the access to the First Tier and Lejja's eyes for surreptitious attack from an enemy that had never come—until now. For two centuries, Lejja had held preeminent place in the City because she kept such guardians, reaping the advantage of Kiiri's elevation to First among scientists to perfect her machines, as Koyil used Niintua's ferocity to intimidate the other tier leaders. Law against Song, a rivalry as ancient as the leadership of *Quevi'ali* itself, Kiiri had said, perhaps as ancient as ancestral seas on some remote world even the Avelle little remembered. As they approached the portal to the First Tier, Jahnel drew Austin into convenient shadow and made him wait behind her as she studied the group of Avelle ahead. She counted four, all armed with dis-rifles, high-caste by the arrogance of their posture, and probably Niintua's own brood-kin, servants or not. They had the look of the Battle Leader.

Twenty meters nearer loomed the upper exit of the fallway she had used earlier, the narrow access tunnel dividing First and Second Tiers. If matters went poorly, they could try to flee downward—but any detour around the Gate by that way would be seen. Could she bluff? But for what reason would a Faon overtly go into the First Tier, something that would go unquestioned by a servant Avelle? She thought of a reason, then smiled.

"Come," she whispered. She drifted them through the pool of shadow beneath a projecting coaming, then casually inverted into the narrow accessway, pulling Austin behind her. Forty meters down, she glided into a blind tunnel, seeking its shadows. "Behind me," she whispered. "Say nothing to the Avelle."

A few seconds later a bulking shadow moved across the

access tunnel. "You!" the guard demanded in badly spoken
francais. "Why are you here?"

Jahnel pulled herself forward, pushing Austin back with a
shove on his shoulder with her boot as he tried to follow. She
drifted slowly toward the guard, deliberately coming close
enough to brush his electrostatic field. He retreated slightly in
distaste.

"Ward off," he said harshly.

"I am Jahnel Alain of the Faon, a breeding female. Your
affiliation?"

"I am Servant Pagudi of Fourth Tier." Niintua's kin-
alliance—she had guessed that right. She edged forward still
more, watching the guard intently. Pagudi retreated still further,
drifting into the middle of the accessway. He regarded her with
wary eyes. "Why come you here?" he asked.

"It is my time of season for breeding and I require privacy—
have you not heard of this strange way of the Faon?"

The Avelle grunted and relaxed the tight curl of his wing-
flaps. His eyes flickered redly in the gloom. "I have heard—and
of other things, Faon."

"You are of Niintua's brood, are you not?"

"How do you know that?" Pagudi huffed.

"Who else has the guarding of the upper ways in these diffi-
cult times? You have the look of your kinsman, Servant Pagudi." Pagudi puffed himself a little, thinking that a compliment;
Jahnel left him to his misperception. "Leave me to give *my*
look," she said coyly, "to new Faon of my brood."

"Breeding does not need privacy," Pagudi informed her
pompously. The Avelle bred in public view, the breeding adults
showing their primacy in that open privilege as their servants
looked on wonderingly, rarely taught anything about such mystery until infrequent fortune brought them to breeding rank in
their own right. It was not a tradition the Faon had chosen to
copy, and Jahnel used that difference now.

"Faon are strange in their ways," Jahnel advised him loftily.
"We require privacy for necessary attention; distracted, mating
may be unsuccessful."

Pagudi hesitated. "I am not versed in breeding matters."

"With your look of your kinsman, perhaps that will change,"
she said in outrageous flattery. Not likely, she thought: a Faon
loose in the First Tier, and he just looks puzzled. She risked a
glance upward, hoping this servant's senior was not following
to investigate the delay. She had to get rid of Pagudi quickly.

She wiggled her arms in sinuous display and watched him gawk. "I feel instinct overcoming me. Will you not grant me privacy?"

Pagudi flinched and gestured an embarrassed apology. "Your pardon, Faon. I leave immediately." And he did. Before he could report to his senior, Jahnel signed to Austin and soared with him down the access fallway to the first cross-way, then fled into the maze of the First Tier. She took a winding path, sometimes falling dozens of meters downward, then slowly working back upward, heading for the outer edge of the tier. Austin followed docilely, no doubt utterly lost in all the turnings and twists. Finally, she found a refuge in a wide access port and stopped to rest.

"Where are we?" he asked.

"In the First Tier. A little further and I can take us straight up to the Downlift."

Austin looked around elaborately. "Privacy for breeding?" So he had overheard. She scowled at him.

"Don't get ideas, miin," she muttered.

He laughed at her, his teeth showing white in the gloom of the tunnel. "I picked up the gist, though I didn't catch all the words. Avelle have an interesting society. So do you."

She looked at him. "Are you mocking us?" she demanded angrily. "Since when do your rules of morality govern us?"

He did a strange thing then, touching her face with the lightest of touches, then laying his palm softly along the curve of her cheek. She promptly moved backward, eyeing him warily. It occurred to her that Pagudi might not be the only one ignorant of another's breeding customs. He dropped his hand and she heard him expel his breath in a sigh. "You are beautiful," he said, a wistful tone in his voice. "No, I'm not mocking, Jahnel. On *La Novia*, 'privacy' is taken to such extremes that everybody pretends 'breeding' happens hardly at all. It's bad form to even discuss it—Latinos take their morality seriously, especially the women, and Anglos have their own sidestepping. I find you a refreshing change."

"That *is* strange, Austin, to pretend. Is that what you meant by your words, a marveling?"

"Yes." He abruptly leaned forward and kissed her before she could react. "In case we don't have time later." She raised her fingers to her lips, surprised, and still suspected him of mocking.

"You are too bold," she said, half-angry at him.

"Just running out of time, my lovely."

"I'm not your lovely, Austin."

"I know." He looked away. "I've been thinking about that, most regretfully." Then he grinned at her again.

"You're such a miin," she said disgustedly.

"And you're a Faon," he retorted. "Now that we have affirmed our basic identities, what exactly am I supposed to tell *La Novia*?"

She settled back comfortably on her heels. "To go away. Would they do that?"

"No, not permanently. If they did, that would mean your people would be stuck here."

"So?"

"Well, yes, that. Ask for something less, too, just to give me an option. Boland is stubborn, almost as stubborn as you."

She scowled at him, then thought a moment. "Then retreat and stay away for a time, at least until Lejja can regain the advantage she has lost. Lejja is Principal of Songs," she explained, as he looked puzzled by the name. "We live in her tier; she protects us. Koyil is Principal of Laws and is our enemy; he and Lejja have contested for decades for control of the City. Do you understand now, Austin? Your ship is Koyil's weapon against Lejja, and he will use it like a great-claws snaring a shrimp, just as Lejja once used our *Phalene* as a weapon against him. It is a fitting revenge he won't resist. And, Austin"—she pointed at him—"pay attention when the Avelle say, as they will the next time and the next, that they don't want you here."

"All right, I hear that. How long away?"

"Three dozen days, at least."

"Won't you even *consider* returning with us?" he urged suddenly. "What if the Avelle turn against you? What happens then?"

She shrugged. "Return is an option—but Quevi Ltir is our *home* now. If you know anything about *Phalene*, you know why we left Mu Carinis."

"That situation's been eased."

"Oh?" she asked skeptically. He grimaced, confirming her suspicions about the bland reassurance. If she were Latino, she'd not give up advantage so easily, either, not with captive colonists dependent on PAS transport and a discriminatory scale of fees. "Has it changed?"

"But it'd be different now, Jahnel, I promise you. The Faon are the only humans who have solid contact with the Avelle—"

"*And* their knowledge of their science—and their weaknesses if they resist human intrusion. What physical law says the Avelle owe Earth contact, Austin?"

He shrugged helplessly. "I'm only thinking of you. I'm not Elena—I don't want your science. But if it's the only choice, Jahnel . . ."

She turned her shoulder to him, ending the discussion. "Three dozen days, if you can. Give us that and perhaps," she added reluctantly, "if all goes poorly, we might consider the other."

He blew out a breath and paused to think. "I might manage it. And when *La Novia* comes back, Jahnel, can we meet again?" He seemed strangely earnest, as if much lay in her answer. She wondered about his life aboard his ship, to turn so easily to outsiders; she suspected, among other things that his ship did not have kin-bonding at all. Was that why the first Faon had so easily chosen to become Avelle? Or was it only the Latino habit of building barriers out of arrogance? She had seen the contempt in Rivera's face as he had looked at her. At least the Avelle were honest in their dislikes.

"I don't know," she told him truthfully. She looked away. "My people don't approve of what I am doing, Austin—in fact, they do not know. Your promise is important in lesser ways, too."

"Will you get into trouble?" And then: "What was their alternative?" he asked in an altered voice. He had not believed in Benoit's threat, then, for all his defiance; he did now. It sobered him.

"We are much Avelle, we Faon," she answered obscurely. "Come, I will return you to the surface."

She led him to the far wall of the First Tier and drew him upward along the access fallway. Lack of care showed here, too, with tarnished fittings and robot housings that had corroded into fixed place, their alert-panels darkened. She detoured around a live monitor, not wishing to advertise their presence. As they neared the upper levels, she hunted for another entrance into the First Turning, a different entrance than the one, now probably guarded, that had brought them downward. They emerged into a subsidiary fallway that joined the primary fallway only a few meters below the First Turning. She slowed, studying the shadows above them. It would do, she decided.

Speed counted now. She linked her arm in Austin's and set her belt jet to full power. Still accelerating, they approached the First Turning and rocketed out of the circular shaft. She inverted quickly, dragging Austin around with her, and collided feet first with the ceiling, angling for the recoil. She burst into the farther room, prepared for anything that waited. The room was empty.

Kiiri's doing, perhaps, she thought, wondering what other games the Science Leader might be playing with the Principals. By all rights, Niintua should have stationed a guard here—he had many guards to spare.

"Suit up," she instructed Austin, then cycled them both through the air lock into the Downlift. Again they soared upward, flashing past the empty access tunnels, alarming the protectors but leaving them well behind before they completed ward-off sequence. The movement of the robot canisters rippled along the wall, pacing them. Still striving for speed—the robots might signal, bringing the Avelle—she hurried him to the exterior Portal to the surface.

Austin looked curiously at the control panel for the energy shield, his interest obvious. She ignored it as she released the door shield and hurried him into the rubble of surface ruins, keeping to shadows under the glaring sky. If Austin meant treachery, he now knew the entrance to the City and something of its defenses. If Austin meant treachery . . .

At the edge of the ruins, she stopped in a pool of shadow and left Austin to skip forward to the crater-edge. With a sigh of relief, she saw the ship's lander again in low depression, lights blinking—these miin were a stubborn breed. She ran back quickly to Austin. "The lander is there. Give me your belt. If you run quickly, you can make it to the crater."

"It would be easier to keep the device," he countered, one hand protectively over the ward-off unit on his belt.

"I give the miin nothing of that kind, Austin. You forget who you are."

"Not that." He unlatched the belt and handed it to her. "Quickly, eh?"

She smiled grimly. "As if your life depended on it." He caught at her arm as she turned.

"You're sure you don't want to go back to Earth?" he asked. "If you can get the Faon to the surface, we can get you all away from here, away into safety. There's a whole universe out there, Jahnel, new places to choose as home and to build again. Isn't that an option?"

"*This* is my home-space," she said stubbornly. "It is what I hold and what I defend."

"With aliens who kill you on the slightest excuse—or none

at all? Aliens who betray you?'' He twisted his mouth. ''What kind of 'home-space' is that, Jahnel?''

She smiled, knowing he did not understand. ''When I was six years old,'' she said musingly, ''I was chased half the length of the tier by a servant-guard from the level across the fallway from ours. I had spent all the morning signing insults at him, just to see what he'd do—'weed-face' was one of the milder ones, as I remember. He could have caught me in a few wing-strokes, but he let me get away. The Avelle indulge their children to excess, even young reprobates like me, for children are their future and their being. What makes a home-space, Austin? And is love the less because it is fierce?''

He scowled, then shook his head, unconvinced. ''Hmmph.''

She tried again. ''You see only violence and denial, but you come from outside. The Avelle come from a proud and violent brood, one that has honed itself with millennia of conflict—but within, Austin, *within* is the kin-bonding. For eighty years we have learned that bonding, and have finally seen within to what they protect so fiercely. An Avelle will die to defend his brooding, will not yield a centimeter of home-space—because he loves fiercely.'' She shrugged. ''Of course, Avelle are also maddening in their subtleties, and not even the closest Avelle friend can be fully trusted—kin-bonding to his iruta intervenes. And they are dangerous—you are right in that. So? Is safety all-important?''

''Stupid deaths, that's what 'so.' ''

''The miin have made their own stupid deaths among us.''

''Touché, Faon.'' He looked away.

She touched his sleeve to regain his attention. ''You have seen little of us and even less of the Avelle. Perhaps, if the Songs allow, you can see more later—if you still wish to understand. And perhaps you can tell me of your Earth; I will listen.'' She smiled gently. ''But I don't think your arguments convince even yourself, however you protest. You sense what is here, with practically no acquaintance at all.''

''I let you get away, you know.''

She smiled more widely, liking this miin. ''I know. Good faring, Austin.''

''Good-bye, Wolf.''

She moved backward deeper into the shadows and watched him rise to his feet. He looked out across the rock-strewn plain a moment. Then he was off, running a counterpattern across the rubble, bounding awkwardly with all the speed that low gravity could lend him. Jahnel looked toward other shadow pockets along the face of the ruins, guessing that the robots waited there, hoping she was right about the hesitating. To confuse the machines further, she shifted position several meters along the wall, then ran to another pocket of shadow, distracting them with her movement. Seconds might count for Austin in that distraction. She looked out toward the crater and saw him leap over the rubble at its rim, careless with his suit on jagged rock.

He has a certain stupidity about risks, she thought—and so do I. She looked up at the star-strewn sky with its deadly haze, then faded backward into other shadows, heading for the Downlift.

☙ Chapter 9

AUSTIN SKIDDED DOWN the broken rubble to the crater floor, then caught himself against a jutting rock when he nearly overbalanced onto his face. Tricky, just like Luna, he reminded himself. He pushed himself upward, cautious about recoiling too far in the light gravity, then moved at a slower pace toward the lander in crater-center. He didn't see any crewmen outside the ship, but he knew that Chief Paige would have the exterior monitors on. He stopped twenty meters from the ship and waved, then fumbled with the dial on his helmet radio, without a clue as to the readings he was getting in the dial window about frequency.

"Austin here. Do you read?"

He shifted settings and repeated his hail, then gave it up and tramped toward the exit ramp.

A spacesuited crewman promptly appeared in the lock, armed with a laser rifle. He waved it warningly. Austin slowed and put both hands up; that earned him a rifle cocked and pointed straight at his head. Austin stopped short and glanced nervously over his shoulder at the crater-rim, half expecting a row of nasty little boxes perched on the lip, ready to blast him to powder.

"Damn it," he muttered, and tried dialing helmet frequencies again. "Austin here. Put that damn thing away, will you?"

"Greg!" a voice blatted in his earphones, high with surprise.

"Chief? It's me. Let me in before more little robot friends show up. Please?"

"Let him in, Juarez."

The crewman at the port lowered his rifle, and Austin bounded forward, squeezing past him into the port. As the

121

air cycled, he unlatched his helmet and breathed good Earth air. The inner door opened with a hiss, and Juarez gestured him in with his rifle, his dark eyes glinting through his faceplate.

Chief Paige waited for him in the lander main room, his hands on bulking hips, his look a glare. The chief always glared—likely he had glared at his mother from his cradle, permanently incensed with everything. It made him a good chief, in the sour-minded tradition of all good drill sergeants.

"So you decided to show up," Paige said in disgust. "You're only about six hours late. Boland's fit to be tied." He looked beyond Austin at the lock as Juarez stamped in behind him and keyed shut the lock. "Where's your lady friend?"

"Give me a break, chief," Austin said. "Can I talk to Commander Boland?"

"If you don't have that woman with you, you don't *want* to talk to Boland, believe me."

"Just set up the link, chief. Nice to see you, Raoul." Juarez grunted, his young face noncommittal. Austin followed Paige into the control room; the chief tipped his chin toward a chair.

"It's your funeral."

As Austin sat down in the chair, the radio crackled, then steadied into the contact hum. A few moments later, the video link activated, filling the small screen above the radio set with revolving lines, then the quick snap of a picture. Rivera's aristocratic face looked at him coolly.

"Austin here," Austin said, rather unnecessarily. Rivera's expression did not change, his disapproval apparent in his lack of expression. "Can I talk to the commander?" Rivera turned away from the screen and called. Austin was conscious of Paige standing behind him, probably waiting to witness the feasting. He waited, his fingers tight on the chair arms, until Boland traded places with Rivera. Boland's Anglo face showed even less emotion than Rivera's. "Austin reporting, sir. I've got new data about—"

"Where have you been?" Boland demanded, his voice a harsh bark.

"I was delayed," Austin replied as curtly, his temper rising. God, they acted like he was a small boy who had been off too long playing in mud puddles. He forced himself back into control. "I have important information." But Boland wasn't listening.

"Where's the captive, Austin? Hmmmph, I thought not. Paige will bring you up; there've been new developments and I need you here." Boland half turned from the screen in dismissal.

"Sir!" Austin's shout brought Boland's head quickly around. "Sir, we have to leave this star system. *La Novia*'s presence is pressuring the alien society into violence, with the Faon right in the midst of it."

Boland scowled. "Our mission is to make Contact."

"You're making Contact, sir, but not the kind we want. It has to be done a different way, and the first thing we have to do is leave—visibly, apparently permanently, until things calm down here."

Boland thought about it. Though a bit of a tight shirt, Boland had brains, enough to win a captain's post in a Latino service. Austin counted on that.

"Is that what the woman told you?" the commander hedged, then looked to the side at somebody else.

"Yes, sir. She took me down into the City, then brought me back here to warn you. I don't think the others agreed, but she brought me back. She says *La Novia* could personally arrange the death of everybody down there, just by hanging around. Is that clear enough, sir?" Austin twined his fingers in his lap, pressing hard enough to be painful. If he says no . . . Austin didn't want to think about the possibilities.

The commander turned away from the screen and muttered to somebody, then stepped slightly aside and back to allow another face into screen-sight. "Are you all right?" Elena asked, her face concerned more than he expected.

"I'm fine. Tell him, Elena—we've got to withdraw."

Elena shook her dark hair impatiently. "Your data doesn't match up with ours, Greg. The aliens aren't upset at all. Their leader has invited us into the City."

"What!"

"As far as we can understand, that is," she amended, making a pretty face. "Pictures only tell us so much, and our pidgin French—what we other crewmen can scrape together from some old high-school learning here and there—isn't enough to be sure. That's why we need you up here. Apparently this Koyil speaks fluent French."

"Koyil? Wait a minute, Elena. Koyil has invited you into the City?"

"Yes. He says he'll turn off the defenses so we can send a

Contact party down.'' Elena's thin face filled with enthusiasm. ''Greg, this culture is millennia old—you wouldn't believe the technological marvels we've seen in the aliens' transmissions. It could advance our science by centuries—gravity control, total environment control, genetics, chemistry. And *La Novia* is the Contact ship that starts it all.''

''And Lejja's tier is the first tier off the Downlift,'' Austin said, trying to keep calm. Careful, Greg: do it right. ''These aliens carry territoriality to the outer limits. Do you know what will happen when your party invades the City? It'll be open war, with Koyil pouncing on Lejja from the other side. Listen, Elena—this Koyil is the political enemy of the Avelle Principal who protects the Faon. He's using you to start a tier war.''

Elena shook her head, smiling. ''Nonsense. He's quite friendly, Greg.''

''I've been down there!'' Austin shouted. ''He's using you!''

Elena flared back at him instantly. ''Oh, really. Let me tell you something, Greg, about your precious Faon and their Principal. She's enslaved them with drugs—Koyil told us so. We found those drug traces in the corpses, after all. And the captive's behavior just bears it out—obviously she's been conditioned to return at any cost.''

''Enslaved? They aren't enslaved, Elena.''

Boland's narrowed eyes shifted back and forth between them, but he said nothing.

''You're such a great authority?'' Elena jeered. ''Did you talk to any Avelle down there? I thought not. We have. How do we know *you* haven't been tampered with?''

''Good Christ. One more time: the aliens are territorial with attack instincts. Koyil is using you.''

''Imprinted instincts don't survive sapience,'' she said pompously.

''And where's *your* authority, Elena? How many alien races do you know, BioOfficer?''

''That's irrelevant. Don't you see the opportunity here?'' Her pretty face again suffused with excitement as she lofted off into lulu-land about ''possibilities.'' Could somebody lust for Contact, any Contact at whatever price? Apparently Elena did—and had the influence to turn Boland. Austin looked quickly at the commander standing behind her, seeing no encouragement but not yet a decision either way.

''Koyil is the Faon's enemy,'' Austin repeated desperately. "He wants the Faon eliminated. And the best way is exactly what he's encouraging. The pressure is building up, and the target is the very colonists we're supposed to rescue. Contact is secondary; we've got to get out of here—at least for a while."

"According to your Faon," Elena said dismissingly.

"Who else would you believe?" Austin asked angrily. "Koyil? Why believe an alien over humans? Hell, Elena, if you want gravity control and the Avelle's other tricks, get it from the Faon. They have the knowledge, too."

"Unfortunately, you lost us a Faon to ask. I don't see her with you, so I assume she's permanently lost."

"She ambushed me," Austin muttered.

"You let her go."

Austin didn't deny it. What was the point? It wasn't exactly true, but it wasn't exactly false, either, and his uneasy guilt about it would make any protests unconvincing.

"I'm reporting what I discovered," he said sullenly. "My recommendation as liaison officer is to get *La Novia* the hell out of here."

"And *my* recommendation," Elena said, giving him a disgusted look, "is to continue the Contact we have made with the Avelle. Your report is just rumor; mine is fact." Austin studied her arrogant expression and wondered what he had ever liked in her. Lust for Contact, indeed—with anybody sacrificed.

Boland looked thoughtful, then nodded. "Continue contact with Koyil, Officer Sanford; ask him about Austin's data—"

"No!" Austin objected. "Don't do that!"

Boland scowled at the interruption. "That's enough, Austin. When you've returned to the ship, prepare a report. Boland out."

Austin stared at the blank screen. Even if Boland countermanded that last order, Elena would ask to ingratiate herself with Koyil. Mr. Koyil, one of our crewmen has visited your lovely city and told us . . . And the Avelle would know. He had picked up enough from Benoit to see the fear—no, not fear, the man was too self-possessed for that. Dread, if the Avelle knew Jahnel had brought him into the City. He guessed, probably accurately, why Jahnel had stolen him away.

She saved your life, he thought. And it'll come down on them without warning, a full-scale invasion by miin into Lejja's tier.

And who, exactly, just fancifully assuming, pick it out of the air, would Koyil say let them in? Only one group in the City was human. He swiveled back and forth in his chair and sighed for effect, then turned casually toward Paige. "Well, it was worth a shot." He shrugged. "Guess I'll ride in the back with Juarez, chief. That okay?"

"Sure, Greg." Paige gave him an odd look. "Elena sure backed you up, didn't she? I thought you two had a thing for each other."

Austin made himself shrug. "Sometimes."

"Latinos," Paige muttered. "Loyal to the last. Go buckle yourself in. Lift-off in two minutes."

"Right." Austin pulled himself out of the chair and drifted through the door to the rear compartment, then casually closed it behind him. Lift-off regs were useful. He snagged his helmet from the chair where he had left it, and Juarez eyed him curiously as he lifted it to put it on. Austin gave him a lopsided grin. "Yo, Raoul. Dropped something important beyond the crater-rim and Boland wants it. Be back in a sec."

"Okay, Greg." Juarez smiled faintly.

All those honest times, he told himself as he cycled through the lock, true-blue and true-spoken, and it pays off now. He jumped down the ladder, raising a puff of white dust, and bounded easily across the crater-floor and vaulted over the rim. He stopped and looked over the ruins, watching for movement, then loped forward hastily. Without the ward-off device, he would have to stay alert.

"This could be your last dumb move, Greg old boy," he whispered, then remembered and snapped off his helmet radio with a curse. The last thing the Faon needed was a radio fix on their Downlift. Think, Austin: use your brains now. He looked behind him for one last look at the crater, then moved into the ruins at a bounding trot.

A hundred meters in, he saw movement ahead and darted into a pool of shadow beside a wall, then pulled himself onto the top of the wall. As a boxy shape rolled toward him down the rock-littered street, the blue light-haze glinting off its sides, he edged himself over the narrow ledge of stone and hung half down the other side, supported only by a hand and a bootheel wedged into a crevice. Subnormal gravity had its advantages, too, he reminded himself. And you're going to die, Greg.

He felt a steady vibration through the wall as the robot came closer; then it faded. After several minutes, he cautiously raised himself to look over the wall—and looked straight into the bore cannon of a canister robot. He froze as it regarded him with a single lensed eye. He saw dial lights flicker on its upper panel, then a waxing light glow through a central seam, pallidly yellow in the harsh blue starlight. Panicked, he thought of throwing himself off the wall, running, but knew the thing would blast through the wall the instant he moved, as it had blasted through the metal walls of the first lander, crisping everything inside. Seconds passed in their silent standoff; then, to his amazement, the robot's interior glow faded. It swiveled on its treads and moved off.

As it rolled on down the ruined street, Austin felt something touch his foot from behind and recoiled violently. He squawked as he lost his grip on the wall and fell, landing on something that shifted away from beneath and then shoved him hard against the wall. He rolled away, trying to get to his feet on the shifting gravel, then recognized Jahnel. She stood a meter away, glaring at him through her helmet faceplate, a laser rifle slung in the crook of her elbow. He saw her lips move and raised his hand to his helmet, then stopped, realizing he had jogged it off her frequency. He raised a finger up in front of his mouth, then jerked the thumb hard in the direction of the crater. She studied him, obviously confused, then spoke again. Frantically, he tapped the helmet aerial and signed again urgently at the lander. She stepped up to him and calmly adjusted his neck controls. He heard a click over his radio circuit.

"The radios are directional, Austin. Just don't talk while facing the crater."

"Oh."

"But thank you for the warning. What did Boland say?" She reached a hand to help him to his feet.

"Koyil's invited us into Lejja's tier. He's going to turn off all the defenses so we can come right in. Genial guy, huh?"

Jahnel's eyes widened. "Miin invading the tier? With Koyil's help?"

"Right."

She looked shocked.

"And something else, maybe," he added reluctantly, not liking to upset her further, especially when he knew she had gone out on a limb for it. "Listen, you made it clear that bringing me into Quevi Ltir was some kind of mistake with the Avelle."

"With the Faon, too," she said dryly.

"What will Koyil do if Elena tells him about it?"

"She mustn't!"

"She might. I'm sorry. She's hipped on Contact. She'll do anything to ingratiate herself with Avelle." He shrugged. "Hell, she'll think he'll be pleased."

"Oh, he will, believe me." Jahnel's lips tightened in anger and she glared again at him, as if it were Austin's personal fault. Lumping him in with all the miin again, he thought in despair, intruder and outsider and unperson. For a while, he had thought Jahnel liked him. He sighed.

"Elena never did listen to me much; she's too fixed on who's in charge. And now Boland won't listen either, not when I've run off like this. He'll think I'm demented or something—or drugged."

"Run off?"

It distracted her from her glare. "Unauthorized departure. I lied."

"And nearly got yourself crisped by a nindru."

"So?" He stared at her.

"Go back to your ship, Austin," she said wearily. "Thank you for the warning." She took the other ward-off device from her pocket and hesitated, then looked in the direction of the lander. "No, I can't. You'll have to take the risk again like before."

"I'm not going back."

Her head jerked back around in surprise.

"Listen, I'm your only link to my ship. *La Novia* isn't listening now, but they might later." Sure they will, Greg, he thought—but he could always hope. "You don't have a surface-to-ship radio link—right?"

"Niintua controls that—and he belongs to Koyil." She looked around vaguely. "I suppose we could build a mobile transmitter and bring it to the surface, but the robots would hear it and bring the Avelle. But if your Boland and Elena won't listen to you, why should they listen to us?"

"True. Anyway," he said earnestly, trying to persuade her, "I'm an asset to the Faon. Perhaps if you argue enough at your seniors, they might see me that way, too."

"Not likely. Faon are a stubborn breed."

I'm looking at a perfect example, he thought irritably. What a woman! "I'll take the risk."

"Papa Benoit wanted to disrupt you, Austin, toss you in after your spacesuit. End of problem."

"I know."

"He still could," she threatened.

"So?"

She threw up her hands. "I don't understand you at all. Go back to your ship. But one thing, Austin: don't include yourself in the Downlift party. It will not survive."

"No. I'm not going back."

She eyed him suspiciously. "I know these ruins, all the escape routes. I could lose you in ten minutes and let the robots take care of the rest."

"True," he said. "But you won't. You didn't before."

"Once is not always, miin."

From beyond the edge of the city, the sky filled with a sudden flash of light as the lander ignited its engines; an instant later, the small ship shot into the sky and vanished over the horizon, climbing swiftly.

"Shouldn't we be getting back?" Austin asked brightly.

She stared past him at the departing lander, then gave him a rude word. He grinned at her, and she looked like she could throttle him for it.

"If I bring you down again . . . ." She pointed a finger at him. "You ought to be disrupted, Austin. Life would be far simpler for me if you were. If you insist on arranging it, come on." She tossed him the ward-off device and stamped off. He hurried after her, nearly falling on his face as he tried to attach the ward-off without watching his feet, then just tried to keep her in sight. As they approached the Downlift, she finally slowed and let him catch up.

"I mean well, Jahnel."

She glanced at him angrily. "I know that—and I don't like it. It would be easier if you fit the prejudices, acted truly like a miin. Do me a favor, Austin: change."

She preceded him into the Downlift and raised the energy barrier—Boland would give his eyeteeth for the technology, Austin thought, then watched her curiously as she twisted a collar band on her laser rifle. She leaned the rifle against a wall, then hurried him down and through another sequence of turns and twists in the First Tier. They had descended about a kilometer when the tunnel walls suddenly trembled, a long rolling murmur that ended with a palpable air concussion down the shaft. *Thump!* Austin caught at a projecting section-rib and held on, wondering what the hell had happened, then realized that Jahnel must have blown up the Downlift.

"Weapon overload?" he asked.

"Quiet!" Jahnel pulled him onward and then whisked him aside from something he didn't quite see, then began moving even more quickly, hurrying him along, impatient with his awkwardness. He kept silent, trying to cooperate, knowing that her agreement was grudging, his presence not appreciated. Did you expect her to cheer, Greg? he asked himself wryly. Hoorays for a miin?

What was it like to see all outsiders as intruders, he wondered, a taint to be driven off? To have no interest, none at all, in other people? Elena was eager for that Contact, though her reasons ran more to career-building and personal acclaim than a genuine interest in the Other. Boland, too, had his reasons, as did most of everyone aboard *La Novia*. The drama of rescue, the shining glory of First Contact—real Contact for the first time ever—all of it forever associated with their ship, their crew, the beginning of a bright future. Whenever historians spoke of that beginning, they would cite *La Novia*'s name, perhaps certain crew names, too, spoken with awe, respect, drama—the new Christopher Columbus and his *La Novia*, their names taught to schoolchildren for centuries to come like the children in centuries past. Glory.

He saw Jahnel pause at another portal and gesture him to stop. He watched her cautiously drift outward, inverting gracefully like a porpoise in water. And would those historians mention the Faon, that little footnote of mistake and regret? The Faon, too, had a beginning—only we never pay attention to those other beginnings, he thought, especially those we so carelessly ended.

What do you want out of it, Greg? What's your glory?

He looked around the narrow confines of the tunnel and sniffed at the strangely scented warm air that blew across his face. His body had a lightness that was intoxicating. He lifted an arm, moving it against the air, seemingly bound only by the air, and that lightly, not the heaviness that dragged, the limits that restricted. This was an alien place, with strange rules, a curious rightness to itself. What do you want, Greg? Is it even relevant what you want?

He recognized a certain alcove then and knew they were close to where she had left him before, down by the guarded back portal into the Faon levels.

"Wait here," she said.

He caught at her boot. "I'd rather go with you. Last time I got assaulted by two heavies in black capes—not that you'd get that allusion." She made a dismissive gesture, her face troubled and wan; he pulled harder, bringing her back even with him. "I know I'm a miin; I know your people don't want me. But if I'm to be of any use to the Faon, it doesn't help to stuff me in corners, like laundry to go out."

"Laundry?"

"Well, skip that." He spread his hands. "Let me be a person, Jahnel, not an intruder to be explained away and barely tolerated, not disrupter trash."

"I never said you weren't a—"

"I know—and neither did your Papa Benoit; you didn't give him a chance, and maybe he wouldn't have. But I'm a *man*, not an object. *La Novia* is part of you, what the Faon are in the fundamentals. You can deny it and chase after the Avelle ways—maybe even you're right in the important parts—but I can't help the Faon if you keep me as your pet miin."

"I never said *that*, either." She scowled at him, her pretty face deeply troubled.

"Not that I wouldn't mind being your pet in certain ways," he added, greatly daring. He smiled, but she did not respond. He was suddenly aware again of the gulf between them, a gulf of eighty years and a human community pressured to adapt away from the human, breaking the links to everything Earth thought normal. Maybe she couldn't think of him as a man; maybe, to her, he would always be a miin, nothing more. "Even if you don't understand," he said, feeling defeated, "allow this, please."

Her face was shadowed. "All right," she said finally. "Come with me."

He followed her down the narrow tunnel and emerged into the narrow fallway that ran down the outside of the next tier. Jahnel looked down and gasped, then grabbed his cape and yanked him upward. They shot up the side of the fallway at full belt speed; after a dozen meters she yanked at him in a rough invert and hauled him into a side tunnel. Together they arrowed onward at reckless speed through the nearly lightless tunnel. Austin looked back and saw the tunnel opening suddenly masked, then fill with a black and gray shape, coming rapidly after them.

They crashed around the next turn, Jahnel getting more of

the impact than he did, then accelerated again into blackness, a pitch dark that strained the eyes. He tightened his grip on her and closed his eyes, concentrating on the tenseness of her muscles, hoping for a signal of the next wild invert. It came several meters later, a smashing into metal and recoil in a new direction—and acceleration again. Half dazed by the impact, Austin hung on, knowing he dared not lose hold, not now, not with an Avelle close behind.

An Avelle by the Faon's secret doorway. What did it mean? He remembered back to that fragmentary glimpse downward before she grabbed him, and remembered the portal had stood open, gaping, with no Faon on guard—only the Avelle, who now pursued them relentlessly.

Another smashing turn, one that impacted full on his elbow. He yelped involuntarily and lost his grip on her with that hand, his arm numbed and throbbing. She adjusted immediately, shifting her grip on his belt to steady him. "Hold on, Austin," she muttered.

"Leave me if you have to."

She swore. "You don't know what that guard will do to you when he catches you, even not knowing you're a miin."

"Let's say I can make a good guess. Save yourself, Jahnel."

"I save both of us. Shut up."

She took the next corner at reduced speed, then accelerated again straight downward. Austin flexed his hand, trying to get the feeling back, then winced at the agony shooting from shoulder to palm. They fell downward at dizzying speed, falling straight, accelerating hard against the air. When she felt the touch of his injured hand on her arm, Jahnel reached down and flicked on his own belt jet. They immediately veered right as Austin's jet kicked in at an oblique angle. He hastily corrected, crowding as closely to her as he could. The darkness was so complete he could see nothing beneath them. They fell, faster and faster, plunging hundreds of meters into the unknowable dark at full speed.

"Are we going to hit anything?" he said, trying to sound never-may-care. He doubted if he had brought that off. Rocketing at thirty klicks into pitch darkness was hard to ignore. "Just for nerves' sake." He heard her laugh softly.

"This fallway goes three kilometers deep, Austin. With a head start and both our belt jets pushing, we can maybe outdistance the guard, then get enough time at the bottom to find a hide-hole.''

"An Avelle guard at your secret door, Jahnel.''

"Yes.'' Her voice sounded very bleak, with an undercurrent of fear. He had never heard fear in her voice before, not even at her most helpless. "Let's escape first—if we don't, whatever happened in my Home-Space will be irrelevant for both of us.''

"True. How do we know when we're near the bottom?''

"Backpressure from the air currents—only we're going too fast to feel it.''

"You're guessing, then.''

"Right.''

"Hell on wheels, woman,'' he said weakly. He closed his eyes and resigned himself.

Ten minutes later, she cut power to both their belts and talked him patiently through a slow invert to face feet-downward; they decelerated rapidly. Austin looked up, half expecting a gray-and-black shape to loom out of the darkness above them, pale clawed hands ready to snatch, then blinked as he recognized a flicker of shadow in the blackness as they fell past a tunnel opening. Light—not much, but some light. He looked down hastily, straining to see what lay beneath them. "Light?''

"We are nearing the lower levels that stretch beneath the City's tiers. We'll turn soon.'' She looked quickly upward. "Avelle see into the infrared farther than we do. Pull your cape over your head for a shield. Show nothing to above.'' She released him and flipped her cape upward, covering her head and arms. He copied her awkwardly, falling parallel with her. "You'll have to do this invert yourself, Austin. When I tell you, raise both feet quickly, tuck them as you spin, then push out hard on the wall that will be behind you. You'll be parallel to a tunnel; I'll take the portal immediately below. The tunnels join at an angle several dozen meters from the fallway. Do you understand?''

"Yes.''

"Do not let your body show beyond the cape. He'll see where you've gone—and he'll catch us this time.''

"I understand.''

"Counting. . . . one, two, three. . . .''

He saw the circular shapes of access tunnels passing by them on the wall to the side. "On six, Austin. Four, five, six!''

Austin whipped his boots, spun, and struck out frantically with his feet. His boots hit the wall hard and he rebounded at wild speed, barely missing the metal edge of the tunnel opposite him. An instant later, he heard the reverberating clang of Jahnel's own invert behind him in the fallway. He pulled himself hastily down the tunnel, newly infected by the sense of pursuit, then found the junction. A few moments later, she loomed up in front of him. More light here, almost enough to see her face. He looked down the common tunnel and saw a gray paleness suffusing the walls at a far turning, reflecting metal on metal from some exterior source.

"Come," Jahnel said grimly. "If we have luck, we will now see what has happened to the Faon."

❧ Chapter 10

AUSTIN FOLLOWED JAHNEL cautiously toward the pale light. They emerged into a low-ceilinged room more than a hundred meters long and nearly as wide. The metal walls gleamed in the soft illumination, shadowed into a dozen shades of gray by the dim ceiling lights. Along the walls tall machines stood in long banks, some with lighted dials, others dark. Between the machines in room center a vast spiderweb of metal rods and dark oblong box-joints stretched from floor to ceiling; he heard a faint humming from the structure. Jahnel moved slowly toward the spiderweb, her head turning from side to side as she watched empty doorways spaced along the walls. She circled the spiderweb and vanished into a doorway on the left.

The next room was hollowly empty and without features except for several wide circular plates spaced at regular intervals along the ceiling. As he passed beneath one of the plates, he felt a current of uprising air, cool and moist. Ventilators, perhaps. They must be beneath one of the tiers, with these rooms the basic environmental controls. He marveled at the complexity of the technology, trying to take it all in at once. Jahnel proceeded cautiously, watching all corners, and led him through the single door on the opposite wall to a narrow upward fallway. She rose on her belt jets ten meters above his head, then pulled herself into a side portal. As Austin joined her, he saw a vast expanse of open air above them surrounded by the dim shadows of circular walls, and recognized the central fallway of Jahnel's home tier.

Jahnel looked out and upward, then soared into the fallway, not hurrying. As Austin followed, he saw an Avelle turn in an access portal far across the fallway and examine them leisurely. With the dark wing-flaps wrapped tightly around its pallid body,

135

its white-skinned head made odd contrast above, a dark tulip shape against the dim light behind it. He saw a flash of red eyes as the Avelle turned its head, looking elsewhere. Austin touched his belt jet and then spread his cape with his arms, as Jahnel did. Together they rose against the air, mimicking the posture of the Avelle aloft in the fallway.

What would it be like, he mused, to take all this as customary, the goodness of one's home, the beloved spaces to hold forever and wanting no other? He had left Caracas as a young man in anger, never to return, but its images often returned to him in his dreams: the boulevards and parks, the white-stone streets, the rise and fall of gentle Latino voices, the brilliant sunlight. *La Novia* had not filled the void. No sunlight here, he thought— I would miss the sunlight. He turned his head to look at another Avelle lounging on a platform; the guard stirred as they rose past his guard-station, then relaxed and gestured a casual greeting. Jahnel signed back, just as casually, and Austin wondered if she had called him weed-face once. He looked the part.

Is love the lesser because it is fierce? she had asked. He curled his fingers into his palms, suddenly wanting to be part of this city, this place, so deeply that it caught his breath.

Impossible, he told himself. Be real. You can't have it. But still the wanting clutched at him. With an effort, he shoved it away.

As they rose steadily past the levels, Avelle became more frequent, some flying in groups, others drifting near the access portals and gesturing to each other. As he passed a group of three, he heard their rasping speech, liquid vowels that flowed together in an undulating pitch, punctuated by strange clicks and pops. As the Avelle still ignored them both, he relaxed a little more, but followed Jahnel's exact path up the fallway as she swerved gracefully around passing Avelle, giving each group a wide berth. The strange scents were stronger here, a strange perfume with musky overtones, not exactly pleasant yet not noxious, the collective scent of the aliens. As they passed one level, he caught a whiff of vegetation and dank water, then another scent, cloying, that he could not identify. The warm air sighed against his face and hands, changing direction subtly as he and Jahnel slipped sideways across the fallway, slowly weaving their way upward.

Jahnel angled inward and inverted gracefully in front of a portal; as Austin caught up, he saw a Faon in the alcove beside the port. The Faon gestured at Jahnel, then looked at Austin coolly, his face expressionless. "Benoit is waiting for you," he said to Jahnel, then looked away, ignoring Austin completely. They floated across the threshold; even though he was prepared, the gravity snatched at him and nearly took him into a tumble; he caught himself with only a slight stagger to the side, then tried to cover it with a quick step forward, not entirely successfully.

"Not bad," Jahnel said.

"Thanks."

"Not good, either," she lectured him. "You can betray yourself with too much awkwardness, Austin; the Avelle know us too well, and we are born to this environment."

"I understand."

He saw a Faon stop ahead and stare, then rush away toward the central stairwell thirty meters ahead. "We are announced," Jahnel said sourly. "Let's get out of earshot of the portal in case Avelle drift by, and we'll wait for Benoit."

She stalked along on her long legs for several meters, then parked them both by a door to one of the living units—vayalim, he remembered, their word for both the family quarters and the marriage within it, as if both territory and relationship were the same essence, an undivided fundamental. Perhaps for the Faon it was, in this alien place: certainly it explained why they had little interest in the rescue urged by *La Novia*. In the Tiraamu, another word he remembered and perhaps only now began to understand, nothing else is needed, for all is held. He watched Jahnel's profile, regretting what he had forced her to risk, wishing he had understood, wishing . . .

You *are* a miin, he thought disgustedly, using the word the way she used it, and felt ashamed.

It took only a few minutes for the senior Faon Benoit to come rattling up the stairway. On the top riser, he stopped and stared at Jahnel, his seamed face flushed with displeasure. He walked forward, his anger apparent in his stride.

"Where have you been?" he demanded.

"Avelle guard our back portal, Father. I think Niintua's brood; they must have found the door when they were searching the First Tier."

"We know about that. I plan to send a protest to Lejja and have them removed. Our children have a right to play in the First Tier."

"The miin ship is talking to Koyil," she added in a flat voice. "He's invited the miin into our tier—he'll even turn off the defenses." Benoit jerked in surprise, his eyes widening and Jahnel

went on. "Had I not taken Austin to the surface, we would not
know that. And you would not know why Avelle guard our back
portal."

Benoit's anger cleared abruptly and he shot Austin a quick
glance of reappraisal. "Indeed," he muttered. He turned to
another Faon nearby, a young woman with blond hair like Jahnel's and vivid blue eyes. She, too, inspected Austin coolly, but
without the animus, then gave Jahnel a quick gesture past Benoit. Whatever it meant, it didn't improve Benoit's mood when
he saw it. "We go down-level in an hour, Nathalie," he said
sternly. "Inform the iruta—and ask Celeste and Arnaud to join
us."

"Yes, sir." Nathalie hurried off.

Benoit looked Austin over. "If you took him back to the
surface, why is he here?" he asked, not friendly.

"He calls himself an asset, our one link to the miin. Are you
in a mood to listen this time?" She glared at him.

"A miin," he said disgustedly.

"A person," she countered. Austin glanced at her in surprise, but she was focused on the older man. Benoit sniffed and
turned away.

"Perhaps. Come with me, both of you."

He led them down the hallway. Austin followed, very conscious of being watched and resented by many eyes. As Benoit
stalked into the conference room, his cape flapping, Austin
watched the older man's back, then nearly collided into him as
Benoit whirled to face them.

"What do you mean by 'down-level,' Papa?" Jahnel asked
coolly. Papa? Austin looked back and forth and suddenly saw
the resemblance.

"The preparations have been in progress for hours," Benoit
answered. "Lejja has received a challenge from Koyil. Lejja
has received many such challenges, but under the circum-
stances, it was thought best to prepare. With your news of Koyil's talking to the miin, it gives a context. This time Koyil may
indeed invade our tier."

"Aiming for the Faon," Austin suggested, greatly daring.

Benoit ignored him loftily, then decided to notice him, after
all. Austin couldn't decide which was worse, being noticed or
not by this proud old man. "We're just the excuse, Austin,"
Benoit said. "An able one in Koyil's dislike, but an excuse nonetheless. Koyil is Lejja's chief rival, as Law always is to Song.
We can serve our tier by mixing up the situation." He looked

away into the hallway, then scowled at Jahnel. "I don't like this."

"Better to act now when we have time," she said, "than to wish we had acted when we don't."

Benoit grunted. "True." He grimaced.

A woman of middle years with silvering dark hair walked in from the hallway, followed by a brown-haired man about the same age. Both had an air of authority like Benoit's—and Jahnel's, he realized abruptly. He looked at her sharply, wondering what else he didn't know about her and these Faon. The woman caught the last of Benoit's comment and took in Austin's presence with a sweeping glance. "Nerup has strength," she offered.

"Nerup is not Principal, only sister-daughter, Celeste."

"She watches everything with those eyes of hers. In her youth, Lejja waited for the right moment and won; perhaps Nerup can, too, when Lejja finally fails." Celeste smiled gently at Benoit. "We've known this would come, Benoit. We've known a long time; the miin ship, too, is an excuse."

That gained Austin another irritated glance from the older man. Celeste chuckled low in her throat.

"Jahnel has the right of it, Benoit, for all your bias and history of wills with your daughter; I argued that before and say it again. You can't ignore the miin; they are here and a weapon that can serve several hands." She turned to Austin and studied his face a moment, then smiled without restraint. "You may regret coming to us again, Austin. It may cost you your life; Quevi Ltir allows few mistakes without penalty. But you are here—and we will use you."

Austin bowed slightly. "Madame, I tried to convince La Novia to go away—at least for a time. They didn't listen. I understand the stress it's causing in your society, but our commander prefers our Contact officer's enthusiasm to my warning."

"Does your commander often ignore prudent warning?" Celeste asked, her voice carefully neutral.

"The drugs we found in Faon bodies create problems in his belief."

The woman's eyes were suddenly amused. "The battle drugs? You don't use them? But then, of course, you don't. We seem to forget so easily where the line between Avelle and human lies. This must be all strange to you, Austin."

"As my world would be to you, madame." He bowed again. "No doubt," she said without interest. "Jahnel?" Jahnel looked at her, her face strained. "Go see Sair, please. You are stressing him with these sudden disappearances."

"I doubt if Sair is interested in seeing me right now," Jahnel said in a low voice. "Or any other of my own."

"You are senior wife; it is your duty to mend the family—and Sair's duty, also. Melinde is perhaps incorrigible, my dear, but you are senior wife and have the duty. You have a little time before we leave the levels. We will keep Austin here with us until then—if Sair agrees, and I expect you to have him agree, your vayalim will have the keeping of him."

Jahnel looked down, obviously distressed.

"I don't understand," Austin said.

"It is not your affair, Austin," Benoit said abruptly. "Do not offer your help except where it serves a purpose." A stubborn man, Austin thought, trying not to resent it. As stubborn as his daughter. Benoit pointed at a chair by the central table. "Sit there for now and wait."

Austin walked to the table and sat down, pulling his cape around him into neat folds. Aal, she had called it, and protective camouflage in this place. It had a silky feel and moved heavily in the Earth-normal gravity. He fingered the fabric, noting the heavy metallic threads that strengthened both woof and warp, and remembered its lightness in the fallway. At a distance, except for size, a Faon would visually resemble one of the native aliens—a purpose in that? Why had the Faon changed their humanity so markedly to live in this place? Why did they have little interest—make that zero interest—in returning home? Strange, something Boland would not understand even if he could be persuaded of it. It was all too easy to put it on the drugs, call the Faon enslaved and mind-bound, and take them out of this place despite themselves. He sneaked a look at the three Faon still talking by the entranceway, their stance proud, their looks fierce. Slaves? Not hardly. Boland would not find it easy to extract the Faon from their City—or this Koyil to drive them out of it.

Okay, Greg, he said to himself, and interlaced his fingers in his lap, then studied them intently. You're liaison officer to the Faon—self-appointed, true, but contact nonetheless. What's the strategy? Do you persuade the Faon to be rescued and help *La Novia* complete First Contact? Or help them keep their place in the City, whatever the cost to *La Novia*? Elena wouldn't have a doubt about her answer, and he guessed Boland wouldn't be far off her choice, either. A ship officer's decisions ran strictly to ship interest, always. Why are you even tempted to go the other way? With a pretty woman in the picture, his shipmates would have as easy an answer as the drugs. Is it that easy? God, she thought he was part of the walls—worse, actually. Give it up, Greg. And she was married—very much married, in a very different sense than the usual. Three husbands—amazing. He thought about certain sleeping arrangements it probably wasn't polite to think about and wondered if they did. What would *La Novia*'s precious Latino morality think of that? They would think anything, even if it wasn't true, when they heard about how the Faon crafted their marriages. Did they?

Cut it out, Greg, you loon. Think about strategy.

"Austin!"

He looked up, slightly startled, and saw Sair in the outer doorway. The man beckoned at him curtly, his dark eyebrows drawn down into a scowl. Austin felt his face grow hot despite himself and abruptly banished all of the pleasant speculations about Sair and Jahnel and the others. He stood up and walked stiffly toward Sair, trying to get his face into better order.

"Come with me," the other man said.

They lead you around like a child, Greg, he thought as he followed Sair back into the main corridor. Sair stomped down the stairway, not looking back, his anger apparent in his posture. To them you are a child, worse actually. And suddenly Austin did not want to be "worse, actually," with a different yearning, one he had known before in adolescence, when yearnings had a poignancy rarely repeated in maturity. When he was a boy, he had yearned to be part of the crowd of other boys, sharing in their laughter, their confidences—had yearned for years to belong until that crowd of boys had finally beaten the hope out of him. He had left it all behind, bitterly alone and content with it, he thought. He wanted . . . what?

I never had a brother, he thought, looking at Sair. Shipmates, friends—but not a brother. Not in the truest sense. Sair turned back to Austin at the doorway to Jahnel's—what was the word?— vayalim. Even their marriage had an Avelle name.

"I don't like this, miin," Sair said furiously.

"I know that. Your pardon, Sair. I don't know your rank title, or I'd use it. Your pardon for that, too." The apology seemed to startle the angry man in front of him. Sair studied his face a moment, his expression still displeased.

"I don't need apologies from you," he said resistantly. Austin sighed, and suddenly wished he could sit down again and study his hands. Something restful that required little of a culture-shocked pilot. He looked away. Strategy, Greg. He couldn't think of a single idea.

"You say nothing, miin," Sair said.

"I figured that seemed best." Austin hooked his thumbs in his belt and faced Sair more directly. "Will you want my help in the preparations, or am I part of the baggage?"

"Your choice."

"I'd like to help."

"All right." Sair led the way into the vayalim. In the central room, a large pile of boxes and packs lay against a wall, several hundred pounds—but then they would be carried in light gravity in the fallways, Austin realized. He saw a squat mechanical device, its interior glowing with a pallid gleam, lighting a spiderweb of delicate wires; beside it, another device he couldn't fathom. The boy Evan spotted him and straightened from bending over the supplies, his expression promptly copying Sair's scowl. Jahnel's husbands kept their united front; Jahnel must be at odds with all of them, and he knew it distressed her greatly. He looked around for her, wishing she didn't have that burden, not because of him.

"What's he doing here?" Evan asked angrily.

Sair waved him to silence and joined him by the piled supplies.

"Leave the gravity field on until we're ready to exit the levels," he instructed. "Benoit wants gravity-up to be simultaneous as we leave; we'll reintegrate the fields later when we find a holding space." He bent over the machine with the gleaming spiderweb and tapped a dial, then straightened and looked over the other supplies. Austin backed up and parked himself by the wall, watching them both. Elena would give her eyeteeth to be where he was right now, to know what he had suspected: the Faon had a working knowledge of grav control. He curled his fingers into his palms, pressing hard enough to cause pain.

And he had let Jahnel get away. What had Boland really intended to do with her? Entice more of the Faon to the surface, hoping to catch at least one with the grav-control specs? Bargain with the Avelle for her return? You give us that and we'll give you her. Or maybe a threat of execution to up the stakes? The Faon had attacked the lander twice and killed *La Novia*'s crewmen, with Jahnel caught with a laser rifle in her hands right after the second attack. As descendants of *Phalene*'s personnel, the Faon were legally still under PAS authority; surely Boland could

find a PAS statute that fit. Deliberate murder. Riot and mayhem.
Wanton destruction of PAS property and personnel, with malice
by stealth. You give us grav control, or we'll kill her.

Ridiculous, he told himself. Boland wouldn't—but suddenly
he wasn't sure. Boland could, with these stakes. Elena would,
certainly: he knew all too well the ruthless streak in her ambitions, and Boland was listening to Elena. With gravity control,
Earth could leap a thousand years with the technological appli-
cations of a unified field theory—the *right* theory, finally—that
stated the fundamental truth of space-time; Elena was right about
that. Men would kill for such science, would sacrifice anything.

You knew it, too, without knowing you knew. You felt uneasy
and helped her escape by not trying that hard to stop her. And
now you're down here with her, still trying to stop it. But how?

He saw Jahnel appear from one of the radiating hallways,
glance at him, then walk on to deposit her parcel beside the
others. A little blond girl ran out after her, then flung herself,
laughing, on Jahnel to swing from her aal, wrapping herself
round about in it and dragging down on Jahnel. Jahnel turned
swiftly and caught her up, then turned her upside down to dan-
gle.

"Luelle, you're a pest," she said, and laughed, then bounced
the little girl lightly. Luelle caught at Jahnel's cape again and
buried her face in it. Jahnel extracted the girl and righted her,
then kissed her soundly, her face soft with affection. "A pest,"
she told the child sternly, and set her down on her feet. "Go
help Mama Solveya pack your things, like I told you to."

The little girl ran into the hallway, vanishing like a minnow
into the reeds, silver-quick and flashing. Jahnel saw Austin
watching her. "My daughter, Luelle," she said.

"She is a lovely child."

Evan marched up to Austin and thrust a pack into his
hands, then released it before Austin had a full grip. "You can
carry this," he announced. Austin's knees promptly buckled
under the weight and he nearly dropped the pack, then juggled
it carefully into a shoulder carry, trying not to grunt with the
effort it cost him. "And other packs," Evan said, staring at
him. They were nearly of a height, for all Evan's half-formed
body. He had a gawky strength and the same grace of the other
Faon, even in Earth-normal gravity—and a fearsome stare.

"Glad to help," Austin said mildly. Evan snorted to himself
and stalked back to Sair. Jahnel watched the byplay, looking
from Austin to Evan and back again, then scowled and turned

away. Scowled at him? Or at Evan? He walked over to the two
Faon men, balancing his load carefully. "Where do I carry it?"

"Just follow us," Sair said, lifting one of the other packs.
All the adults in the room trooped out of the vayalim and down
the hallway. The corridor was crowded with people, all working
in near silence. An occasional low command, the soft tramp of
boots on the metal flooring, but a tenseness, a deliberation to
the transfer of possessions that Austin noticed and guessed he
hardly understood. Down-level, Benoit had said. What did that
mean?

He followed Evan's example and put the pack near the wall
in the large conference room. The available spaces were filling
up quickly as Faon came in and out of the room, piling the
bundles high. A few were tying line between the bundles, gathering them in long chains, with brightly colored markers tied to
each bag. Sair led the way out of the room and Austin followed,
trying to keep his eyes on everything. A few of the passing Faon
recognized Austin—he could see the shock of resentment in
their eyes—but most hardly looked at him, so completely did
the aal help him to fit in. Didn't that show something about miin
and human? At the door to the vayalim, he touched Jahnel's
elbow.

"What does 'down-level' mean, Jahnel?"

"We're evacuating our levels, going downward."

"Oh," he said, pretending he understood.

She smiled at him.

"All levels below us in this tier are occupied by Avelle, Austin. Either we take away levels that Lejja has given to other kin-
groups, thereby violating her kin-bond with us, or we go down
into the bowels of the City and strike upward into another tier."
She looked beyond him at the solemn procession of Faon. "Lejja
has been good to us and we remember our kin-bond. We will
go downward and strike elsewhere."

"So they just let you walk in, those other Avelle?" he asked
ironically.

"No. Invasion of another iruta's Home-Space is resisted to
the death. When it is tier against tier, an entire iruta can die,
thousands of deaths in the worst wars. The wars keep the balance in the City, weed out the weak." She shrugged. "Right
now, we're among the weak. Koyil won't expect us to leave our
levels like this; it's not something an Avelle can do."

She turned and preceded him into the vayalim and picked up

another parcel off the stack of bundles. Austin followed her and took the parcel she indicated.

"If you'll have war here or there," he asked her, "why leave at all?"

She looked at him bleakly. "When Koyil's kin-alliance comes, Austin, they will come in the thousands—and Lejja's kin-alliance will rise in the thousands to defend. This tier war has been brewing a long time, probably longer than the Faon have even been here. Law and Song are a basic Avelle conflict; their history usually revolves in the interplay—and the wars. Like Papa Benoit said, we're mostly an excuse. *But* if we remove ourselves unexpectedly," she said earnestly, "it may help Lejja; the unexpected is a well-known weapon among the Avelle, a defter one for them than for us. We're too flexible to be utterly surprised for long; they lack that flexibility. And it will save us. In the lower levels, we have a chance at winning a new place elsewhere, at least until the conflict resolves in our own tier: here, if Lejja fails, we have only death. Do you understand now?"

"Yes. My ship doesn't know *anything* of this, you know."

"They didn't ask." Jahnel shrugged and turned away.

"That's hardly fair," he argued. "We were in the middle of it before we even knew who you were."

"And your commander isn't listening now, either," she said sharply.

"That's not my fault."

She turned back to him and lifted her eyes to his face, then seemed to shake herself. "I'm sorry."

He followed her back into the corridor as she and the others continued the long transfer of everything the Faon could take with them. At the last, Sair carefully packed the spiderweb device; as the internal light dimmed, Austin felt the gravity lessen. Sair and Evan carried the device toward the doorway. "Careful of the threshold, Austin," Sair said over his shoulder. "The corridor is still heavy."

"Thank you."

Finally all the Faon assembled in the conference room, some lined up in the corridor: over two hundred adults and children, all dressed in the black hood and cape of the aal, all standing silently, their packs and parcels gathered neatly along the wall near each group. Benoit climbed on the table and raised his arms. "Vayalim! Iruta-bond is divided here; look to your family if all is threatened. Descend as quickly as you can to the lower levels and assemble in the duct room."

''The Avelle are outside,'' a Faon man said.

''We will divert them. Wait until the word is given.''

Several Faon nodded.

''Austin, Jahnel, come with me,'' Benoit ordered. Feeling very much under scrutiny, Austin followed Jahnel through the small door opposite the portal beyond. Three Faon waited beside the portal, which was now closed again. Benoit looked behind him to check that none of the assembled Faon were visible through the inner doorway, then nodded at one of the guards. ''Open the portal and let's see what we see.''

The Faon worked a mechanism in a panel by the portal and it irised open onto darkness. Benoit stepped forward, easing lightly over the gravity barrier, and drifted into the open space. He looked upward and gestured, then nodded for Jahnel and Austin to join him. ''Ask the first group to come forward, no burdens yet,'' he instructed the guard, then waited, floating easily in the fallway, neatly inverted at a slant to watch whatever hovered overhead. Austin handed himself outside the door and moved aside, keeping a cautious hold on a nearby projection. Above them, three Avelle were dimly visible against the backlit shadow, one high above them in the fallway. Another floated downward, approaching Benoit.

''My greetings, Niintua,'' Benoit drawled. ''You stray far from your tier.''

''My affairs are not yours to say, Benoit,'' the Avelle rumbled in understandable French. ''Since when do the Faon have an exit portal into territory not their own?''

''Who owns the First Tier? None now. Who can complain?''

The Avelle eased closer, and Benoit casually dropped his hand to his belt and slipped away, maintaining their separation. Niintua stopped with a graceful turning of his wing-flaps, his large eyes flickering redly in the gloom.

''Still, I demand answer. Someone destroyed the Downlift—someone I suspect is *you*, Benoit.''

''Me? Was that what that was?'' Benoit snorted. ''Why would I do such a thing? We come into the First Tier for enjoyment—and possibilities. Our population is expanding—perhaps in time the First Tier will be a grand Faon kin-alliance, a rival even to Lejja herself. Would that suit you, Battle Leader?''

Behind them, several Faon issued through the port and gathered beneath them, followed by others. More Faon poured through the portal, slipping easily into formation beneath Benoit. The second Avelle drifted sideways, closer to the fallway edge, shifting position. Austin watched him nervously as he came downward toward them, wing-tips sculling, then saw Jahnel drift an equal distance to the side and down from Benoit, outpointing him. Austin remained wisely where he was, guessing he understood about half of what was going on right then.

"Your ambitions outstrip your brood," Niintua sneered, retreating upward several meters, then flaring his wide wing-flaps.

"Perhaps," Benoit agreed equably. "But it is our right to try, is it not?"

Suddenly a small dark shape darted out of the exit portal, followed by the child Luelle, moving as gracefully as a seal. The fur-bird squawked as it saw the hovering Avelle and darted aside into a small recess. Then Luelle saw the hovering servant Avelle, too, and promptly headed for him, her hands outspread in delight. The guard flashed his wing-flaps as he saw the child soar toward him, his eyes glittering.

"Luelle! No!" Jahnel cried out, her voice sharp with panic.

The alien launched at the child, and Austin pushed hard off the wall with his feet, blundering awkwardly between the Avelle and Luelle, swinging an arm wildly at Luelle to push her backward toward Jahnel. The hand connected and swooped the little girl away and down. Stranded by the invert of his swing, Austin floundered in midair and felt a rush of warm air as the Avelle pounced on him, seizing him with powerful hands. He was overwhelmed by the sweet-odd smell of it, by the furious alien eyes inches from his own, and struck out in terror, puny in its grasp. "No!" he cried, as the alien raised a clawed hand to slash at his throat. He struck the claw away desperately, deflecting it to his shoulder. He felt the burning tear at his skin as it penetrated muscle, opening a wide gash. The Avelle raised his clawed hand again, to slash downward at Austin's bowels.

An instant later, the Faon mobbed them. Austin saw a confusing blur of black-garbed bodies around him, of hands pulling at him, striking at the Avelle who held him, of being wrenched free. He heard a shout, and the Faon flung themselves backward, dragging Austin with them; a laser-blast gutted the Avelle an instant later, slicing through segmented skin, spilling a nauseating mass of coiled gut, charred and burning from the laser-blast. As the Faon pulled him rapidly back, Austin heard other laser-blasts and saw Niintua literally disintegrate in midair. Two Faon launched themselves to chase the third Avelle racing upward.

"Down!" Benoit shouted. "All Faon down to the lower levels.'' Austin was pulled downward in his group and struggled weakly as one Faon yanked too hard on his injured arm.

"Careful," he muttered. The Faon looked at him—it was Sair, Austin realized suddenly, his thoughts strangely sluggish with shock—then glanced down at his arm.

"Merciful Song," Sair said. "You *were* slashed." He spoke to the others and they abruptly slid sideways to the wall, stopping there. Sair flipped back the edge of Austin's aal and peered at the wound, then grabbed a package from a Faon who darted up. As he tore open the flap, he shot Austin a fierce glance. "You have about three minutes before the poison kills you if I don't do this." He extracted a knife from the parcel. "Hold him."

Austin stared at the knife. "Amputation?" he asked unsteadily.

Sair looked up quickly and smiled. "No, brother," he said gently. "But prepare yourself."

Sair slashed down with the knife and laid Austin's shoulder open to the bone. Austin cried out in shock and struggled wildly.

"Greg! Hold still!" Sair shouted.

Gulping, Austin obeyed, his head throbbing with shock and pain. Blood gushed from his shoulder into a viscous cloud; he watched it numbly. Sair took a device from the parcel and tossed it to one of the Faon holding Austin; the other quickly removed the cloud of blood with a suction device. As Sair began packing the wound with a plastic-like gel, Austin drifted away toward unconsciousness, his surroundings expanding and contracting in dizzying waves, his vision narrowing to a single black tunnel. Tunnels: the symptoms suited Quevi Ltir. He chuckled insanely at his own joke, then gave in to the darkness, safe in Faon arms.

® Chapter 11

JAHNEL CAUGHT THE sobbing Luelle into her arms and cuddled her. Across the narrow fallway, the Faon descent began in earnest, the mood turned grim with Niintua's death. They were committed, even if the Faon who pursued the other Avelle servant could catch him and stop him from bearing word to Koyil. A flow of dark-suited bodies, nearly all laden with equipment, issued from the fallway portal, falling effortlessly in the darkness and vanishing into the depths. Jahnel hovered above Sair, watching him dress Austin's shoulder as she comforted Luelle. Sair checked Austin's pulse and shook him slightly, but the man was obviously unconscious, from shock or Avelle poison or both—or perhaps dying. She bit her lip in worry. Slash wounds were unpredictable, as much affected by the depth of the wound as the Avelle's blood level of attack chemicals when it slashed.

As she watched, Luelle sniffled to a stop and then complained, which abruptly earned her Jahnel's angry attention. She paddled Luelle, then caught her easily as she tried to squirm away; she shook her daughter vigorously until the little girl's blue eyes welled with new tears.

"I'm sorreeee. . . ." Luelle wailed piercingly.

Jahnel took a breath and forced herself into control of her own fear.

"How many times have I told you about the fallways?" she demanded angrily. "You were nearly killed, Luelle. Do you understand?"

"But Smart-Mouth got away . . ."

"That Avelle would have made you dead, Luelle. Do you *understand* me?" She gave her small daughter another shake.

Luelle's eyes widened and the small mouth distorted in hor-

149

ror, working soundlessly toward a terrified wail; Jahnel pulled her close and hugged her. "Darling, darling girl," she murmured, "it's all right. Just be more careful." Luelle's shriek burst out next to Jahnel's ear.

"Ouch," Jahnel muttered. Over Luelle's shoulder, she saw Francoise move quickly toward them. "What happened, Aunt? How did Luelle get into the fallway?"

"Solveya turned her back and she was off, chasing that damned fur-bird of hers. I missed her by half a meter as she ran by. Luelle, you bad girl!" she said sternly. Luelle wailed anew.

"It's all right, Luelle," Jahnel said, patting her. She looked upward quickly, hoping the noise did not attract new Avelle before the Faon had escaped. Sound carried far in the fallways. "Calm down now; that's my girl." Luelle's sobs lessened and she tucked her face into the curve of Jahnel's neck, sniffling herself into hiccups.

"Smart-Mouth," Luelle whispered plaintively.

"I'll find Smart-Mouth," Jahnel said, exchanging an amused look with her aunt. "Will you take her, Aunt? Perhaps Luelle has the point now—at last." She smiled at Francoise's unconvinced expression. "I know—I had as pointed a lesson several times and remained as stupid. Too bad that Austin caught the brunt."

"Austin?" Francoise turned in surprise and saw the group bearing the unconscious Austin downward. "He was slashed?"

"Yes. I don't know how bad it is." Jahnel lifted her chin. "We have an obligation to Austin," she said defiantly.

Francoise smiled. "Your vayalim will come around, Jahnel. Give them time. I was never in opposition, only abstaining until I could think further." She took Luelle from Jahnel and gave the child a quick hug. "Come along, little one, and stop your sniffles. They are not becoming to a Faon, however young."

Francoise inverted gracefully and swooped downward, joining the stream of dark-suited Faon that still flowed from the portal. Jahnel looked for her family and helped Eduard bring the last of her vayalim's possessions, then found Smart-Mouth clinging to an overhang several meters up the fallway; she caught him deftly and wrapped the furious pet in a fold of her aal, then soared back down to Eduard.

"Let's go," Eduard said. Together they followed the last dozen of the Faon in the plunge downward. Behind them, their Home-Space stood empty, perhaps abandoned forever. Who could know? she thought, and wondered what new chance—if any—lay ahead. Once a human ship had taken the chance among aliens and earned a new place for themselves; now *Phalene*, what remained of her in her children's children, took flight again. It would not be easy to win the next space.

Several hundred meters deeper, she kissed Eduard and bid him look after Solveya and the children, then cajoled him to accept Smart-Mouth's custody. Eduard took the fur-bird gingerly and with distaste, an emotion fully shared by his small captive. Smart-Mouth cursed vividly as Eduard tried to stuff it in a small bag, then bit him hard.

"Ouch! You damnable thing! Why don't I just wring your neck?"

With a renewed effort, Smart-Mouth squirmed out of his grasp and bolted for freedom; Eduard swiped out an arm and grabbed it, then stuffed it away quickly.

"Smart-Mouth was *your* idea, Jahnel," he reminded her. "I've a better idea: fur-bird stew."

"I'll vote for that—but I did promise Luelle."

Eduard grunted and tied the bag on his bundle, then gave her a quick kiss. "See you below."

Jahnel accelerated past the flow of people to catch up with Sair. The Faon descended in an orderly haste, speaking little, with even the children hushed into solemnity. She slowed abreast of the Faon carrying Austin and looked anxiously at Sair.

"I think he'll be all right," Sair reassured her. "The wound is bad but no seizures as yet—that's a good sign. There might not be any brain damage at all."

"You moved quickly, Sair." She entwined her arm in his and let herself be pulled along. He squeezed her hand against his side and smiled at her, his dark eyes alert.

"Love you, Jahnel. How's Luelle?"

"Distressed, mostly about getting in trouble again. Many wails and dutiful sobs, but I'm afraid not much more than that."

"It took a while for Francoise to teach you proper contrition, if I remember correctly."

"For which I am forever marked, judging from how frequently that is mentioned—not always, but enough to notice." She smiled as Sair chuckled. "I remember a few scrapes of your own, boy Sair. We survived; we will survive this."

Sair's smile faded. "Perhaps."

"We *will* survive. I won't permit the alternative." She lifted her chin, posing for him, and eased some of the worry from his face.

"You won't permit," he said ironically. "I've yet to see an Avelle deterred solely by a Faon's wishing."

"I expect you to help, husband."

"Oh, I will." They both felt Austin's body tremble, then jerk through a mild convulsion. "Damn," Sair muttered. He tightened his grip on Austin and checked his pulse, then asked Yves to find another slash kit. His brother darted away toward a nearby group.

"Too much antidote can cause its own convulsions," Jahnel offered.

"I know."

Austin's body trembled again but stopped short of a second convulsion. They waited anxiously as they fell rapidly downward, but he did not convulse again. Yves brought another slash kit, then left with the others to rejoin his own vayalim. Arm in arm, Sair and Jahnel bore Austin downward at an easy pace. Austin's pale face was slack, his eyes partly open and unseeing. Jahnel closed them, then laid her palm on his cheek. "No fever yet."

"We'll ask Celeste to look at him." The councilwoman had a special skill with Avelle wounds, a gift she had cultivated since a loss of a beloved in a tier war two decades before.

"He saved Luelle's life," she said tentatively.

"On impulse, I saw. It says something about a man that he reacts instinctively to protect the helpless, even more that Austin hadn't a clue about what he was risking. Blundering into the path of an attacking Avelle!" He shook his head wonderingly.

"Man?" she asked pointedly.

"Miin. Pardon me."

"Oh, Sair. . . ." she began, but then saw the amusement in his eyes.

"When we have time, my love," he said, "I can listen to why you've acted as you did. I admit I wasn't listening before, so I'm not complaining about you flitting off—or blowing up the Downlift. That *was* you, wasn't it? But I'm not conceding anything yet. This situation is too damned complicated with too many unknowns—I want to think it over. Fair enough?"

"Fair enough."

"I have the feeling we get only one chance to get it right— only one pattern that we can fly safely. And I don't know what it is—I don't think your father knows either." He sighed. "I'm afraid it's the beginning of the end, that events are in motion beyond our control. I'm afraid for us." She tightened her hand on his arm and did not reply, knowing that he knew she shared the dread.

They neared the bottom of the narrow shaft and followed the others through an air duct into the ventilator room. Utilitarian and nearly empty, the lower levels were rarely visited except by Avelle technicians and then only with cause. The Avelle preferred their machinery to be self-tending, like the defense robots in the First Tier. Most of the Faon had stopped in the machine room, waiting while a party went forward into the next of the long rooms underneath Lejja's tier, exploring cautiously. Then the group moved again, passing quickly through five long rooms before descending into a wide well, the short fallway that led to the second lower level immediately over the sealed underlevels.

They settled along the walls in family groups, their possessions piled among them. Jahnel touched fingers with Solveya and took Didier from her, cradling the infant boy as her junior wife shifted some of the parcels into better order. Didier kicked his feet wildly, alarmed by a light gravity he had rarely experienced, then put his fist in his mouth to cry. Jahnel hushed him, then unbuttoned the top of her bodysuit and let him suckle, rocking back and forth in a calming rhythm. Though she had weaned Didier three months before, he still found occasional comfort from her breast.

Luelle sat near them by the wall, leaning back against Eduard and encircled by his arms; she smiled tentatively at Jahnel when she saw her mother looking. Jahnel winked at her, probably risking incalculable damage to Luelle's newborn caution, but her daughter's smile of immense relief justified the risk. Perhaps Luelle had learned something this time—but would she and Didier have the years ahead to practice the knowledge? Jahnel bowed her head over her suckling child, tickling the baby's feet to make him smile, and tried to push away that jab of worry.

Celeste came to examine Austin, then conferred in low voices with Sair. Across the room, Jahnel saw torment in Melinde's face as she watched Jahnel and the baby; when she saw Jahnel looking back, Melinde quickly turned away and began talking animatedly to Philippe. Is it only that? Jahnel wondered sadly—wanting what I have and you don't? Why can't you be patient, my own? Or do you wish so intently, my little sister, that I be stripped of what I have to ease your jealousy? Has it gone that far?

Calmly, she took Didier from her breast and wrapped him

warmly in her aal. Wish what you will, Melinde—it won't be that easy.

She saw Austin's first movement with her peripheral vision. He woke up slowly, dazed and obviously confused, his eyes moving over the faces nearby, then the large room. He mumbled a question in his ship language, then woke up enough to speak francais. "Where are we?"

"In the lower levels," Sair told him. "Rest easy. Don't try to move too much."

"Luelle?" Austin started to sit up and Sair firmly pushed him back.

"Safe. Lie still."

Austin turned his head and saw Jahnel, then relaxed. She leaned toward him.

"Thank you, Austin, for the life of my daughter. I am grateful."

It embarrassed him and he tried to smile, then twisted his mouth wryly. "You're welcome." He thought perhaps to say more, but finally turned his face away. They all waited in silence, thinking their private thoughts, until her father came to room-center and raised his hands. All heads turned toward him.

"Hiboux reports the lower levels ahead are empty," he said. "It has been suggested that we find a place of concealment for the children until we can take a new Home-Space in another level."

A senior wife of the Hiboux objected. "I would not want the children in any place of danger—we must know we can keep the new levels before we shelter our children within them."

Benoit nodded. "I agree." He indicated the room with a sweep of his hand. "But the lower levels are not defendable. We need a place the Avelle will not look immediately; once they discover our absence, they will search the lower levels. Suggestions?"

"We could retreat into the First Tier," another elder offered.

"Or try the underlevels now," yet another suggested. Benoit shook his head.

"The First Tier isn't safe. We didn't catch the other guard, and likely Koyil will attack Lejja immediately when he hears of Niintua's death. As our protector, Lejja is responsible for our actions—Koyil will demand satisfaction for the murder of another Principal." He shot a look at Jahnel, as if she were responsible. Jahnel sighed—in a way, she supposed she was.

"Do you suggest, Benoit," Nathalie asked acidly, "that we

should have allowed Niintua his guard's unprovoked attack on Jahnel's child?" So it had been Nathalie's laser, among others, Jahnel thought, grateful to her friend. "Since when do we sit passively and allow our children to be slashed?"

"The deed is done," Benoit said heavily. "We cannot recall it now."

"Even if we could," Nathalie retorted, "why would we want to?"

Benoit tightened his lips, displeased, but let it go. "The underlevels are unknown to us; we don't know anything about the environmental conditions. They might even be maintained in vacuum." He shrugged. "We may be forced into that, but first we should try to establish ourselves in a tier. I see no other way to protect the children." He half turned, looking at several specific faces. "Are we agreed? Good."

He counted off various groups, and Jahnel found herself and Eduard included in the advance party of a half-dozen Faon, including Jean and Marie from the Hiboux, Etienne Tardieu from Ruisseau, and Nathalie Jouvet from Etoile; Nathalie pressed Jahnel's arm and smiled rather grimly. Nathalie had always been more serious than most; this crisis had settled the line of her mouth into firmness. The six Faon took a portable drill with them and slipped forward through the succession of empty rooms with wide ventilator ports on every ceiling, the occasional environmental console in midroom, then slowed as they reached the vicinity of the next central fallway. Eduard gestured at the others, and they clustered along one wall.

"What do we know of the next few tiers?" Nathalie asked.

"Sarama's tier next to us is strongly held," Jean answered. "They've allied with the tier immediately overhead and have some connection with Koyil himself, enough to trade a few breeding females. Or so they've been boasting on the City-Net lately."

Marie, one of Jean's junior wives, grimaced. "I've heard the neighbor has strength also, with the allowance of breeding adults cut back, even against caste lines, because of overcrowding. They'll war soon against Sarama."

Young Etienne looked thoughtful. "I have some gossip, too," he said tentatively.

"Whose?" Nathalie asked sharply.

He shrugged. "Inai." The old Avelle guard had fallen in the habit of comfortable gossip, less inclined than the other guards nearby to keep to instincts. All of the Faon present had talked to him while on guard duty over the years. Thinking of how she had once called him weed-face, Jahnel smiled.

"He's fairly informed," Eduard conceded. "Doesn't he have a brood-sister that joined Nerup's staff?"

"The last I heard," Jean offered, "was that Nerup had granted her breeding rights this season. What's her name?"

"Sochip or Socha or something like that," Etienne said. "Anyway, Inai told me that that Kaali, the tier leader three tiers over, has lost breeding strength; her kin-alliance considers itself the unpolluted descendants of the first Star Leader, for all that Pakal resides elsewhere after the rank shifted to a collateral line. They don't share breeding females."

"Great for inbreeding," Eduard muttered. "A kin-alliance doesn't have enough variation to avoid deformities; all the recessives turn up."

"Exactly. Inai says there are rumors of deformities in every brood now, a lot of stillbirths, with whole levels going dark. A kin-alliance can keep that a secret for a long time, but the rumor's out now for Kaali. One of the other kin-alliances is bound to challenge her soon."

"If it's true," Eduard said, then grinned wolfishly. "Hey, here comes the kin-alliance. Who would have thought it?"

"Right." Etienne twisted his mouth. "Anyway, I heard that rumor; maybe it's true."

Jean shrugged. "We need a vulnerable tier with empty levels we can appropriate without the Avelle noticing; we can't dare take on an open invasion. They'd mob us in any instant."

"Empty *lower* levels," Nathalie amended.

"And ripe for pressure from the nearby tiers," Eduard warned. "We may not be the only iruta testing Kaali's defenses."

"Avelle always evacuate the outer levels of their tier first," Jean argued. "For this bank of tiers, that's down-tier. Kaali would focus her population strength nearest the primary fallway and the three nearest tiers, or she would just invite invasion. Have you ever heard of a tier war starting across the lower levels?"

Nathalie scowled, then turned to Jahnel. "What do you think? Has Kiiri ever mentioned anything like that?"

Jahnel frowned. "I don't have anything express—it's something I never asked him. He's not interested that much in tier warfare so long as Lejja keeps winning, thus preserving his freedom to do what he likes—everything else is his research or us." She shrugged. "He hears things and remembers them, but he uses other tools."

Jean looked impatient. "We have to choose correctly. If we invade a tier and are driven back out, the other tiers will find out immediately and guard the lower accesses. We don't get a second chance at this."

Jahnel gestured. "Sair said that, too. We have to choose right the first time." She thought a moment, then traded glances with the others.

"Kaali's tier it is," Eduard announced after several nodded. "Nathalie, you take point and keep to shadows. Remember, all, to shield your face as much as you can with your hood to keep the infrared down. We're looking for a vacant level low in the tier. We sneak in and drill an access portal to the fallway between the tiers, then bring our people up to the portal and in."

"If we find a vacant level," Nathalie said.

"If," Eduard agreed.

He gave them the Avelle gesture for good fortune, and they set off. Jahnel pushed off after Nathalie and followed the younger woman through the succession of long empty rooms; every few hundred meters, a Faon slipped up a shaft to check their progress along the tiers. Each time, the Faon had to slip partway into the tier fallway to read the Song on the interior walls, but with care each managed to avoid immediate interest.

Jahnel took point at the fifth stop and rose cautiously into the central fallway, creeping from projection to projection for the shadows they lent. Far above her, she saw isolated words of the inscribed Song ringing the fallway; some of the words, each several meters tall, enclosed a level access; others stood isolated, single thoughts given special emphasis by their placement. All her life Jahnel had grown up among the Songs and had asked Kiiri to teach her their meanings; he had indulged her by explaining a few words, but eventually he had lost interest— or had thought better of explaining such mysteries to a child who had no reason to know. Other Avelle had been of similar reluctance, but together the Faon had learned the Songs, piece by piece from whatever Avelle felt genial enough to explain.

Sing of the Home-Space of Quevi'ali, she read high above her. This was the right tier. A tier that had once hosted the Star Leader would not give up the rank-words merely because a failure of birthline had sent the honor to another tier. Though Lejja held great precedence in the City as Principal of Song, the Star Leader, the hereditary successor to *Quevi'ali*'s captain, had once held superior rank. But Star Leader Pakal was not as crafty as Lejja and had lost some kind of advantage to her long ago—only the Principals knew what. Jahnel floated in a deep shadow beneath a jutting tier-support, picking out other words of the Song of the Ship. If Kaali kept to her disdain and continued abusing her brood strength as she was—if she was—whoever eventually took away her tier would remove the words; such major rank shifts could take decades to work themselves out in the visible Songs of the City.

She hesitated, watching the several platforms above her. She saw nothing for two dozen levels up—no guard, no activity at all. Twenty meters beyond, at last, an Avelle guard stirred lazily into view, stretching his wing-flaps with a casual invert off the platform, then quickly retook his post. The Avelle across the fallway reacted, leaning into view as he studied his opposite, then relaxed. She could discern heavier shadows far above of normal Avelle traffic in the fallway, but activity lower in the tier was markedly reduced. In Lejja's tier, the constant to-and-from extended from top to bottom level: not here. She rose carefully to the lowest level's platform and eased upward around the platform edge, then slipped over the threshold into the darkness within. She floated just inside the level portal, facing inward, all senses alert, sniffing at the air. The air smelled dusty, unused; she sensed nothing moving within the darkened level. But then the lack of challenge itself at the portal showed it unoccupied.

The Song of the Faon might just get a new verse, she thought wryly, and explored a few meters farther, thinking wilder dreams of a whole tier of Faon, a Faon voice in the City to be measured, to be courted. A kin-alliance won such honors by deft play in the tier wars; Lejja had built her position in the City by building upon earlier triumphs by her predecessors, only the immediate previous two holding Song-rank. She retreated to the doorway and cautiously slipped under the platform, then returned downward to the waiting Faon. Eduard saw her discovery in her expression and relaxed visibly.

"You didn't believe," she teased him.

"Of course not. Inai's rumor is true, then. How far up is it dark?"

"At least a dozen levels, with maybe gaps above that."

"I wonder what the other kin-alliances would give to know what we know."

"It was so easy to find out, though," Jean said, confused.

"Why don't the Avelle—well, of course. Invading another tier has too many instinctual implications. They'd be impelled to display. Look how Niintua reacted when Benoit suggested our taking First Tier. Full threat-display.''

"Exactly," Jahnel agreed. "Benoit will be interested in this, I think. It's another unexpected difference, like our abandoning our Home-Space. It makes us an unknown quality—Lejja will love being given new proof of that and weave it into her maneuvers.''

"Sneaks for hire?" Nathalie asked with a grin.

"Why not?" Jean answered. "In Quevi Ltir, it would be quite useful. The Avelle would never think of it, can't do it. Maybe it's time to try the opposite tack and *remind* the Avelle of our human advantages.''

"It would be different to be universally wanted, I admit," Eduard said. "Nathalie and Etienne, you go back to Benoit and report. We'll start drilling the new portal into the other fallway." The two pushed off and hurried away.

Eduard led the way into Kaali's tier, and the four Faon slipped unobserved into the vacant level Jahnel had found. Eduard left Jean near the central portal to watch awhile for any belated reaction from the tier. The others drifted through the darkened corridor, noting the vacant vayalim gaping on each side. The Avelle had stripped out the air converters and other environmental support equipment when they left, leaving the level open to the central fallway to prevent deterioration. From the dust on the floor and every surface, it was obvious the level had been abandoned for many years.

"Kaali won't have long, not with these losses," Jahnel murmured, looking around at the empty space. Although Kaali's misfortune had benefited the Faon, it still grieved Jahnel to see a kin-alliance fail, so long had the Faon been conscious of their own sheer edge into oblivion. The death of a kin-alliance could disturb the City for a generation, however inevitably such death accompanied other growth. But flux gave opportunity, she reminded herself; if the Faon had learned nothing else from the Avelle, it was that—and they had learned to pounce on the opportunities. "Did we tell Lejja we were leaving?" she asked Eduard.

"No. But she checks on us all the time—and I wouldn't put it past Kiiri to plant devices in the machines he's repaired. Alavu serviced one of our gravity generators lately; we left that one behind." Eduard glanced at her. "Why the face, love? Criticism of your precious Kiiri?''

"He's not *my* precious Kiiri."

"Tell somebody else that, Jahnel; I know better."

"So? Are you complaining?"

"Hell, no."

"I think the Avelle are affecting your mind, Eduard. Yes is no, and no is yes, and . . ." He playfully lunged at her and she slipped out of reach, then inverted to show her scorn. It seemed an age since she had so mocked Kiiri's servant. Eduard took another swipe, missing her as thoroughly as Alavu had. She snickered at him.

"That's enough, Louve," Jean drawled, coming up behind them. "Breeding activity at its proper time."

Eduard promptly turned and swooped on him, making Jean dodge him into a vayalim doorway. As Eduard turned his back, Jean swooped out again and flipped Eduard through a full invert. The two crashed into the opposite wall, tussling. Finally Eduard pushed him away.

"Duty, friend." His eyes danced with amusement, their common relief at finding a safe haven bringing smiles to all.

"Yes, duty," Jean said. "Marie, my love, bring the drill. We'll look for the best spot on the inner wall to drill our hole." The two moved onward and vanished into the darkened corridor ahead. Eduard and Jahnel systematically searched the rest of the level, checking every room, then met again in the central corridor.

"When this is truly ours," Eduard said, glancing around, "we will inscribe our Song on the walls. Appropriate, no?"

"Why not?"

"Would your miin understand why, I wonder?"

"He's not my miin, Eduard." Jahnel pulled her eyebrows together and gave him a scowl.

"To the contrary—he is definitely your miin, wife. Everybody knows it—but we've had time to think about it." He shrugged and slipped an arm around her waist, then kissed her. "I have, just to let you know. I like this Austin, Song knows why. Maybe it's aging disease. Evan and Solveya still oppose, though, and Melinde, well—she does what she wills. Give us time."

"Solveya?" Jahnel asked in surprise.

"She thinks him a threat."

"Well, he is—so are you, so am I. Everybody's a threat to somebody." She caressed his face. "But I grieve for the divisions I caused—I was in the middle of it before I even knew, no time to think of it and consult, to know for sure. I'm sorry, Eduard."

He wrinkled his nose at her. "Few of us had time. But we have a breathing space now—if we can keep it. It'll work out. You worry too much, Jahnel; goes with the bloodline."

"You worry too little, my Eduard. That goes with yours."

"Suits." He looked around the darkened corridor. "Come, let's go quietly watch the front door. An open portal makes me nervous."

"We can't close it, Eduard—the portal is visible from above."

"I know. So we'll keep watch until the Faon arrive. Come."

✒ Chapter 12

A T THE PORTAL, Jahnel and Eduard could hear a faint whine
behind them as Jean began drilling through the back wall,
a sound not perceptible to any Avelle above. It was further reassurance, and they kept the watch comfortably in the shadowed
doorway of the level, careful to avoid quick movement that might
attract attention from any Avelle guard looking in the wrong
direction at the wrong time. As the minutes passed without any
reaction, they retreated several meters inward, not wishing to
invite discovery with too much vigilance. Eduard playfully
pulled her farther into the first vayalim on the left, then pretended concern as he peered around the doorframe, looking out
into the fallway. He was incorrigible.

"Whatever are you doing, Eduard?" she asked.

"Checking for Faon spies," he said grandly, then swept her
dramatically into his arms for a passionate kiss. After a minute
or so, the kiss grew less playful. She threw her arms around his
neck and pressed him close, aroused by his intensity. After a
while, he broke it off.

"Tonight it's my turn—promise me," he said.

"I forget who was last."

"It was me. Thanks very much." He scowled at her fero-
ciously.

"I only meant that so *much* has happened, Eduard, that I
simply *haven't* a mind left to remember unminded things like
sex with you."

"That's an apology?" he growled, and checked in the corridor, looking left and right.

"I only meant that you take me beyond thinking, Eduard,
with your skills."

"Hmmmph." His blue eyes twinkled. "But you still love Sair

162

more. I know it, Jahnel; you can't protest your way out of it.''
He thumped his hand on his chest. ''Despair, desolation, what
you do to me, Jahnel, knowing such a thing . . .''

''And you love Solveya more. I know it, Eduard, I just—''

He lunged toward her, and she flipped herself away, mocking
him with a gesture.

''You'll have to move faster than that to catch me,'' she told
him airily, catching his mood. After so many hours of tension
and shocks, with miin above and Austin below and Koyil aloft
on the prowl, she relaxed gratefully into playing with Eduard—
and knew he knew it, and knew he had started it because he
knew.

Eduard puffed his chest out, posing for her. ''I'm content with
the memory of the time I *have* caught you, Jahnel. Luelle and
Didier are the proof.'' He grinned fatuously.

''Each time is a new adventure,'' she admitted. That earned
her an outright laugh, which she quickly shushed.

He caught her hand and pulled her against him, smiling down
into her face. ''Have I ever told you how much I like being
married to you, Jahnel?''

''A few times, now and then. But you tell Solveya that, too.
I know it all too well.'' They smiled at each other contentedly.

''It would have been nice if the kids matched up the other
way,'' Eduard said. ''If Luelle were Sair's, and Solveya's baby
mine . . . but I suppose it just gives us all the more reason to
try again.''

''True, but Sair doesn't mind—neither do I. Are you worried
it was resented?''

Eduard shrugged, probably bothered more than he would ever
admit.

''You listen too closely to Melinde,'' Jahnel said. ''The blend
is why the vayalim has its strength, Eduard, don't you agree?''

''Spoken like a true senior wife. Is it true the miin have only
two-adult marriages?''

She shrugged. ''I'm not sure *what* they have; Austin was too
busy teasing me. He hinted the miin might find us offensive in
our arrangements—but who cares? I won't give up what we have,
Eduard, whatever the miin think. Now are you worrying about
that, too?''

''Me?'' he boasted. ''I never worry. But let's keep the Avelle
from taking it away first. We can fight off the miin later, I think.''
He checked the corridor again, then stilled, his ear cocked toward the level's interior. ''I hear movement. The iruta must be

arriving. I'll go warn Papa Benoit that the central portal is open.''

"All right.'' Jahnel drifted out to station herself just inside the central portal. She felt the current of warm air, scented with all the life of the City, brush across her face, stronger now that Jean had pierced the rearward wall. Faint noises came from the darkness behind her—a murmur of low voices, rustlings, a clank of machinery striking a wall, a shushing sound. Several Faon loomed up beside her, her father among them.

"Well done, Jahnel,'' he muttered, as if he disliked giving the praise.

Jahnel tightened her lips. "If we can hold it, Papa.''

Benoit made a wry face and turned to the man beside him. "I want a barrier erected across the corridor just inside the hallway, enough to be concealed by darkness from casual inspection.'' He toed the floor beneath them, then tested it with a stamp of his foot. "And put a gravity inductor underneath this floor. If they are foolish enough to attempt entry, we will crush them with our grav fields. Yes, daughter,'' he said to her sharp look. "Gravity as a weapon. Kiiri gave us many weapons, perhaps knowing full well what he did.''

"You speak as if this were a tier war, Papa. Faon gravity, sprung unawares, would kill an Avelle. I thought we only wanted concealment.''

"Invasion of another tier is not a benign act.''

"We are not Avelle, Papa Benoit.''

"In this instance, we *are* Avelle.''

She turned to face him squarely. "And if we face defeat, what do you propose to do?'' In the worst of the tier wars, the Avelle on the edge of defeat took horrible measures, once even pocket atomics that had threatened the whole City. Every kin-alliance in Quevi Ltir had reacted instantly, throwing tens of thousands of Avelle into the responsible tier and destroying its inhabitants to the last nestling.

"What?'' she asked. Her father smiled thinly and turned away. She caught his arm. "What?''

He shook her off. "When the order comes, daughter, you will obey as kin-law requires. We will not be destroyed lightly.''

She watched him move off, alarmed by the inexorable expression in his face. Her father had always been stern, sparing of affection, but not implacable. He reminds me of Koyil now, she thought sadly: unforgiving and unswerving. She looked around the corridor, now filling with Faon as they moved into the vacant vayalim. A Home-Space or death trap? And death for whom?

I told myself I would defend fiercely; why do I doubt what would be necessary? Am I not Avelle enough?

Seeing Solveya waving at her from a doorway, Jahnel nodded to the Faon who stepped to take her guard-place, then joined her family. Austin sat lumpily in a corner, still looking dazed and obviously in pain from his injured shoulder. As she walked in, he looked up, his face lighting suddenly. He had been in Evan's and Solveya's care; she could understand his depression: both were scowling.

"Where is Sair?" she asked.

"With the Etoile," Solveya answered, shaking back her hair. "They're going to rig some air converters after we've sealed the level, then tap the water reservoirs to fill the tanks. We could bring precious little food, a few great-claws in water bubbles, some plantings. How can that feed all of us for long?" She looked around helplessly, her hands unconsciously cradling her stomach, then focused on Austin with distaste.

"It's not his fault, Solveya."

Her sister-wife's head jerked back. "Oh? I wonder about you, senior wife, and your strange affection for this miin. What did he tell his ship when you took him to the surface? What is his ship telling Avelle?"

"And your solution?" Jahnel asked hotly, stung by Solveya's tone. "His death? What would that solve?"

Solveya's beautiful face settled into stony immobility. "Perhaps it might cure what is wrong here, Jahnel." She turned and moved away, putting distance between them. Jahnel thought to go after her, then gave it up for the moment and moved to Austin. Perhaps I will lose both junior wives, she thought. Melinde fears the Avelle, Solveya fears for her unborn child—and both have the right in that. There is cause for fear.

"I'm sorry," Austin muttered as she knelt beside him. "I'm sorry she doesn't like me."

"It's not you; it's the danger that threatens us. How's your shoulder?"

"I've felt better. What is this place?"

"Another tier. We are undiscovered for now; I fear it won't be for long. Even a kin-alliance under breeding stress still makes its patrols."

"Come again?"

"Never mind. Rest there. You'll need a time to recuperate

from the slash poison. Celeste's antidote works slowly, but if you can wait it out, it works. If you feel faint or feverish, let us know.''

"Okay.'' He smiled almost shyly. An odd shyness, she thought, looking down at him, fitting it with other things she guessed about his ship people. Had *Phalene*'s humans also lived in such loneliness? Or did Austin live more isolated than others? The Sanford apparently found the connecting, though Jahnel still didn't understand Austin's story about her, not completely.

"Where do you come from, Austin? On Earth?''

"A place called Caracas, in South America. A Latino homeland. I'm half-Latino myself.'' Austin shifted his shoulder slightly, then winced.

"Caracas?'' Jahnel rolled the word curiously. "A harsh-sounding name for a home-space.''

"But a beautiful place—gardens and white stone, wide streets, gentle-mannered people.''

"And you miss it.''

"Not that much—not enough to go back.'' He looked away from her to watch Luelle playing with Smart-Mouth. Jahnel waited patiently, saying nothing, until he sighed and met her eyes again. "I had an argument with my father. My parents divorced when I was nine, and my father cut her off from me. I never saw her again. I heard later that she went back to France and eventually emigrated to a new colony-world in Vela.''

"Cut you off? How could he do that?''

"Venezuelan law. Latino society has rigid statutes about rights to children, a definite order of things you break at your peril— and its culture doesn't encourage husbands to forgive. My father never did. Neither do I.'' She saw the muscles shift along his jaw.

"This, too, is part of morality?''

Austin smiled. "I suppose so.''

"And this Boland? He thinks in these patterns?''

"Boland is Anglo, but—sometimes. If nothing else, the ship's command directives have a similar slant.''

"Anglo?''

"From North America. There's a political union, but *La Novia* comes from a Latino port and has mostly Latino crewmen.

Jahnel thought about that, wondering how "unions'' matched kin-alliances—if they did. Though she had studied the First Generation's oral history tapes as a girl, the knowledge had seemed mostly irrelevant to a Jahnel more interested in her latest "tier war" with Sair. She should have paid more attention, she supposed, a hindsight that didn't bother her much. She was more interested in the personalities aboard *La Novia*. She saw Austin look at her curiously, as if he wondered at her interest. She shook her head irritably.

"You are Latino."

"Half-Latino—and I don't admit that very often." His jaw set stubbornly again, his dark eyes glinting.

"But you won't admit the French, either?"

"Who wants to be a foreigner? Especially among Latinos; they're a stubborn group about who's what." He shrugged. "But then *Phalene* knew that, didn't they?" He glanced bleakly around the room. "I've made a great trade. I'd say a miin in Quevi Ltir is the ultimate foreigner."

"No more than we Faon would be among your 'unions.' "

"It doesn't have to be that way," he protested, then gave it up. "Well, I can't argue it much. Boland and Elena are rather unmistakeable types." He looked glum. "Won't you even think about it?"

Jahnel reached and touched his face. "Here is kin-bonding, Austin. Here is family. Don't judge too quickly from your loneliness." He looked startled, then quickly dropped his eyes again, a slow flush spreading upward from his collar. What had she said to so disturb him? She shook her head in confusion, not understanding him. "Rest," she told him. "All is at peace for the moment."

"I let you escape," he muttered.

"I know. And saved my child's life. There was good in these things, whatever may happen after. I hope your 'fee' is not too onerous, Austin. Rest now."

She glanced at Solveya as her co-wife busied herself with settling Luelle and Didier. Is she right? she wondered bleakly. Have I changed so very much that even now, when all is at stake, I have doubts? She moved over to Eduard and let him wrap his arms around her, then leaned back against him to rest. As he tickled her ear with his finger, she wished they could steal away into some nearby room and forget everything for a time. Eduard kept up his tickling, tempting her toward her wish; after a few minutes of his insisting, she sighed and turned to smile at him, then led him into the darkened hallway to an inner room, conscious for some reason that Austin's eyes watched them leave.

Eduard looked around the bare sleeping room, squinting into the shadows. She snapped on a wall light.

"Where's the bed? I expect some comfort here," he complained, making a show of peering around.

"Oh, Eduard."

"I love it when you say 'Oh, Eduard' that way. It reminds me that you're older than I am—a comfort in itself to me, Jahnel. We'll go through life with those three years between us, you ahead, me following."

"This has a point?" She wrapped her arms around his waist and laid her head on his shoulder.

"Not particularly. What are you going to do about Austin?" He tilted up her chin with a finger and kissed her.

"Does *that* comment have a point?"

"Not at all." He smiled, then sobered. "Always and ever, Jahnel. I promised that; we all did. You shouldn't worry so much."

"Is that why you were so insistent to lure me away—to take me from my worries?"

"Well . . . I have a few other reasons." He kissed her again, then cupped her breast gently. "Love me, Jahnel," he whispered urgently.

"Always and ever, my Eduard."

He smiled and drew her downward to the floor.

Afterward, she lay contentedly against Eduard's bare chest, drowsing. When he began to snore softly, she quietly disengaged herself and dressed, then left him to wander into the hallway. Two guards stood inward and outward by the level portals, with the Faon settled quietly into the vacant vayalim, family by family, as if this space were proper to them. As the hours passed into nighttime, Jahnel sensed a restlessness growing among her people. Many lay awake, gathering in small groups in and out of the vayalim rooms, conscious of their constriction into silence and immobility. The Faon were accustomed to freedom of movement—a safe home-space with familiar surroundings, but freedom to roam the wide fallways of the tier, even to explore surreptitiously the empty shadows of the First Tier. Some of the younger Faon grumbled among themselves in the darkness, quickly silenced by their elders, as all settled down to wait, not certain what they awaited.

After a time, Jahnel tiredly returned to her own vayalim. Solveya's pallet was empty, she noticed. Perhaps Sair had returned and the two had sought their own privacy for lovemaking. She thought to look for them both, anxious for them, but instead sat down between Evan and the children. She leaned forward to check Didier as he slept fitfully, still unhappy in the lighter gravity he had rarely experienced, then settled back again with a yawn. I should sleep, she told herself, and tried to rest. As she drowsed, Evan cried out in his sleep and she touched his shoulder, caressing him; he quieted, escaping whatever dream had oppressed him. Evan's nightmare disturbed Luelle; sleepily, she climbed into her mother's lap. Jahnel kissed her and rocked her gently until she slept.

We all dream fitfully, Jahnel thought sadly, oppressed by a sudden despair that throbbed dully in her throat. *La Novia* had offered the Faon another place, a place of safety, though few of the Faon would wish a return to the economic dependence and limited future that their grandparents had risked oblivion to escape. How much worse to return to human space, odd in their alien ways, without resources save those given in charity? On Mu Carinis, the *Phalene* colonists had secretly pooled their savings for nearly twenty years, waiting patiently until they had enough to buy *Phalene*, hindered always by Latino taxes, colony surcharges, minimal pay, after-the-fact legislation, Latino arrogance. To go back to that? To be paraded as oddities, then to be used to crack open Avelle society for the science Kiiri could give them? For the Faon would be used; that promise was implicit in Austin's reluctant acknowledgments of *La Novia*'s intentions. Rescue might have brought the ship to Quevi Ltir, but other matters now kept them, too. She bowed her head and cradled Luelle more closely.

Return would be safety for you, Luelle, whatever the price. In the Faon stubbornness, as much her own as Benoit's, that option had been cut off. She herself had had a number of years of full life as wife and mother, lover and friend, but Evan was just beginning his adulthood, and the children might never know theirs, a light extinguished, a life ended. How to face such choices? Did Benoit meet this horrible doubt in every choice he made for the Faon?

When I blew up the Downlift and cut off our access to the surface, she realized uncomfortably, I thought only of countering Koyil. I thought like an Avelle, looking only to the immediate riposte, the quick slash. I thought only of that and nothing else—and destroyed a future that might have saved us. I bound us to the Avelle and forgot we are also human.

And who pays, my Luelle? Who pays? My precious daughter, she thought, and rocked slowly back and forth.

What is wisdom? How do we ever know?

As the next hour passed, Jahnel remained sitting on the pallet, nodding off in brief snatches, her head sinking forward, then catching upward with a jerk. I should sleep, she told herself again, but kept herself awake, not knowing why. Stubbornness, she supposed, or an unwillingness to dream. I do not want the dreams this night would bring.

She heard soft footsteps approaching in the corridor outside, then a brief silence as the steps stopped immediately outside the door. She looked up and waited, then heard the steps resume, entering her vayalim. A shadowed form approached her. Her father sank down to his haunches beside her, his arms balanced on his knees, large hands hanging loosely. He looked older, with wider streaks of gray at his temples, deepened lines around his mouth. He regarded her gently, arousing her interest merely in that.

"Papa Benoit," she said in a low voice, greeting him.

Benoit sighed, and arranged himself more comfortably by sitting against the adjoining wall, then stretched out his legs in front of him. "I've been thinking, daughter, of your words to me this afternoon—and the consequences you fear. Tell me, Jahnel, why did you bring Austin into the City?"

She hesitated, wondering what he wanted of her. "I didn't want to leave him for Niintua's robots."

"He is only a miin, one of those who have killed our people."

"He is human like we are, and I'm not quite sure whose fault that was—miin or Avelle. But you see only miin—and behind that, Latino."

"So? Have you forgotten why *Phalene* left Mu Carinis?"

She shrugged. "No. But perhaps you forget other things you should remember, my father. You are leading us into an ultimatum, an Avelle solution that has decimated whole tiers. I brought Austin to give us flexibility."

Her father considered it. All Jahnel's life he had pushed her away, denied her the acknowledgment as his heir. That he would come to her now, so mildly, without demands, without anger, showed more than anything else how much lay at risk—and how much Benoit Alain feared for the Faon. She warmed toward him, putting aside their many quarrels for the sake of that gentleness.

"Can Austin contact his ship?" Benoit asked.

"You disintegrated his radio," she pointed out, then relented. "Not that we dare send such a signal from here. But he tried to tell them—they won't listen. They prefer Koyil's winning ways.'' She twisted her mouth and focused on brushing Luelle's hair back from her small face.

"We could always give Austin suval," Benoit said.

"Without biotesting? And with his consent or without it? Papa, I'm fully acclimated to battle drugs and the suval nearly killed me. Let's be more honest in how we kill him."

Benoit shrugged. "It was just an idea," he said, retreating, though she knew he had meant it more seriously than he now pretended. "It's hard to think in new patterns. I am second-generation, daughter—our parents taught us survival in this place—survival by becoming Avelle. Perhaps you can be different, restore a better balance."

"Irrepressible human?"

He smiled slightly. "Tell me then, Faon, about flexibility. Tell me why the younger are restless, ill-content to wait here."

So he had sensed the restlessness and felt its challenge to his judgment. She bowed her head again, wishing he had come to her for other reasons, too, that there might finally be peace between them. She sadly suspected that only the restlessness had brought him, a questioning of his choices that disturbed, not a wishing for peace with his daughter, never that. She took a sharp breath of pain, then stilled it. "We can't wait here forever," she said softly.

"I agree. We will be inevitably discovered, if only by a tier-by-tier search if the Principals finally league against us, if they do. Now all is in flux, with kin-alliances maneuvering to their strongest positions. I have decided we need something stronger— I can listen when I need to."

"I've noticed that, Papa," she said sourly.

He grunted noncommittedly, too fatigued to argue about it. "I want you to take our restless young and find a better place. And I want you to take Austin with you—for his flex-i-bili-ty." He drawled the words, taunting her and not too kindly.

"What place?" She stared at him.

"You found this place; find us another."

"The underlevels? We don't know what's down there."

"Exactly. You will find out."

"Break the seals? I can't think of a better way to flag our path for the Avelle."

"So find an inconspicuous corner to break the seals, some-thing they won't notice. We know nothing about the environment there—nor really why the Avelle don't go there. Hints, perhaps. I've checked our report tapes back to our first explorations outside the tier.'' He shrugged. ''The Avelle let the defenses in the First Tier deteriorate, too. Maybe it's only disinterest in other automatic machines.''

''Or maybe the underlevels are as radioactive as the Avelle imply they are.''

''That's a possibility.'' He shrugged.

Jahnel looked down at Luelle. ''When we went to the surface into danger, the Avelle sent us. Now you send Faon into danger, too.'' She leaned forward. ''Papa, Avelle subtlety has its charms, but Faon kin-obedience asks more honesty. What do you really want in the underlevels?''

''Control of the City's reactors,'' he said flatly.

She stared at him. ''I see—all too well. Benoit Alain as a true Principal? That kind of control would give you the rank, I'll hazard. But what virtue would that claim for us? Song is taken; so is Law and Mind. We have no ship and we killed the Battle Leader. That doesn't leave much to take.''

''A sufficient Name takes time to show itself,'' he said dismissingly.

''Hmmmph,'' she said.

''Kin-loyalty without questions is useful.''

''Not from me, Papa.''

He chuckled then, and she distrusted that sound as much as his pride.

''Give us other options, Jahnel. We cannot hide in shadows, careful of careless noise. We need a place to stand, to defend—only then can we bargain in strength.''

''You *will* bargain.''

''Of course—but only with strength. Find us that place.''

''All right,'' she said tiredly. ''All right.''

''Good,'' he said briskly, and she wondered why her father had little doubted her agreement. Was his mildness all pretense? Did only Jahnel have doubts? ''Choose your party from whomever of the restless you prefer. It is time for the young to find the way.'' He rose lightly to his feet and stood looking down at her. ''You choose.'' She watched him walk away, feeling herself ensnared in plots as thoroughly as she had been caught in Kiiri's word games in the fallway.

She rose to her feet and lay Luelle down next to Evan, then left the common room to find Sair. He answered her sleepily as she called from the doorway, and then joined her in the corridor, pulling his clothes around him. She explained Benoit's request.

"He asked you to take Austin?" Sair asked, puzzled.

"Better he be found with us few than all the Faon, I guess. Who can tell? Will you come, too, beloved?"

"Yes." Sair shook himself, trying to wake up completely, then quietly shut the door to the inner room where Solveya still slept. "How about Jean and Nathalie? They have practical heads and good experience in skulking around."

"Yes. And Evan."

"Evan? He's only fifteen."

"And restless, Sair. That apparently is the key to getting picked to swan off into radioactive zones. And I'd like to take Melinde—she's been avoiding me and I'd like the chance to talk to her when she can't easily stalk back to Philippe."

"All right." He studied her for a moment. "What is disturbing you, Jahnel? What else did Papa Benoit say?"

"Oh . . . I don't know. I keep waiting for Benoit to want a daughter someday, someone to trust—stupid me, I suppose. Benoit will never willingly share power; he's learned too well from the Principals."

"Nonsense. Lejja has always encouraged Nerup—this is strictly Benoit's choice, what he does and what he doesn't do." He frowned at her. "Here I am now, defending the Avelle. Where did we lose our balance?"

"Not you, too, Sair."

They looked at each other plaintively, then chuckled at the same time.

"Love you, Sair."

He smiled. "Enough of that, wife," he said briskly. "Let's straighten up, clear eyes, aals flared, Faon to the alert."

"Right. You first."

He snorted at her. "Some respect, please. But watch Melinde around Austin, Jahnel. Philippe's still arguing for solving Austin permanently—I've put a few spies into his group—as if disrupting Austin would make his ship go away and make Koyil our friend." He scowled. "Philippe never has been noticed for rationality. I think the battle drugs have warped his brain."

"Kiiri says the drugs are safe. The Avelle have fine-tuned their chemicals for millennia."

"For Avelle, not us. Our biochemistry may have its similarities, but there *are* differences, however subtle Kiiri's knowl-

edge. I knew Philippe when he was younger—he didn't have this
bloody-minded side to his emotions back then. Watch him, Jahnel. He's not rational. Neither is Melinde right now.''

''Melinde has the excuse of being young, however you scowl
at me—I *will* defend her. Neither she nor Evan has ever fought
in the tier wars. Violence at a distance lacks a certain impact.
In any case, I'd like to give them something to do instead of
spinning in place while everybody waits.'' She smiled. ''See? I
am a Principal-in-waiting already practicing my motives within
motives. Next vast ambition will begin to corrode my bones.
In time you won't know me at all.''

''Beloved,'' he said gently, ''corrode away, if you will. But
I will always know you.''

He followed her into the common room and bent to shake
Evan awake, then sent him off to find Melinde. Jahnel woke
Luelle, then gathered Didier from his cradle and took them both
to Eduard to watch. Once again her vayalim sent too many of
its six into danger, she thought—only now the six had become
five. All the Faon had noted Melinde's change of company; if
Jahnel let it go much longer, some might argue that it was more
her failing than Melinde's.

I am senior wife, she reminded herself. I have the responsi-
bility to keep my family together. But it would help if Melinde
cooperated a little. She stepped into the darkened room she had
shared with Eduard and roused him, then watched as Luelle
cuddled in Eduard's arms and both fell asleep. She tucked the
baby's blankets around him, then straightened.

I wish for too many things, she thought, but still the world
unravels as it would. Oh, Song, I'm tired. Every muscle in her
body ached, a dull throbbing that dragged at her. I should have
slept better than I did; I knew it.

She watched Eduard and the children sleep peacefully, safe
for now in this hidden place—but for how long? When will it
end? And how will it end? Why do I feel we are plummeting to
the end I fear the most, the end of everything, the deaths of all
I love, Faon and Avelle alike? She curled her hands into fists.

We love fiercely, she had told Austin, and the love is not
lesser, she had said, because it is fierce. We Avelle and Faon,
together. If anything has meaning, it must be that—or all is lost.
But how?

Am I human—or Avelle? Can't I be both? *Must* there be that
choice?

''Jahnel?'' Eduard murmured sleepily. ''What's the matter?''

"Go back to sleep, beloved." She bent to caress him, then left to join the others, not knowing where she would find her answers, if answers even existed with all in doubt.

❧ Chapter 13

AUSTIN AWOKE AS someone touched his shoulder. He stared upward into Sair's face, still dazed from dreams he had already half forgotten. "What is it?" he asked stupidly. Had the Avelle found them?

"We're going exploring again. Benoit wants you to come with us."

"Benoit? I thought he didn't like me."

Sair looked amused. "He doesn't. Welcome to Quevi Ltir and its convoluted rationales, Greg. And Papa Benoit is only an Avelle-in-training; the Principals have been masters of the game for decades. Come."

He called me Greg, Austin noticed, with a pleasure that warmed him. But he called me Greg before, he remembered, right after I got slashed. And brother.

Sair looked down at him patiently, his face shadowed by the darkness of the room.

"Are you awake?" he asked, prodding Austin's ribs with a toe. Austin obediently got to his feet, muscles cramped from sleeping on bare floor. He was used to softer mattresses. He walked around in a circle, stretching his legs. "Is Jahnel coming with us?" he asked casually.

"Yes. Why do you ask?" Sair's dark eyes suddenly gleamed suspiciously in the semidark of the room.

"Just asking."

Sair grunted and turned away. Austin followed him, gliding more easily in the low gravity. He felt he was getting used to light grav, though likely he would never have the grace of these people born to it. He caught himself on the edge of the doorway as Evan slipped by impatiently, then followed at his own sedate pace.

In the corridor outside the vayalim, he saw Sair, Jahnel, and Evan, and three Faon he couldn't name, a dark-haired man, a blond woman, and a brunette teenaged girl. The girl gave him a disdainful look and pointedly turned her back; the other Faon didn't bother to introduce themselves, either. Sair gestured at him and led them inward toward the portal the Faon had cut into this level. They passed quiet rooms and some Faon sleeping in corridors, a jumbled pile of parcels and equipment, then two Faon working quietly under a small lamp on a black-and-silver device Austin couldn't recognize. In the small room immediately before the portal, Sair hunted through another stack of parcels, then uncrated two laser rifles from a container alongside. Austin thought of asking where they were going, then decided it would make him sound like a miin. He wondered if Evan had asked when he awoke—if not-asking was some proof of interior control or something. If you've modeled your society on a brood-oriented and territorial alien, how does the human mix in?

He still felt odd from the poison in his shoulder, with the world seemingly stretched tight at odd angles. His shoulder ached, but whatever anesthetic Sair had packed in the wound seemed to work; he could move it a little and even hold something in his right hand—a little. Sair handed him a parcel, and he automatically took it with his right hand, then had to shift it quickly to his other hand. Jahnel noticed it and gestured at him— something Avelle, probably, for the gesture meant nothing to him—then took her own parcel and spread the shoulder straps. Austin looked down at his parcel and tried awkwardly to put it on under his cape. Sair came to help him, then raised a hand for attention.

"I'll take the point. Keep alert for any Avelle that might observe us."

"And if they do," the dark-haired Faon said, "our reaction?"

"I'd rather not kill Avelle if we can avoid it. We aren't in our home-space and lack the right." Sair scowled, reconsidering. "This then: while we are close to this level and the Avelle might discover all through us, we pursue and destroy. In the lower levels, let them chase us. Agreed?"

The other Faon nodded. Austin felt confused and knew he showed his bewilderment. Sair's eyes shifted to Austin.

"A watch on Austin, shared in rotation—for your safety, Austin. You are still awkward."

"I've had a whole day to adjust," Austin muttered. Sair shrugged, not interested in his complaints.

"Nathalie has the first watch on you." Sair nodded toward the blond woman, who gave Austin a cool look. I feel like a bumpkin at a society ball, Austin thought. The distaste, the wondering looks, the amusement are exactly the same—and he knew the Faon wouldn't have the faintest idea of the accuracy of the allusion, either. Maybe someday Jahnel could tell him the Avelle equivalent; surely they had one.

"Let's go." Jahnel and Sair glided smoothly through the portal and inverted gracefully, vanishing downward. Keeping close to Nathalie, Austin followed, not yet informed why he was going—or where.

The group fell swiftly down the narrow fallway and flashed into the open, then darted down one of the access tunnels to the level below. Sair slowed and edged back upward, peering over the lip of the tunnel, looking in both directions carefully, while the others floated beneath him. He pushed himself downward and inverted to join them. "No movement," he said calmly. Jahnel nodded, and they resumed their flight downward, quickly transversing room after room. Austin did his best to keep up, though the speed of their flight gave him little opportunity to experiment with his belt controls. Finally Sair inverted around him and took his left arm, pulling him along.

Austin's sense of direction was all mixed up. He didn't know if they were retracing the Faon's flight earlier that day or proceeding farther along under the tiers. He knew only that they went fast. After several hundred meters, Evan pointed to the right, and the group swerved toward a corner of yet another large empty room. Set in the corner was a black circle about a meter wide. As they came up to it, Austin felt a current of cool air issuing from it.

"We only know of two lower levels, and we've never come this far," Nathalie commented. "Is there a third open level under this one? I thought the underlevels were sealed."

"So the Avelle told us, Nathalie," Sair replied. "It would be like an Avelle to pretend to give information inadvertently, just to misdirect. But I tend to believe they are sealed. There must be another level, maybe not complete, but the air current's coming from somewhere." He leaned forward and looked down the access portal. "Room for an Avelle to pass through, if he squeezed."

"Let us squeeze," Nathalie said, her lips quirked upward. She drifted over the portal, inverted, and pulled hard on the edge of the portal, arrowing herself downward. Jahnel followed, and Sair waved Austin over.

"Do your best, Greg. It's a tight fit."

Austin maneuvered awkwardly to get his feet upward and then copied Nathalie's quick movement. He shot forward into the darkness, then tried to pole himself along with his uninjured arm as Jahnel had done in the First Tier tunnels. Several meters below him, he saw the gray circle of the other end. As he sank through it, hands took him and pulled him aside. His head spun dizzily a moment.

"Careful, Austin. Are you all right?" Jahnel asked. "You look pale."

"How can you tell?" he joked, peering at her through the gloom.

The dark-haired girl stared at him contemptuously. The expression made her look prematurely old, arrogant, and sour; he bristled automatically, giving her glare for glare. The girl sniffed. "I don't even see why you brought *him* along," she said to Jahnel.

"Benoit's orders, Melinde," Jahnel said with an edge to her voice. "You do remember orders, don't you?"

"Keeping him is *stupid*!"

"If the Faon decide to kill him," Jahnel said coldly, "would you personally take on the task? Talking and killing are different things, Melinde—and you haven't even fought in a tier war."

"I fought on the surface!"

"I know—but real battle is more than target-shooting from a distance. It means blood and pain, destruction and loss. Philippe forgets that—or remembers and doesn't care."

The girl lifted her chin. "I happen to agree with him."

"About what? Revenge at any cost?"

"It's all *stupid*! And so are *you*, Jahnel, whatever you think of yourself!" The girl flounced off angrily. Jahnel let out her breath in a sigh.

"My sister-wife, our youngest," she explained to Austin. "I wish I had wiser ideas of how to deal with her."

"She's very angry," Austin said tentatively.

"Many are angry." She gestured to him and moved toward Sair. Austin followed slowly behind.

Above their heads, dim telltales spread shadows in dim circles of light, not enough to illuminate far corners. He looked around at the bare room, which was practically identical to the dozen they had traversed. On one wall, a doorway gaped and he could sense another current of cold air flowing from it. Sair followed the air current through the doorway into a second wide room, the others drifting after him. Before them on the far wall stood a pair of huge metal doors nearly five meters tall, gleaming dimly in the ceiling lights. The metal seemed mottled somehow, as though melted into place with odd variations of composition in whorls and incised edges. As he came closer, he saw the inscribing in the metal, and remembered similar incised patterns in the walls of the fallways.

"Do you know that word?" Sair asked Jahnel, pointing at one of the block shapes in an upper corners.

"No, I don't. It looks like 'song' but it's shaped squarely, not round. Inflected—hmmm. How do you inflect a primary word?" She pointed to another word on the other panel. "But there's 'Star Leader.' What would the Star Leader have to do with the underlevels?"

"I don't see any door controls."

"They might have wards," Jahnel warned. "Personally, I'd cut through the wall, not doors that might have sensors built in."

"Hmmm. Evan, bring up that drill and let's try a test hole over there." Sair glanced around and shrugged off his pack; he was promptly copied by the others. "Unhook your pack, Austin. It has protective gear inside."

"Protective? Against what?"

Sair shrugged. "Radiation, maybe. The City's power generators are sited in the underlevels—beyond that door. Maybe inert gases, maybe even partial vacuum. It's best to be prepared." The others had pulled thin-fabricked suits from their packs, the surface glinting with metal threads woven into the synthetic. Austin found a similar bundle inside his own and unrolled it, revealing a close-fitting bodysuit with enough stretch to fit and a breathing mask. With quick glances at the others for guidance and hampered by his injured arm, he stripped off his aal to the undersuit and pulled the new bodysuit over it, then refastened the aal and connected the mask straps, pulling his hood tight over the edges of the mask.

"This keeps out radiation?" he asked, fingering the close weave of the shimmering suit.

"Airborne or contact particles," Jahnel replied. "The Avelle have hinted that the environment is dangerous. Maybe." She pulled a cylindrical object out of her pack and tossed the empty bag toward the far wall. It drifted loosely, billowing slightly against the air pressure, and finally sagged into the wall and slid downward. Austin tried to copy her but had lots of room to miss; his bag settled two meters to the left.

"Retreat to the far wall," Sair ordered. "Evan, you begin the drill-hole."

The young man lifted a long rifle-shape in his hands and waited for the others to move back, then ignited the drill. The laser shot out, lancing toward the blank wall, and struck, clinging incandescently in a tiny point of brilliant glare. Austin looked aside to watch with his peripheral vision but even then had to squint against the brilliant diamond glare of the laser. The wall gradually changed color at the point of impact, becoming a cherry red and then melting slowly, a spreading trickle of glowing metal that traveled several centimeters and then froze into serpentine shapes. Sair drifted up and touched Evan's arm.

"You're through the wall," he said. "Hold up a minute."

Sair moved cautiously toward the glowing aperture, which was still fiery red at the edges, a gap onto emptiness in the middle. He held a device toward the aperture and edged forward, noting the readings.

"Jahnel," Austin whispered. "Why am I here? What are we doing?"

Jahnel's eyes sparkled with amusement. "You waited all this time to ask? Courage doesn't require such restraint, Austin."

"Well, I didn't know," he retorted. "Why are we here?"

"We're exploring. These are the underlevels, the lowest caverns of the City. The Avelle keep them walled up, but we know the City's power plant lies within—perhaps that is the reason." She noted Sair returning to Evan for a muttered conference. "We have a temporary safety in our new level, Austin, but it is not a secure one."

"So Benoit wants to come down here?"

She made a face. "We probably can't maintain environment. We don't have the portable machinery, not for two hundred of us. But it would be a place of refuge—if we can get to it."

"I see."

Evan was widening his beam, blasting at the wall above and around the initial penetration. Sair came back to the group.

"Some airborne radiation, but slight," he said. "Whatever the Avelle's reason for sealing the underlevels, it isn't lethal atmosphere. But it's cold, warm enough for machine graphite but not for us."

"How cold?" Nathalie asked.

Sair shrugged. "Maybe ten over zero."

"We can dress against that."

"True." Sair turned to watch with the others as Evan completed melting a hole just short of a meter square, large enough for human entry but too small for the larger Avelle. Smart, Austin thought, providing the Avelle don't have another access. Evan turned off his drill and they waited for the metal to cool, then passed one by one through the hole into the pitch darkness beyond.

"Lamps," Nathalie said, and unlatched a pocket lamp from her belt, then snapped it on.

The light leapt outward and vanished, swallowed up by an immense distance. Austin had a sense of a vast space outward and down; sound echoed hollowly with strange reverberation. They picked their way along the wall, Nathalie's light preceding them, a steady current of cold air blowing against them from below. Jahnel and Sair added their own lights, but it did little to show the dimensions of the place. Austin found his own lamp in his belt and pulled too hard with his injured arm, making himself wince, but got it turned on. Surrounded by a sphere of yellowish light, the Faon explored along the wall until they met a corner and another wall at right angles, then explored in that direction.

"Portal coming up," Sair muttered. At the edge of the lights, Austin saw a rectangular black shape several meters ahead, unledged but open. The group halted several meters from the doorway while Nathalie explored ahead, then called them. As Austin floated through the doorway, he saw her raise her lamp to study a panel on the wall just inside the door. She pointed mutely at a symbol by a double bank of raised buttons. Sair looked, too, and there was a muttered discussion.

"Well," Sair concluded, "if they have alarms hooked into the systems here, we'll have to trip them. We need light."

Nathalie spread her fingers and pressed four of the midbank indicators at once, two above and two below. A reddish light flared into the room, glancing off tall machine panels, illuminating other doors leading to inner rooms, each bracketed by more of the tall metal symbols the Faon had named Avelle Songs.

They all stayed by the doorway, heads turning as they examined the large room, similar to those above them in the lower levels, but equipped with different machines. On several of the instrument banks, red and blue telltales glowed dimly, and Austin could sense a subtle palpation in the air, now that they were out of the strong air current of the central cavern. Jean pushed off and headed toward one of the doors with other machines visible beyond. Sair gestured to Nathalie and Evan to move toward other doors, then turned to Austin.

"Do any of these instruments seem familiar to you?"

"How could they?" Austin asked in surprise.

Sair looked impatient. "Benoit sent you with us for whatever technical expertise you might have, which I assume you have. We're familiar with Avelle technology, but not main power systems. So I ask again for your input."

Jahnel touched Sair's arm.

"Yes, yes, I know." Sair studied Austin's face a moment, his expression noncommittal. "However it came about, you're in this with us."

"And not very welcome," Austin said, too loudly. Melinde gave him another of her dark glances.

"Well, of course not," Sair said, frowning himself. "What did you expect?"

"Nothing, Sair. I expect nothing." Austin looked past him at the instrument banks, then pushed off the wall and drifted toward them. The bank reached to the ceiling, a pattern of lights and symbols, instrument covers, and strange configurations. He turned and looked toward the other rooms, then headed for a door not chosen by the others. Sair and Jahnel followed him curiously.

This room had shelving along all the walls, with a litter of equipment, wires, and devices scattered at random along the shelves. A ceiling light threw sharp shadows downward, concealing the recesses. He ran his eyes over the strange equipment in despair. They expect miracles, he thought; how am I supposed to know anything about this stuff? Then on a high shelf he spotted a familiar shape and immediately swooped up to it, catching himself neatly on a shelf support. He lifted out what looked to be a microwave guide, a narrow metal tube with a globular torus at its middle, a small power source at the base of the tube. It had to be. He stopped himself from hastily peering down the tube-end—an excellent way to radiate his brains, he reminded himself, if the Avelle used a continuous source. He swung the guide toward the devices, seeing if it affected any of the other machines.

"What is it?" Jahnel asked.

"A microwave guide, I think. With a piece of lead to stagger the emissions, I could signal with this."

"Signal whom?" Sair asked suspiciously.

"La Novia." Austin eyed Sair. "Listen, our computers are geared to notice patterned communication—hell, Earth has been looking for other intelligent life for decades. Put a microwave pattern–signal in her path, and the computers would ring every bell on Boland's board. Maybe he'd listen this time."

"To what?" Jahnel asked. "To go away? Not while Koyil is talking to him."

"It's worth another try. I can tell him the situation down here, that the Faon have had to vacate their Home-Space, that you are all in danger."

"Would he care?" Jahnel asked pointedly.

"Probably not." Austin let the guide sag. "But it's worth a try."

"So send the signal, Austin," Jahnel said.

Sair made a convulsive move, then thought better of his protest.

"We'll have to get closer to the surface," Jahnel went on. "I assume your signal can't penetrate a kilometer of rock."

"True."

Sair stared at her. "Go up through a tier? With every Avelle in the City looking for us?"

She shrugged. "We'll have to find another way." She thumbed over her shoulder at the main door into the cavern. "Why is there such a wind? How can a sealed cavern have such freshness to the air? We expected something depleted, heavy with radiation. I'd like to know where that air current goes, if only to make sure this place is defensible."

"Beloved, Papa Benoit sent us here to reconnoiter."

"And we are. Listen, you stay here with the others and explore these rooms, like Benoit wanted. Austin and I will follow the air current. Maybe it leads upward, closer to the surface. We need this chance, Sair."

Sair glanced at Austin. "But he says he doesn't think it will work."

"If we don't try, Austin won't have much chance to be wrong."

Sair blew out a breath. "All right. Be careful, love." He tugged at her arm, bringing her to him to press her close. Austin looked away.

"Come on, Austin," she said.

"Perhaps you could call me Greg."

She looked at him, her expression unreadable. "Austin will do." She touched Sair's face, then inverted gracefully and headed for the cavern. Austin spotted a small square of metal and hefted it, then turned it in the light. It looked like lead; whatever it was, it had enough specific-gravity weight to block microwaves—he hoped. He cradled the guide in the curve of his injured arm and tucked the plate into his belt, then followed her into the cone of light spilling into the cavern from the instrument room. Jahnel slowed and hovered in midair, then turned toward the left until she faced away from the vigorous air current. "That way," she murmured.

She headed straight ahead across the gulf, following the current. Austin glanced back at the lighted doorway as it receded, conscious of a great depth below them. Ahead was only a brief cone of light emitted by their belt lamps, then an empty blackness beyond. They steered by the steady wind at their backs, following the air current across the vast cavern. Behind them, the lighted doorway of the power room dwindled to a tiny square, then a sharp point of light. Austin tried to guess at the dimensions of the cavern, awed. After fifteen minutes, they came abruptly upon another wall and a wide portal onto more darkness. Jahnel caught herself on the lip of the opening, nearly pulled into the tunnel by the rushing air. She peered upward, hesitating.

"Give me your hand. I don't want us to get separated." She grasped his hand firmly, then pulled them sideways to face the center of the tunnel. The air moved them forward, pushing at them, and they passed over the lip of the tunnel. Jahnel balanced on the air, then touched her belt jet. They flew upward cautiously, trying to not outspeed their lamps.

They ascended steadily on a sharp incline, the bore of the rock tunnel unvarying. Time lost meaning as they rose, lost in the sameness of the walls, the darkness that enclosed them. After more than a half kilometer, Austin guessed, the transition came abruptly. One moment they were still entombed by the tunnel walls, the next they had flashed by another portal lip into a dimly lighted space, another cavern. He gasped as he recognized the long and bulbous shape of an interstellar colony-ship, three hundred meters from engine modules to prow. High on the metal hull gleamed a word he recognized, then a series of numbers.

"Phalene," he breathed. Jahnel pulled them to a sudden stop, hovering as she stared at the ship. Austin pointed beyond it. A wide boxy shape, four times the size of *Phalene*, stood beyond in the far reaches of the cavern, a hulking shape of gleaming metal, crystalline connectors, and massive engines. Jahnel seemed to shrink back, her expression filled with dread.

"Quevi'ali," she breathed. "Song preserve us!" She turned and would have darted back into the tunnel if he hadn't checked her.

"Why?" he objected.

"The Songs," she said obscurely. "Come!"

He yanked back hard, stalling them in midair. They sank slowly downward as she tried to pry his fingers off her arm.

"Austin! Will you pay attention?"

Then she stopped, staring past him over his shoulder. He twisted to look behind him and saw the looming shape of an Avelle drifting toward them, sculling effortlessly with the edges of its wing-flaps. Strangely, Jahnel made no attempt to flee. Austin took one look at her calm face, gulped, and remained still. The Avelle rose gracefully, descending around a high arc, like a raptor about to pounce. Jahnel turned slowly in place, facing the Avelle as it approached still closer.

"Greetings, Kiiri," she said in a normal voice. Austin released part of his death grip on her arm, wondering if he would *ever* understand this place. The Avelle's reddish eyes shifted to Austin, measuring him.

"Ah, this is the miin," the Avelle rumbled in a deep voice, speaking French in an understandable but an odd watery accent.

"In another life he was."

"And in this continued life," Kiiri said in a reproving tone. "Let us not warp reality." The Avelle drifted closer, then backed easily on the air with his flexible wings, hovering in front of them. "He seems to have adapted well."

"Faon came from the same stock as he has. Why should he not?"

"True." Kiiri actually sniffed, and Austin suddenly had the mental image of a crotchety old gentleman dressed in a tuxedo and cape—or a vampire with those eyes. The second thought was not an image that consoled. Kiiri shifted his gaze to him again and twitched a wing-flap. "Perch him somewhere, please. I want to talk to you."

Jahnel tugged on Austin's sleeve. "How about on *Quevi'ali*? He can explore."

"Mind your obscenities, Jahnel. I have every right to be here, considering I own Pakal by knowing a certain secret. Two of my personal attendants are guarding the other door, so your miin will be safe. Hmmm. And leave the microwave device here, miin."

"What if he wants to call *La Novia*?" Jahnel asked sweetly.

"Who *is* this?" Austin demanded.

Jahnel laughed. "This is Kiiri, the Science Leader."

Kiiri bowed gracefully in midair, and even Austin could detect the mild mockery in his flickering eyes.

"Kiiri is one of the Principals who rule Quevi Ltir, Austin. His name is Austin, Kiiri; mind you be polite. When Kiiri's in an honest mood, which isn't always, he is Lejja's ally and the chief protector of the Faon—most of the time. Why are you here?" she shot at Kiiri.

"I set an infrared warning beam at the other end of the ship tunnel. It summoned me quite nicely. *Why* I'll explain to you alone. Perch him, Jahnel."

"All right. Austin, wait at the tunnel edge." She pressed his arm. "It's all right, really."

"If you're sure."

"I'm sure."

Austin handed her the microwave guide and drifted apart from her, then made a wide detour around the Avelle. Kiiri sculled himself to turn with him, definitely amused. Amused? Why amused? Austin reached the tunnel edge and caught the lip, then edged out of the airstream to avoid losing his position. Uncertainly, he watched the Avelle soar away, leading Jahnel toward *Quevi'ali*. She takes risks, he thought, then realized that the Avelle must have several faces to the Faon—Jahnel had hinted at as much before. All he had seen was Avelle in attack; was there a softer side? He looked around the massive cavern, amazed at the engineering of it. On the metal wall nearest him marched row after row of the inscribed metal letters, each two meters tall, of what Jahnel had called Songs. Songs implied artistry—creativity, gentleness, reflection. Were the Avelle that also?

I could live my whole life here, he thought, and perhaps still not understand as much as half the whole—but I would like to understand. I would like to know. He settled himself to wait patiently, guessing that this waiting without explanation fit well here in this place. He set to learn it conscientiously.

❦ Chapter 14

JAHNEL FOLLOWED KIIRI down the floor of the massive cavern, her thoughts in a turmoil. If the Avelle could so easily second-guess the Faon, all might be at risk. Perhaps even now Kaali's tier was massing above their refuge, ready to swoop. Kiiri soared gracefully, spiraling down to the massive engine pods of *Quevi'ali*. He hovered and allowed himself to sink the last meter, then coiled his tail into a comfortable seat. Jahnel touched down lightly in front of him and wrapped her aal around herself. She glanced up curiously, made slightly dizzy by the huge structure looming above. Kiiri watched her benignly.

"How did you know I would come here?" she asked suspiciously, unable to conceal her anxiety.

"No one is currently stalking the Faon, wherever they are, if that concerns you."

"You don't know where we are?" She raised a sardonic eyebrow.

"Oh, I could guess." Kiiri curved a wing-flap idly. "Both Kaali and Serup have brood problems, according to rumor available to you. But neither matriarch suspects secret invasion, not yet." His thin lips curved upward, mimicking a human smile. Whatever he intended with it, it did not reassure Jahnel.

"What *is* your game, Kiiri?" she demanded.

"Once you trusted me." Kiiri pretended disappointment.

"Claws, I still trust you," she said impatiently. "I just don't know what you want. But I *do* know when you're playing games."

Kiiri flicked his tail and looked amused. "Always direct, my Jahnel. But you mistake me—you are right about the games, but you're wrong that I play them with you, Faon. Let me tell you a tale, kin-sister." He gestured upward with a clawed hand

189

toward the huge Avelle ship. "This is *Quevi'ali*, as you know, the most sacred focus of our existence. All our Songs center on this ship and our roving life. It is Avelle destiny to rove, to prey on other ships, to make our way in the universe as Predators, singing new songs of our exploits as we achieve them. It gives us strength and purpose."

"To destruction," she summarized flatly.

"To achievement," he amended gently. "Don't quibble. Sometimes we are the prey of stronger ships—and nothing hones a race better than pursuit by a great enemy. And so *Quevi'ali* sought this refuge here. We had caught the worst of a skirmish with four other Predator ships and fled before them, then went to ground here. In time, we would rebuild and birth a daughter-ship, giving *us* the strength of two for a time. The force of an Avelle city-alliance immediately after resurgence cannot be withstood. Those are the times the Avelle rise in strength and make themselves a shining terror."

Jahnel snorted. "Like I said, destruction."

"Competition." Kiiri drifted to the side, his eyes studying the smooth hull of the ship. "Let's avoid the more perjorative words; I prefer the neutral but accurate terms, especially from you. The young are always emotional."

"But Quevi Ltir has enough kin-broods to fill three ships like that."

"Exactly." Kiiri swiveled back to her, his red eyes glinting. "Ah, the secret. Would you like a secret, little Faon? A secret that you could sell to the miin, betraying us to their ship?"

"They aren't a Predator ship, Kiiri. They're just exploring, looking for us."

"A ship is a ship," he said dismissingly.

"Bigot."

"Am I? What do the miin want here, truly?" His eyes glittered dangerously.

"Gravity control." That surprised him, she could see. "Great Songs, Kiiri, they don't want Quevi Ltir—they want your science."

"How could one *not* have gravity control and travel from star to star?" he huffed.

"The miin managed. You had our ship to study—you must know better than you're pretending. Can't another species lust for something besides territory—and 'shining terror'?"

"Hmmm. I had assumed the enabler machines had been damaged." He glanced at *Phalene*. "Interesting."

"I'd call it a whole new complexion. Why such surprise? If anybody knows how different we are, it's you."

" 'We'?" he asked, jumping on the word.

She looked back at him levelly. "We are human—you knew the miin were, too, and you didn't say. I have a grievance with you, Science Leader."

"Noted—and regretted." The Science Leader did not seem too concerned, Jahnel thought, doing her own noting.

"What's your dread secret?" she asked.

Kiiri drifted a few meters away, his attention on *Phalene*.

"Kiiri . . ."

"Oh . . . your pardon, Jahnel. I was abstracted."

"You are many things; abstracted isn't one of them."

"Little skeptic. Why can't you believe I am what I appear? Haven't I always assisted the Faon? You called me 'protector' before Austin."

"Assisted for your own reasons, some of which I know. Avelle never do anything gratuitously."

"Of course not. That would be inane." He smiled at her again, overtly amused. "Let me continue my tale, then. On a Predator ship, the ship itself is a common asset owned by all. Within this ship the kin-alliances, for there are always several bloodlines to keep a genetic prudence, these iruta compete and push and generally annoy one another—for the benefit of the race. But the ship itself is too great a weapon for one kin-alliance, too great a temptation when nothing but ship systems lie between a rival and the void."

"So you appoint a captain, the Star Leader, and arrange the other Principals about him to balance your politics."

"Correct. Other Principals may rise by political maneuver and personal force, as I did, but the Star Leader's rank always descends by bloodline. Only the Star Leader has the passwords to the ship systems, passing by oral tradition from father to child through the generations."

Jahnel's eyes widened as she caught the slight emphasis. "Oral tradition?"

"Machines can be penetrated, their data abstracted by foul and devious means," Kiiri said matter-of-factly. "There must be passwords, to protect all from devious intrusion."

"And Pakal doesn't know the passwords." She looked up quickly at *Quevi'ali*. "And you know he doesn't. *That's* how you got the Principals' vote to let us stay!"

"Please," Kiiri said mildly. "Spare my ears with your shouting. But, yes, the previous Science Leader discovered the Star Leader's negligence and created a little oral tradition of his own. Pakal is my creature," he said flatly. "I hold his life in my claws, ready to squeeze." He extended one hand and spread his claws, his anger savage and abrupt. He trembled. "One word from me spread abroad and his entire kin-alliance won't last an hour." Kiiri controlled himself with an effort and rotated to face *Quevi'ali*, inspecting its silver hull without hurry. "Unfortunately, that doesn't help a certain essential. *Quevi'ali* remains closed to us, confining us in this prison of a world."

"But how can *we* help you? We don't know your passwords, either."

"You always were quick of mind, leaping easily from fact to motive. How? I haven't the faintest of ideas. But you are unpredictable and think in different patterns." He regarded *Quevi'ali* soberly. "The tier wars grow worse with each generation. We can drill new tiers, of course, but with each new kin-alliance, the complexities grow. We aren't meant to stay in one place so long, Jahnel. We will tear ourselves apart, confined in this place." He lifted his chin, his gaze bleak on the Avelle's beautiful ship. "I have tried everything I can think of—so did my predecessor, with the terrified help of a certain Star Leader. But random choice has no logic. Science fails." He crossed his arms and let his head sag downward.

"You've never told Koyil this?"

"He is Law. He'd be in the vanguard of the revengers raging into Pakal's tier."

"He is practical."

"Not that practical. He finds in himself an aversion to Faon that eats at him; he'd never consider you a solution. Even a Principal can be ruled more by emotion than logic. Both are tools; emotion is merely more predictable and thus the weaker tool."

"If you tell the miin, Kiiri, they will exploit you."

"I am telling Faon, not miin."

"But half the City is chasing us."

"Not yet. Lejja declared you had left her tier and displayed your empty levels to one of Koyil's truce guards. Since you were the excuse for the invasion, Koyil had to withdraw. Being Principal of Laws can have its pinches; you have to stay moral. A smart move by your father, totally unexpected, like most best moves."

"He knew it was smart."

Kiiri glanced at her, amused again. "I didn't like my father, either. He had your basic arrogant egg-mold mentality." He stretched his wing-flaps and coiled them around his body neatly.

"But they will chase."

"Maybe. Koyil is thinking about it. He is an able thinker." Kiiri made a rude gesture and dismissed him as a topic. He drifted closer to Jahnel. "Little Faon, we have been friends, have we not?"

"We still are friends, despite a few of your less inestimable moves."

He chuckled, and flipped her a rude word. "I am Avelle, I won't deny it. But I have always felt the Faon were a key, a binding still concealed in shadows—and you are at grave risk, Faon." He gestured at the microwave guide. "I wouldn't recommend that quite yet. Koyil controls the surface defenses, and the robots would pick up the signal and track it here, then downward to the underlevels. All is in flux right now among the Principals: give Quevi Ltir contact between a Predator ship and a kin-alliance that we can't control and you will unite us instantly against you." He put out his clawed hand. Jahnel hesitated, then handed him the guide.

"I have doubts in giving you that," she said.

"There are other tools in the underlevels storeroom. Let your miin scrounge a little more."

She scowled at him. "He's not my miin."

"He is indubitably your miin. Tell Benoit to find another use for your Faon unpredictability that confounds even an Avelle and think of a better move that uses the miin. This was too obvious."

"Any suggestions?"

"Am I a Faon?" He drew himself up in mock offense. "Song perish the thought."

"*That* you aren't, I agree."

She began to turn away, then was caught by his clawed hand. He pulled her closer, deep within his body-field, an outlandish contact a Principal never permitted, and brushed her face with a clawed finger. She stared into his eyes, startled, then abruptly threw her arms around his neck, hugging him close.

"Good faring, Jahnel," he rumbled into her ear.

"Good faring, my Kiiri." She broke away and hurried toward Austin, not looking back. Austin looked his questions as she reached him, but she only tugged at his sleeve, guiding him back into the tunnel access. "Come, Austin." Her tone annoyed him, but she hadn't time to get enough control to think of miin sensibilities. She touched her belt jet and arrowed down the narrow tunnel, returning to the depths.

With Austin in tow, they reached the underlevels' main cavern and jetted toward the point of light across the abyss. The light spread into a small rectangle, then a doorway. As they came within a hundred meters, she saw a human shadow silhouetted across the light. Jean raised his hand in greeting.

"Did you make contact?" he asked.

Jahnel gave a quick look to Austin. "Not with the ship. Where is Sair?"

"Looking over the possibilities of rooms beyond this power room. We found several half-levels, none adapted to environment, of course, but more defendable than open space." He waved irritably at the abyss behind them. "Come."

Jahnel and Austin followed him through the wide power room; Jean vanished into the middle doorway. "Why did you give the Avelle the microwave guide?" Austin asked her in a low voice.

"Not now, Austin."

"How long am I supposed to just go along?" he asked in obvious anger. "Is that the way it is down here? Just do it, no matter what you think. I haven't noticed you following those rules."

She swiveled toward him, her own anger rising.

"Well?" he asked. "Who do you think I am?" He did not give her a chance to answer. "Just some sack of potatoes to loft here and there? The ultimate dispensable? A *tool*?"

"I acknowledge that you are angry," she said to him, setting her face. "Even that you have cause. And, yes, you *are* a tool. So am I. We are all tools, Austin, even the Principals. Accept that fact."

"Well, maybe I don't want to be a tool anymore."

She crossed her arms and stared at him. "How do you propose yourself elsewhere?"

He stared back in frustration, then thumped his chest with a forefinger. "I am a person."

"Of course."

"You admit it?"

She shrugged, then softened toward him. "I am in your debt for Luelle. We may all be in your debt if you can help us further. Kiiri spoke of keys, and some keys lie in shadows. But temper tantrums—and I have my own at inconvenient times—do not help. Please, Austin: be patient with us."

He thought about it, his face a study of conflicted emotions. A proud man, in some ways as stubborn as Melinde, for all his compliance with orders and unavoidable situations among the Faon. And, for whatever reason, he cared for the Faon, had proved it by putting himself in risk of death for a Faon child. Would Jahnel Alain, she wondered candidly, act the same if the situation were reversed? Could I care so easily for outsiders with no kin-bond to me? Does that make him the better?

Heretical thought, to doubt kin-bond. Is he the better?

Austin shrugged at last, though his expression was still angry. She drifted closer to him and took his sleeve. "I am distracted and thinking of too many things. Forgive me, Austin."

He looked nonplussed at her closeness, and she abruptly remembered his embrace in the First Tier—mockery, she had thought at the time, typical miin behavior that meant nothing. He saw her expression change and flushed, then backed off hastily.

"Don't do me any favors, Jahnel," he said harshly.

"You are still angry."

"That's a surprise?"

"Not at all. It would be gracious to accept my apology."

"I don't feel gracious."

She smiled at that, then laughed outright. Austin flushed again and looked truly furious, as if he might strike her. But, then, no doubt they had tried him severely, this proud miin.

"We share a common humanity, Austin, that is clear," she told him gently. "Be at peace and one with us." She spread her hands in the Avelle gesture. "Join our kin-bond and be Faon—until you must go away again. And *do* forgive me, whatever your ungracious feelings." He eyed her suspiciously and it made her laugh again; it was exactly what Sair would do, had done. "Come, if you would."

"When do I get answers?" he asked resistantly.

"The price for kin-bond is kin-obedience—though we don't exact that price as rigorously as the Avelle. Understand us, Austin, through them. An Avelle never questions certain matters, never asks, never yearns, never doubts; it is bred into his genes and constantly reinforced by environment—and outright compulsion. They are predators, but prey as a group through their bonding, their force magnified a thousand times in that bonding. It is their strength—and their weakness. *We* are predators and borrow their strength by copying what they are, but we are human, too—and no one knows if our humanity is a weakness in this place.'' She sobered, watching his face. ''Now comes the crisis to discover if it is weakness, my Austin, a weakness that will kill us all—or will save us. Do you still want your answers?''

He hesitated. ''Eventually, I would like my answers.''

''Eventually you will have them.''

''This is the *weirdest* place I've ever seen.''

''I'll take that as a compliment. Come along.''

They caught up with Jean and the others in the short tier beyond the power room. Sair wrinkled his nose at the lack of environmental consoles, though the floor bore marks of equipment removed long before. Likely Avelle had lived here while building the complex, then had returned to the warmth and spaces of upper tiers. Or perhaps the rooms had another function, quite different from the uses the Faon would put them to. ''It's still cold,'' Sair said, looking around at the half-lighted corridor.

''But defendable,'' Nathalie said firmly.

''All right, Nathalie. We'll tell Papa Benoit it's defendable.'' Nathalie smiled.

''And a weapon of strength,'' Melinde muttered, glancing at the power panels. Jahnel suddenly doubted her wisdom in bringing her sister-wife to carry such news to Philippe, as she surely would. Melinde gave her a level stare, confirming her suspicion.

''Let us go tell Benoit,'' Jahnel said, with slight emphasis on the name, and looked straight at Melinde. Melinde smiled thinly, saying nothing. Control your irritation, Jahnel reminded herself: patience. She watched Melinde glide gracefully out the portal, then speed toward the wall exit. Truth be told, Jahnel thought, I'd like to give Melinde a good shaking, hard enough to rattle her bones. It wouldn't help at all and likely make things worse, but how I'd like to shake her hard.

Was I that arrogant, she wondered, when I was younger and knew better than anybody who said differently? Probably—almost certainly. Papa Benoit had his trials with me. And I still think I know better—only the risks are higher now, dangerously high. She felt a tingle of dread snaking up her spine, a fear that her willfulness might bring unintended disaster to the Faon. Kin-obedience has its reasons, she told herself, in an elder's need to temper the foolish young. And you are young, Jahnel. Remember that, when your choices bear risk for more than yourself. She shivered, then set out after Melinde.

* * *

They left Jean at the drill-hole as guard and retraced their route to Kaali's tier, cautious for any Avelle observers. They saw no one and quickly slipped up the narrow fallway between the tiers to the waiting Faon. Celeste welcomed them warmly, then listened placidly to their news. "I thank you for looking, Jahnel, but we think the crisis has passed." She smiled widely, almost airy in her visible relief. "Koyil has sent us a City-Net summons to a Council. All Quevi Ltir knows."

"A Council!" Jahnel said.

Celeste only smiled even wider. "Lejja also invites us." She waved her hand happily. "The currents must have turned against Koyil. Song is again triumphant!"

"Did Kiiri join in the invitation, Celeste?"

"That wasn't mentioned." She studied Jahnel's face. "You think that has significance, Jahnel?"

"I don't know," Jahnel said uncertainly. "A Council? With what agenda?" She could think of several topics Koyil might choose, none of them fitting Celeste's happy conclusion and most of them by Jahnel's own arranging.

"Whatever he chooses. We can't refuse, child—that would be a direct challenge to the Laws and Koyil personally. A minor kin-alliance does not refuse invitations from the Principals."

"Sometimes to their intense regret. Didn't Koyil abscond with part of a neighboring tier a few years ago by calling a parley?"

"He had a kin-brood claim."

"Koyil has kin-brood claims all over the City," she said sourly. "He lends his females everywhere."

Celeste eyed her, obviously surprised by Jahnel's skepticism. Several Faon had drifted into the room to listen, seniors and juniors both, and Jahnel saw the same division in opinions. So did Celeste. Her mouth tightened in displeasure and she quickly sent Nathalie to find Benoit. "Well, if you don't believe me, Jahnel, you can discuss it with your leader."

"As you wish," Jahnel responded, conceding nothing. And that, too, displeased Celeste. The older woman made an irritable gesture and turned away.

It fits too well what we wish to believe, Jahnel thought sadly, especially what the seniors want so desperately to believe—that Law is honest, that customs are always observed, that our rights in the City are truly protected. Benoit would pounce on that conclusion, finding his own affirmation as kin-leader in trusting Avelle ways, in an easy return to normalcy. Perhaps seniors wish more for what they will, she thought, trading the young's easy

confidence in their own immortality for other protections against
pain and the ultimate loss.

But I am young and I no longer feel immortal—not while we
lie within reach of Koyil's claws. If I wished, she realized, I
could challenge Benoit now and force a division among us when
he most needs our unity. And if Benoit is right and I am wrong
. . . I could be wrong. Perhaps wishes are true.

She sat down on a stack of parcels by the wall to wait and
leaned back against the wall, then shifted her feet so Sair could
sit against her. Austin hesitated, then took his own seat a short
distance away, his eyes flicking from her face to Sair's. It was
all strange to him, she could tell: Song knows, it's becoming
strange to me. She leaned forward and wrapped her arms around
Sair, resting her chin on the top of Sair's head. He relaxed back
against her, offering the comfort of his presence, and she wished
for privacy to ask his advice. But too many eyes watched her
now as other Faon drifted in, others out, waiting also. She
sighed.

If I tell Papa Benoit about Pakal, she thought, he may be
tempted to use it at the Council. What better accusation to fling
at Koyil to counter accusations against the Faon? The ultimate
negligence, there in Avelle holding; all the Faon have done pales
in comparison. Yes, he would use it. But Kiiri warned against
exposing Pakal. Would Benoit heed that warning, know the intensity I saw in that warning? Will he believe me? He didn't
listen about Austin, isn't listening at all. I doubt if he would
listen to Kiiri's warnings.

And what about Austin? If I tell Papa Benoit about Austin's
plan to contact his ship, will he tell Koyil that, thinking it some
kind of advantage? Will he admit Austin's presence among us?
Will he tell, in his wish to please the Avelle after Koyil murmurs
his rolling assurances, none of them trustworthy? Benoit will
play the game by Avelle rules—and their rules put us in weakness, make us predictable. She fastened on that thought.

Unpredictability, Kiiri said, that is our strength now. We are
human, too—something we have tried to forget and Benoit still
wishes to forget. An Avelle would tell such knowledge to a
senior—kin-obedience would demand it. What if you do not tell,
Jahnel? What then? Is it arrogance to think of not telling? Benoit
would never forgive me if—when—he found out. Would Sair
understand? Would anyone understand?

Will I lose everything? For I fear to tell Benoit either of these
things.

I could challenge him for the Leadership now, in this place, she thought, greatly tempted. And if the seniors remain with him, denying me, I would divide the Faon into two parts, robbing one part of youth, the other of experience. In Quevi Ltir, a kin-alliance without balance invites unavoidable destruction.

Benoit strode in and shot a glance at Austin, then ignored him pointedly. That is getting old, Papa, she thought. Disdain pricks only as long as it affects the object—and Austin had already learned to ignore Benoit back. She watched Austin leaning casually against his stack of parcels, his head turning to watch others come in and out of the room, looking anywhere but at Benoit, and repressed a smile. You learn quickly, my miin.

Benoit listened politely to Sair's report about the refuge in the underlevels, nodded at all the important points, even smiled in approval—but his attention was not on it, she could see that. He radiated a confidence that had made him abstracted, uninterested in options. He assumes Lejja has won; he truly believes that the parley will give us safety again, that we have won. Oh, my father. How can you so easily forget the dangers?

She let the moment for challenge pass, keeping her face down and meeting none of the eyes that watched her expectantly, some with dread, others with anticipation. She would not divide the Faon, not now.

Benoit gave brisk orders, then strode out of the room again, all confidence in himself, knowing he had the right understanding of all affairs. Do I look like that when I'm wrong? she wondered. How tiresome. If I ever become Leader, I must remember to doubt myself occasionally. She sat lumpily, no doubt looking as sour as she felt. Sair stirred uncomfortably within her arms.

"I think we should go to the underlevels," Jahnel said into his ear. "I think Koyil means treachery—and we could be trapped here, all of us."

"But Papa Benoit is so sure of himself," Sair murmured back, his eyes on the Faon that still shifted in and out of the room, still watching them. "How can we deny such exquisite certainty?"

"You, too?"

"Let's say you're contagious, my love." The idea did not comfort her.

Nathalie drifted in, then several others of the third generation, all juniors among the Faon. Silently, they arranged themselves in front of Jahnel and Sair until more than twenty, Hiboux and

Etoile, Roche and Ruisseau and Louve together, sat looking at Jahnel. Philippe and Melinde took a position in the back, their expressions most challenging of all. Jahnel looked back defiantly.

"I sense a game adrift on the air," Nathalie said quietly. "And I wonder why Jahnel Alain of the Louve has not told her kin-alliance what she knows."

"I don't trust Koyil," Jahnel admitted, meeting Nathalie's eyes. "But of knowledge I have nothing specific, not about Koyil's parley." She raised her hand, palm outward. "Truth."

"Then another matter?" Philippe demanded, pouncing on her wording.

"Yes. But different—and I'm not telling that, especially not you, Philippe." Jahnel tightened her lips. "Am I Faon Leader, who must tell what I know? Take your demanding to the proper ears."

"But this is madness!" Philippe raged. "Benoit trusts the Avelle! He'll kill us all!"

"I also trust the Avelle," she shot back, "though perhaps to a lesser point. And Benoit may be right—and he is Leader. Remember your kin-obedience, Philippe."

"Yes, kin-obedience—right into the slaughter!"

"And what's your alternative?" she demanded. "You're very loud in complaining, Philippe, but I don't hear any solutions."

"We should fight!" Melinde cried.

"With *what*? Two hundred Faon against ten thousand Avelle? We wouldn't last an hour. Grow up, Melinde."

With a chopping gesture of disgust, Philippe swept out of the room, Melinde firmly in his wake. Jahnel felt Sair stiffen as Melinde left and knew that he might not forgive this public rebuff. Melinde had chosen her allegiances, and Sair might not permit second thoughts, not after this. She sighed, grieving for her sister-wife. The divisions had already begun, driven by fear she could not control. It ruled her father into believing wish-dreams, ruled Melinde into other dreams of blood and destruction, even ruled herself—into what? Trust against all reason in a cajoling miin and a scheming Principal. She bowed her head in despair.

"Now that the children have left," Nathalie said dryly into the silence, "it seems to me that this refuge of ours is an excellent trap—should Koyil know where we are."

"I doubt he knows yet," a Ruisseau argued.

"He may know soon," Nathalie countered. "We are desperately exposed."

"My elders think differently," a Hiboux said unhappily. "They follow Benoit and his assurances."

"What do you think, Jahnel, of your father's assurances?" Nathalie pressed at her.

What does she want of me? Jahnel wondered, angry at the insistence. "I am kin-loyal," she protested.

"You have the makings of a Principal—hasn't Kiiri cultivated you to that rank all your life? Don't we all know it, Jahnel? Why don't you?"

"That's ridiculous," Jahnel said with a real anger. She lifted her chin and stared at them at all. "Principal? What have I heard since I brought Austin into the City? Did any of you speak up when my father doubted? I am irritated with you all, my Faon; I am a-rustle with wing-flap shivers."

Nathalie chuckled low in her throat, irritating Jahnel all over again. She stared at Nathalie, then at the others, one by one, challenging, but saw only a level gaze, a waiting. She took a deep breath. "All right—you want my opinion. I think it's time we left this tier." She shifted her gaze to the Ruisseau, challenging him particularly. "And I think Koyil knows exactly where we are; he hears the same rumors we did."

"Then we shall certainly leave," Nathalie said equably.

"Why are you forcing this?" Jahnel asked, troubled. "Benoit has been a good leader—he still is, whatever my doubts."

"I thank you for your support, daughter."

Jahnel started and half rose to her feet. Her father stood in the doorway, his expression thunderous. He looked around at the assembly of Faon, his mouth drawn down in fury. No doubt he saw another cabal developing, far more dangerous than Philippe's angry declarations. What else had he heard from the hallway? Likely all of it.

"Return to your vayalim, Faon," he said harshly, then stabbed a finger at Jahnel. "*You*, Jahnel, will accompany me to the parley."

"No, Benoit!" Nathalie said. "She is your heir!"

"That's enough!" Benoit roared. "I remind you what you are, Nathalie—and I have never named my heir. You presume too much." He glared at them all. "I *demand* kin-obedience in this—I demand it!"

"Demand?" Nathalie asked acidly, then caught Jahnel's

warning glance and backed off. Benoit, too, saw that prompt compliance and it infuriated him all the more.

We war with ourselves, Jahnel thought in despair. We make our own destruction. Her shoulders sagged. Stop—this must stop, and quickly, before all unravels. "I will go, my beloveds."

"Jahnel . . ." Sair said in anguish.

"I will go." She disengaged herself from Sair and stood up, then moved to face her father. "You ask for obedience; I obey."

Benoit harrumphed, only partly mollified, then whirled toward Nathalie. "The Faon will remain here until we return. Is that understood, Etoile?"

Nathalie nodded coldly, her eyes glittering. Benoit moved away briskly toward the portal, not looking back to see if Jahnel followed. Jahnel slowly took her place in the parley party, her face stiff and controlled. As Benoit conferred briefly by the fallway portal with Celeste and Arnaud—he was taking both his councilors, she saw, more idiocy—Nathalie drifted up to her and calmly slipped a vial of battle drugs into Jahnel's hand.

"You will find the Faon in the underlevels, Jahnel," she murmured. "Return to us."

Jahnel glanced at her father and thought to protest, then knew it would do little good. "I will try."

"Come," Benoit said, his strong voice ringing through the room. "We haven't much time." Mutely Jahnel followed him through the portal, the vial clasped tightly in her hand.

❧ Chapter 15

AUSTIN WATCHED JAHNEL leave with Benoit, wondering exactly what had just happened. The Faon seemed to be in a ferment, with much bustling and conversation. He backed up to a wall to listen to the conversations he could catch and puzzled over Benoit's decision. Wasn't Koyil the Faon's enemy? Or were the Faon duty-bound in some way to walk into a stupid risk? Jahnel thought it stupid—he could tell that—but somehow Benoit had won by some Faon rule. He hadn't caught the Avelle word Jahnel had used to Benoit. He knew many Avelle words now, though with a few he only guessed at the meaning. I wish she had time to tell me things, he thought, watching the faces. I'm a little tired of getting parked.

Some of the Faon, mostly elders, seemed relaxed and at ease against all sense, though they said little among themselves. Philippe and two women moved from group to group, arguing, gesturing passionately. Nathalie and Jean made their own circuit, drifting in and out of the room to other Faon gathered in the hallway. Something is definitely going on, he thought. Will I ever understand this place?

Sair came through the doorway and looked around the room; his eyes met Austin's, and he wound his way through the gathered Faon to Austin's chosen vantage point. "Watching the ferment?" Sair asked in a low voice, his dark eyes unreadable. "So do we all."

"Why did she go?" Austin asked abruptly.

"An Avelle reason." Sair studied Austin's face for a moment, opened his mouth to speak, then turned away abruptly as he blinked against sudden tears, his mouth twisting harshly. Austin reached out his hand but stopped short of touching, then pulled

it back. Who am I to offer comfort? he thought. I don't belong
to this place; I don't belong to him—or her.

"It was an honorable reason, I'm sure," he offered awkwardly. "One that fits this place—and one that fits the Faon. I
don't know what it was, but I believe in Jahnel." He shrugged.
"I'm only a miin, Sair, but perhaps my believing counts as
something."

Sair looked at him askance, then dragged together his self-
control, quite raggedly; Austin hoped Sair felt no embarrassment to be so vulnerable before a miin. He looked down quickly
at his hands, not wanting to add to Sair's burden.

Sair recalled his attention by touching Austin's sleeve, a quick
touch barely felt and quickly gone. "Thank you, Greg," he said
quietly.

Austin looked up into Sair's face—and saw the acceptance
there, a smile in the eyes, a quiet strength that suddenly encom-
passed Austin within its protection. They were nearly the same
age, but Sair's life in Quevi Ltir had given him more than Austin's junior pilot's berth and its irrelevancies, more than one
defiant act as a youth that had cut instead of mended bonds. Yet
Sair now offered. Austin looked his surprise, startled by the
sudden understanding between them. Sair's smile deepened at
Austin's expression.

"In this place," he said musingly, "there is no sunlight, only
the lamps and the shadows between—and so we find our sunlight
in each other. Jahnel is my sun." He moved his shoulders
slightly. "I have other kindred, of course, other beloveds, but
. . . still. . . ."

"I know; I've seen it between you. I envy you, more than
you probably know." Now it was Austin's turn to flush and look
away. He heard Sair laugh low in his throat.

"You envy *me*? You have all the universe to explore in your
great ship, your worlds. We live narrowly, we Faon."

Austin met his eyes. "You think so? I don't agree."

"Indeed?" Sair seemed to laugh more at himself this time,
then turned away. "She said that you could understand. She
said—well, that's not important right now, I suppose. Rest
here for a time, kin-brother, while we wait." Austin watched
Sair move off, then vanish through the doorway. He doubted
Sair would rest, not until Jahnel returned safely, if she did.

He sat lumpily on his seat of parcels. Rest: sit and wait, Sair
had said. All Austin had done, it seemed, was sit or follow
around, with his very presence a risk to the Faon, his ship an

outright threat that Koyil used against them. He fretted, dissatisfied with himself. I don't like being a miin, he thought rebelliously.

Why had Jahnel given the microwave guide to that Avelle? He couldn't fathom why—nor had she bothered to explain, as usual—but probably she had an Avelle reason for that, too. Even so, he had to talk to *La Novia*, get some of the pressure off the Faon. He had to convince Boland somehow. He got to his feet and a bump from a passing Faon nudged him to the left; he continued the movement, drifting casually toward the rearward portal, then eyed the guard on watch. The Faon stared back impassively, his dark eyes gleaming in the shadows of the fallway.

Impossible, Austin told himself. The guy probably had fifteen eyes, and he had already seen Faon reflexes. He slumped back against the wall, discouraged.

Several minutes later, to his surprise, a number of younger Faon began drifting in his direction, laden with parcels and their children with them. He watched a group pass him and leave through the portal, right past the guard. Austin promptly attached himself to the next group, keeping his hood pulled closely around his face. He floated down with the Faon group, wondering where they were going. How could he explain this to Jahnel? He felt half-inclined to turn around and find Sair, but kept going down, keeping his face concealed. The Faon, now a steady stream from the portal above, drifted down the narrow fallway, bunched momentarily at the intersection with the lower levels, then slipped downward, retracing the path the exploration party had taken earlier. They're evacuating to the underlevels, he realized. His nape tingled at the implications.

Who had decided this? Why didn't they wait for the parley? What *is* going on?

At the narrow portal into the underlevels, the Faon slipped one by one into the vast chamber beyond. Without hurry, two Faon proceeded to drill a wide portal on the other side of the sealed door to pass through equipment. No one spoke, not even the children. Austin edged forward with the line and then followed the Faon woman ahead of him through the portal. On the other side, he quickly sideslipped to the left, moving deep into the shadows. As he edged backward, he watched the Faon go the other way, seeking out the refuge by the power rooms. He hesitated, not sure at all of his next action. He had thought to rummage in the storeroom for more communicator makings, but he would never get past the inevitable inquiry, certainly never be permitted to leave the area. With a whispered curse, he turned and plunged backward into the darkness, heading for the long tunnel he and Jahnel had taken before.

Fifteen minutes later, he slowed as he approached the end of the tunnel, then crept as quietly as he could, using friction off one side to propel himself slowly. He edged up to look cautiously into the cavern, studying the shadows, then lofted himself over the edge and sank slowly toward the floor a dozen meters below, his eyes alert. Nothing moved in the chamber. In the far end of ship cavern, *Quevi'ali* stood glinting, but Austin's object was *Phalene*, if he could get inside. Had the Avelle rigged another "light alarm"? If they had, his goose was truly cooked.

Not much time, Greg, he told himself. Make it count.

A single light shed some illumination into the cavern from the wide access portal set midway up the wall. He could hear the humming of machines through the portal, though at a distance, like some great highway. The air had a warm and silky touch, moving in a steady current from the doorway to cycle through the ship cavern. He touched ground on the metal floor and moved slowly along it, keeping an eye on the portal above and anything that might await him in the shadowed corners. He passed machine housings and thought nervously of mobile robots. Jahnel had shown an awed fear of the ships, but it seemed more a taboo to her, not physical threat. Maybe: he watched shadows, anyway. But why had she feared this place? And what had that Avelle told her?

He looked at *Quevi'ali* and its sleek menace, the lofting stabilizers reminiscent of an Avelle in flight, the squat power of its nose-tip weapons. A magnificent ship—a ship that said even more about the Avelle than their complicated City. Predator ship, she had said. Who were they, these aliens? He felt another longing to know, to know them as Jahnel did. He doubted he would get the chance, not now. Both Avelle and Faon alike would think his presence here a treachery to the Home-Space—and punish instantly.

He stopped in the shadow of a machine and took a deep breath. You could go back; nobody knows you're here—yet. He thought about that, then shrugged it off and moved on. It didn't matter—he would give the Faon this one extra chance, if he could. He approached *Phalene*'s air lock at an angle, using a series of banked machines as cover, then paused behind the last hulking machine to study the thirty meters ahead to *Phalene*'s hull. He could see the hull damage from this vantage—great ripping scores across the upper third, a badly wrecked engine module, a twisted spidernet of meteor screening. He was surprised that the ship had managed to limp in-system with that kind of damage. *Phalene* herself told of the Faon's beginnings— and how they had arisen from literal disaster. He circled cautiously, trying to get the ship between him and the doorway above his head, alert and on his toes about being seen—if anyone was here to see.

Near the ruined engine module, he saw the outline of the service hatch and headed toward it, crossing the last dozen meters in a quick rush. He opened the control panel and peered at the dials, then checked above and below again before risking a quick flash of his belt light. He studied the image of the control-panel interior in his memory, trying to match it to what he knew of ship systems. Different, but he could recognize part of the pattern—some things in ship design didn't change much when they worked. He cautiously reached within, touching the buttons lightly, finding their arrangement and matching them to the words he had recognized. He pushed one button hard and waited.

A narrow crack appeared along one side of the service hatch, then widened with a squealing sound that echoed through the dark cavern. Austin shrank against the cool metal hull, his heart pounding as he waited, half expecting a swooping shadow from above, talons outstretched. After several minutes, he moved again and looked inside the narrow accessway, reaching upward into the darkness for the wheel and lever that should be there. He pulled himself into the hatch, then rotated the lever and pushed. The hatch sprang open, raining rust particles into his upturned face. He muttered a curse and brushed his eyes and mouth, then entered the ship, closing the inner hatch behind him.

He turned on his belt light and found himself in a cannibalized engine room. Coils, disemboweled machines, engine panels with covers stacked to the side—someone had disassembled *Phalene*'s engines almost down to the bolts. He picked his way through the debris to the ladder across the room and propelled himself quickly up the rungs to the next level. The comm station should be in Command, traditionally in the nose of the ship. He stayed on the ladder, rising through level after level. Some levels had been torn apart, others less interesting left largely intact. Whatever damage *Phalene* had suffered in her accident, some-one—probably the Avelle—had completed the job of making her a total wreck. To be spaceworthy, she would need a complete refit, so much so that any Earth dockside chief would argue starting anew from hull inward.

He reached the uppermost level and pulled himself out of the ladder-well, touching down lightly. His heart sank as he saw the ransacked condition of the room. Did the Faon even know that the Avelle had done this to their ship? Would they protest if they knew? Perhaps they had paid the Avelle with *Phalene* and had given up any claim to it. He looked around in the glare of his lamp, then noticed a single burning light far off to the left. He craned his head, trying to track on that greenish gleam. He picked his way through the debris, losing sight of it, then catching it again as he circled the middle control consoles. He reached a narrow door open several inches; beyond it, he saw a telltale burning on a small console. He put his thumbs in his belt and studied that light, then ran his gaze around the edges of the doorway, looking for a tripwire, anything that might spring this too-obvious trap.

Trap? Or opportunity?

Kiiri, she had called him, Science Leader. Likely he knew this ship from top to bottom. And she had trusted him, enough to drop their plan without a look back, even giving Kiiri the microwave guide when he asked. Why?

How in the devil did Kiiri know I would come here? he thought in frustration. And what did he expect me to do? And what's smart—to do it or not?

He reached out a hand tentatively, then pulled it back and studied the doorway edges again. No help for it—he had come this far. He put his hand on the edge of the metal barrier and eased it backward, giving him room enough to enter. No electric shock, no alarm bells. The small light burned onward, beckoning. He stepped into the small room and looked around. Barely two meters wide, it was obviously a workstation—radio comm, he decided. What else?

How did Kiiri know?

He sat down at the console and put his belt lamp on the top ledge, then studied the array of dials and buttons on the tilted panel. Recognizable French words, amp and frequency dials, everything, including a small light over the power signal. He smiled grimly and snapped a tilt-lever with a finger. "Signal on," he muttered. "Radio Faon on the air."

He adjusted the frequency dial to *La Novia*'s main channel

and heard a squawl of static, then spotted the hand mike on its cord reel. The mike pulled out with a whirring sound.

"Austin calling *La Novia*. Come in, *La Novia*."

That committed him. Right now several thousand Avelle, Austin advised himself, are rushing toward you, laser robots in the vanguard. The radio crackled badly with static as he pushed the receive button—dust in the receiver, probably. Kiiri could use a good maintenance manual. "Calling *La Novia*."

"*La Novia* here," the speaker blatted, making him jump. He hastily dialed down the audio. "Who is that?" the voice demanded.

"Gregory Austin. I want to talk to Commander Boland—right away. I don't have much time."

"He's asleep."

"Well, wake him up, you idiot! This City is about to explode into open war and maybe explode you, too. Wake him up!"

He heard a mutter and open static, then Elena's breathless voice. "Greg? Are you all right?"

"I'm fine. Are you still having nice chats with Koyil? Somehow I guess you're not. Jahnel blew up the Downlift and the timing would be interesting." Her surprised silence was all the answer he needed. "I thought so; Koyil is calling the Faon to a parley, so who needs you anymore? He's playing you for a fool, Elena, using us as a way to stir up the City and rearrange a few things down here."

"He said he wanted Contact!"

"I guess it's not against the law down here, ho-ho, to tell outrageous lies, especially when you *are* the law. Get it? Where's Boland?"

"Coming."

"I probably don't have time to wait. You have to get *La Novia* out of this star system, Elena. Do you understand? You *have* to or everything down here is going to explode. I'm not drugged, I'm not conditioned, and I'm not wrong. The Avelle are territorial predators to the nth degree—they live, eat, breed, think territory. Just being up there is pressuring them into hysteria, and Koyil is using it against the Faon. Get out of here."

"But—"

"No buts." He jerked as he heard a clang far beneath him. "They're coming. *Leave*, Elena! Austin out." He snapped off the mike and hastily powered down, extinguishing the radio link. Then he was out of his chair and out of the small room, circling the middle consoles. He heard more noises below, a scurrying and a sharp clang. He looked wildly around him and realized he had nowhere to go. Well, you knew it, Greg. You knew it all along. He backed up to the wall and looked vainly among the wreckage for a length of iron, something heavy.

A dark shape shot up through the ladder-well opening and hovered in front of him, wing-flaps spread. It hissed at him as it hovered, red eyes glinting, then drifted slowly forward. Austin dodged to the right as it pounced, but it caught him easily. He struggled wildly, striking out at the huge alien, then froze as it poised a taloned hand directly over his throat.

The Avelle said something Austin didn't understand, but the meaning of the words wasn't hard to guess. He stared at the taloned hand with horrified fascination, as if poison already dripped from the claws. His stare seemed to please the Avelle; he clucked to himself and tucked Austin close to his hard side, then flashed backward, arrowing down the ladder-well at dizzying speed. Within seconds, they had swept out of the ship and climbed effortlessly toward the cavern exit. Austin closed his eyes helplessly as they swept over the chamber threshold, narrowly missing the door-rim by a scant wing-tip, then looked again, exhilarated despite his terror, as the alien accelerated into the fallway beyond. With great sweeps of its wing-flaps, the Avelle soared into the City's principal fallway, the inscribed walls flickering by in a blur.

So incredibly fast: Austin blinked against the rush of the blood-warm air, then craned to look ahead, only to get his neck wrenched as his head was pushed back against the alien body. He inhaled the odd smell of the Avelle's skin, overwhelmed by it. The muscles of the segmented body moved smoothly, supporting the rapid beat of the wing-flaps, an exquisite grace of movement he had never imagined possible. To fly like this! To move like this without a ship! Half suffocated by the Avelle's grip, he panted for breath, hyperventilating. The Avelle noticed it and loosened his hold slightly, a solicitude Austin found encouraging. But, then, if the Avelle intended to kill him, he would have done it already.

"Where are we going?" Austin ventured, then flinched as the Avelle threatened him again with a taloned claw. "Uh, never mind."

The Avelle's eyes flashed redly, but he withdrew the claw. They accelerated once again, soared at a prudent distance around a group of Avelle sculling placidly down the middle of the wide avenue, then dashed through another group, parting it like a scythe through grain. Austin looked back at the scramble left behind them, bemused. Hell, who needs flight rules? He'd hate to be a traffic cop in this place.

As they darted around another clump of Avelle, Austin peered backward again, trying to see any obvious reason why they were spared the scythe treatment. The Avelle squeezed Austin more tightly in response to his movement, hard enough to make Austin's ribs creak. Austin squirmed in his grip, then poked at the muscled chest. "Hey! Ease it up a little."

The guard raised his claw. "One more word, Faon," he declared in rather decent French, "and I'll slash you to shreds." His large eyes flashed again. "You dishonor me with your Faon filth-talk. Speak Avelle or don't speak at all!"

"But . . ." As the alien's eyes flashed warningly, Austin shut up. Weed-face, he thought angrily. How can I speak a language I don't even know? And since when is French an insult?

His irritation stopped abruptly. The guard had called him Faon. He looked down at his aal. Well, of course: if it looks and talks like a Faon, it must be a . . . Maybe Elena hadn't told Koyil that Austin was in the City. Or maybe Koyil knew but had not told his guards. But maybe, in the chance, he could somehow avoid hurting the Faon. Maybe.

The Avelle turned abruptly, wrenching Austin after him in another wide swoop across the fallway, accelerating even more. Wherever they were going, it would be over soon.

Jahnel followed her father and the others—his councilmen and two Hiboux guards—through the lower levels to Lejja's tier, then rose with them past the many familiar levels. Avelle gathered at each platform to watch the Faon pass, but without friendly gesture. She saw the tension in their coiled bodies, the glitter of their deep-set eyes. She let the others get slightly ahead and palmed a set of battle drugs into her mouth, then casually closed the gap again. Celeste turned to look at her, then drifted downward to Jahnel's side.

"Jahnel . . ."

"I am here, Councilor, as obedience demands."

"But why do you doubt?" Celeste's blue eyes were deeply troubled. "Surely Koyil would not . . ."

"Because we wish it too much, Celeste—and Koyil knows we would wish earnestly. As long as we are predictable, we play his game, not ours."

Celeste looked thoughtful. "Yes, I do wish, very much."

"So do I." Jahnel smiled gently at the older woman and touched her hand. "Perhaps Benoit is right. Let us wish for that, Celeste."

They passed through the high gate and turned into the principal fallway of the City, making a stately progress between the tiers. The Principals' Council Chamber was sited in neutral space at the base of the fourth upward tier, although Koyil owned that fourth tier through breeding bonds as well as the tiers on either side, one of them his own birth-tier. Only custom ensured Lejja's safety among such numbers when she came to Council; the other Principals had similar disadvantage, but Koyil himself had disadvantage as keeper of the very Laws that protected his rivals. Of all the spaces in Quevi Ltir, the Principals' Council Chamber was truly neutral space. Benoit counted on that, Jahnel knew; she also knew Koyil had already bent his laws to maneuver against the Faon, a fact her father chose to ignore. She felt the battle drugs begin to course through her body, elevating heartbeat and reaction time, sharpening vision, impelling her to violence.

Strengthen me, O Songs, she prayed, for the sake of those I love.

They soared into the Fourth Tier and entered the Council Chamber, Benoit leading, the others arranged by rank order. Jahnel herself took last place between the guards, demanding nothing. As one, the Faon drifted downward and bounced slightly as they touched the floor, facing the Avelle gathered there.

A hundred Avelle ringed the room, wing-flaps wrapped tightly around their bodies, every eye upon the Faon. Immediately before them on a low bench reclined the Principals, as tightly controlled, as silent and still, as the others near the wall. Benoit took a step forward and gestured deep respect.

"The Faon have come," he announced in a clear strong voice, "at the Principals' bidding and in kin-loyalty to Lejja, Principal of Songs." He bowed courteously to Lejja at one end of the bench. "We have come to parley, to the easement of kin-alliance struggles, to the peace and order of all things." He straightened and waited expectantly.

Jahnel had seen each of the Principals many times on the City-Net, but had never herself come to Council; even Benoit had been summoned only once in twenty years. Next to Lejja to the left reclined Suuryan, Principal of Mind, gray-skinned from his long-standing addiction to mind-enhancing chemicals;

beside him sat Koyil, vigorous in his maturity, malignant in his hatreds. To Koyil's left, Kiiri reclined lazily, his eyes hooded, flanked by a smaller Avelle, Pakal, who blinked constantly. At the end of the bench, Niintua's seat-flap remained empty, either a position still unfilled or pointed reproof to the Faon, probably both. All the Principals sat unmoving, saying nothing as they stared at Benoit.

After a silence, Lejja stirred weakly, her wing-flaps falling open as if she lacked the strength to wrap them about her; Jahnel saw her eyelids sag as her head drooped. Her visible decline pained Jahnel, as it had before, only this time the alertness did not return to that old frame, the eyes did not ignite. Lejja shifted her body fretfully, then lapsed back into immobility. Jahnel caught the glint of triumph, quickly masked, in Koyil's clever eyes.

The pause lengthened to uncomfortable silence. Finally, Suuryan forcibly nudged Lejja. She sat up with a start, then rose gracefully, swaying only slightly. "I see the Faon and welcome my kinsmen," she said in a wavering voice. "I am Lejja, Principal of Songs, and I welcome their Song." She sank back onto the cushion, panting a little. Benoit bowed again.

"I am Suuryam, Principal of Mind, and say not."

Jahnel immediately sensed the wave of tension among the Avelle ringing the hall. These were each kin-leaders of rank and position in their own tiers, a weight of authority and knowledge, of craft and strength, that supported the kin-alliances of the City, all Principals in the making. They know something, she thought, scanning the room. Since when does Suuryam's alliance with Koyil cause a stir like this?

Koyil rose in his turn. "I am Koyil, Principal of Laws, and make challenge."

Kiiri rose before Koyil could even resume his seat. "I am Kiiri, Science Leader," he called out in a voice that echoed throughout the chamber, "and I defend Lejja and all the Faon." He turned to Pakal and glared at him.

"The Star Leader also," Pakal muttered.

"Also *what*, Pakal?" Koyil barked.

Pakal lifted his head and stared back at both Koyil and Kiiri. "Also—only that." He sent a defiant glare at Kiiri. Kiiri slowly sat down, for once his dismay apparent. Jahnel calmly palmed her vial of battle drugs to the Hiboux on her right.

"Be ready," she whispered. He gave her a startled look, then arranged a small cough seconds later. The vial passed back to

Jahnel and to the other Hiboux guard, then forward to Arnaud. Jahnel tightened her lips as Arnaud firmly pocketed the vial, stopping the exchange. That stubbornness may kill you, Councilor, she thought, her own blood pounding in her ears with the urgency of the drugs. Soon—it would come soon. "Save Celeste—if you can," she whispered to the Hiboux.

The answer was barely more than a breath. "Yes."

Koyil rose slowly, his wing-flaps pulled tightly against his body. With magnificent dignity, he turned to face each part of the huge chamber, returning at last to face Benoit. "The challenge is unanswered," he intoned. "The Law requires—"

"The vote is even!" Kiiri corrected sharply. "When the Principals are evenly divided, Law cannot act; you must preserve what is."

"I see only five Principals," Koyil said silkily. "How can our vote be even?"

Kiiri flipped a wing-tip with a word rarely offered to a Principal, especially the Principal of Laws. "Quibble as you will, Koyil. Pakal refuses to vote—and that divides us evenly, two against two. You cannot act."

"The Faon murdered Niintua, the Battle Leader!"

"His guard attacked one of their nestlings—the defense was justified. You cannot act!"

"The Faon failed to drive away the miin!"

"So have you," Kiiri retorted. "Why are the greater surface weapons inoperative, Koyil? Look to your own failings first before you judge others. You cannot act!"

"Can I not?" Koyil sneered. "Bring in the prisoner!"

A tier guard swooped in through the doorway and dropped Austin unceremoniously from several wing-heights up. Austin sprawled on the floor, unhurt, then clambered uneasily to his feet. Jahnel saw Benoit's head turn toward him, his face utterly stricken. Claim him as Faon, Father, she wished him urgently. Deny he is miin. Play the game as it should be played!

"And who is this?" Koyil drawled, his eyes glinting. He advanced on Austin, who had the good sense to not cringe away. "Dressed in Faon clothes, yet talking to the invaders of our Home-Space from *Phalene*—your ship, Faon."

"As you have talked to miin, Koyil!" Benoit declared angrily. Jahnel closed her eyes, appalled. Predictable—it was predictable. You have studied us well, Koyil, especially my father.

Koyil drew himself up in outrage, his wing-flaps flaring. "I? I talk to intruders. You insult the Law? *You* are intruder!" His finger jabbed out, not at Austin, but at Benoit. "Intruder! I summon the Law to defend us! I summon the tiers to defend us! Even now Kaali has discovered invaders in her tier, an invasion without cause, without law . . ." Shouts drowned out Koyil's denunciations as the Avelle ringing the walls reacted, some in support, some in contention, a wild confusion as kin-leaders left their proper places and surged forward into the room.

"*Now!*" Jahnel cried and launched herself at Austin, dragging him after her as she flung herself past Koyil. For a startled moment, the Avelle did nothing, giving her just enough time to escape out the chamber doorway, the two Hiboux and Celeste close on her heels. Flying in a close phalanx, the four Faon soared into the main fallway and accelerated to reckless speed, missing startled Avelle by inches. She heard a cry behind them and dared to look back, then groaned as she saw Benoit and Arnaud floundering in midair, struck aside by the Avelle pouring out of the Council Chamber. Other Avelle mobbed them instantly, tearing the two Faon to ribbons.

"No!" Jahnel cried out, and heard a cry of dismay from Celeste.

"Benoit!" The older woman slowed, though she could do nothing for those lost.

"Come on!" Jahnel called tightly, and grabbed at Celeste's sleeve, impelling her onward. "We go down the next fallway at full belt speed. Better to hit wall than suffer that. Hold on, Austin. Faon, invert!"

They made a rapid turn down a vertical fallway and fell, accelerating faster and faster, the walls flickering past in a dizzying pattern. The battle drugs erased anguish, erased fear, impelling Jahnel to their imperative of violence. She hurtled down the fallway, her hands curved into talons to attack any who blocked her way, the other Faon closely behind her. Beneath them, alerted by the harsh cries of their pursuers, the Avelle in the fallway scattered out of their path.

"Yaaaaaaa," Jahnel screamed, adding her battle cry to the Avelle's confusion, her companions screaming with her. A tier guard launched at them and missed, then another nearly caught Celeste. The older woman struck out as she flashed by the Avelle, raking the guard's face with her fingernails, then flipped herself aside neatly. Together, the Hiboux closely behind, Celeste and Jahnel plunged down the rest of the fallway, inverting in a flash to brake at the last instant, and emerged into the lower levels into the midst of a pitched Avelle battle. Jahnel swerved, then dashed into the whirl of darting, struggling bodies. Behind them, Koyil's pursuers crashed into the midst of it, attacked instantly by every Avelle within reach.

Jahnel dodged among the fighting Avelle, her breath coming raggedly. Austin held on for dear life, knowing it was his life, their lives, trying awkwardly to guess her next invert and not unbalance her as she twisted and turned. "Hold on, Austin!" An Avelle lunged at them from above, hissing, his wing-flaps spread. Jahnel darted aside, nearly colliding with Celeste, then snatched at the older woman, pulling her out of range of a slashing claw.

"We can't make it, Jahnel!" Celeste cried.

"We must! This way!" They surged off in another direction, only to dodge again seconds later. Behind them, one of the Hiboux was caught and disemboweled with a single blow. He screamed, a thin agonized cry, then spun away downward.

"Let me go. Save yourself!" Austin yelled at Jahnel over the din.

"Shut up!" she shouted back. They plunged through an access portal to the level below, reckless of any traffic coming upward, and fled sideways through the succession of large rooms. A murmuring ahead warned them of another pitched battle before the sealed doors to the underlevels. Jahnel kept on speeding ahead, heading straight for it, her two companions at her heels.

"Arrow down," she called aloud. "Crash-field left and down."

"Right with you," the Hiboux cried back. "Counting to invert . . . one, two, three . . ." Ahead, Jahnel saw a square doorway with bulking shadows within, flashing across the limited view, black on white. Jahnel accelerated still more. "Four . . . five!"

They flashed through the doorway and inverted as one, hitting an Avelle mid-body at nearly thirty klicks with their booted feet. The Avelle screamed and spun away, crashing into several others. With the recoil, the Faon flipped themselves aside as another Avelle lunged at them and collided with an Avelle on intercept course. The room turned into chaos as every Avelle responded by attacking whatever moved beside them. Jahnel fended one off by flipping her aal cape into its face and dodged across the room toward the port.

A laser cracked through the air, burning Avelle flesh, then cracking again, clearing a path through the flashing, screaming bodies. Jahnel swooped toward the portal; as she slipped through the narrow hole, a shadow ahead dodged aside, clearing the way. One, two, three—all through, and Eduard sprang back into place to shoot his laser-bolts into the room beyond. Jahnel soared outward into the wide cavern and switched off her belt jet, coasting outward a hundred meters into open air.

"Welcome, Austin," she said, panting, "to Quevi Ltir. *That* was a tier war."

"Thank you for saving me—again."

"I owed you the debt of Luelle's life," she said simply. She rotated in place, still drifting outward, to see her companions. Celeste was cradling her arm gingerly, but the slash looked minor; the other Hiboux seemed untouched. Jahnel released Austin and spread her arms wide; quickly Celeste and the Hiboux embraced her, all amazed to be alive. Several other Faon came out from their positions by the cavern walls, surrounding them.

"Papa Benoit?" Melinde asked tightly.

"We lost him, Melinde," Jahnel answered, and saw tears spring into Melinde's eyes. They looked at each other in anguish, for one moment bonded again. "Arnaud, too."

"I grieve for them, too," Philippe said harshly, his dark eyes flashing. "We will be revenged!"

Jahnel closed her eyes wearily, too winded to deal with Philippe now; her heart pounded frantically as the battle drugs still stressed her system. She took three sharp breaths and relaxed loosely, following battle drill, drifting as she rested. Philippe began to blat again, and Celeste shut him up with a single vivid word.

"I'm tired of you, Philippe," she said contemptuously. "Take yourself away."

Philippe gave Celeste a nasty smile and swerved away toward the power room. Jahnel watched him go for a moment, then dismissed him with a shrug. She caught at Melinde's arm as her sister-wife made to follow him.

"What happened here, Melinde?"

Melinde's mouth twisted uglily. "Kaali's tier guards attacked as we crossed the lower levels; you were right, Jahnel—Koyil knew exactly where we were. The noise brought down soldiers from the next tier and started a war. Some of our vayalim were cut off and trapped in the tier."

"How many did we lose?" Celeste asked quietly.

"Who knows? Sair is counting now." Melinde made a short chopping gesture, her narrow face distorted as her grief changed to a blinding rage. "The Avelle must pay. They will pay for this—promise me, Jahnel."

"Melinde . . ."

"Promise me!" When Jahnel said nothing, she darted away, plunging after Philippe.

Celeste shook her head. "I'll talk to her, Jahnel."

"If you would, Celeste," Jahnel said heavily. "Thank you. Lately I haven't found much to offer her, at least nothing that makes a difference." She signed at Celeste and other Faon, bidding them toward the lighted safety of the power room, then watched them move off.

"I believe in you," Austin said quietly from behind her. "Whatever you choose to do, I believe, Jahnel."

She turned to him, surprised. He regarded her soberly, his brown face further shadowed by the darkness, a question in his eyes. Impulsively, she reached to touch him in thanks and found herself pulled against him roughly, his lips on hers with a strange urgency. For an instant she thought of resisting, then relaxed against him, surrendering to his embrace for a long moment. Then he pushed her away from him, looking elsewhere.

"I'm sorry," he muttered.

"For what?"

He looked surprised in his own turn. "You're a married woman, Jahnel."

"Overmarried, as you have commented," she said drolly.

"But—oh, hell, I don't understand this place at all. Aren't you offended?"

"Not in the least."

"Would Sair be offended?" he asked then, quite uncomfortably. A slow flush crept upward from his collar line as he visibly squirmed.

Austin worried about the oddest things, she thought, amused; she couldn't resist teasing. "I don't know. Why don't you ask him?"

Stark horror crossed Austin's brown face, making her laugh outright. He scowled, then pulled himself up into dignity, posing for her. "I'll skip that for a while, thank you."

"I'm not offended, Austin," she reassured him.

"Well, uh . . . good." He laughed then, too, probably at himself. It had a nice sound, she thought, liking this miin more than she had ever expected. She touched his sleeve.

"Thank you for your loyalty—and the compliment. Did you talk to your ship again?"

"Yes, but I don't know what they'll do. That Avelle guard showed up too fast." He gestured awkwardly. "I'm sorry I messed things up at the Council by getting caught. I'm sorry about your father."

She sighed, and gestured her thanks. "Koyil had his counters neatly arranged; I suspect you were only an unexpected boon. One way or another, it would have ended as it did." She grimaced. "It was predictable."

She looked away from him toward the cavern wall, then turned to the lighted portal of the power room. Benoit had bid her find this place, then had gone to the Council thinking it unneeded, believing in the pattern he had lived all his life. Now we will never have peace with each other, she thought sadly, grieving for him; now he will never know if he was right or wrong in withholding his naming of me. We ran out of time.

Eduard had sealed the accessway, and he and other Faon on guard now slowly dispersed along the cavern wall, watching for any new drilling by the furious Avelle beyond. Their holding might not last for long, but for the moment it brought a kind of safety. How long can we hold this place, here at the end of things? she wondered.

Austin shuddered in the cold darkness, caught by the chill. She touched his hand. "Come," she said. "It is cold and grows colder." Together they moved across the abyss toward the lighted doorway.

We will do our best, Father, she promised silently. Perhaps you wouldn't approve of what I do; perhaps you were right all along about me—but I will try, too, for the sake of all you loved, all that I love still.

℞ Chapter 16

JAHNEL LOOKED FIRST for Sair, worried about all her family. She found him inside an inner room, supervising the assembly of a heating unit. He turned as she neared him and swept her into an embrace.

"How many did we lose?" she asked.

"Eighteen, including three children. None from our vayalim, though Evan has a bad slash. Kaali's tier guards saw us crossing the fallway and attacked; Evan went back to help and got into the midst of it."

"Where's Melinde?"

"With Philippe," he said sourly. "Where else?"

"Be patient with her, Sair—please."

Sair shrugged tiredly. "I'll try—though it's getting harder the more she emotes." He looked around the small room and at the Faon busy at the heating unit. "Well, we're here now. We can hold off the Avelle at the sealed doorways for a while, but they'll eventually come across the gulf from the ship tunnel. We can't survive a long seige—we don't have enough food with us."

"How long a seige?"

"Several days maybe. Aside from the tunnel to the ship cavern, there are no other doors into this power complex and we can hold the main door indefinitely—until we run out of food or they try atomics."

"This close to the reactor? The Avelle aren't stupid, Sair."

"True." He shrugged again. "Where's your father? He'll need to be informed." He saw her expression and sighed. "So it's true. Melinde is demanding vengeance; she's not the only one. Jean has figured out the symbols for the power banks, knows what connects to what. Philippe wants to shut down power to Koyil's tier, maybe others."

220

Jahnel twisted her mouth. "We don't dare. If we take violent action of any significance, the Avelle will respond in force. The tiers have eight thousand guards to throw at us through the ship-cavern tunnel."

"They wouldn't empty the tiers," he protested.

"If we present mortal threat? Without power, the ventilators won't work, the heaters won't work. You've got atmosphere imbalance within an hour, cooling within two. Several hours of that and the brood chambers could have fifty percent mortality. You know how fragile newborn Avelle can be, especially with inbred bloodlines. Of course they'll attack. They're *Avelle*, Sair. They prefer to die rather than be defeated, especially with their broods at risk."

He grunted. "I hadn't appreciated that. Your Austin is contagious; I've begun to think too much like a human."

"He's not *my* Austin."

"Actually, I rather like him," Sair said absently. "So what do you suggest, my love and Principal?"

"I'm not Principal, either," she said tiredly.

"Oh?" He smiled at her. "Nathalie thinks otherwise; so do other kin-leaders. You can't avoid it, Jahnel. Even with the loud talk among our firebrands, the vote is rather obvious. You're Benoit's obvious heir, despite his prideful refusals; that's one point. More importantly, you're Kiiri's protégée—we need a link to the Avelle, like Benoit had with Lejja. You brought Austin into the City against opposition; you ordered the right retreats. Wisdom in retrospect is a mark of a Principal."

She made a rude sound. He ignored it, intent on making his point. "So you need a plan." He looked at her expectantly.

"Plan?" She looked back at him, then tried to cudgel her tired brains. Finding no help in his face, she looked beyond him through the doorway at the tall power panels, the groups of Faon gathered in the corners—and saw their covert attention on herself and Sair. He's right, she realized. They will look to me. She felt a sudden panic. "Help me think, Sair. What is the essence of a Principal?"

"Treachery for advantage."

"Be constructive, please. One Principal's treachery is another's deft move; it's a question of point of view. What is the essence?"

He thought a moment. "Applied strength—at the right time."

"Right. And what is our strength as Faon?"

"Holding those power panels."

She shook her head. "The power panels are neutral, both strength and disaster, depending on how we use them. We, as Faon and human, what is our strength? We are not predictable, Sair. Kiiri told me that; Austin has proved it—humans can think in different patterns. We can do things the Avelle would never expect." She glanced around for Austin and saw him lingering by one of the power panels, looking rather forlorn. "That was Lejja's strength, acting outside the usual pattern and then springing her trap with the surprise. She rescued *Phalene* and used it; when we abandoned our tiers, she used that. Nerup would respond the same, I think."

"You lost me somewhere in there."

Jahnel took a deep breath, then set her jaw. "I want to meet with the kin-leaders—no, everyone, including the firebrands. And Austin, too. In this we cannot be Avelle and merely gather to hear a Leader's decision; we must all decide when all lives hang in the balance. Can you arrange that?"

"Of course."

She laid her palm on his face, then smiled as he turned his head to kiss it.

"I'll go find the kin-leaders," he said.

He moved away quickly and signed to Jean and Nathalie. After a few hurried words, the three divided and disappeared into separate doorways. Jahnel drifted across the room to Austin. He brightened slightly as she came up to him, then resumed his worried frown.

"This is not a good tactical situation," he said. "Though perhaps I'm looking at it wrong again."

"In this case, you're right." She turned to look at the tall panels. "Do you know machines like this?"

"Reactor pile?"

"And power systems. Some wish to shut down power to a few sample tiers."

"Your Avelle wouldn't like that."

"Right again, more than you know. If we asked, Austin, could you overload these panels, like I overloaded the dis-rifle?"

"You mean blow up the City?" He stared at her, eyes widening.

"Yes—if I asked."

"I could." He frowned. "I'm not sure I would—if you asked."

"Believe me, if we ask, overload might be the preferable choice. When we passed down through the tier war, most of the

Avelle were focused on each other as their kin-alliances collided unexpectedly. Down here they would all focus only on us. And after they had torn us to pieces, they would return above to their tiers, resume their lives, and erase us from their Songs. Koyil will eventually repair his distance machines and blast *La Novia* out of our skies, and there will be peace. A fine goal, worthy of a few hundred servant lives." She shrugged.

"That's obscene!"

"Not in Avelle terms, Austin. Kiiri says the real Predator wars, the ones with ships, are far worse—and these Avelle are descended from that stock. It is their strength, that ferocity, that one-mindedness. Once you understand that need and see beyond it, you see what they preserve with it. When we humans have maintained a technological civilization for twenty thousand years, perhaps then we can comment and make judgments. No?"

"Humans have other options. Better ones."

"Different ones, not necessarily better." He scowled.

"Are you really going to blow us up? How can you kill ten thousand beings just for revenge?"

"Ah, now you worry about the Avelle. No, Austin, I won't—not while I have the choosing. I don't wish to punish Quevi Ltir—I'm not *that* Avelle. But I needed to know if you could make an overload: the Avelle are good at discerning truth in us, especially the Principals. In this City, knowing truth sometimes means living a while longer."

Faon were emerging steadily from the inner rooms and arranging themselves by kin-group, murmuring among themselves. Jahnel saw Melinde among the Louve, talking earnestly to the senior husband of another vayalim, Evan by her side. Solveya brought in Didier, accompanied by Luelle and Aunt Francoise. Her aunt kissed Luelle and settled her beside Solveya, then left to join her own vayalim. My beloveds, she thought, watching them all. What is wisdom? The last Faon issued from the inner doorways, joining with a few others returning from guard duty on the cavern wall. Jahnel drifted down the tall panel complex to the center of it, then balanced lightly as the asteroid's gravity pulled her slowly to the room floor. When all eyes looked at her expectantly, she raised her hand for attention, remembering with a pang her father's own gesture.

"Faon, I present a choice to be made. Will you hear?"

To the left near the rear, Jahnel saw Melinde join Philippe and his cohort, their anger visible in their faces. All of that group

stood apart from their kin-groups, not caring if Etoile or Hiboux
or Louve; this crisis had brought other divisions in other families. When we have time—if we have time, she thought, looking
at Melinde—perhaps we can mend our bonds. She waited until
the room fell completely silent.

"I am Jahnel Alain of the Louve. You all know that the Faon
Leader is dead, killed at Koyil's Council when the Avelle betrayed us. Others have died this day. We have a choice, Faon:
an attempt at life, or a means of sure death. That is the shape of
it. Will you hear?"

"Who are you to speak for the Faon?" Philippe called out,
his voice harsh. "Benoit never named you heir, Jahnel."

"Who are you," she shot back, "to stand apart from your
kin-group? Who are those who stand with you, denying kin-
bond?" She looked away from him to other faces. "He never
named me heir, my kindred—but we have no time for orderly
changes. Change is upon us, like an attack from the heights. So
I speak for myself, Jahnel of the Louve, and ask you to listen."

She stopped and waited for any other challenges. The room
was silent, every eye upon her. Jahnel took a deep breath and
began.

"I sing a Song of the Faon, my kindred. Eighty years ago
Phalene came to Quevi Ltir, rescued against all reason by a
Principal for reasons of her own. To us she gave Home-Space;
to us she gave her strength and protected us from malice that
wished our deaths. Human we were; Faon we became. But now,
my beloveds, we must remember we were human. In that is our
strength." She took another breath and squared her shoulders.
"If we were Avelle, we would choose as Avelle choose: on the
brink of defeat, to lash out and destroy this City as it destroys
us. We control the City's reactors; we have the means. I know
that has been discussed." She shot a look at Philippe and Melinde. "But I argue for another way: a human way. To destroy
Quevi Ltir, we destroy Lejja, our Mother. To destroy Quevi Ltir,
we destroy her Avelle kin-alliance, our Avelle brothers. We destroy to no purpose except our revenge—and I say we, as human
and Faon, cannot do such an evil."

"So we calmly allow our own destruction?" Jean asked from
the Hiboux, his face flushing.

Jahnel smiled. "No. We do another thing, something both
human and Avelle. We play as Principals play, and use our human unpredictability as a weapon." She raised her hand to still
a murmur of confusion.

"You've learned from Kiiri too well," Jean grumped. "You speak in riddles."

Jahnel grinned at him. "Let us bond again, Faon, to Lejja's tier. Let us put ourselves in Nerup's hands as a weapon, a knife she must wield carefully lest it bite her, too. Let us threaten destruction and use the doubt to trouble Koyil."

"Nerup?" Nathalie asked, her eyes thoughtful.

"I want to be Faon," Jahnel said. "I want a place in this City with the Avelle, a place of kinship and shadows, of warmth and safety. We should talk to Nerup." She raised her hand again as a murmuring spread through the room. "And I have another weapon, one given me by Kiiri. We have often wondered why the Avelle have lingered too long in Quevi Ltir. They have no choice. Pakal's kin-line has lost the ward knowledge to enter *Quevi'ali*." She dropped her hand. "Kiiri asked us to help."

"How can *we* help?" Philippe called out. "And why should we, for all your idiot talk of bonding? What has bonding brought us? Exile in this frigid tomb! Over fifty deaths! I say shut down power to the tiers!"

"Lejja's, too?" Jahnel asked hotly.

"Why not?" Philippe crossed his arms and stared at her.

Jahnel flipped her hand, dismissing his rudeness. "Their nestlings would be first to die—would you strike first at children, Philippe? Why not blow the reactors and be done with it honestly?" That created a murmuring. Scanning quickly over the faces, Jahnel saw that Philippe had not yet won over the Faon, for all his talking, but he had swayed more than she had expected. We feel the pressure even more keenly in these last depths, she thought, and now respond as Avelle respond—with a single violent option of mutual destruction. Instinctively, she shied from that answer. She raised her hand for silence.

"Your choice will remain available for a time," Jahnel said heavily. "Let us try this other first. Austin has the knowledge to explode the reactors, we the knowledge of its markings to guide his destruction. But let us talk to Nerup first."

She stepped back formally and spread her hands, giving the Faon the decision. "Ten minutes, my kindred, to decide among yourselves. We will vote by kin-group, as always."

She watched Philippe open his mouth to protest, then shrug and turn sullenly to his companions. There was a brief discussion; then, one by one, his group drifted apart, back to their kin-bondings. Vaar, the kin-law, has its uses, Jahnel thought,

watching Melinde return to the Louve. Evan promptly went up
to Melinde and embraced her, a gesture Melinde partly resisted.
We have the same stubbornness, too, Jahnel thought sadly, and
turned away. Austin was watching her, his dark eyes intensely
interested.

"Do you also have comment, Austin?"

He crossed his arms. "When are you going to call me Greg?"

She eyed him a moment. "Greg." His entire face relaxed
into a pleased smile; she hadn't realized it meant that much to
him. Strange—but not so strange, she supposed. The world
seemed turned on its ears right now.

"Thank you," he said.

She shook her head, amused. "You've had a hard time among
us. Chased up and down the fallways, nearly tossed in the dis-
ruptor, slash-attacked, dragged through a tier war—now we may
blow you up with the rest of us."

"I had my chance to get out." He looked away at the groups
of Faon, then shrugged defiantly. "I don't regret the choice. I
hope you don't regret yours."

"Well, if it works," she said sourly, "I get to be Faon
Leader."

His dark eyes glinted. "You already are Faon Leader."

"Hmmph. Among Avelle such rank is highly desired. I'm
not sure if I want it."

Jahnel waited patiently as the kin-groups conferred, watching
the faces. When the talk had quieted and all eyes returned to
her, she entwined her fingers in front of her and faced them.
"Louve," she said quietly.

"We choose with Jahnel of the Louve," Sair's voice rang out.

"Etoile."

"With the other option in reserve, we agree."

"Hiboux."

"With the other option *not* in reserve," Jean said forcefully, "we also agree." Jean gave the Etoile a fearsome glare,
which was promptly returned. Jahnel sighed. We could talk until
the walls fall down, she thought, and still Hiboux will glare at
Etoile.

"Roche."

"We agree," said a Roche elder. Philippe stalked away angrily to a far corner of the room.

"Ruisseau."

"Abstain." A derisive murmur rolled through the room.

"Come on, Ruisseau," an Etoile called. "Get into the fall-way or out of it. Do you follow Jahnel or not?"

The Ruisseau elder looked confused. "Is that what we're voting on? I thought . . ." The others' derision turned into outright laughter, and he stopped to glower, then glanced around at his kin-group. "Jahnel is Faon Leader," he said firmly. "On that we agree—but we are evenly divided on the other, and Ruisseau still abstains on the choice. Go talk to Nerup, Jahnel, since that is the greater will of the Faon. Then let us see."

"Very well," Jahnel said. "We brought several communicators with us; have we found a feeder line into the City-Net?"

"No outright connection," Jean said, "but we can tap into a monitor system and ask the computer to route it upward."

"Then do it."

Five minutes later, Jahnel stepped into the small systems room off one of the corridors and watched Jean complete the final programming. "Direct into Nerup's chamber," he said, and stepped back, gesturing grandly at the jury-rigged device. Jahnel positioned herself in front of the communicator screen, then waved two Faon out of the monitor's vision. She took a breath and organized her mind. One chance to enter us in the game, she thought. Make it count.

You improve, Kiiri had told her. But she had never expected the burden to come so soon.

"Send the access signal," she said. "Let's hope she's alone."

The communicator screen came to life in a scramble pattern, then steadied into muted grays. The shadows shifted, then became clearer; suddenly Jahnel saw into a small chamber of Avelle design. On a comfortable couch in room center, Nerup turned her head slowly and looked coolly at her monitor screen, her eyes flickering.

"Jahnel," she murmured.

"Nerup," Jahnel replied, deliberating omitting titles. "How fares our kin-mother?"

Nerup coiled her tail out of sight beneath her wing-flaps, then gestured noncommittally. "Lejja did not survive the Council meeting. There are many in my tier that blame Faon for that death. And now Koyil's tier warriors beseige our gate, as they will beseige yours, Faon." She shook her wing-flaps and rose, displaying her slim body for a moment, then wrapping herself tightly. "All is ending."

"Song, I bring new weapons."

"I am not Song," Nerup spat, "any more than you are Faon Leader." She drifted toward the monitor screen, her wing-flaps outspread in threat.

"Do you live within such narrow walls, Nerup? We are the Faon, your kin-brothers, and we control the power systems of this City."

"Not for long." Nerup's deep-set eyes flickered with sharpened interest.

"Long enough," Jahnel said casually. "My miin is deft with machines, my Faon familiar with Avelle constructions. We have more than enough time to do what we could do. Tell Koyil so."

Nerup considered, her clever eyes focused on Jahnel's image in her monitor. "In all the City's history, such a threat has no match," she mused aloud, "and extreme threat invites stark response. Koyil's reaction is predictable: he controls five tiers, more than enough to overwhelm your position even if I withhold. When a kin-alliance dared to use pocket atomics in the tier wars, all the City combined to destroy it."

"I have a pocket atomic that gives little opportunity for that, no?"

"Would you, Faon?" Nerup asked, bemused. "Truly?"

"Tell me, Song, which answer serves you best: to doubt and bear that truthfulness to Koyil's ears, or to know and seem unpersuaded?"

Nerup flicked a wing-tip. "I withdraw the question. Why don't you call Koyil yourself?"

"Koyil has a twitch when it comes to Faon—and since when should a junior bear a Principal's message?" Jahnel raised one hand and gestured kin-obedience. "Bear my message, Song. Use my weapon."

Nerup regarded her a moment, her face unreadable. "I shall consider it." Then she raised a clawed hand and returned the respect, accepting what Jahnel had gestured. "When this tier war has ended, Faon, return to my Home-Space and dwell with us."

Jahnel bowed. "Our respect, Song."

"*My* respect, kin-sister." Nerup stretched out an arm and blanked her screen.

Sair drifted through the doorway from the corridor and slipped his arm around Jahnel's waist. "Well played, beloved."

"Maybe." She turned and kissed him. "We shall see. How are things in the power room?"

"Restless. Philippe is busy talking again, and Melinde's gone back to his group." He scowled. "If she doesn't watch it, we may divorce her before she divorces us. Even Evan's angry at her now."

"Well, we'll see," she hedged. "Matters aren't usual right now."

"Vayalim loyalty is a constant, Jahnel, whatever matters apply." Sair looked severe. Jahnel felt a jab of pain for her sister, seeing his expression. She took his hand and pressed it, then turned away.

"How is Evan?" she asked.

"Not comfortable, but tended. He's watching over Solveya and the kids. Eduard's come in from guard duty on the wall. Not even he's finding much to joke about."

"True."

Sair studied her face. "Do you think it will work?"

"Your guess is as good as mine, Sair. We're walking the edge of an abyss, and only the Avelle can say how they'll react. Coming from Nerup, the threat may be less provocative. Maybe. Do we have guards on the ship-cavern tunnel?"

"Etoile took care of that—not that a few Faon blocking the tunnel will do any good."

Jahnel bit her lip. "Maybe we can barricade it."

"With what? We have some laser tools, but that tunnel is twenty meters wide. Where do we find the spare metal?"

"Rip out the walls."

Sair chuckled. "I'll talk to Nathalie; she'll enjoy leading the destruction. Any suggestions about which walls?"

"Well, never mind. A laser cannon would turn any barricade into vapor, anyway." She scowled. "This place is not defensible, not in a tier war."

"Still, I'll talk to Nathalie." He shrugged. "We're back to our problem of inadequate weapons again." He gestured at the door toward the power room. "The weapon we have is too big, not exactly a problem I expected. What else do we have? Maybe something humanly unpredictable?" He smiled at her.

"I will always love you, Sair," she said suddenly. "I only wish Luelle had been given an opportunity to grow up."

"We haven't lost yet, Jahnel," he said lightly.

"Maybe." She drifted over to the communication monitor and dialed randomly through a few channels. The Avelle instructor still droned on, as if nothing were amiss. The City continued, as the Principals disputed, as guards tested nearby tiers, as females cuddled their nestlings, as always. And the Faon? The Faon abided, preserving their place in an uncertain City. She set the monitor to receive and settled herself to wait.

⧼ Chapter 17

THE WAIT CONSUMED a long hour. Faon came and went, finding unconvincing reasons to look into the side room and to raise an eyebrow at Jahnel; Sair chased them off, then left to check on Philippe's mutterings. Gradually, the kin-leaders assembled in the corridor, out of sight of the monitor, and joined Jahnel in the waiting. Etoile brought news of their erection of a flimsy barricade across the ship tunnel, and of an Avelle scout they had dispatched violently as he fled upward; Jahnel worried, wishing they had determined his kin-alliance first for any clue to Koyil's maneuverings. A slight touch on the balance scales, poorly applied, could undo what slender advantage the Faon had. Ruisseau reported to the kin-leaders on supplies; Roche, highly irritated, suggested that Philippe be put on guard duty to shut him up. Hiboux concurred, then started its own argument with Etoile. The tension grew, making everyone quarrelsome. Jahnel waited, becoming more convinced with each passing minute that her gamble had failed.

She looked up quickly as the carrier signal chimed on the City-Net monitor; the screen lit into bands of shadow, then steadied into a picture of the Principals' Council Chamber. She moved forward, her heart pounding, and faced the Principals of Quevi Ltir. A new Avelle had taken Niintua's place, one she did not recognize—but she had no doubt of the new Battle Leader's allegiance, not after Song's recent reverses. At the other end of the bench, Nerup reclined impassively, her tier still strong enough to allow her to take Lejja's place without significant dispute. Koyil glared at Jahnel from the center of the Principals' bench.

"I am the Law," he announced. "Give up the underlevels, Faon."

231

Jahnel's tension eased slightly—it was not outright attack, not yet.

"Look to Song for that decision, Koyil," she said with deliberate arrogance. "Or vote among yourselves, as you will."

Koyil pounced on the offer immediately. "We shall vote."

Jahnel stopped him with a gesture. "I claim right of speech."

"Then attend this Council in person," Koyil said, "as the law requires."

Jahnel smiled ironically and gestured vast amusement. "After the murder of our prior Leader? After your treachery to a kin-alliance of Quevi Ltir? Has your brain grown diseased, Law?"

"Insolence!" the new Battle Leader declared. Koyil shut him up with a fierce look, and Jahnel felt a new wave of confidence. Or was Koyil only stalling as his tier soldiers poured into the ship cavern to the assault? Balance, she reminded herself, mine to keep and Koyil's to disturb.

"I claim kin-right and call on the Principals to hear me," she declared in a strong voice. "Why were we not informed that the miin were human?" she challenged. "By denying me that knowledge, you forced me to bring a miin into the Home-Space to preserve my brood. When were we given proper weapons to repel the miin invasion? By neglecting the surface weapons, you permitted the miin superior advantage and caused unneeded deaths among my Faon. Why were we denied our right of Home-Space and forced to flee our levels and hide in the depths? For what cause? When have the Faon ever denied kin-allegiance? When have the Faon ever played treachery to our Principal? Since when do the Principals of Quevi Ltir move against a minor kin-alliance without cause?"

"Cause? You have a miin with you!"

"That happened afterward and you know it, Koyil. Do the Principals know you have spoken to the miin ship with words of welcome, with fawning good will, keeping them here to stress the kin-alliances? Do the Principals know you invited the miin into the City, an obscenity prevented only by my destruction of the Downlift? Yes, I destroyed it—to save the City from your treacheries, Koyil."

The startled glance at Koyil from the Star Leader and even Koyil's new Battle Leader showed she had struck home. At Koyil's left, Kiiri folded his wing-flaps in satisfaction, like a teacher nodding approval to his student, then nearly ruined it with a triumphant glance at Koyil. She prepared another slash, distracting the Principals quickly.

"Or do you lust after the miin ship, Koyil?" she asked. That brought confusion to all—and panic to Pakal's eyes. Kiiri gestured slightly to warn her off. She obeyed instantly, wondering if she lost everything by trusting that guidance. You trust Kiiri too much, Faon had warned her. She threw all into the balance. "We are the Faon, kin-alliance with Nerup's tier. We submit to Nerup, the Song of Quevi Ltir. Vote." She heard a stir behind her among the listening kin-leaders, a quickly stifled protest.

Koyil eyed her distrustfully. "And your threat to explode the reactors?"

"What threat?" Jahnel pretended surprise, then a sober reflection as if the idea was newborn to her. "Since when does a kin-alliance of Quevi Ltir propose such obscenity? All broodings in the City would be harmed." She thumped her chest. "Never have the Faon considered such evil."

Koyil snorted, not believing a word of it. Good, she thought.

"Tier soldiers in the ship tunnel," a voice whispered urgently from the corridor. She acknowledged the warning with a slight movement of her hand.

"Indeed," Koyil said unpleasantly. "A vote, then." One by one the Principals spoke, as before, Song and Mind and Science and Battle, until the choice came to Pakal. The Star Leader looked uncomfortable, his eyes darting from Kiiri to Koyil, then fixing on Jahnel with open hatred. When he said nothing, Koyil turned to him.

"Star Leader!" he prompted.

Pakal started violently, then rose with dignity. "May the Faon live in peace among us," he spat.

"What!" Koyil shouted.

Nerup stepped in smoothly. "The vote is three and three: the Principals are undecided." She rose gracefully. "When the vote is even, the Songs decree that mercy rules, that matters return to as they were." Her eyes focused on Jahnel. "Return to my tier, Faon, and be welcome."

"No!" Koyil shouted. "I challenge!"

Nerup turned to face him, icy with disdain. "Then it is war."

"As you wish," Koyil said menacingly.

"I have had an idea proposed to me," Jahnel said, breaking their tableau. "The more I think of it, the more I like it." She smiled grimly as every eye in the Council Chamber turned to her. "If the kin-alliances are to destroy each other, let Faon do the favor of quick death. Why delay the agony? You have ten minutes. Prepare yourselves.'' She leaned forward and snapped off the monitor.

A babble broke out behind her as the Faon kin-leaders reacted. She turned to face them, her jaw set.

"Is that a bluff?" a Roche asked, his eyes wide. "I thought you said . . .''

"I don't know," she said. "Have those tier soldiers attacked the barrier?''

"Not yet. If they do, they'll get a nasty surprise.''

Jahnel stared blankly at him a moment, then understood him. "Benoit's gravity weapon.''

"Benoit had good ideas.'' The man stared at her defiantly, and Jahnel knew control might slip from her far too easily. The disminded ferocity of the tier wars would grip Faon as easily as Avelle, here at the end of things. Behind him she saw Philippe's eager face, already tinged with a flush of triumph. She saw the ferocious demand in his eyes and wondered if he had been fool enough to take battle drugs on top of it. For fear of that, she changed tactics, countering her opponent before he even knew the game had engaged.

"I want to see Austin," she said firmly. "Bring him.''

Austin arrived a few minutes later, his brown face an open question.

"We may have lost our gamble," she told Austin. "Are you prepared to do what I bid you to do?''

Austin looked wildly around, as if he sought escape from the horror she imposed on him. His shoulders sagged. "I protest, Jahnel. You can't . . .''

"Yes, Jahnel!" Philippe cried. "Kill them all!''

Jahnel ignored his outburst, all her attention focused on Austin and the kin-leaders gathered around them.

"Our choice narrows," she said. "Would you prefer death by slash—prefer that death for our children, all our beloveds? Your ship brought this down on us, Austin. Don't you think it's fitting that you bring the solution?''

"Jahnel . . .''

"Don't you?" she pressed at him, but still he resisted. "If you would be one with us, miin, choose our obedience.''

"Benoit asked that kind of obedience," he spat at her, his brown face flushing darker with his anger.

"And I obeyed him," she flung back. "Do you obey, Austin? Are you Faon enough to obey?''

"I—what kind of person *are* you?" Austin cried out. "*La Novia* may want to loot their science, but she won't destroy them. What kind of 'fierce love' is that, Jahnel? I would never do that, you said." He waved his arm at the power room, all around them. "Everything they've built here, everything they are, a sentient people—to *kill* ten thousand people! And you think that means you don't lose?" His voice was a cry of anguish.

"Do you obey, Austin?" she asked softly, her attention on the shocked faces of the kin-leaders behind him, on other faces in the other room who had overheard.

"No, I won't help you," he declared with frigid contempt.

She nodded. "Then we must certainly stop the Avelle in the ship tunnel, my kindred." She spread her hands. "Austin will not help. Let us prepare for what we can do to defend our own."

She dismissed the Faon with a nod, then caught Austin's sleeve as he also turned away. "Greg, wait."

He shook her off angrily. "Leave me alone!"

She sighed and let him go after the others. When the side room was empty except for herself and Sair, she allowed herself to sag against the wall.

"Jean says he's traced the reactor leads to an exposed flux," Sair commented. "If we pulse a gravity field underneath the coupling, we could blow the reactors ourselves."

"I expected as much." She turned away. "He spoke well, didn't he?" she said softly. "Sometimes we need to be reminded we Faon are human, even here in this alien place."

"You mean you never intended . . ." He frowned, disturbed. "That was rather rough hauling around, even for a miin, Jahnel. You play at Principal with a deft hand."

"I told you to watch for the corrosion," she said unhappily. "I had to distract Philippe to give us time, beloved, make him think only Austin could explode the reactor. If Philippe knew we had the knowledge, he could not be controlled."

Sair reached for her and drew her close, his breath warm upon her cheek. "It was necessary, I think."

"Perhaps. I hope Greg will forgive me."

Sair sighed and shook his head.

Through the doorway, Jahnel heard a murmuring, then the sound of laser-fire. "It has begun."

Jahnel and Sair watched from the portal into the vast cavern. In the distance, laser-fire lit up the darkness, showing the first of a horde of flashing winged bodies descending down the tunnel. As the Avelle crossed over the tunnel threshold, the Faon gravity fields snatched at them, crushing them to metal, breaking bones, exploding organs, folding the segmented bodies into a sickening tangle that tipped slowly into the abyss, falling into the darkness. With cries of dismay, the Avelle in front tried to turn back, only to be forced into the fields by the press of other bodies descending fast behind them. Jahnel held onto Sair, horrified, as the slaughter began. The Faon had chosen their weapon better than any had expected.

The Faon by the tunnel-mouth retreated into open space, their laser rifles suddenly irrelevant as the Avelle in the tunnel panicked, turning on each other to slash and destroy, tearing each other apart even as gravity crushed them into death as they fell into the fields. Dozens of Avelle, mad with the violence, threw themselves into the fields, dragging others with them, and still the tier soldiers pressed from above, rushing downward. It was madness, it was slaughter—it was death.

Several of the Faon threw away their dis-rifles and fled back across the abyss toward the power room, weeping. Melinde flung herself into Jahnel's arms, sobbing wildly. "I saw Inai!" she cried. "Our own tier guards! Crushed! Oh, Jahnel, it was horrible!"

"Koyil would put our tier guards in front," Jahnel muttered grimly. "But grav fields can't hesitate, can't have second thoughts—he expected to use our love against us." Melinde buried her face in the curve of Jahnel's neck, clinging tightly as she was racked with sobs. Jahnel held her closely and kissed her hair, comforting her. She was so very young, so young to face the realities of death. "Turn off the fields," she said quietly.

"The soldiers are still coming down the tunnel, Jahnel," Sair warned.

"Turn off the fields," she repeated firmly. "We've made our point."

The order was carried across the cavern. As the Faon shut down the fields, a few Avelle lunged forward into empty space and were scissored apart by laser-fire, but the others—hesitated. Jahnel felt her tension relax almost like a sudden pain. Even Avelle can be affected, she thought, and turned to a new pattern—when we are unpredictable. Even Avelle.

"Leave this place!" Nathalie shouted at the tier soldiers, her voice echoing in the darkness. "Leave or we shall crush you all!"

Jahnel waited until she saw the first movement backward

among the Avelle to retreat, watched a few moments more to make sure, then gave Melinde into Sair's arms. "Take care of Melinde, beloved. I'll be in the monitor room," she said, trying not to hope too much, not yet.

"We'll come with you," Sair said.

"Yes," Melinde declared, wiping the tears off her young face with her sleeve. "I want to hear." She smiled raggedly at Jahnel, a crooked anguished smile that expected rebuff. "I want to hear, Jahnel."

"Then come, sister-wife," Jahnel said gently. "We will listen together."

The comm screen lit twenty minutes later, then steadied to show Nerup lounging easily on her chamber couch, her deep-set eyes flickering.

"There is a truce," the Principal said simply.

"And are we the item bartered away, Song?"

Nerup gestured friendly admonishment, nearly equal to equal. "After all you've done to set it up, Faon Leader? Why didn't you carry out your threat against the City? Or will you still?"

"You doubt that?"

"Do not joust with me, Jahnel," Nerup said. "You offered kin-obedience. Since when does a mother sacrifice her kin-brood to strangers?" She turned away from the monitor and spoke to someone else in her chamber. "Bring Kiiri. Perhaps she'll believe him, since she doesn't believe me."

"Kiiri is there?" Jahnel asked.

"Of course he's here. He is part of my tier, as are you. I thought we agreed on that."

Jahnel crossed her arms and allowed herself to look skeptical.

Nerup chuckled. "In the end, my Jahnel, a Principal of Laws cannot bend the laws he protects." She gestured wryly. "The vote was even; your defense of the ship tunnel added to its legality. And the miin ship has withdrawn beyond detection—that helped greatly. Is that what your miin asked them to do?"

"He's not my miin."

Nerup ignored her protest. "Balance has returned, with Law and Song in matched contention."

"But not victory."

Nerup shrugged. "Even it were, kin-sister, no victory lasts for long among Avelle—but there *can* be a space of peace, a time for quiet living, the care of nestlings, and a sharing of kinship. Share it with us."

"You believe her?" Philippe asked sarcastically from behind her.

Nerup scowled, her eyes glinting. "Who speaks?"

"The vote was even closer than you think, Nerup," Jahnel said frankly. "But I want an escort of your kindred to take us through the lower levels to our tier—and only your tier soldiers to guard this place in our stead."

"Granted—but the second must be temporary. The protocols have already begun between the iruta to reseal the underlevels. This weapon we must deny even ourselves—the Avelle are ever prudent." Only then did Nerup's good humor show itself in her open satisfaction of a triumph, an ending of threat. The Principal of Songs was greatly pleased—and had cause for it, Jahnel supposed. She rubbed her face tiredly.

"Your answer, Faon," Nerup prompted. Kiiri moved into view behind her, his face impassive.

"Let me consult with my kin-leaders for a brief time. My greetings, Kiiri. Our respect, Song." She blanked the screen and sighed.

Had she hoped for victory? She couldn't remember. But a space of peace was enough.

"And that's all? Just like that?" Melinde asked acidly from behind her.

Jahnel whirled abruptly, startling her sister into a step backward. "To have life again?" she asked coldly. "To avoid the death of everyone? And you think that's not *enough*?"

"But—"

"Yes, always but. Have a care, Melinde. Sometimes stubbornness can lose you the ones you love, lose them beyond retrieving. You're on the edge now, for all my excuses for you to Sair and Eduard. My beloved, when you choose to be willful, be sure it's worth what you risk. Be sure you're *right*."

Melinde's eyes filled with tears. "And were you sure—all the time—that *you* were right?" she asked brokenly.

Jahnel smiled. "Not at all. And that's the fear of it—that you might be wrong and lose everything worth having." She leaned forward, intense. "Don't you understand, Melinde? Now there's time for children, for a future—time we almost lost forever." She spread her hands. "Now there's time for everything."

Melinde hesitated, then looked at Sair. "Time . . . and you weren't sure."

"No."

Melinde smiled then, her tears rolling down her cheeks. Jahnel spread her arms and Melinde came to her, then went shyly toward Sair.

"She is young," Jahnel told him firmly as he hesitated.

"I hear you, O Principal," he muttered, then made himself smile at Melinde. "Let's hope by the next crisis, Melinde, you're a little older."

"Oh, Sair!"

"We can talk about it," he said, more gently, and kissed her. "All you have to do is listen. That's all I ask, all we ask." Melinde clung to him, and Sair looked at Jahnel as he held her, his dark eyes alight.

Philippe made a rude sound, and Jahnel forestalled any comment with a fierce stare. "Take yourself away, Roche. Mend your own bondings."

Philippe bowed mockingly. "Oh, yes, Principal. Anything you say, O Principal." He turned and moved off, his body stiff with indignation.

"Perfection in peace would be nice," Jahnel said resignedly. "No doubt, in time, I'll wish as firmly for unthinking obedience as Papa Benoit."

Sair chuckled. "What a dread thought. Melinde will help us avoid that. Won't you, Melinde?"

"Definitely!" Melinde declared.

Jahnel sighed. "Spare me a while, if you would, beloveds. I need a rest." And she smiled as they laughed at her.

❧ Epilogue

I N THE FAON LEVELS, Jahnel sought out Austin as he continued to avoid her. She finally found him in a corner room of the vayalim, watching Luelle play with Smart-Mouth.

"See, Mama?" Luelle cried as she saw Jahnel in the doorway. "Smart-Mouth can do flips."

"Most unwillingly, I think. Will you take Smart-Mouth into the common room, Luelle? I want to talk to Papa Greg."

Austin's head jerked around at the name she gave him. He quickly looked away again, a muscle jerking in his jaw. She sat down in front of him, arranging herself comfortably.

"I see you," she said. "That is an Avelle greeting, pronounced *alai seertan* in their speech, neutral but lacking in threat. When friendliness is intended, one adds this gesture." She raised her hand and signed at him.

"I don't feel friendly," he muttered. "Leave me alone."

"Ah, a miin greeting that we Faon still share. You are angry at me for pressing you about the reactor."

"Let's just say I realized you aren't what I thought you were." He refused to look at her and studied his brown hands in his lap. A stubborn miin. Stubbornness must be bred into the human brood, she decided. It occurs so frequently.

"But what was the object of my demand?" she asked softly. "Doubt of you? Do you really think, after my speeches, that I wished what I threatened? Perhaps I needed a hard reminder to my Faon about that choice. Perhaps I needed a distraction from the threats all around us, time for my gambit to work itself among the Principals. We know Avelle machines, Austin—Philippe would not have needed you, a fact he never realized." She smiled. "He believed my certainty in looking to you. Unthinking obedience has its uses, even among Faon."

240

Austin looked up at her and scowled. "You always did have clever words," he accused.

"I am much Avelle in that."

He grumped and thought about it. Jahnel waited anxiously for his answer, then sighed as he looked up again, his face cleared of its sullenness.

"Sometimes it's nice to be clued in *before* instead of after," he said.

"I agree. But I can't always promise I will."

He shrugged, accepting it.

"Kiiri says *La Novia* has returned," Jahnel said. "They're sending signals at us again, though your ship lurks on the fringes at a most prudent distance; apparently even miin can listen to sense. The messages are surprisingly meek. Kiiri says the San-ford wants to talk to you."

"Why?"

"Am I a miin to understand her purposes?"

Austin scowled and pointedly shifted his seat to turn his shoulder to her. He studied his hands in his lap, refusing to look at her. "Games."

Jahnel leaned forward and touched his sleeve. "Play," she corrected. "There's a difference. A feint and counterfeint, a dalliance, a testing of wit—it's very Avelle. They cannot em-brace casually; they cannot visit one another easily—but they, too, find a means for playful affection."

Austin shook his head in bewilderment. "I can't keep up with this."

"You can learn."

His eyes met hers with sudden intensity, then shied away again.

"*La Novia* will need a liaison down here, Greg, a trade for Nathalie—she's volunteered to go educate Boland on attitudes."

Austin grinned wolfishly at that, as if he enjoyed the idea. Likely he did, very much so.

"I imagine she'll do quite well," he commented.

"You've wanted to learn more of us, to understand us. Here is the opportunity. I'll have time now, we all will, to give you your answers, if you still wish to ask."

He looked up at her, his dark eyes thoughtful in his brown face. "I'd like that."

"Then it is settled." She unwound her legs and stood up, then reached out her hand to help him to his feet. "This time, my miin, contact must be on Faon terms, for we are the bonding between human and Avelle. Do you think you can convince your ship of that?''

He smiled broadly. ''I'll try.''

''Solveya needs some help with dinner,'' she suggested.

He bowed to her, making a ceremony of it though he still smiled, and left the room, his shoulders square. Austin, too, was young. Do I feel old? she thought. Not really.

Jahnel sat down again with a sigh, then twined her fingers in her lap. Well, Papa Benoit, she mused, I have tended everyone and made the peace among my kindred, Faon and Avelle and miin. It may not last, but for now we have kept what is ours. And I feel peace with you, Papa, because I understand now what you protected when you were Leader.

Jahnel looked around at the small room, knowing her be-loveds were safe in their Home-Space, the place they defended, the life they had re-won. We should add a few new words to the Song on our walls, she thought. Words about miin and the stranger ship that came for us—and found the unpredictable. And later there may be other words to add, words both human and Avelle that blended as the Faon. She smiled.

What is wisdom? ''To love fiercely,'' she whispered to the empty room, knowing she had the right of it.

About The Author

Paula E. Downing is an attorney and municipal judge in Medford, Oregon. She and her husband, fellow SF writer T. Jackson King, live in a large house on eighteen acres of wooded property a few miles south of Medford. *Fallway* is her fourth novel: her first novel, *Mad Roy's Light*, was published in 1990 under her married name, "Paula King," followed by *Rinn's Star* from Del Rey in the same year and *Flare Star* in April 1992. Besides writing SF novels, Paula also writes a long-standing column for the Science Fiction & Fantasy Workshop, a nation-wide correspondence group based in Salt Lake City; edited for two years for *Pandora*, a small-press SF magazine; and recently published five nonfiction articles on writing SF, one of which will appear in next year's *Writer's Handbook*, an annual writer's market guide published by *The Writer* magazine. Paula enjoys cross-stitch and needlepoint, reading, computers, and pretending to garden. Her next novel for Del Rey, *A Whisper of Time*, is scheduled for publication in early 1994.

flew flashed on the whirl of darting, struggling bodies. Behind it a